A dramatic tale of love, intrigue, and divided loyalties, based on the true story of "the man who failed to stop the Pacific War."

In the fall of 1941 a senior Japanese diplomat is sent on a desperate mission—a last-ditch attempt to secure peace with the United States. But, unknown to him, the Japanese military have their own plans. On December 7th, he stands before a furious Secretary of State to deliver Japan's ultimatum, unaware that, an hour earlier, his country has attacked Pearl Harbor.

Around this event unfolds the story of an extraordinary family, caught between two hostile nations. At its head is Saburo, the pro-American diplomat who becomes reviled in America as an instrument of treachery. At his side is Alice, the passionate and courageous American woman who fell in love with him and followed him halfway around the world, only to find her adopted country at war with her own people. And in between is their beloved son Ken, a Japanese Army pilot with a Caucasian face, haunted by his "enemy blood," and fated to do battle in the skies with his other half—his mother's countrymen.

The war intensifies. The bombing of Tokyo begins. The order to fly suicide missions against the B-29s is given. And one of the most powerful and stirring accounts of a family loyal to its principles, and loyal to each other, moves to its shocking climax . . .

Riding the East Wind

RIDING THE
EAST WIND

OTOHIKO KAGA

Translated by Ian Hideo Levy

KODANSHA INTERNATIONAL
Tokyo • New York • London

TRANSLATOR'S NOTE

This is an adaptation, with abridgments made with the author's permission, of the Japanese novel published by Kodansha Ltd. in 1982 under the title *Ikari no nai fune*.

The names of many of the key characters in the novel, which is based on real people and actual events, have been changed, but the authenticity of historical details—including documents such as the official correspondence between the Japanese Foreign Ministry and its Embassy in Washington, and the substance of the talks between the Japanese and American negotiators—has, as far as possible, been preserved.

ACKNOWLEDGMENTS

Publication of this translation was assisted by a grant from IBM Japan, Ltd., Rengo Co., Ltd., the Osaka Gas Research Institute for Culture, Energy, and Life, and other organizations, under the auspices of the Association for 100 Japanese Books.

Distributed in the United States by Kodansha America, Inc., 575 Lexington Avenue, New York, N.Y. 10022, and in the United Kingdom and continental Europe by Kodansha Europe Ltd., 95 Aldwych, London WC2B 4JF. Published by Kodansha International Ltd., 17-14 Otowa 1-chome, Bunkyo-ku, Tokyo 112-8652, and Kodansha America, Inc.

ISBN 4-7700-2049-X
First edition, 1999
99 00 01 02 03   5 4 3 2

I

A HIGHLAND SUMMER

1

"*Banzai!*" the crowd roared, and a hundred little rising-sun flags fluttered together. Women in black kimonos lined the front of Karuizawa Station, alongside old peasant men in the ancient uniforms of the Russo-Japanese War and schoolchildren in gray summer shorts, all raising their arms in unison and crying out, again and again, "*Banzai! Tenno heika banzai!*" Long life to the Emperor, victory on the battlefield!

On a wooden dais a slim young man stood in a crisp new Imperial Army uniform. At each shout of "*Banzai!*" the young recruit bowed deeply to the crowd, his shaven head gleaming in the harsh afternoon sunlight. On a wall behind him hung a long banner with bright red Chinese characters that said: "CONGRATULATIONS ON YOUR DEPARTURE FOR THE FRONT." This was one of a thousand identical ceremonies repeated that August day in 1941 in front of railway stations all across Japan.

Suddenly the crowd parted for a Western woman in a long white pleated skirt, a lace blouse, and an enormous hat with a rose on the brim. For the locals in the international resort of Karuizawa, Western visitors were a familiar sight, but as Alice Kurushima made her way out of the station and through the crowd, the presence of this foreigner in her exotic attire still seemed to astonish them. They forgot their "*Banzais*" for a moment and stepped back as she passed through.

"Tanaka!" Alice called back to her cook in English, oblivious to the solemn ceremony she had just walked into. "Get us a taxi!"

"Oui, madame, tout de suite . . ." Tanaka bowed to her, tipping his white beret, and looked around the little square. There were no taxis.

All he spotted were two rickshaws. "Madame, allez-vous en rickshaw. Board yourself, please!"

"But what about the luggage?" Alice said, turning around. The porters had piled more than a dozen trunks and wicker suitcases in front of the station. Her husband Saburo stood there, dwarfed by the mountain of belongings. Beside him stood their daughters Eri and Anna—one in American-style slacks, the other in kimono—and the maids Yoshiko and Asa. They all looked a bit bewildered.

"Madam," Yoshiko said, speaking an English that was as fluent as Tanaka's was broken, "Asa and I will carry the luggage. Why don't you and the master go in rickshaws?"

"But how can you carry it all? We brought so much."

"Don't worry, madam. We can borrow a wagon from the Peony Inn." Yoshiko pointed to the inn across the square.

Just then the sun burst forth from behind the clouds. Alice quickly covered her arms with a scarf, believing the sun up here in the highlands was harmful. She was glad she'd worn a large hat and long skirt to protect herself.

Yoshiko walked over to the Peony Inn. Instead of a wagon she returned with a wooden oxcart, a relic from another era. When the family had piled all their luggage in, the cart looked absurdly top-heavy, but there was nothing they could do about it. Absurd or not, they set off. Alice and Saburo rode in the rickshaws, followed by Tanaka and the two maids pulling the cart, with Anna and Eri pushing from behind. The rickshaw drivers were both elderly men who moved at a snail's pace, so the others had no difficulty keeping up as the procession made its way down the main road through Karuizawa.

Alice looked around. The highland resort hadn't changed in the five years they had been away. Here and there in the larch woods stood the villas of the foreigners and wealthy Japanese who spent their summer here, each house painted a different color. Beyond the forest she could see the yellowish brown slopes of Mount Asama. A white trail of smoke rose from its crater into the blue sky.

They reached the livery stable and turned onto a dirt path that led through the rice paddies. At the end of the path was the Kurushima family villa. When they saw the house with its red roof and white-washed panels, Eri shouted, "We're home!" and started running. Tanaka and the maids, luggage in hand, traipsed after her across the leaf-strewn yard.

Alice stepped down from the rickshaw and started toward the house. Turning to Saburo, who was following slowly behind, she called out in English, "It's slippery, be careful!" Then to Tanaka, who was crouching in front of the main door, she called out in Japanese, "Why don't you take the luggage in?"

"Because, madame," Tanaka answered, reaching with his index finger to tip his beret slightly over his forehead, "the key—it does not work. Rien à faire."

"There are so many keys," Yoshiko interrupted him. "We don't know which is the one to the front door."

"Let me try," Saburo said. But before he could try them out, he stumbled over a pile of larch leaves. Tanaka barely caught him in time.

"Oh Papa, you're so helpless!" Eri snatched the keys from him and tried each one in turn, but to no effect. "They must be rusty."

"Why don't we go in from the veranda?" Anna proposed.

"Madame Arizumi," Tanaka said, bowing to her, "I already tried, but it is locked from inside. C'est impossible. There is simply rien à faire."

"Maybe you've got the wrong bunch of keys," said Yoshiko. "I'm going to see if the caretaker has another set." Yoshiko ordered Asa to keep an eye on the trunks and suitcases and ran off to find the caretaker, who lived in a farmhouse behind the villa.

"The house really is in terrible shape," said Alice. She had intended the remark for Saburo, but when she turned around her husband wasn't there; he had already made his way to the archery range at the bottom of the garden. It was Anna who answered her.

"Of course it is, Mama. We've been away for five years. And then there was that terrible typhoon that came in the middle of the summer. They say even the station was flooded with muddy water."

It seemed the monsoon had lasted an inordinately long time this year, and on top of that the town had been hit by a typhoon on the night of July 22nd. Rain came flooding down from the mountains, turning the roads into rivers. The square was inundated and water rushed into the station, causing a panic. Even in Tokyo, houses had flooded in the low-lying districts near the bay. All across the Kanto plain the trains had stopped running one after another.

The Kurushima family had been waiting for the rainy season to end, and it wasn't until the beginning of August that they finally left Tokyo to come up to their villa.

But the huge pile of leaves couldn't have been the result of just one typhoon. Evidently the caretaker had neglected the place all the years they were away. The paint had started to peel, the window-panes were clouded with dirt, and the rooftiles were invisible under a thick layer of leaves. Even the bicycle and its trailer were weather-beaten and red with rust. The entire house would have to be re-painted and given a thorough cleaning. Alice peered through the window, frowning at the mess inside.

Yoshiko returned from the caretaker's house with a new key, which immediately opened the door. The maid went in first, followed by Tanaka, Alice, and Anna. The air smelled of mildew, and every-thing was covered with dust. Alice shrank from the sight.

Suddenly Anna screamed and grabbed her mother. "Bugs! Look, it's full of bugs!"

"Where? Oh my goodness, Mama!" cried Eri, grabbing onto her mother as well.

The floor was covered with black spots which were beginning to come alive. Some were tiny, others over five centimeters long. With their black sheen, they looked like crickets. Aroused by the light that suddenly shone in on them, they began to hop about like seeds in a box that someone had shaken, and gave off an eerie hum.

"Do something!" Anna screamed, covering her eyes. "I can't stand them."

She looked as though she was going to be sick, so Eri and her mother, stroking her back, led her to the sofa; but just as they were about to get her to lie down they noticed that the sofa was covered with insects too. Even the ceiling and lintels were twitching with them. Eri took her older sister outside instead.

"We're just going to have to get rid of these things," Eri said. Recovering from the shock, she slapped the dust from her hands and told the maid to come inside with her. Then she called out, "Papa, come —quick—we've got millions of bugs!"

The sound of Eri's voice seemed to rouse Alice. "Let me help," she said. She didn't like insects, either—they were repulsive, filthy, disgusting things—but they couldn't just leave them there.

Saburo came to the doorway and peered in. "Aaagh!" he cried, recoiling at the sight. But then, obviously embarrassed at having reacted like that in front of the family, he picked up a broom and marched into the house like a samurai. "This is war!" he declared.

Everyone joined in the attack. They used flyswatters, newspapers, mops, and brooms. They whacked at the floor, the walls, the furniture. The insects hopped and skipped around them, but they were stupid things and were crushed with ease when their attackers crept up on them from behind. The problem was that the remaining insects then took refuge on the ceiling and at the top of the pillars.

"I've got an idea," said Saburo, who went outside and soon returned holding a souvenir from his trip to America in January. It was a General Electric vacuum cleaner. The vacuum cleaner, with its long neck and a bag attached to the base that swelled with air, was still a novelty in Japan. He switched the machine on, and with a great roar it sucked up the insects from the ceiling, the pillars, and the walls.

"Papa, it's *wonderful*," said Eri, clapping her hands in delight, as the others all gazed at the amazing machine. "Mama, is this a special machine for catching bugs?" she asked.

"Yes, it is, dear," her mother said with a straight face.

"No, it's not. I don't believe it."

"Oh, but it is. There are lots of insects in America. You don't think we catch them all *by hand*, do you?"

Once this problem had been dealt with, it was time for a thorough house-cleaning. Under Alice's direction, everyone wrapped washcloths over their noses and mouths and then set to work. Leaving Anna in charge of the cleaning downstairs, Alice went up to the second floor. In the bedroom where their son Ken had stayed during the family's last visit, she found his clothes strewn about exactly as he'd left them five years ago, when Ken was a teenager. Seeing them made her wonder how they would look on him now, a young man of twenty-two—too small, of course, and probably too flashy. She wasn't sure. That summer in Karuizawa five years before was the last time Ken had lived with them. While the rest of the family went over-seas—to Belgium, and then to Germany—Ken stayed on in Japan alone. Alice had felt terrible about leaving him in Tokyo with only the servants while he went to school. Then, when she had finally re-turned to Japan, delighted at the prospect of taking care of Ken her-self, he had disappeared into the Army.

Alice could hear her daughters laughing and went to the stairwell to see what was happening.

"Hey, look at Papa!" Eri shouted. Catching sight of her husband when she went downstairs, Alice found it hard not to laugh as well: Saburo Kurushima, the former Japanese Ambassador to Germany, was decked out in heavy working gear, but was settled on the couch on the veranda. He had on brand-new overalls—bought in Tokyo to wear while working in the field behind their villa—and in addition to a gauze mask was wearing a straw hat. Knee-high boots completed the ensemble.

Anna shook her head. "I'm amazed he can even move in an outfit like that."

"He's *not* moving," Eri laughed, "—His Excellency is tired already."

After applying the mop to half the floor, Saburo had put it down and gone out to the veranda for a break. He was about to light his pipe, when he realized he had to remove his gauze mask first. His two daughters smiled.

"It must be from using that vacuum cleaner," Alice said, smiling too.

After a while Saburo closed his eyes in the cool breeze that came drifting from the woods, and dozed off.

In a few hours of feverish work the others managed to make the house respectable again. Alice stood beside a jumble of rugs and futons and blankets hanging to air, and scribbled in the notebook she always kept with her:

1. Completely repaint panels.
2. Seven broken windows—replace.
3. Get handyman (or caretaker) to sweep leaves off roof.
4. Replace zinc lining in sink with stainless steel—completely rusty.

Realizing she had forgotten about the garden, she stepped down from the veranda and inspected the grounds.

The Kurushima villa had once been known for its moss garden, which carpeted the area between two larch groves. The autumn leaves and the winter snow posed the greatest danger to the moss, and the Kurushimas had asked a local gardener to look after it throughout the year. But they had been away for five years now, and the old gardener's son had taken over the job. Their messages apparently had not gotten through to him, for the garden had been totally neglected. Under a heavy blanket of rotting leaves, the moss had died.

Alice added another item to her notebook.

5. Redo moss garden with turf.

Eri had wanted a lawn to play tennis on. In order to create the space for it, they would have to cut down two trees, no, more like four. It would be expensive. Alice had her doubts. They would have to get the gardener to make an estimate first, and then think about it. But now as she stood there, somewhere in her mind's eye she could see her daughter hitting a tennis ball across a bright green lawn. She decided they *would* have a lawn, no matter what it cost.

Alice walked to the edge of the garden. There was a shallow pond there, surrounded by rocks, which they had built as a pool for the birds. The water itself was clear. If the leaves were raked away, it could still be used. Just beyond the pond was a fence, similar to the white picket fence at Alice's country home in Connecticut. In Japan most houses had stone walls. Occasionally one saw a fence around a neighboring villa, but it was never painted, for the Japanese preferred to leave the wood plain. Alice's white picket fence was half buried under the tall grass.

6. Repaint fence.

On the archery range some of the grass had been uprooted. The target with its triple bull's-eye stood uncovered. The wooden stand had rotted, and the target, bearing the scars of numerous arrows, tilted to one side. Saburo had taken to the sport back in the days when he was head of the Trade Bureau, before he was appointed Special Envoy to Belgium. He was a physically awkward man not given to athletics, but he had nonetheless tried his hand at golf and tennis like everyone else. These, however, had soon lost their appeal, and it was only archery that held his interest. Japanese archery was an austere exercise, more like a Zen ritual than a sport. It was done in a ceremonial kimono, each shot preceded by elaborate bowing. The Kurushima family had built a small archery ground behind the main house in Tokyo, and Saburo had practiced there religiously. But when he was posted overseas he had given it up, and now hadn't shot an arrow in five years.

7. Repair archery range.

Saburo had brought his bow and arrows with him, so Alice wanted that done for him. But there were so many other things to do as well. She sighed, then crossed out "6. Repaint fence." She thought some more, then crossed out "4. Replace zinc lining in sink with stainless steel." They would have to economize.

Japan had been at war with China for four years now. When the Kurushimas returned to Japan at New Year's, the first thing that struck them was how everyday items like food and clothes were now in short supply. Before they left Germany, Alice had scolded Tanaka for buying up huge stocks of canned goods and wine, telling him it was silly. She had had to apologize. Germany had also been under wartime conditions, with food severely rationed, but it was nothing compared to Japan. Alice couldn't buy meat or eggs, and there was no cheese or butter to be found. Imported wine had completely disappeared from the shops. If anything, she should be grateful to Tanaka: the cook had secured them enough canned goods and wine to last a year.

Alice placed a blanket over Saburo, peacefully dozing on the veranda, then began sorting through the luggage with Tanaka and the maids.

She had planned to get the house in order in three days, but it ended up taking ten. The roof was covered with a thick crust of rotten leaves, which stank. Alice really needed several strong men to clear the roof, but the local handymen who did that kind of work were all away at the front in China. In the end, she found one retired laborer to do it. It was all the old man could do to climb up there, and his heart just wasn't in it; after three days he was still crawling slowly around the roof.

"Well, damn it, I'll do it myself," said Saburo, leaning a ladder against the wall. Alice talked him out of it. After the workman finally managed to get the leaves cleared off, they found the tiles badly damaged; at least half of them would have to be replaced, but finding someone to do this was quite a job in itself. Yoshiko, who was from a nearby village, asked her mother Toku to inquire among the locals, and after a great deal of negotiation they finally got someone to come and work on the tiles. To plant the turf, Toku also found them an old field hand, but this wasn't a time in history to be planting new lawns, and the fellow had to bring some grass from a corner of his own pasture with him. As for windows, the glassmaker was off at the front, and his wife was unable to handle the order for seven by herself. And no house painter would come at such short notice. The town was simply too short of men to accomplish all the things Alice had scribbled in her notebook.

It was Alice's habit to jot down her thoughts in her notebook immediately. She did this because too many ideas would crowd into her head at once, and she was afraid that if she acted on one she would forget the others. But when it came to implementing her various plans, she tended to forget the tiresome details that were involved: negotiations, payments, paperwork. It was Yoshiko who took care of this. Yoshiko had been with the Kurushimas for more than ten years, since Saburo's stint as Director of the Trade Bureau, and she had lived with them all the time they were abroad. She had become indispensable to Alice, and she alone had the privilege of reading her mistress's notebook. Clearing the leaves, fixing the roof, planting the lawn, replacing the windows, repainting the house—it was Yoshiko who turned all of her mistress's dreams into reality.

When the house itself was ready, Alice turned her attention to the interior. She changed the wall hangings in the hallway and repaired all the torn mattresses in the bedrooms. Then she inspected the large area in the center of the house, which served as both a living room for the family and a parlor for entertaining guests, and decided to redo it in a style she called "Flemish."

They would take out the Italian china cabinet and bring the Dutch ornamental chest down from the second floor. The rattan table would go out on the veranda, and the old-fashioned dining table, hewn from a single piece of wood, would be brought in from the kitchen and set in the center of the room. They would replace the chairs with the wooden ones from Brussels. The carpenter and painter were recruited to help move the heavy furniture. After much fuss, when everything was finally in place, the Dutch chest somehow looked wrong next to the table, so out it went and back came the Italian china cabinet. Now everything looked perfect. Alice draped the room with some lace she'd found in an antique shop in Karuizawa Old Town, placed a flowery centerpiece from Brussels on the table and, as a final touch, added a little model windmill they had picked up in Rotterdam. In Alice's mind at least, the room was now "Flemish."

After four days spent redoing the parlor, Alice was ready for guests. There was no need to send out any invitations, though, for open house on Saturdays at the Kurushima villa was an old tradition. Once word had gotten around that Saburo Kurushima had brought his family up to Karuizawa for the first time after five years abroad—three and a half as Special Envoy to Belgium, and a year and a half as Ambassador to Germany—old friends summering at the resort began to arrive.

They came one by one and they came together: Alice Grew, the wife of the American Ambassador, with her youngest daughter Elsie; Kazuo Yoshizawa, the former Japanese Ambassador to Great Britain, with his only daughter Wakako; the Wolffs, who owned a German trading company in Yokohama, with their son Peter; and Father Hendersen, pastor of the local Anglican church, his wife Audrey, and daughter Margaret. Alice, who loved to entertain, showed them into the "Flemish Room." Tanaka, who had cooked for the Kurushimas since their time in Berlin, was sensitive to the tastes of each guest, and planned his meals accordingly. Usually he liked to serve a Japanese meal, with sashimi and tempura, to Westerners, and treat the Japanese to the *petite cuisine* he had mastered in France and Germany. But while the Kurushimas had a plentiful stock of canned goods and wine, it was hard to come by fresh meat and vegetables. Especially vegetables. The weather had made for an unusually poor crop this year, and vegetables weren't be found in the shops. The Kurushimas managed to obtain enough fresh food for their dinners only because Yoshiko's mother approached the farmers in the surrounding villages.

2

One Saturday morning toward the middle of August, a postcard arrived by special delivery from their son Ken at the Army flying school in Kumagaya. His military duties had kept him from getting away, he wrote, but he had finally received a week's leave. He would arrive on Saturday evening. Clutching the postcard in her hand, Alice danced her way over to Saburo.

"Ken's coming home," she announced.

"Oh," Saburo nodded, engrossed in his newspaper.

"Sa-bu-ro!" she shouted. "I said, Ken is coming home."

"Ah, yes," he responded, lifting his head and glancing curiously at her from behind his thick glasses. But his dark eyes still showed no glimmer of understanding. He was completely absorbed in his own thoughts.

"It's Ken," Alice repeated for the third time. "Our *son* is coming home."

"Really?" Saburo answered and smiled at last, taking the postcard Alice held out to him. Beneath the message in Japanese were several lines in English: Japanese for his father, English for his mother. "That's nice."

"It's not only nice," said Alice, stamping her foot on the floor like a little girl, "we'll have to have a big dinner for him."

"Yes, we will, won't we?"

Alice was about to go on about Ken's homecoming celebration, but before she had a chance Saburo held up the newspaper and said, "Alice, look, the German Army appears to be stuck. The Russians are putting up a stiff resistance. It doesn't look as if Stalingrad will fall any time this year."

This time it was Alice who was deaf to him. Who cared about the German Army? Her son was coming home. They had to have a real feast for him.

"German evacuees from the United States and the Dutch East Indies have landed in Japan," Saburo went on. "They've been split up into several groups, and are being put up at various resorts around the country. Here in Karuizawa they're staying at the Mikasa Hotel and the Mampei."

"Oh, really?" Alice said, settling herself next to her husband on the sofa. She opened her notebook. What was she going to feed Ken? He probably wasn't getting anything decent to eat in the Army.

1. Beef, 1.5 kilos. Send Yoshiko to butcher in Ueda.
2. Vegetables. Buy from old black marketeer when she comes on her rounds.

"Sounds like those Germans, all right," Saburo said, continuing his commentary on the news, heedless of his wife's concerns. As Alice's ability to read Japanese was limited, every morning Saburo would digest the news for her. "They lead a strict communal life—get up at six in the morning and do group calisthenics in the square in front of the hotel. I bet German calisthenics are different from our radio exercises."

"Yes," she nodded, "I'm sure they are." She put an arm around his shoulders and smiled, kissing him on the cheek, knowing he followed a fixed routine. "That's all well and good about the Germans, but Saburo, listen, you've got to choose the wine."

"Okay, okay." Saburo put his arm around his wife's plump shoulders, and she pressed her face against his chest. Then he kissed her, not in the way a fifty-six-year-old man kisses a fifty-one-year-old woman, but the way a newlywed man might kiss his bride. Alice's eyes were closed, her lips parted. She could feel him gazing intently at her. It occurred to her suddenly how much she'd given up—her parents, her home, her country—to follow this man around the world for the last thirty years.

"Yes, the wine," said Saburo, stroking his wife's shoulders. "Shall we make it a 1936 Moselle?"

"Fine." It had always been Saburo's prerogative to choose the wine from their cellar, and she never questioned his choice. Now she voiced her agreement with enthusiasm, for he had finally shown some interest in welcoming their son home.

But there was something else Alice had been wanting to discuss with him, and she hesitated, unsure how to bring it up. In June, at their house in Tokyo, in the middle of a meal celebrating his promotion to lieutenant, Ken had suddenly announced, "I want to go to flying school. I want to become a pilot." Alice had been stunned. She was willing to accept that, as a male, he was subject to conscription, but she had always detested the military profession, and it broke her heart just to think that her son was a soldier. Her one consolation had been that Ken was a technical officer, applying what he'd learned as an engineer to military aircraft, and not involved in any actual fighting. Now he suddenly wanted to be a pilot.

Alice was determined to make him change his mind. But instead of trying to talk Ken out of it, as Alice hoped, Saburo had simply told him, "If that's what you want to do, go ahead. You have to choose your own path."

Alice had cut in angrily: "There's no reason for you to fly. An aircraft engineer doesn't have to be a pilot. You can stay right on the ground and do your job."

Ken had said softly, "Mama, a good engineer needs to fly the plane he's designed. You can't really know the result of your work until you take the controls yourself." As always, he was gentle with her, but he spoke with resolve. His mind was made up. He had that same quiet insistence his father displayed when he got really angry.

It was then that Ken's intention suddenly became clear to Alice, and it made her feel faint. Her son wanted to be a *test pilot*. The most dangerous job in the world, a flier riding with the angel of death. An Army test pilot. "No!" she told him. "I'll never let you. Ken, please understand. You're my only son."

But Saburo had simply repeated his opinion, this time in English: "Ken, just do your duty, on your own."

"Duty?" Alice cried. "Why is being a test pilot a duty?" Things then began to blur, and the next thing she knew she was lying on the sofa, with her husband and children all staring down at her . . .

"Is there something on your mind?" Saburo now asked her as they sat close together.

"Yes, I want you to warn Ken of the danger, to make him give up the idea of becoming a test pilot." Alice's determination was as strong as Ken's had been in June. His visit was a rare opportunity to talk him around.

Saburo shook his head firmly. "That's not possible."

"Why? He's our son. We can't let him die."

"Alice," he said, pulling her toward him, "Ken's Japanese. He's a soldier serving the Japanese Empire. Listen, I know what you're going to say, that it's not his duty to become a test pilot. But a soldier is under orders, and ultimately those orders come from the *Tenno*."

The *Tenno*. Alice felt a jolt go through her. She knew the word *Tenno*—not the English "Emperor," but the Japanese "Son of Heaven," in all its solemn majesty. Saburo revered the Emperor. For him a command from the *Tenno* was absolute. When he was made Special Envoy to Belgium, he was given an ivory fan from the Emperor, a gift for the wives of diplomats appointed to ambassadorial rank. On his return from the Palace, he had shown it to her, holding it with great reverence. Alice had taken it from him, and proceeded to mimic a Peruvian fan dancer they'd seen in Lima. Saburo was furious. "This isn't something you fool around with!" he shouted. "It's a personal gift from His Majesty the Emperor." Alice stopped and, treating the thing with as much care as Saburo had done, returned it to its paulownia box. She was half joking when she did this, but Saburo seemed to find the gesture appropriate. His feelings on the subject were something she would never understand. For her the Emperor was the chief of state, no more. As Saburo's commander in chief, that squat little gentleman with a stooped back was owed her respect, but it went no further.

Alice twisted away from him. "I don't care if he is the Emperor, he has no right to command my son to die."

Saburo looked at her as if looking at a stranger. He removed his glasses and wiped them with his handkerchief. In an almost inaudible voice, as if addressing the glasses instead of her, he said, "Just because he's a test pilot doesn't mean he's going to die. If Ken designs a safe, high-performance aircraft, then naturally it'll be safe for him to fly, too. We have to trust Ken. He's a grown man now."

"A man," Alice murmured. "Yes, I suppose you're right." She felt the lingering warmth of Saburo's hand in her palm. His hands were always warm, even when he had been out in the middle of winter. And his skin seemed even whiter than hers. His hands were smooth and hairless, like a woman's, but without the luster that the soft down on her own hands had. Ken's hands were hairy, like those of his grandfather James Little or his uncle Norman. They were a man's hands.

"When's Ken getting in?" Saburo asked, eager to change the subject. He got up and went to look at the garden. Pearls of light shone through the larch trees and the white birches, glistening on the newly laid turf. Cicadas buzzed in the wind.

Saburo came back and extracted the railway timetable from the bookcase. "He's on duty until noon. That means . . . he probably won't make the twelve o'clock train from Kumagaya. The next one is the 1:32, which gets into Karuizawa at 4:28. So he should be here a little after five."

"Oh my goodness," Alice said and peered at her notebook. "I've got to get everything ready."

She swept out of the parlor, and was about to go upstairs to put Ken's room in order when she saw Yoshiko and went straight over to her, walking with long strides, not the dainty footsteps expected of a Japanese lady.

"Ken–is–coming–home," she announced happily, stretching each syllable as if singing a phrase from an opera.

The mistress's mood was infectious, and Yoshiko, who was in her thirties, was genuinely delighted. "Master Ken's coming home? That's wonderful!"

"Yoshiko, you and Tanaka decide on the preparations for dinner. Just follow what I've written in my notebook. Everything else I leave to you. Don't forget to call the market for some sashimi, and try to get us some beef somehow."

"We're in luck, madam," she said after a glance at Alice's notebook. "Five hundred *momme* of beef just arrived. My mother was able to get it for us in Ueda." Five hundred *momme* was the equivalent of two kilos, and the source of the beef was a black market slaughterhouse.

"It's filet, a very good cut. I put it in the refrigerator right away."

"Yes, we *are* in luck," Alice said, echoing her.

Tanaka entered the room with his sleeves rolled up and wearing a rubber apron. He had probably been doing the laundry. His gray, receding hair made him look older though he was only in his forties. With a smile on his ruddy face, he asked, "Madame, what were Master Ken's favorite dishes?"

"*I'll* tell you," Yoshiko interrupted, in a tone of voice that suggested she knew all there was to be known on the subject. "It's all right, madam. Just leave all the details to us. I'll go get his room ready now."

"No, no, I'll do it myself."

There were four bedrooms on the second floor of the house. One was Saburo and Alice's, one was Eri's, one was Anna's, and the bedroom in the middle, which overlooked the garden, was Ken's. Anna had asked if she could use it when her husband came to stay with them, but Alice had flatly refused. "This room belongs to Ken," she said.

The maid had apparently taken great pains with her cleaning, for the room was spotless. Hanging on the wall were Ken's riding whip, his tennis racket, and a German air gun, which he had kept meticulously polished. But the first thing to catch the eye was the extra-long custom-made bed. Alice touched the sheets with her hands and found them slightly damp, so she pulled them off and replaced them with a fresh set.

There was a faint smell she recognized as Ken's still lingering in the closet. A man's smell, she thought. The shirts and trousers seemed to sigh on the hangers, as if he'd just hung them up. They were all things Alice had bought for him long ago, and they seemed much too childish for him to wear now. It occurred to her in fact that she hadn't bought any clothes for her son in several years.

Unlike Anna and Eri, Ken had spent more time apart from his mother than with her. He had been born when Saburo was the Consul in Chicago. He spent the first years of his life in America, and was eight when he first set foot on Japanese soil. He had stayed in Japan ever since. A month after they brought Ken back, Saburo and Alice, together with the girls, left for Athens where Saburo served as Consul General, before going to Peru, where he was the Minister at the Embassy in Lima. By the time they returned to Japan for Saburo to take up a post as head of the Trade Bureau, Ken was thirteen. The family lived together for four years, after which Saburo was sent as Special Envoy to Brussels, leaving Ken alone again in Japan. After Brussels it was Berlin as Ambassador to Germany. They had finally returned this April, but shortly before they arrived Ken was drafted into the Army. Alice's son, who had spent almost half of his twenty-two years apart from her, was coming home tonight. Alice smelled Ken in his old clothes, and she longed to see him. He was her only boy.

When, many years ago, Saburo had first told her he wanted to have Ken brought up in Japan, Alice had opposed it. If anything, it was because he was a boy that she wanted him by her side. But Saburo wouldn't budge. He wanted Ken to grow up in the land of his ancestors, as a Japanese. Alice couldn't argue with that, and she gave in. Even so, she had constantly missed him.

Ken had been a beautiful child. The year before last, when the family was in Brussels, Ken had traveled all the way from Japan to visit them. It was just before the beginning of the war, when the last light of peace cast a faint glimmer over Europe. Their son had been a seventeen-year-old boy when they had left him, and suddenly he was a young man of twenty. And a remarkably handsome young man. He was her son, and yet Alice found him dazzling. During a trip by train from Belgium to France Ken had been scouted by a movie director. The military attaché accompanying Ken had brushed the man off, saying it was a downright insult to ask the son of the Ambassador to be an actor. A week later Germany invaded Poland. The war had begun, and Ken was stuck in France, returning to Japan by way of England and the United States. Alice sighed when Ken showed her the business card the movie director had given him; it bore the name René Clair.

"Mama."

Alice turned. The sound of her daughter's voice pulled her out of her reverie. Behind Eri, with her round, teasing eyes, she could see the slanted, anxious eyes of Anna.

"Mama, what are you looking for?" Eri asked, poking her head into the closet. She wore a short white skirt and was carrying a tennis racket.

"I'm just going through Ken's old polo shirts," Alice said, trying not to show any emotion, but suddenly, unable to hide the flush in her cheeks, blurting out, "Ken is coming home!"

Eri flung the tennis racket on the bed and hugged her mother. "Oh Mama, that's wonderful! When's he coming? Tomorrow? The day after tomorrow?"

"Guess."

"I don't know. When is it?" Eri drew close to her mother and looked deep into her eyes.

"I imagine it's very soon," Anna said calmly. "It's written on Mama's face. I'll bet it's today. It's today, Mama, isn't it?"

"Yes," Alice nodded. "He'll be here this evening!"

"Oh, super!" Eri began jumping up and down. The wooden floor echoed like the pounding of a big drum.

"Eri, calm down," said Anna.

"Anna, it's only natural to get excited. Look, my legs are trembling, they're going *pyon pyon!*" Eri squealed. She fell back on the bed and bounced up and down as if on a trampoline, then let loose a fierce stream of chatter, mixing English and Japanese. "What'll we do when Ken comes? Oh I know. *Mazu issho ni* tennis *wo shite*, then we'll go to the pool, then we'll go riding. *Uma ni noru no.* You know how to ride, Mama, so you can come with us to the Shiroito Cascade. Too bad you can't ride, Anna. *Zannen ne!* Oh, we can play poker, too. Mama, let's all play poker!"

"Eri, please be quiet. Mama, how long is Ken staying?"

"He didn't say, but I think he got a week's leave."

"That's super!" Eri exclaimed, flinging her legs in the air and turning a backward somersault. "Mama, I'm off to play tennis," she announced, and ran out of the room.

"What a silly girl," said Anna, as she carefully smoothed the sheets and straightened the pillow. She drew back to survey the bed, then adjusted the sheets and pillow slightly. Even by Japanese standards, Anna, as her mother well knew, was a perfectionist.

"The pillow has to be exactly at the center. Mama, do you think it looks all right?"

"Why, yes. It's right in the middle."

"No, it's not. It's still off."

"It's fine the way it is."

"It is not. Look," she said, measuring the distance from the edge of the bed with her fingers, "it's about seven centimeters too far over on this side." She moved the pillow over a bit. Finally she was satisfied.

That settled, her mother proceeded to pull Ken's polo shirts out of the closet. She studied each one before draping it over her arm. She looked dubious about something.

"Are they dirty or something?" Anna asked.

"No, they've all been washed and ironed. They're just too childish for Ken now."

"Really?" Anna picked up a shirt and examined it. "They look all right to me."

"But Ken's a man now. He's a Lieutenant in the Army. An Army officer would look ridiculous in a shirt like this."

"That's not true. The German men at the Mampei Hotel wear even flashier shirts. The problem is the size. Ken's probably a lot taller than when we last saw him."

"Yes, he probably is," said Alice. "But where can we go to buy some shirts these days?"

"Why don't we worry about it after Ken gets here? If necessary, we can borrow a few shirts from somebody."

"I suppose we could," she conceded. She put the shirts away and glanced around the room. Everything seemed in order. The only thing left was dinner. But then, turning to Anna, she noticed that something seemed to be preoccupying her. While Anna had the same short, stocky figure as her mother, she had inherited her facial features from her father. She had Saburo's thick eyebrows. But Anna's clear, narrow eyes were hers alone. Whenever she was concentrating on something the brown pupils would be touched with green; they had that strange flickering light one sees in an opal.

"Mama," Anna whispered, "there's something I want to talk about."

"What is it?" her mother said, feeling a constriction in her chest.

"Let's go to my room, shall we?"

Anna's room was spacious, but it faced north and was dimly lit. It had twin iron-frame beds and a sofa and chairs of sculpted wood in the Karuizawa style.

"You've fixed it up nicely," Alice said, looking around. Anna took the chair across from her. She was silent, consumed by her thoughts.

"Is it something secret?" Alice prompted.

Anna just sat there, expressionless.

"I know . . . you're pregnant, aren't you?"

"No." Anna winced. Finally she began to speak. She told her story slowly and reluctantly, as if pulling out, one by one, things she had hidden away in a drawer. "Yoshiaki and I haven't been getting along. We didn't have a fight or anything. It's just that there's a coolness in our . . . marriage. He's a journalist, so I always knew his life would be irregular. And I accepted the fact that he likes to go out drinking a lot. But lately it's gotten really bad. He often doesn't get home till morning, and sometimes he's away for two or three days at a time. Last month, when the Cabinet resigned and Foreign Minister Matsuoka had to quit, he didn't come home for ten days. Later he told me he'd stayed at the Press Club at the Foreign Ministry. I thought that was a bit odd, and I called his office about it. They said, no, he never stayed there, he always . . ." Anna's voice trailed off. She averted her eyes.

Her mother felt her chest tightening further. "Anna, tell me. Please tell me everything."

"All right," Anna sighed. "He has what they call a *mekake*. Do you know what that means, Mama? He's keeping a woman other than his wife. He ransomed a geisha from one of those establishments, and set her up in a house he bought for her in Iidabashi, which is right on the way from the Foreign Ministry to our house in Nagata-cho. He'd tell his colleagues he was going home, when every single night he was staying with her in Iidabashi . . ."

"Anna, are you sure about all this? You're not just imagining it?"

"Yes, I'm sure," she said, the pain evident in the deep lines on her forehead, which made her look ten years older. "When I called the Press Club, nobody knew where he was. They thought he'd gone home. I thought it was very odd. Then one day I was shopping in Kagurazaka and I saw them. Yoshiaki walking with a woman close beside him. It was raining, and I hid my face under my umbrella and followed them. I felt ashamed at the mere idea of following someone, but I had no choice. I kept following them until they disappeared inside a house. I could see their silhouettes in a window on the second floor. I couldn't move. I just stood outside in the pouring rain. Then people began looking at me suspiciously, so I went home."

"Why didn't you go in and confront him? I certainly would have."

"I couldn't," she answered weakly. "Doing that would be publicly exposing his infidelity, and it would mean the end of our marriage. I don't want to leave him. Mama, isn't there a way to make him give that woman up, so we can get back to our life together again?"

"That's impossible!" said Alice. What was wrong with this girl? How could any woman forgive an unfaithful husband? Had her daughter turned into some traditional Japanese woman, ready to choose a life of submission, willing to bear her sufferings in silence?

"What's impossible?"

"It's impossible to forgive him. He's abandoned his duty as a husband, and you no longer need to fulfill any duty as a wife. Don't you agree?"

"Mama, I love him."

"Oh dear." Alice vigorously shook her head, and began to pace the room. Oh yes, love. Love was the problem. She had always disliked that man Yoshiaki Arizumi, ever since the days when he started coming to their house as the Berlin correspondent of the Tokyo News Agency. A thin man, feeble-looking, always making a display of his not very fluent German, and joining with the military attachés in preaching the Axis pact between Japan, Germany, and Italy. A man who'd had the gall tell her pro-American husband that Hitler was the greatest man in history. When he was drunk his little opinions became absolute truths, and he never knew when to shut up.

When he asked for Anna's hand in marriage, Alice was absolutely opposed. Saburo answered, vaguely and reluctantly, that if the two of them wanted to get married he and Alice would just have to accept it. Anna started crying. She had been a timid, obedient child, but when she wanted to get her own way she resorted to tears. Alice was helpless when this happened, and often felt like crying herself. But Alice hated tears.

"Anna," she now asked, "what can you still see in that man? He's betrayed you, you know."

"I know he has, but I still love him. If he showed the slightest sign of remorse, I would forgive him. I truly would."

Alice gave her daughter a hug. "If that's how you feel, then that's all you can do."

"Should I tell Papa?"

"I don't know." Alice thought about it as she held her in her arms. Saburo was a cautious, moderate man, but he had a quick and violent temper. Instead of sympathizing with his daughter's unhappiness, he might explode at the man who was its source. No, Alice herself should talk to Arizumi. She would try to convince him to give up his *mekake*. That would be the wiser course.

"Does he know that you saw him with the other woman?"

"No, I don't think so."

"Did you mention anything about it to him?"

"No, not a word."

"What if I had a talk with him first?"

"Well, . . . No, Mama, I'll talk to him myself. Then if it's necessary, you can talk to him too, all right?"

"Oh Anna, my poor child." Alice stroked her back tenderly, wishing she could somehow take on part of her suffering.

3

Tilting his head to keep his tall chef's hat out of the way, Tanaka put some firewood into the stove. When Asa blew into the bamboo pipe to fan the flames, Tanaka's ruddy features glowed like the face of a scarlet demon. The smell of meat and vegetables, spices and oils filled the air. Anna nodded her approval, and Tanaka bowed deeply. Chatting with the young mistress, who understood French, was something he always enjoyed.

"C'est délicieux, sans aucun doute, Madame Arizumi."

"It certainly smells good."

"Yes, madame. C'est la cuisine de Bourgogne. The perfect cuisine for red wine, j'en suis sur."

Anna smiled at Tanaka. The sight of this earnest but rather foppish man never failed to cheer her up.

Tanaka had originally studied painting in Paris, but a friend convinced him that war was about to break out and that they should take refuge in an Axis country. Tanaka went to Berlin, where he ended up leading a Bohemian existence. After the Tripartite Pact was signed, the Japanese Embassy suddenly found itself with more banquets than it could handle, and Tanaka was hired as a cook on a temporary basis. It turned out his true talent was cooking, not painting, and the skills in French cuisine he'd picked up in Paris led to his being hired as the official chef. When Saburo resigned as Ambassador, he brought Tanaka back to Japan with him as his private cook.

According to Yoshiko, the reason Tanaka gave for accepting this job was "my attraction to the personnalité of Madame Alice Kurushima." At other times it was, "If I stayed in Germany I would've been caught up in the war, and this was a good chance to get out." Sometimes, when he indulged his weakness for the bottle at night, he'd say, "When you work for the Kurushimas it's good for your English." Indeed, even as he took great pride in his knowledge of French, he would also force his rather broken English on people, especially on Anna and Eri, "the madame and mademoiselle blessed with foreign blood and perfect English," as he put it.

"Madame Arizumi, today I will concoct your favorite dish. C'est ce qu'on appelle du punch en français. Good peaches, watermelons, grapes, and apples have been assembled. I also have good rum . . ."

Ever since that evening in Berlin when Anna had praised Tanaka's punch, it had become a pleasure for him to prepare it for her, no matter what the occasion. According to Tanaka, Saburo's favorite fare was sushi, Alice's was rice salad, Anna's was punch, and Eri's was rolled cabbage. Nothing could convince him otherwise. Whenever the family gathered for dinner, one or two of these items would always be on the menu. It was Tanaka's practice to announce which special dish he had prepared for whom, and it didn't seem to bother him if that person never even touched it.

"Asa, lay some more wood on the fire." Asa responded to Tanaka's command by pouting and moving sluggishly toward the fire in her baggy white uniform, a hand-me-down that the cook made her wear. This country girl from Chiba prefecture was fourteen or fifteen years old, about the same age as Eri. She was shorter than Eri, but had a much bigger frame and large breasts. She didn't speak a word of English, and her Japanese was so thickly accented that the Kurushimas had a hard time understanding her. Yoshiko, who was accustomed to the family's polite Tokyo speech, would often scold her: "What's wrong with you, girl? If you speak, speak proper Japanese!" The result was that Asa stopped saying anything at all.

She had a plump face, and her cheeks sometimes looked puffy with pouting. Whatever the Kurushimas ordered her to do, she would respond with a syllable or a grunt. She was a sullen girl, but men were scarce, and they needed her strong arms. She was more than a match for any man at hauling water from the well, carrying sacks of vegetables, chopping firewood.

In anticipation of Ken's arrival, the kitchen was a scene of great activity. Anna found this the first cheerful thing to have happened in a long time. Like her father, she was bad at sports and games, and she spent her days in Karuizawa reading and embroidering. Since she had been abroad most of her life, attending Japanese schools only for the few years when her father was head of the Trade Bureau, it was hard for her to get through a Japanese book. She read mostly in English and French. But lately it tired her to read more than a few pages of anything. She had never had any friends in Japan, and now her only acquaintances were Ambassador Yoshizawa's daughter Wakako, whom she had known in Europe, and Ambassador Grew's daughter Elsie. The three of them would get together to talk, or take Elsie's dog for a walk, or sometimes join in the poker evenings at the Yoshizawa household.

Yet the fact that she was living alone, away from her husband, and that he was leading a life of dissipation, made Anna feel dissatisfied and restless. Her days had become unbearably monotonous. She even considered going back to Tokyo. But then she thought of being confined day and night in a dark, cramped house, with her husband almost never there, in the hot and muggy summer, and she decided to stay in Karuizawa.

And now Ken's imminent arrival had brought the whole house, even the kitchen, alive. It occurred to Anna that she had been able to reveal her long-held secret to her mother because Ken's coming home had made Alice so happy, and that she'd felt she could reveal *any-thing* to her, no matter how unpleasant. In any case, just to have unburdened herself was a relief. Her step lightened, and, seeing her father reading in the living room, she tiptoed up behind him and suddenly pounded him on the back.

"Anna, you startled me! . . . What are you looking so cheerful about?"

"What's that you're reading?" She glanced at the book, then peered at its cover. It was a biography of Franklin Delano Roosevelt in English. "Is it interesting?"

"Why, yes, it is. The character of the President of the United States is an interesting subject."

"Really?" Anna sat down diagonally across from him, where she could get a good look at his face. He was a book lover, and his reading time was the most precious thing in the world to him. He never allowed anyone to interrupt, not even his own family. Anna had often seen her mother and Eri being scolded for interfering with his reading, but she also knew that she was the only exception. Ever since she was a little girl, not once had he scolded her for disturbing him while he was engrossed in a book. If anything, he seemed to be delighted that his daughter was interested in what he was reading.

"Tell me, Papa, what sort of character does Roosevelt have?"

"Well, he's a complex personality. You can't describe him in a single word. He's certainly not a simple man, he's what in music you'd can 'polyphonic.' You think he's easygoing, and he turns out to be tough. You think he's indecisive, and he turns out to be resolute. If you had to define him, I suppose you could say he always has a precise sense of where things are heading, therefore he's flexible enough to adapt to circumstances. And he prefers action to words. He's the type who acts while he thinks, instead of thinking first and then acting."

"He sounds pretty complicated. But he's a great person, isn't he?"

"Oh yes, he's a great man."

"Have you ever met him, Papa?"

"No, I haven't. I did meet the Secretary of State, Cordell Hull, once at a conference in London, when I was on my way to Belgium."

"What kind of person is Hull?"

"Serious, scholarly—an idealist."

"Hull is older, isn't he?"

"Yes, by about ten years. What is this, Anna? Why are you suddenly interested in Roosevelt and Hull?"

"No reason, I just . . ." The fact of the matter was that Anna had often heard her husband cursing Roosevelt and Hull, and she was curious as to what kind of men they really were. He had told her that "Roosevelt's family are Jews, you know, from Holland. That's why he jumps at every chance to make money for America. Look at the huge profit he's making by selling arms to Britain." He'd said, "Hull's family are poor whites with a dubious background. He might be Jewish too, for all we know." Also that "in order to protect their vested interests, the Roosevelt–Hull combination, the Jewish plutocrats, are oppressing the poorer countries of the world, Japan, Germany, and Italy . . ."

"Papa, is Roosevelt a Jew?" Anna asked.

"No, I don't think so. He's of Dutch origin. I don't recall his being Jewish."

"What about Hull?"

"Hull's mother is Irish. I don't know about his father, but I think he's of English origin."

"Might he still be Jewish?"

"I rather doubt it." Saburo's soft black pupils glimmered behind his thick, silver-rimmed glasses. He obviously found something rather admirable about the way his daughter asked question after question, like a clever student, something Japanese girls normally did not do.

As if in apology, Anna went on, "Arizumi says the Jews have to be destroyed. He says the Jews are the root of all the evil in the world."

"Well, young Arizumi *is* a fan of Hitler's."

A fan? thought Anna—*he's absolutely intoxicated with Hitler. He has a copy of Mein Kampf, of course, but the house is full of other Nazi tracts. Instead of a wall hanging he has a swastika flag, and beside the Shinto family altar he's hung a portrait of Hitler he brought back from Berlin and one of the torches the party members use. When he comes home drunk he sings the Horst Wessel Song to himself.* "He's turned into a complete fanatic," said Anna with distaste.

"How is his work going?" asked Saburo, changing the topic slightly.

"He's still running around, as usual. He's so busy he hardly ever comes home. Last month, when the Cabinet resigned, he was away for almost two weeks."

"Well, it's a busy time. Every day brings a new, unexpected development. The whole world is moving at a gallop."

"Where's it going, Papa?"

"I don't know," he sighed. "I hope it's not war. I was just reading the joint communiqué issued by Roosevelt and Churchill following their shipboard conference. This is the first time they've overtly mentioned Japan as a possible enemy."

"Papa, Arizumi . . . ," she started hesitantly. "Arizumi seems to have forgotten about me these days." Despite her agreement with her mother, she had decided to tell him something of what was happening.

"Oh?" Saburo blinked, not quite understanding. "Is he too busy?"

"Yes, I guess so. I hope that's it."

"You think it could be something else?"

The worry on his face had the effect of weakening Anna's resolve. She couldn't tell him the truth. Her father had a simple trust in people, and when he was betrayed his anger could be frightening. He would certainly turn that rage on Arizumi, but Anna still didn't want to leave her husband.

"Yes, there is something else," Anna nodded, carefully concealing the turmoil inside her. She spoke as if making an important confession. "Lately Arizumi's joined the pro-German rightists. They force their way into the Navy Ministry and other pro-American offices, and threaten the officials. A dozen of his friends came to our house for a secret meeting. They had headbands on, with daggers in their belts. He frightens me, Papa. He goes around carrying a banner with slogans like 'JAPAN MUST DESTROY AMERICA, ENGLAND, AND RUSSIA!' and 'BE FAITHFUL TO THE AXIS PACT!' I wish he would just stick to his reporting."

"He's obviously disturbed."

"Yes, he is." Then she added quietly, "I'm scared. It's as if he's gone mad. He only talks in slogans."

As she spoke, Anna suddenly recalled a conversation with her husband just before she set out for Karuizawa earlier in the month. In an unusually gentle tone of voice, Arizumi had said, "Could you ask your father to do something for me? You know I'm the secretary of the Iron Cross group, and we're trying to promote the Tripartite Alliance. Do you think you could get your father to accept the chairmanship? He wouldn't actually have to do anything. He'd be chairman in name only."

"My father was opposed to the Tripartite Pact," Anna had answered forcefully. "Since he resigned as Ambassador to Germany right after it was signed, there's no way he would agree to be head of your group."

"But things are different now," he had said. "America and England are putting great pressure on Japan. They've started an economic blockade. Freezing Japan's financial assets and banning the export of petroleum—these are outrageous acts. Even your father must recognize that."

"I don't know anything about politics," Anna had told him, flatly refusing her husband's request. "If you really want to have him as your chairman, why don't you ask him yourself?"

It wasn't until now, with her father, that she remembered this conversation. "Papa," she asked casually, though the question was important to her, "you were opposed to the Axis pact, weren't you?"

"I certainly was," he replied with visible emotion. "Hitler's special envoy Stahmer negotiated the treaty in Tokyo with Foreign Minister Matsuoka while I was in Berlin. It was all carried out by my superiors behind my back. All of a sudden the order to sign the treaty was thrust at me. So I . . ."

". . . resigned as Ambassador."

"Anna, you've become something of an expert in politics."

"No I haven't, but I've always been interested in your work. I saw everything that was going on while we were in Germany. I just never talked about it." Anna gave him a smile.

The members of a diplomat's family are often privy to secrets of state, but they can't ever reveal what they've learned. The motto in the Kurushima house was "Keep your eyes open and your lips sealed."

Her father returned her smile. There were deep wrinkles in the corners of his eyes. He was only fifty-six. But after his resignation as Ambassador—an almost unheard-of event in the Japanese Foreign Ministry—he had been given the special status of semi-retirement known in the diplomatic service as *en disponibilité*. It was the ministry's way of letting the world forget about him before they pushed him out entirely. It meant a limbo of awaiting orders that never came, and it had rapidly aged him. Confined to his house and never exercising, he had developed a pot belly. His skin began to sag, and his hair turned gray.

"Papa, what are you going to do from now on?"

"I don't know. Perhaps a time will come when they'll need me again . . . I don't feel like doing anything. I've been in the diplomatic service for thirty years, and twenty-five of those years I've spent abroad. I just feel tired. The other day . . ." He hesitated, then looked Anna straight in the eye. "Don't tell anyone about this, but the other day the new Foreign Minister, Toyoda, asked me to return to the service as his Vice-Minister. I turned him down. The real reason I did this is that diplomacy nowadays, especially the complex and bewildering course of negotiations with the United States, is too much for a tired old man like me. That was the real reason, but I just told him I wasn't feeling well."

"Papa, how are you really?"

"Not too good. My blood pressure is high, and I often get short of breath."

"You've got to exercise more."

"Hmph," Saburo laughed. "It's funny to hear that from you. You're not exactly an athlete yourself."

"With Ken and Eri, it's as if they were born for sports. Not me."

"Anyway, I think I'm going to take your advice and go out to the archery range." Saburo closed his book. He stood up, lifted his arms, and stretched.

4

Anna was immersed in a book. It was a nineteenth-century English novel, one of those tales of a country maiden led astray by her young master where the girl invariably ends up bearing his child. Anna had taken it from her mother's bookshelf. It was one of a dozen novels mixed in among her many books on plants and animals, and its red jacket was torn, its pages browning at the edges. It had been published in 1911, three years before her mother was married. So the daughter was reading the same book her mother had read as an unmarried girl some thirty years before. As she read, she imagined her mother's feelings back then, and before long it seemed that not she herself but Alice Little was reading the book. Certain sentences that Alice had found especially moving—mostly psychological descriptions—were underlined in pencil. These Anna read with special attention.

She could hear arrows whistling through the air in the garden, and the wind in the trees. Shafts of sunlight swayed in her room, and a breeze blew in, touching her cheeks. Anna gazed out the window, looking beyond the larch trees standing straight and symmetrical toward Mount Hanare, with its prosaic shape, like an inverted bowl.

Someone was shouting. Someone was running along the corridors—running to the front door. Ken was back! Anna dashed from her room. But when she reached the stairs, she assumed a slower, more dignified pace. Against the flood of backlight, Ken's tall figure stood out bold and dark. Anna made her way past the women surrounding Ken, past Eri and Alice and Yoshiko, and was about to rush up and kiss him, when she was blocked by the figure of a man standing next to him. It was Yoshiaki Arizumi. After a moment's confusion, she gave her husband a challenging look, tossed him a greeting and, with him watching her, flung her arms around her brother's neck and kissed him on one cheek and then the other. The Kurushimas were probably the only Japanese family who kissed each other with an American exuberance. It was a greeting Anna had never given Arizumi.

Along with Ken's distinctive personal odor there were soldierly smells—tobacco and leather and sweat. "Oh, Ken, you do look grand!" she said, pulling away and admiring him in his uniform. On the right side of his chest were blue wings, the badge of an Air Corps officer. His stripes were a little more worn than in June, when he had just been promoted to lieutenant. Other than the small white circles around his eyes—the area that his goggles covered—most of his face was tanned a deep brown. He was the very picture of a pilot.

"Ken, come on in!" Eri shouted.

Ken wiped the white dust from his boots and handed them to Yoshiko. Alice and Eri followed him in, leaving Anna and her husband behind them. It was only then that Anna noticed that Arizumi was wearing a white hemp kimono with a dark blue waistband. She was used to the casual Western clothes everyone wore here at the resort, and her husband's attire seemed rather pretentious. She felt a little sorry for him. After brief hellos to Arizumi, Eri and her mother had become totally absorbed in Ken. Anna forced herself to be pleasant to her husband.

"If you had told me you were coming, I would have made all sorts of preparations."

"Actually, I'm up here to do a story. It was a sudden assignment, so I didn't have time to tell you I was coming. The German evacuees from the U.S. and the Dutch East Indies have been put up here in Karuizawa. I'm going to interview them." As he spoke, Arizumi turned his head, like a toy tiger, twisting his thin lips. "I want to wash the sweat off—take a dip in the bath—then I'll go find an inn."

"An inn? No, you can stay here. There's a room for us on the second floor."

"Oh, would that be all right? It would certainly be most convenient, I must say."

When he spoke like this, Anna could never tell if he really meant it or was being ironic. Had he forgotten the letter she sent him right after her arrival in Karuizawa, telling him there was a bedroom for them here and he could come up anytime? Or was this merely one more way of mocking her?

"The train was pretty crowded. Full of *gaijin*, as I expected," he said, using the word literally meaning "outsiders." "I heard someone speaking German, so I went over to talk with him. It turned out to be a man named Wolff, who lives right next to your villa. He said he owns a trading company. You know him?" Without waiting for her answer, he went on: "Then at Kumagaya, this tall soldier got on. It was Ken. Amazing! The last time I saw him was at our wedding, and he was wearing a suit. So Ken and I came up here together . . . Okay, I'm off for a quick wash."

While her husband was in the bath, Anna set about tidying up the bedroom. There were open books and magazines lying about. She put them away, then hurriedly wrapped the college notebooks, filled with her poems and essays, in newspaper, taking care to tie the package firmly with string. For a moment she panicked, not knowing where to hide it. She finally chose the wardrobe in her mother's dressing room. Before she could finish changing the sheets, Arizumi came upstairs.

"Oh, this room, eh?" he said, looking around. "What luxury. Very Kurushima." Arizumi had changed into a casual short-sleeved shirt and shorts. Anna was surprised. Only wealthy Japanese visitors wore European-style shorts in the summer. Her husband, a farmer's son from the northeast part of the country, had never displayed such fashionable Western tastes before. Anna sensed the influence of the other woman: of course a geisha *would* be attuned to the latest styles.

"That one's your bed. I put your trunk in the closet."

"Yes, this is quite luxurious." Arizumi took in the scenery from the window. "Big garden. Lots of trees. Yes, quite a view. I wouldn't mind being rich enough to have a villa like this myself. By the way, did you talk to your father?"

"What about?" said Anna, feigning ignorance.

"You didn't ask him, did you?" He made a sour face. "That's too bad, too damned bad. Here's your husband knocking himself out for this movement. For the nation. For Japan. You've always been disappointing in that respect. You *are* Japanese, aren't you?"

"Of course I am." The smile quickly faded from Anna's face. Arizumi had never talked like this before. "Just what are you saying?"

"I told you. You're disappointing—unpatriotic."

"Why don't you come right out and say what you mean?" Anna's voice had at last turned harsh.

He gave her a bitter smile, which he evidently meant to convey pity. "I don't think I should. It'd hurt too much."

"Nothing you have to say can hurt me." She spat out each syllable.

"Oh, let's forget it. It's been quite a while. Why waste time on a stupid quarrel?"

"I agree." Anna tried to smile, but the smile wouldn't come. She had once longed to see her husband, had stored away this longing through the nights she slept alone, but now the man disgusted her. Why were his lips so thin and rubbery, like strips of raw squid? Why did he twist them in that nasty way?

There was a knock. Eri bounded in like a puppy.

"What's the matter? Everybody's waiting for you downstairs. They've already sliced the watermelon. Mama told me to call you. And I think Papa wants to talk to you, Mr. Arizumi. He didn't say so, but I have a feeling he wants to." Eri ran out again and romped down the stairs.

Arizumi pulled Anna to him and tried to kiss her. Anna refused, but the man was stronger, and when he locked his arms around her she could feel herself weakening inside. She began to reconsider. Would she ever manage to leave him, she wondered.

Then he whispered in her ear, "Little Eri's turned into a big girl," describing two breasts with his hands. He had always said the best thing about Anna's body was her large breasts.

Anna felt the disgust returning. "She's still a child!"

"How old is she, anyway?"

"Eleven years younger than me. She's still fifteen."

"You mean fifteen by the American count, Kurushima-style?"

"No, by the Japanese count, Arizumi-style." In Japan a child was considered a year old at birth, and therefore always a year older than in the Western way of judging age.

"She's already a grown woman. I bet she'll have men all over her."

Anna did not respond.

5

Dinner was served in the "Flemish Room." At either end of the long table sat Saburo and Alice, with Arizumi on Saburo's right and Ken on his left. Anna and Eri sat to the left and right of Alice.

Yoshiko served the dinner. Awkwardly trailing the hem of the long dress Alice had made her wear, she brought out plate after plate of Tanaka's creations. Alice, who was the same height as Yoshiko, had dug the dress out of her clothes chest. It was an antique, something she had worn a decade ago, which she had decided would be appropriate because its collar was embroidered in the "Flemish" style.

The hors d'oeuvres of tempura and tuna sashimi were followed by a beef stew brimming with vegetables, then rice with red beans and sea cucumber soup to complete the marriage of Japanese and Western cuisines. From the wine cellar Saburo had brought up a 1933 Burgundy and a 1936 Moselle. Arizumi, smacking his lips, exclaimed, "What a feast, especially considering the food shortage! It's un . . . precedented!" Anna thought she heard her husband start to say "unpatriotic" instead.

The center of attention was of course Ken.

Everyone wanted to hear about his life. Three months ago he had entered the Army flying school at Kumagaya, and he had been learning to pilot a 95-1 trainer, nicknamed the Red Dragonfly. The plane had two seats, the student riding behind the instructor. The two control sticks were connected, so that the instructor could correct the student's errors. Ken flew twice every morning. He had already flown solo several times.

"That's pretty fast," mumbled Arizumi, chewing on a slab of meat. "If you can go solo after three months, how long does the whole course take?"

"Six months. It used to take a year, but because of the military situation it's been shortened." Ken put his knife to a large potato, slicing it cleanly in half.

"Well, is that enough?"

"It has to be enough. The world won't wait."

Arizumi nodded energetically at his reply.

"Hey, Ken!" Eri broke into the adults' conversation in her high-pitched voice and, without pausing, asked, "What was it like when you flew by yourself for the first time? Were you scared?"

"No, I wasn't, I just concentrated on doing what I'd been taught and not making any mistakes. Actually, once you're up in the air it's relaxing. It's sort of like a rugby game. You train and train, but once you're in the actual game you don't think about anything at all, you just keep your eye on the ball and the opposition."

"You know," Arizumi put in, "Ken was a star fly half in his school rugby team." Because the Kurushimas had been abroad during Ken's high school years, they had never had a chance to see him play. But Arizumi had, and he proceeded to recount the details of a match Ken's team has lost because he—the key player on his side—had been singled out and worn down by the other team.

"But Ken," Eri started again, unwilling to let Arizumi steal the conversation, "once you're up there, what do you see? The earth and the sky, I know, but do they look different up there?"

"Of course they do. Clouds floating in big puffs. The earth looks beautiful from that height. Over Kumagaya the most prominent landmark is Mount Asama. You can make out its shape right away."

"Wow! So if I climbed to the top of it I could see you in your airplane!" Eri sat with her arms folded in front of her. This was a gesture she'd seen the heroine make in a Berlin opera, and she believed that was what you did when you were dreaming about something. "Fantastic!"

"Ken, I've always wanted to ask you," Anna said softly, "—which do you prefer, designing airplanes or flying them?"

"Of course he prefers flying them," said Eri, stretching her arms like wings and rising from her seat.

"No, I don't think so." Anna calmly scrutinized her brother. "I remember you loved making model airplanes. Your room used to be a little airplane factory. I think you really do prefer designing." True enough, Ken's bedroom walls had once been covered with blueprints and photographs, the desk and floor piled high with silver paper, glue, and rubber bands, with half-finished models and bamboo sticks ready to be whittled into little fuselages. Hanging from the ceiling was a jumble of transport planes, fighters, and bombers. Ken's school books had lain untouched in a bag in the corridor.

He had often taken Anna along when he tried out his model planes. In summer he used to try to catch an easterly wind, which would carry them from the bluff by their house west toward Akasaka. How many times had she gone with him as he carried an airplane he'd just finished to the open lot overlooking the Sanno Hotel. The propellers shone as the model, painted exactly like a real plane, with a pilot and an instrument panel and a control stick, rose higher and higher, until suddenly the rubber band went slack and it drifted down to land in a treetop or sometimes crash on the roof of the hotel. When Anna mourned the loss, Ken would say, "We can always make another one. Anyway it's great it flew this far," and laugh it off . . .

"When I built them I imagined myself flying them. So I guess even back then I preferred to fly," Ken told her now.

"But if that was all, you wouldn't have spent all that time and effort designing them. You could have made a simple plane out of chopsticks. Those fly better anyway."

"I guess you're right," he admitted.

"But flying a plane *is* more fun than building one, isn't it?" Eri, still excited, wouldn't let it go.

"Not necessarily," Ken said gently, as if afraid his little sister might not understand. "All a pilot ever does is fly. After you've flown, you leave nothing behind, but when you make a first-rate flying machine, you really leave something in the world."

"Oh," said Eri vaguely.

"Then you really ought to give up flying," said Anna, "and concentrate on designing."

"I can't. It's not up to me. I'm a soldier, I follow orders." Ken glanced at his mother, then turned toward his father, whose eyes were now on Alice. Anna, aware of the furious arguments between her parents over Ken's entering flying school, felt the tension in the air. Alice had been happily listening to her children chatting away in Japanese, but a shadow now crossed her face. She managed a faint smile, and scooped some of the rice salad from the bowl Yoshiko was holding for her.

"If you disagree with an order, can't you say no?" asked Eri, as if the whole business was strange to her.

"Of course not," said Arizumi with a condescending smile. "In the Imperial Army an order is a command from His Majesty himself. You can't refuse it."

"Well, Ken, what if you were ordered to kill yourself?"

"Of course I would have to do it."

The more Eri pondered this notion, the stranger it seemed to her. Her education in Japan had been brief, and she had no idea how the Imperial Army worked. Nor did Anna, either, but at least she knew from books, and from Arizumi's remarks, that the Japanese military had their own way of doing things.

Abruptly, Eri asked her mother, in English, "Mama, is that true in the American Army too? Can they order you to kill yourself?"

"Well, I've never been in the Army, so I can't say for sure, but I don't think they give that sort of order in America."

"I didn't think so. Thank goodness!"

"Oh, by the way, I just remembered," said Saburo, wiping his moustache with his napkin. "We received a letter from Lauren, forwarded from the Tokyo house. She says George has been drafted."

"Did he go into the Army or the Navy?" asked Ken.

"Guess."

"Let me see," said Eri. "I'll bet he joined the Air Force."

"Exactly. Your cousin George is in the U.S. Army Air Corps."

A sigh of admiration rose from around the table. George and Lauren were the children of Alice's older brother Norman. Anna had known them only when they were children, but Ken had seen them the previous year on his way back to Japan from Europe.

"Then George is the same as Ken. Imagine, both of them airmen!" Eri exclaimed. She was so excited at this thought that she jerked back in her chair, knocking her fork to the floor. "Who's taller, Ken—you or George?"

"We're about the same."

"You look alike too," said Anna.

Saburo, when returning to Japan via the U.S. earlier in the year, had visited the Little family in Chicago, and brought back photographs which showed George to be the spitting image of Ken; they could have been brothers. In other words, Ken, with his prominent nose, his chiseled features, and deep-set eyes, looked almost completely Caucasian, with hardly a trace of the Oriental in him.

"What are they talking about?" asked Arizumi a bit suspiciously.

"Oh, I'm sorry," Anna replied and began to translate the gist of the conversation into Japanese for him. The rule at the Kurushima house was that if there was a guest who didn't understand English, out of politeness they would speak in Japanese. But there were occasions when the conversation became so animated that everyone—except the guest—would suddenly break into English. When that happened someone would usually serve as an interpreter, but Anna seemed to have completely forgotten her husband.

"I see," Arizumi said, keeping his voice down. "Cousins on both sides of the Pacific—it's certainly unusual—but if war breaks out between Japan and America, then Ken and George would be enemies, wouldn't they? And given the international situation, there's a pretty good chance of that happening. And when that happens, Ken and George will be in combat—mortal combat—whether they like it or not. I wonder if Ken is mentally prepared for that. You ask him in English, go on. I'd also like to know how your mother feels about it . . ."

"I can't . . ." What was this man saying? A war between Japan and America? Even to imagine it was painful. And to suggest that Ken and George might have to kill each other—what a callous thing to say! Anna shook her head and grimaced: no, nothing would induce her to ask that question.

The conversation at the table had continued, and no one else, fortunately, had heard what Arizumi said. Now talk turned to George's younger sister Lauren, who was studying Oriental art at the University of Chicago and apparently had developed a special interest in Japanese art. Most of the Littles were Japanophiles. Norman was president of the America-Japan Society in Chicago, and Saburo had first met Alice when he started visiting the Littles' home to practice his English. Lauren corresponded frequently with Alice and Anna, and when she and Ken got together again in Chicago for the first time in a dozen years, a new friendship had blossomed between them. There was a picture in Ken's room in Tokyo of him and Lauren dancing together at a party the Littles had thrown for him. Eri decided in her girlish mind that Ken and Lauren were in love, and teased her brother about it relentlessly.

"Hey," Eri started in again, "when you were dancing with Lauren, what was it like? She was good, I'll bet—I'll bet she was a *great* dancer. How did you feel, huh, Ken?"

Ken had been through this before with her, so he turned it into a joke. "She was as light as a breeze, as fragrant as a flower, and the best dancer in all of Chicago. One dance with her and I fell in love!"

"Really? How fantastic! Oh, I can't stand it! I'm going to go to America for Ken and Lauren's wedding. Oh, why can't I go to America? Everyone else has been there. It's not fair!"

It was true. Anna and Ken had both been born there, but Eri was born in Italy, when her father had been First Secretary at the Embassy in Rome. She had always wanted to see her mother's country, and at the end of last year had begged her father to take her along. But it would have been too expensive, and her wish had not been granted. *She was obviously disappointed*, thought Anna, *but even so, the way she talks is a little too fresh. After all, she's still a child, with bony shoulders and hips.*

"Anna, why are you staring at me? Is there something on my face?" Eri shrank from Anna's look.

"I'm not staring at you."

"Eri, I'll take you to America someday," her mother said. "I want to take all of you. In fact, I'd like to go there myself. It feels like a century since I've been back."

"Mama, it can't be a whole century," Eri objected in her over-emphatic way.

"It is a century. Try counting and you'll see."

"Then how old are you, Mama?"

"Why, two hundred, of course."

Ken whistled.

"All right, Saburo, how many years has it been by your count?"

"Well, we left America in 1927. That was fourteen years ago."

"Only fourteen years!" Alice exclaimed. "No, you must have made a mistake. Look how old I've become. I'm an old hag already, I must be at least two hundred."

"Mama!" Ken and Eri shouted together, giving each other a knowing glance.

"Just once, just once," their mother said more seriously, "I wish we could all go to America together."

"Papa ought to become Ambassador to the United States," said Eri.

"But Uncle Tonomura already is the Ambassador," her sister said reprovingly. "I remember he used to visit us when we were in Chicago."

"So Papa can be the next Ambassador, after Uncle Tonomura."

"Anyway," said Alice, sighing, "just once I hope we can all travel there together."

Everyone fell silent.

"In zese times . . . ," Arizumi started saying, but his English soon failed him, and he turned to Anna. "I want you to tell her something. Ever since the United States froze Japan's assets, all the Japanese in America have been leaving. The businessmen in New York and Los Angeles have already started coming home. At a time like this, your mother's wish would be very difficult to realize."

Anna hesitated, but then proceeded to translate the comment.

Alice's discomfort matched her daughter's as she said: "I'm fully aware that, in the present situation, my hopes are unrealistic, perhaps impossible."

"And another thing," Arizumi continued, addressing his wife in Japanese. "Given the present situation, it's more likely than not that Ken and George *will* be fighting in some air battle. Just think of it, the two of them locked in a duel above the South Pacific. A dogfight—up and down, round and round!"

Arizumi's braying laugh was cut off by the heavy silence that fell around him. For Anna, it was excruciating. The man she'd married seemed to have no regard for her family at all.

It was Ken who broke the silence. "If there was an air battle, I'm sure George would win it. He was a gymnast in college, he's used to doing somersaults . . . By the way, where's dessert? Oh, here it is!"

With a thud as she set it down in front of Anna, following Tanaka's instructions, Yoshiko produced a large bowl filled to the brim with fruit punch.

"Okay, turn the lights out."

Everyone waited expectantly in the darkness. Anna lit a match, but it went out. On the second try she got a fire started around the edge of the bowl. The blue flames spread, fueled by the liquid below, and before long cast a pale blue light on the faces around the table. Eri leaned over to peer at the flames, then pulled back with a squeal only just before her hair caught fire. The flames spread across the entire bowl, illuminating the peaches and grapes and apples floating below, and making them look as if they had just ripened there in that unearthly, magic light. The flames rose higher above the pieces of fruit, until the whole thing flickered like a mirage of Gothic towers short and tall. Eri clapped her hands, and everyone else applauded with her. Finally the little towers of light collapsed one after another into the punch, and the room was dark again. Even after the lights came on, the mirage stayed with them for a moment.

Anna saw Tanaka standing bashfully in the corner, and called out to him, "C'était très bien." Tanaka walked over with a mincing step.

"It was superb," repeated Anna.

"Did you like it? Je suis très heureux. It burned with great beauty. Madame Arizumi's fire power was magnifique."

"Oh, I wish it wasn't over," said Eri. "I want to see it again."

"Well now, mademoiselle, you should drink it before it get cold. Tout de suite!" Tanaka helped Yoshiko serve the punch. When Alice praised every stage of the night's dinner, Tanaka curtsied like an embarrassed girl who has gained a boy's attentions, and covered his blushing face with his hands.

A cheerful, animated mood returned to the table. As Ken blew on a piece of apple balanced on his spoon, Anna said to him, "Do you remember the house in Chicago where we used to live?"

"Of course I do." There was a hint of nostalgia in his voice. "The year before last, I walked around trying to find it. I asked at the Consulate, but they said it was too long ago, and they didn't know. So Lauren and I went out to look for it." At the mention of Lauren's name Eri gave her mother a wink. "Lauren hadn't been to our old house in a long time either, and her memory was pretty dim. All we could remember was that there was an old-fashioned hotel nearby, and that you could see the lake from our window."

"Then how'd you ever find it?" asked Eri, pressing forward.

"Incidentally," Saburo interrupted, "I also went looking for it when I passed through Chicago this year."

"It's like a detective story."

"Ken's right: it was a three-story house, painted white, right on Lake Michigan. It was near an 'old-fashioned hotel,' called the Drake, where upper-class Europeans often stayed. Yes, three stories—the first was the consular offices, and the two floors above were our residence. There weren't many Japanese in Chicago back then, so we made do with the one house. Anyway, the result of my own investigation was . . ." His eyes lit up, and he smiled at Eri. "Sad to say, our old house has been torn down to make way for a highway."

"Oh, what a gyp!" cried Eri.

"However," said Saburo, his smile still directed at Eri, "after the white house, we lived in another house. It was on the University of Chicago campus. That house is still there, and that's where Ken and Anna grew up."

"Papa," Ken said excitedly, "was it right by the Roble House?"

"Yes, it was."

"I thought so! I found it too. It was an old two-story building, with steps leading up to the door from the street. So it *was* the place we grew up in!"

"Papa, what's the Roble House?"

"It's a strange brick building that looks a lot like the Imperial Hotel. Eri, you know the famous architect Frank Lloyd Wright, don't you? Well, Wright built Roble House too. It's on the campus, and the university maintains it. I think they use it as a student meeting hall or something."

"I remember!" Anna sounded equally excited. "I'd forgotten the name, but I remember a brick house with a strange exterior. Mama used to take me walking by there. I thought it was haunted! It gave me the creeps—it had staircases in funny places, and it reminded me of a castle or a prison."

"Anyway," Ken continued, "from the Roble House I turned into the third side street, and one block down I saw it, the twelfth house on the right. There was a sign with the current owners' name on it. It was very old, with curved windows. The porch was all covered with dust, but it looked as if people were living in it. Lauren suggested we go in, but I said no, let's just look at it from the outside. It was like a dream, and I didn't want to be woken up. What about you, Papa? Did you meet the current owners?"

"Oh no. I felt the same way—I didn't want to spoil the dream. I did, however, go around to the back to see if it still looked the same. The elm in our garden had grown into a huge tree."

"It's so nice hearing about it," said Alice. "Let's all go visit that house together someday."

"Someday," Eri echoed.

6

The family decided to take their after-dinner coffee on the veranda, but found a swarm of big striped mosquitoes and moths there. Only after insect repellent had been lit and the maids had chased them away with flyswatters were they able to drink their coffee in peace. As long as they ignored the occasional mosquito buzzing around their ears, they were able to enjoy the cool, refreshing breeze and the rich taste of Tanaka's espresso. When the evening air turned chill, they moved into the parlor. Just then the Hendersens arrived for a visit: the pastor of the Anglican church, his wife Audrey, and their daughter Margaret. The three of them were old friends of the Kurushimas, but they had never met Arizumi.

When he was introduced to Anna's husband, Father Hendersen bowed and said, "*Hajimemashite*," before telling him in fluent Japanese, "I've known Anna since she was a little girl. What a fine young woman she's turned into." Audrey and Margaret also greeted Arizumi in Japanese. Margaret had been born in Japan, attended a local primary school, and then became a classmate of Eri's at the Futaba Girls' School in Tokyo. Her Japanese was flawless.

Father Hendersen, who wore a black clerical robe, was Swiss. He was slightly older than Saburo, but he looked well over sixty. His aging was most conspicuous in the white patches of hair on his head and his wrinkled, sagging jowls, but he moved about briskly, as if his tall, thin frame were mounted on a spring. Audrey, who was English-born, had blond hair with a touch of red to it, which Margaret seemed to have inherited.

"Audrey, have a seat," said Alice, motioning her to the sofa.

As the pastor's wife sat down, she happened to pull off the Flemish lace behind her, revealing the frayed upholstery beneath. Anna discreetly reached over and put it back in place, lightly grazing Mrs. Hendersen's back as she did so. The touch seemed to be taken as a gesture of affection, and she turned to Anna with a smile.

"How are you these days, Aunt Audrey?" Anna asked.

"Well, the doctor told me to get plenty of rest, but, my dear, how can I?"

It was clear that she wasn't very well. She seemed pale, and there was some swelling around her eyes. Anna explained to her husband that early in the summer Mrs. Hendersen had had a third heart attack.

"Have you ever tried Chinese medicine?" asked Arizumi abruptly.

"Why, no," Mrs. Hendersen replied, looking somewhat startled.

"I used to have heart trouble myself. My face was all swollen too. But then I tried some Wu Ling Powder and Ta Chai Hu Extract, and I completely recovered."

"Oh . . ." Mrs. Hendersen stared open-mouthed at Arizumi as he scribbled down the names of the medicines.

"You don't want to keep going to the hospital, do you? Let me introduce you to a specialist in Chinese medicine."

"Thank you, but . . ."

"Western medicine has had its day, you know. It's the turn of Oriental medicine now."

"Yoshiaki," Anna broke in, "would you pass me that cushion, please?" Anna then arranged it on the sofa so that Mrs. Hendersen could rest more comfortably.

On the other side of the room Ken, Eri, and Margaret were engaged in an animated conversation about something. Suddenly Eri clapped her hands. "Hey, why don't we dance?" she announced.

Margaret clapped her hands too. "What a great idea! Let's dance!"

Eri's innocent suggestion brought a look of disbelief to Arizumi's face. No one danced in Japan these days; parties and dancing were considered unpatriotic.

Anna raised an objection, too. "Not everyone here is up to it," she said. "It would be rude."

"Oh, that's all right, dear," said Mrs. Hendersen from the sofa. "Go ahead. I like music."

"Those who can't dance can watch," Ken put in. "Come on, give me a hand." And he began pushing the dining table and chairs to one side of the room. The youngsters and the maids pitched in, and soon they had a small dance floor.

Ken then brought in a portable electric phonograph. It looked like a little suitcase, but it opened to reveal a turntable with speakers. He placed several records on the tall spindle, and when he pushed the switch, the bottom record dropped onto the turntable, the arm moved automatically to the edge of the record, and suddenly there was music. Arizumi was startled at the sight of this new invention.

"Papa bought it in America," said Anna proudly. "He always likes the latest things."

It was a bright, cheerful, obviously American tune.

" 'San Antonio Rose.' It's Ken's favorite," Eri announced.

"Okay, let's go!" said Margaret, grabbing Eri by the waist and starting to dance, taking the man's part. Margaret's culottes revealed her long, thin, boyish legs as she skillfully led her partner, who only just came up to Margaret's nose, across the floor. She was deliberately a little rough, and Eri swayed her hips languidly in response, then Margaret spun her about, making Eri's skirt flare out around her. When the music ended, Alice clapped loudly with delight, and everybody else joined in.

With a loud click, the next record dropped and automatically began to play. Arizumi peered into the phonograph, impressed with its magical precision. In this, he decided, America was ahead of Japan; it had this wonderful technology.

" 'Changing Partners,' by Bing Crosby," Anna announced. "This is Mama's favorite song. Oh, look everyone, she's going to dance." There was a girlish playfulness in Anna's voice that Arizumi had never been allowed to hear before.

Alice stepped onto the floor, her shoulders bobbing lightly up and down to the beat. Without a moment's hesitation, Ken grabbed his mother's hand and the two began to dance. Ken was a superb dancer. His narrow hips and long legs reminded Arizumi of a flamenco dancer. As for his mother, her movements were stiff at first, but gradually relaxed. The way she seemed to glide from step to step, the vivacity in her eyes, the way she spun on her heels—no one would have taken her for a woman past fifty. Tanaka and Yoshiko poked their heads in to watch Madame Kurushima and Master Ken dancing, and Father Hendersen clapped his hands to the beat. Eri and Margaret stopped their own dancing to watch, entranced.

When the song ended, there was a burst of applause, but Alice's voice rose above it. "*Banzai*! We were great! We were terrific, weren't we?"

The tempo of the third piece was fast. Eri, unable to contain herself, demanded that Ken dance with her. Father Hendersen asked Anna for the honor. Margaret was left without a partner, but spotted Tanaka behind a pillar and dragged him onto the floor.

"Oh no, mademoiselle, I really can't, je ne peux pas danser," he protested. But when Alice nodded to him that it was okay, he became more confident, moving with a curiously supple swaying of his hips. It made him swell with pride to be dancing with this beautiful blond girl, and he led her past Yoshiko and Asa again and again as if to say, "Look at me, you peasants."

Arizumi slipped away from this boisterous activity and went out to the veranda, where he found his father-in-law sitting alone, smoking his pipe. Arizumi took the seat beside him and lit up a Homare cigarette. He kept a smile on his face for Saburo's benefit, but privately he was thinking, *What a bizarre family, what a strange night.* He'd seen things here one never saw—or at least no longer saw—going on in an ordinary Japanese family. Last October all the dance halls in Japan had been shut down; at a time of national emergency, the "unhealthy pursuit" of dancing had been banned. It took daring even to dance inside one's own home. But here, with no qualms at all, they were dancing away as if it were the most natural thing in the world.

Moreover, the evening meal had been scandalously lavish. Rice was being rationed, the distribution of vegetables was severely restricted, and meat and fish were almost impossible to obtain. Of course the Kurushimas must have saved up for the occasion, but even so, to put such a banquet together was impossible for any ordinary family. Their stock of wine and cognac must have come from their long stay overseas, but how did they get their hands on all the fresh meat and vegetables? Obviously this was a privileged family. No doubt they were being financed by wealthy American relatives.

American. *Yes*, he thought, *Mrs. Kurushima is one hundred percent American. Her blood is Scottish, pure Anglo-Saxon. You can see it in Ken and Eri. If Ken didn't wear the uniform of a soldier in the Imperial Army, and didn't speak Japanese, no one would think he was Japanese.* In fact, when Arizumi had shared the large bath with him in the afternoon, it had been quite a shock. He knew that Ken's arms were hairy, but he had never seen a chest covered with such thick black hair. Certainly no Japanese ever looked like that—it was a bear's chest. And then there was Ken's body odor—it was repulsive! He could understand why the Japanese, when speaking disparagingly of things Western, said they "reeked of butter." Arizumi swore never to have a bath with him again.

And to think that instead of underpants Ken had worn a loincloth! Even the self-consciously Japanese Arizumi had worn Western-style underpants since childhood, and there was Ken in that most Japanese of undergarments, a white *fundoshi*. Not only that, but his favorite foods were sashimi and tempura, and he spoke the language without a trace of an accent. When they met on the train at Kumagaya, the sight of this Japanese officer with an American face had seemed distinctly odd at first, yet once they started talking he'd found nothing "foreign" at all about Ken's general outlook.

But now this Japanese officer had become completely American— look at the way he was dancing.

Eri also looked far more Caucasian than Japanese. The only Japanese thing about her was her black hair. When Eri and Ken were dancing together, they looked exactly like a couple of *gaijin* who happened to be in Japan.

Arizumi stared at his wife across the room. Of the three Kurushima children Anna had inherited the most from her father. Arizumi had always thought her small mouth and narrow eyes were very Japanese. But now as she danced with Father Hendersen, he could see that

Caucasian blood ran thick in her veins too: it showed in her lively movements, the gleam in her eyes that made them almost look blue, and—it suddenly occurred to him—her powerful body odor when they made love.

Arizumi surveyed the scene inside the parlor. Could this lively, happy family, dancing their American dances, really be living in 1941?

July 7th had been the fourth anniversary of the invasion of China, and Arizumi had attended the press conference given by General Hideki Tojo, the Army Minister and Director of the Manchurian Agency. While taking notes, Arizumi had been riveted by the sight of his round, shaven head and the sound of his crisp, high-pitched voice as he intoned: "*Ima yaaah sekai no josei waaah . . .*"

> In these times, when the international situation is fraught with confusion, its shifts beyond calculation, our celebration of the fourth anniversary of the China Incident fills me with profound emotion. In the course of this Holy War in which we have been engaged for four years, through the brilliant sacrifices of our officers and men in the service of His August Imperial Dignity, and with the sincere support of the people on the home front, we have seen a few brave soldiers defeat a horde of Chinese troops. And radiant with the light of that August Dignity, our Imperial Forces shine upon the nation of Japan, and will bring glorious victories without precedent in the history of warfare . . .

Tojo's speech was a pastiche of sentimentality and flowery language, but if one listened carefully, his prediction of future victories was clear in its intent: to warn the nation of the prospect of a world war and the need to be prepared for it.

Sullen clouds lay thick over the Japanese islands. In the ten years since the Manchurian Incident, a national consensus had gradually formed: to "solve" the China problem by force, then to create the Greater East Asia Co-Prosperity Sphere, and to promote "harmonious cooperation" among the nations of Asia under the aegis of Japan. Only the United States stood in Japan's way. The United States had opposed Japan's actions to date, and would no doubt oppose them in the future. What Tojo called "the brilliant sacrifices of our officers and men" was denounced in America as "the rape of Nanking." In February a new Ambassador, Heiji Tonomura, had been sent to Washington, and since spring he had been involved in continuing negotiations with President Roosevelt and Secretary of State Hull. But there was no sign of any improvement in relations between the two countries.

Arizumi turned to look at Saburo, who was enjoying the sight of his family dancing inside as he blew smoke from his pipe into the night air. He seemed completely relaxed, without a care in the world, as he sat back in his wicker armchair.

The man was a mystery. Arizumi had certain pegs he used to classify people — ambition, thirst for power, passion for money, personal cravings. Saburo didn't quite fit any of them. Arizumi couldn't fathom what his father-in-law was thinking, what his purpose was in living.

He had first met Saburo during the February 26th Incident in 1936, an attempted coup d'état by young rightist officers. Arizumi, a rookie reporter, had gone to Nagata-cho in central Tokyo, where many of the government offices were located, to see what was going on. He was keeping an eye on the rebel soldiers, who had taken over the Sanno Hotel, when he saw several women appear in one of the side streets below the bluff. The women were carrying some pots, and as they placed them on the sidewalk, they gestured to the soldiers. In the snow, this all looked like some strange shadow play. Arizumi was intrigued. He cut through the Sanno Shrine to the hill behind it, then made his way down the steep slope beside the middle school, and came out into the alley. There he saw a foreign woman directing the other women as they dished out *miso* soup and rice balls to a platoon of rebel soldiers. Arizumi watched from a distance, then followed as they picked up their empty pots and made their way back up the slope, disappearing into a mansion in front of the Mexican Embassy. The nameplate at the gate read Saburo Kurushima. Arizumi recognized the name. It belonged to the Director of the Trade Bureau, whose wife, Arizumi recalled, was American. In the midst of a coup, with the Army mobilized against it, here was the family of a senior official distributing food to the rebels.

Arizumi smelled a scandal. The next day he paid a visit to the Trade Bureau. At first, Kurushima responded positively to the reporter's request for an interview, but when Arizumi proceeded to ask a pointed question about his wife's activities, the mild-mannered Director exploded. "How dare you! What's wrong with my wife giving food to some hungry people? You're a reporter covering the Foreign Ministry, you say? How dare you come in here and raise this idiotic issue! Get out, get the hell out of here!" Secretaries and assistants came running over, and Arizumi was unceremoniously removed. The article was never written.

Three years later Arizumi encountered Saburo Kurushima again. Arizumi was a correspondent in Berlin for the Tokyo News Agency, and Kurushima was the Ambassador to Germany. It was a turbulent time. The German Army had invaded Poland the month before, and Britain and France had declared war on Germany. Arizumi was competing with reporters from other agencies for any information he could get. Whether Kurushima had forgotten their previous encounter or whether he pretended it hadn't happened, he treated Arizumi with the same civility he showed toward any other reporter he was meeting for the first time.

One day, Arizumi walked into the reception hall in the Japanese Embassy to find an enormous bouquet of roses there, reaching right up to the ceiling. The combined scent of hundreds of these flowers was sweetly overpowering. To a Japanese sensibility, accustomed to the careful arrangement of three or four blossoms in a simple vase, the effect was more outlandish than beautiful, more oppressive than pleasing.

Just then a young woman, evidently the Ambassador's secretary, appeared. "My father has a visitor right now," she told him. "Could you wait a few minutes, please?"

"Yes, certainly," Arizumi replied, quickly switching to polite speech. "Would you happen to be the Ambassador's daughter?"

"I'm Anna Kurushima. How do you do."

He was immediately attracted by her narrow, tapering eyes. Not wanting to seem forward, he looked away, toward the bouquet of roses.

"It's gorgeous, isn't it?"

"Yes. But my father dislikes it."

"Well, yes, there are rather too many of them."

"It's not just that. He despises the person who sent it."

"Oh, and who might that be?"

"Hitler," she said quite casually.

"Why does he despise him?"

"Because Hitler's fond of war. My father hates war."

"I see." Without the slightest hesitation, the Ambassador's daughter had expressed a critical opinion of the most powerful man on earth. Arizumi took this as a sign of her youth, and found it rather charming. "But your father did accept the ambassadorship to Germany," he said teasingly.

"Only after refusing it several times. He kept telling them he didn't want to go to Germany at a time like this. Uncle Tonomura begged him to accept." The girl went on to explain that Foreign Minister Tonomura had been a friend of her father's since their Chicago days, when Tonomura, who was the Naval Attaché at the Consulate back then, used to pick her up and carry her around. Tonomura was a tall man, so the ground had seemed terribly far away, yet she'd felt quite safe.

This was Anna and Arizumi's first encounter, and before long they were seeing each other frequently. As a result, the doors to Nazi society in Berlin began to open for him, not as a correspondent but as a friend of the Japanese Ambassador's family, and eventually as Anna's fiancé. With Anna at his side, he even went to parties at the homes of Foreign Minister Ribbentrop and Luftwaffe Commandant Goering. The excesses of Goering's private mansion, he remembered, made it seem less like a politician's residence than the castle of a daydreamer whose dreams knew no limits. There was a heated pool in the cellar, next to which was a large room whose floor was an intricate network of electric trains running through a landscape of mountains, lakes, and valleys. If one looked closely, one realized that the entire room was a miniature model of Germany. When his guests had all assembled, the Air Marshal made his entry wearing a green Alpine folk costume, complete with lederhosen and a Tyrolean hat, and began directing his trains. A servant threw a switch. Whistles blew. And little locomotives pulled out, one after another, from stations all across the country. After a while, an artificial dusk fell over the room, with a red sunset slanting across the model hills and dales, so the headlights came on and the trains raced through a nocturnal Reich.

After the show, which ended with a burst of applause, the guests were led upstairs to admire the "Portrait of Frau Goering" painted by His Excellency himself. This large picture—it must have been two and a half meters by three—showed the young and beautiful Emmy Goering seated on a Ludwig II couch with her newborn baby. The gilt frame glittered in the spotlight, filling the room with refractions of light. What most impressed the guests, however, was the fact that the furniture was all two or three times the normal size. The women squealed with laughter as they stretched out on sofas that were designed for giants and found themselves sinking into massive cushions. In the dining room was a gargantuan refrigerator donated by an American company. The Commandant opened it to reveal an immense and colorful array of food gathered from around the world. Then they were shown the bedroom, which, His Excellency explained, was kept at a constant 0° centigrade. Stroking his plump red face, he told them that with the temperature at freezing point the skin was constantly stimulated; this was the secret of eternal youth.

Arizumi and Anna wandered together through Hermann's fantasy world, with Arizumi translating for her. Anna knew almost nothing about politics, but she couldn't help wondering how Japan ever found itself allied with such eccentric creatures. She watched from a distance as Goering, with his paunch and his hairy legs, offered cocktails to the guests.

"What a peculiar man."

"Yes, he is strange. But because of him, the German Air Force is what it is today."

"Do you like him?"

"More than liking him, I'd say he's a necessity," Arizumi answered, giving a little bow in Emmy Goering's direction, who was approaching them with a plate of Dutch strawberries. "These times demand exceptional men. Your run-of-the-mill politician won't steer us through the stormy seas ahead."

"I suppose not," said Anna, somewhat surprised at the sudden conviction in her fiancé's words.

Anna looked straight into the transparent features of Emmy Goering's face, thinking how they reminded her of a woman just after she has given birth. She then turned to Arizumi and said forcefully in Japanese: "That man is just too childish for my taste."

Unaware of what her guest was saying, Emmy offered her some strawberries, mentioning that their refrigerator was capable of keeping last summer's fruit perfectly fresh.

Unlike the Goerings' party, the guest list of a banquet they attended at the Ribbentrops was limited to Ambassador Kurushima, a few other diplomats attached to the Embassy, and several selected members of the press. Frau Ribbentrop greeted her guests at the door, but from then on they were in the constant presence of ten uniformed men who stood rigidly behind them. The men were all tall and powerfully built, with a certain gleam in their eyes, and dressed in darker uniforms than those worn by the regular Nazi soldiers. Whenever one of the guests addressed Frau Ribbentrop, the men politely withdrew a few steps, but not so far that they couldn't listen to what was being said. Conversation, as a result, was not exactly lively. Indeed, the whole affair was extremely stiff, with the clinking of cocktail glasses and the heavy footsteps of the waiters sounding unnaturally loud in the room.

At the beginning of April 1940 the German Army had begun its invasion of Denmark and Norway. By May it had progressed through Holland, Luxembourg, and Belgium, then had easily broken through the Maginot Line into France. At the end of May the British Army had pulled out of Dunkirk, and in the middle of July the Germans had occupied Paris.

Following the French surrender, the brilliant successes of the blitzkrieg had inflamed public opinion in Japan. Until then the government had promoted compromise with the United States and Britain, but now the call was heard everywhere for a "southward advance," for Japan to form an alliance with Germany and move into Southeast Asia. The papers were filled with fervent editorials urging Japan to liberate the British, French, and Dutch colonies and to establish a Greater East Asia Co-Prosperity Sphere.

As Arizumi scanned the newspapers and magazines sent from Tokyo, he could sense Japan's eagerness to use the example of Germany's successes in order to solve the "China problem" and gain a conclusive victory of its own in Asia. There was a notable increase among the younger officials at the Embassy arguing for a German-Japanese military alliance. At this moment of historic opportunity, they claimed, Ambassador Kurushima was wrong to cling to a policy of weakness, a policy of compromise with the United States and Britain. Some even dared to say that if Kurushima wasn't replaced with a pro-German ambassador, Japan would "miss the bus."

In July Prince Konoe formed a new Cabinet, which included the pro-Nazi Matsuoka as Foreign Minister. German-Japanese negotiations were carried on without Kurushima's knowledge, as Matsuoka conferred directly with Hitler's Special Envoy in Tokyo, Stahmer, and in the middle of September a meeting was convened in the presence of the Emperor. The contents of this meeting were never divulged, but soon afterwards Kurushima received a telegram from Tokyo ordering him to sign the Tripartite Pact with Germany and Italy. Suddenly Saburo Kurushima was the man of the hour. A man who had had nothing to do with the negotiations, who knew nothing of their terms, had become the main actor in the drama of signing the treaty.

On the day of the signing, hundreds of journalists from the three Axis powers and elsewhere gathered at Hitler's chancellery in Berlin. Among them was Yoshiaki Arizumi. At the center of a huge desk sat Ribbentrop, with the Italian Foreign Minister Ciano on his right and the Japanese Ambassador Kurushima on his left. When it was Kurushima's turn to sign the document, Arizumi was astonished to see him grimace; it was the same expression he'd had when he'd thrown Arizumi out of the Trade Bureau in Tokyo. But that wasn't all. As soon as he was finished, Kurushima flung his fountain pen onto the table, as if he wanted to be rid of the filthy thing. Normally the pen used to sign a document of historic importance is treasured by the signer, or donated to a museum, or presented to someone as a token of high regard. In this case, Kurushima's pen rolled unceremoniously across the desk, and a young official only just grabbed it before it fell off.

Several months later Arizumi learned that Kurushima had announced his intention to resign from the Foreign Ministry. Arizumi asked for, and got, a personal interview.

"Why are you resigning, sir?"

"For reasons of health. My blood pressure has been high. I have dizzy spells. After discussing this with my physician, I submitted my resignation."

"That's unfortunate, sir. Just at the point where Japanese-German relations have become so important."

"Unfortunate?" The Ambassador looked at Arizumi, uncomprehending. The latter was about to explain—that it was unfortunate, in terms of posterity, suddenly to withdraw at the moment he'd reached center stage as a diplomat—but decided against it. Kurushima wouldn't understand.

At the end of the year Alice, with her two daughters in tow, returned to Japan by way of the Suez Canal, and in February 1941 her husband set out on his way home via the United States. Arizumi left Germany in March and arrived in Japan in the middle of April. He and Anna were married at the end of April, in a ceremony at the Imperial Hotel.

The dancers this summer evening in Karuizawa had gone through several records, and the present tune was a Charleston—even Arizumi could tell that much. Ken was dancing with Anna, while Eri and Margaret clapped their hands to the beat.

After a while Arizumi turned to Saburo, who was still smoking his pipe, and addressed him deferentially: "There's something I've been wanting to ask you about, Father—off the record, of course. If it involves state secrets, you don't have to answer."

"Sounds ominous!" Saburo chuckled, as he raised himself in his wicker chair and stretched.

"Is it true that, during the change of government last month, Foreign Minister Toyoda asked you to be his Vice-Minister and you turned him down?"

"Hmm. Were there rumors like that floating about?"

"Rumors? No, sir, I heard it from a fairly reliable source."

"I see." Saburo took a puff on his pipe and blew the smoke out slowly. "Well, it's true. He did ask me, and I did turn him down. For reasons of health."

Reasons of health? This was the same excuse Saburo had given when he resigned as Ambassador to Germany, but he had been at the archery range just a while ago and he didn't seem to be unwell. What was the real reason? It really was unfortunate, as negotiations between Japan and America were at a critical stage. That was why Prince Konoe had resigned, so he could bring down the pro-German Foreign Minister Matsuoka with him. The new Foreign Minister, Toyoda, was known to favor reconciliation with America and Britain. Wouldn't becoming Toyoda's Vice-Minister be a perfect opportunity for Saburo Kurushima to work against the Axis pact in favor of peace between Japan and America? And not insignificantly, wouldn't the post of Vice-Minister practically guarantee his promotion to Foreign Minister someday?

"Let me put it frankly, sir," Arizumi said, raising his voice so as to be heard over the music streaming from indoors. "I think you should have accepted it. At a time like this, what Japan needs is someone who understands America. You, sir, are . . ."

"I'm not qualified for that job. Let *me* put it frankly. In order to save the peace between Japan and America we need a stronger man than myself. In fact the job will be impossible unless it's done by a man strong enough to resist the immense pressure from the military, especially from those fools in the Army who are anti-American to the core.

From Tojo on down, they're all itching for a war with the United States."

"I wouldn't exactly put it that way," said Arizumi. "No, sir, it's America that wants to go to war. All these sanctions against Japan, the embargo on oil, the freezing of our financial assets, all this economic pressure—obviously they're trying to force us to fight back."

"I don't deny that the actions of the U.S. government are driving us into a corner, or that we're surrounded by a network of hostile Western colonial powers. But it's also a fact that many Japanese think the only way to break through the net of sanctions is war. And you're one of them, aren't you? Didn't you applaud the Axis pact? And didn't you say Japan should use the Axis pact to 'smash this Anglo-American conspiracy'?"

"I did say that, and I still believe it. Because of Germany's victories, two major colonies—French Indochina and the Dutch East Indies— have been liberated and are about to emerge as independent nations. If Britain is defeated, India will become one more Asian country with a natural affinity for Japan. It's because the Germans have defeated the colonial powers in Asia that we are allied with them. Japan hasn't the slightest territorial ambitions toward those colonies. We merely want to have harmonious economic relations with them—yes, to bring them into a 'co-prosperity sphere.' But, you see, America is a colonial power, too. Why does it oppose us? It's obvious—because of the Philippines. It wants to protect its own colonial profits, along with those of Holland, France, and Britain."

"Well," said Saburo, "even if you're right, it would be suicidal for us to go to war with the United States. Don't underestimate that country."

"I'm not. I'm saying Japan should become powerful enough to keep America from interfering with our mission in Asia. The Axis pact is the first step, then the invasion of Indochina."

"And the third step, I suppose, is invading the East Indies."

"Precisely."

"Ah, but Britain, which has Singapore, won't stand for that. Churchill will bring the United States into a war with Japan in order to protect

Britain's interests in India and America's in the Philippines."

"That's why you, sir, should act to prevent that from happening. As the Vice-Minister, you'd be the one to negotiate with the Americans."

"No, not me." Saburo gave a weak smile, and knocked the ashes from his pipe. "I'm not the man for it."

Why not? thought Arizumi. *Of course the negotiations would be difficult for anyone. But Kurushima knows the United States better than any other Japanese diplomat, his English is fluent, he's met Cordell Hull, and he is an old friend of Ambassador Tonomura, who is presently handling the negotiations in Washington. Ever since signing the Axis pact, he's withdrawn from public affairs. Instead of serving the nation, he seems to be shirking all responsibility.*

Arizumi thought of the students in the Iron Cross group whom he had recruited from several universities in the course of lecturing about Germany. They revered Hitler and held seminars on *Mein Kampf.* The more they studied, the more militant they became. For Arizumi's pro-Nazi students, Foreign Minister Matsuoka, who had negotiated the Axis pact, and Ambassador Kurushima, who had signed it, were heroes on a par with Hitler. So when they found out that Arizumi was Kurushima's son-in-law, they asked him to try to get the former Ambassador to become honorary chairman of the group.

"But sir," Arizumi went on, "you're still young. Your work as a diplomat still lies ahead of you."

"I'm already fifty-six. I'm an old man. I want to rest."

"Then tell me, do you still regret signing the Axis pact?"

"What do you mean?" Saburo asked, putting his pipe down. He pulled in the footrest of his wicker chair, put his feet on the ground, and, with a quick little clap of his hands, killed a mosquito that had been bothering him.

"I know you were opposed to the Tripartite Alliance, and though you never stated your real reasons in public, I realize that you resigned because of your opposition. But times have changed. Germany has gone from victory to victory, and Japan, through its alliance with Germany, is about to achieve strategic supremacy in the Far East. It won't be long before Russia and Britain surrender to Germany.

Then America will be left standing alone and in no position to oppose the Axis powers. The result will be peace on earth. The world will be divided into three great and equal spheres: the European Co-Prosperity Sphere centered on Germany, our own Greater East Asia Co-Prosperity Sphere centered on Japan, and an American Co-Prosperity Sphere centered on the United States. A perfect balance of power . . ."

"I rather doubt it. You assume that England and Russia will capitulate to Germany, and I wouldn't count on that happening any time soon."

"But sir," he persisted, his voice gaining strength, "Germany *can* do it with *our* help. We can smash the Russians in Manchuria, then smash the British from Singapore to Burma, and then India! With help from us Germany can defeat England and Russia."

"But if you do all that, America certainly won't stand still."

"You're right. Japan and America mustn't go to war. We have to find a way to make the Japanese-German dream a reality—and let's not forget Italy—and to pursue the 'southward advance' without provoking the United States into war. The beginning of that dream was the Axis pact, an event of supreme historical significance."

"I don't want to talk about it any more. The memory of that treaty fills me with disgust."

"But . . . ," Arizumi began, and then fell silent. He'd seen a twitch in Saburo's face, and knew from experience that it was a sign of profound irritation.

"Aren't you going to dance?" Saburo asked gently, as if embarrassed at his own anger.

"I can't. I'm no good at things like that. I can manage a few Noh gestures, though. Why don't you dance, Father?"

"I'm no good at these amusements, either. I can manage a little archery, though."

They looked at each other and laughed. But the younger man couldn't help feeling that the true Saburo Kurushima had evaded him once again. For him, Saburo remained a mystery.

7

Ken and Margaret were now dancing together. Margaret was a tall girl, but her partner was taller, and she didn't dwarf him the way she did other Japanese boys. They made an attractive couple: Ken looking like a teenager in his light red polo shirt with sky blue stripes, and Margaret in her white tennis skirt. As they whirled around the room, Anna was intrigued to see how they looked like children one moment and adults the next. She couldn't take her eyes off them.

"Hey, look at them," said Eri, tugging at her sleeve. "Don't they look fantastic!"

"What do you mean, 'fantastic'?"

"You know what I mean, Anna. Ken and Maggie—they'd make a fantastic husband and wife."

"Are you going to start that up again?" Anna felt exasperated with her. *Just a minute ago you were marrying him off to Lauren*, she thought, looking at her sister's smiling eyes. "Eri, do you realize that once Ken is married he'll live somewhere else? Is that really what you want to happen?"

"Oh no! He belongs to us. So we should never let him get married."

Before Anna could tell her what a fool she was, Eri was gone, and was soon working her way into her mother's conversation with Mrs. Hendersen and saying something that made the two women laugh.

Smoke from the anti-mosquito coils drifted in waves across the veranda. Anna could see her husband and her father talking. They had drawn their chairs close together, engaged in some intense discussion. Had Arizumi actually asked him to become chairman of the Iron Cross? Was he trying to solicit his opinion on some diplomatic news? *Papa, aren't you cold out there? Shall I bring you a sweater?*

She hated the thought that the evening was drawing to a close. For the first time in a long while, she would have to share a bed with her husband. When he reached for her, would she be able to forget about his mistress?

The sky still glowed with the lingering blue light of the day, but the branches on the larches hung coal-black. *It's only been half a year*, she thought, *but I've aged. Look at Ken and Eri and Maggie, in the full swing of youth.*

Nothing could tire Ken, it seemed. With vigorous turns and crisp sashays, he whirled around the parlor, leading Margaret, then Eri, then Anna, without even breaking into a sweat. Glenn Miller, Benny Goodman, Teddy Wilson, Frank Sinatra, Louis Armstrong. Clarinets squealed, drums thumped, an alto sax blew a series of riffs. "Let's Dance," "Moonlight Serenade," "It's Been So Long," "You Turned the Tables on Me" . . . As Anna danced, she could sense her husband's eyes following her around the room. They were the eyes of a man who knew only Japanese war songs and Nazi marches.

In the middle of a dance, the maid Yoshiko entered the room and whispered something into Alice's ear. Anna stopped when she saw the serious expression on the maid's face.

"There are two men at the front door," her mother reported.

"Who are they?" Anna asked.

"I don't know. They're making some sort of demands. They want everybody's names."

Eri, who'd heard the exchange, walked over. "Mama, what's going on?" she asked uneasily.

Alice put a finger to her lips. "It's nothing, just be quiet."

She started for the hall, but Anna stopped her. "No, Mama, I'll go." There was something about the situation that suggested her mother should stay back.

Standing at the door were two men, one in his thirties, the other around twenty or so. Both were dressed in shorts and shirts splashed with gaudy colors, the older man holding what seemed to be a beret in his hand. Their faces were sunburned, their arms and legs muscular. And yet they didn't look quite right in their casual European clothes.

"Can I help you?" Anna asked.

"Yes, miss, we'd like to ask you a few questions." The older man spoke in a fluent standard Japanese that belied his rugged looks. "Is this the residence of Mr. Kurushima?"

"Yes, it is."

"Saburo Kurushima, the former Ambassador to Germany?"

"Yes, that's correct."

The man peered inside. "Are you holding some kind of special meeting here tonight?" He caught a glimpse of Eri, who had peeked into the hallway and who immediately backed away. Strains of jazz could be heard from the parlor. "What nationality is your guest?"

"Nationality?" Anna gave a half-smile. "That's my sister, Eri Kurushima."

"Oh, I'm sorry."

"Excuse me, but who are you? And what do you want?"

"I'm sorry, we've made a . . ."

"*This* is who we are," the younger of them said, waving a black ID card in Anna's face. They were from the Military Police. Anna's eyes opened wide. "What's that music?" the man went on, now almost shouting. "How dare you play enemy music in the middle of a national emergency!"

"Miss, we're very sorry," his partner intervened, still speaking politely. "But we wondered if you could restrain yourselves, out of consideration for public decency."

"Yes, of course . . . ," Anna stammered, wishing she'd turned the music off before she came out. Instead, it sounded as if someone had actually turned the volume up.

"You going to turn it off or not?" The young man had become quite agitated. She'd thought he was just a kid, but seeing his complexion from close up, she realized he could be ten years older.

"Excuse me a moment," she said, turning and signaling with her eyes to Yoshiko, who stood behind her.

Yoshiko went back inside, and in her place Ken came out. To Anna's astonishment he was dressed in full military uniform, with sword and peaked cap. He walked over to the two men with large, confident strides.

Lowering his voice a half octave, he said firmly, "This is the home of an Imperial Army officer. Just what are you doing here?"

"Yes, sir," said the older man. "It's the music, sir. We felt it our duty to suggest it might not be appropriate in a national emergency."

"Why isn't it appropriate? It's German music. Are you telling us not to play the music of an ally of ours?"

"Oh no, not at . . ."

"You can't *dance!*" cried the other man, his voice shaking, as if he'd forced the sounds from his throat. "Dancing is forbidden at a time like this!"

"I know the dance halls have been shut down," answered Ken, tapping the floor with the tip of his sword, "but no one's forbidden to dance. Especially German dances. They're considered a perfectly healthy amusement. Aren't they?"

"Yes, of course, sir," the senior of them said. "As long as they're German, it's all right."

Ken, unsmiling, looked at the two men. "Lieutenant Ken Kurushima is who I am—son of Ambassador Saburo Kurushima. If you goons are really Military Police, state your name and rank!"

"Yes, sir, sorry, sir." They showed him their ID cards. Ken nodded gravely. "Everything's in order. Now get out of here!"

When the intruders had scurried out of earshot, there was a burst of laughter, followed by an awkward silence. After a moment, Mrs. Hendersen remarked how Karuizawa had recently seen an increase in the number of Military Police and Thought Police, and that foreigners were coming under close surveillance. In fact, just the other day her husband had been called in for having read in his Sunday sermon a "subversive" passage from Matthew 5:9, "Blessed are the peacemakers: for they shall be called the children of God."

With a shrug, Father Hendersen said, "It was right after Germany declared war on Russia, so I suppose the police were a little more nervous than usual."

"What did you tell them?"

"Since there was no way I could get them to understand the meaning of 'peace' in the Bible, I said, 'Isn't war itself in the end a means of bringing about peace?' They finally let me go."

"There's been a lot of harassment recently," said Anna, who told them about a visit she'd received from a group of women wearing armbands with "Greater Japan Women's Patriotic League" on them. They had come to warn her that her Western clothes were too ostentatious, and that she should switch to what was called the "combat style," which was either a plain dark kimono or farmer's baggy trousers. "Everybody seems to be telling other people what to do . . . Still, maybe we should cut out dancing for a while."

"No, it's all right," said Ken emphatically. "Don't worry about it."

"It was all right today because you were here to defend us, but what'll happen when you're not around? And if Papa goes to Tokyo we women will be left on our own here."

"We'll have Tanaka," said Eri, "—but that won't do us much good."

"You'll be all right," said Arizumi. "I don't care if it's the Military Police or the Thought Police, they can't touch the Ambassador. And Ken here gave you the perfect excuse. As former Ambassador to Germany, Father naturally has lots of German friends. Tell the police you're entertaining our allies. They'll believe it. They don't know the difference between Germany and America. German and English sound the same to them."

"I don't like it," said Anna, as if to spite him, "—this feeling that it's good if it's German and bad if it's American. We're not at war with the United States, you know."

"But we might be any time now," her husband answered, which earned him a glare from Anna, if only for her mother's sake.

The evening took a new turn with the arrival of Ryoichi Koyama. Ryoichi was the only son of the owner of the Peony Inn, and he and Ken had been friends since childhood. Having had polio in infancy, he had grown up without the use of his right leg, and he walked with a heavy limp. But even with his one good leg he had managed to become a better than ordinary swimmer, rider, and tennis player. After graduating from middle school, he had been helping his family out at the inn.

"Well, well, what a delight this is!" said Ryoichi, putting on an affected voice. "Even our distinguished pastor and his family are with us tonight." He then went over to where Margaret and Eri were standing and peered into the phonograph. "Looks like a great record. Come on, play it for me."

"We can't," said Ken. "The police were just here, and they put a stop to our fun."

"Who, the MPs? Oh, those guys have been throwing their weight around lately. Don't worry about them. They're just a bunch of idiots. Wow, this one's great! Come on, let's put it on." Ryoichi pulled a record from the pile and handed it to Eri; it was "West End Blues."

"If the police come again, we'll tell them it's a German lied," said Ken, still wearing his uniform and sword as he asked his mother for a dance. Father Hendersen led Eri onto the floor, and Ryoichi and Margaret formed another couple. Ryoichi kicked out with his good right leg. It was a strange step, but it was fun to watch, and it fitted the music perfectly.

"Who is he?" Arizumi asked Anna.

"An old friend of Ken's, the son of an innkeeper."

"I see. You certainly get some interesting people coming through this house. What's that music?"

"One of Louis Armstrong's three classic blues."

"Ah yes, I see," said Arizumi. "We're not in Japan. This is America."

Another Armstrong number came on, "Strutting with Some Barbecue," which picked up the tempo and had a lot of bounce to it. Ryoichi's movements became more and more frantic, and Margaret laughed as she leapt away and flung herself back at him.

So the dancing continued for a while, until Ryoichi suddenly sat down at the piano and began playing Gershwin's "Summertime." He played well, his fingers gliding over the keys. Even Arizumi was impressed. Then, for a change of air, Ryoichi suggested they all go for a walk. Eri and Ken agreed, and the Hendersens, who were about to head for home anyway, joined in, so they all set out together. Only Arizumi was reluctant to go, saying he was too tired, but when Saburo insisted he come along, he couldn't refuse.

It was pitch dark outside. The moment they stepped out of the house they couldn't see anything in front of them. Ken led the way with his Army flashlight, shining it on the dirt path that took them through the rice paddies. When they reached the livery stable they were on the main road, with spots of light showing here and there in the houses. But there was no one else out on the road, and it was a little frightening. When they finally got to the shopping street in Karuizawa Old Town, they found the stores still open and visitors to the resort strolling under the streetlamps in various styles of attire. Among the cotton summer kimonos and peasant trousers, there were the casual white outfits of the foreigners.

Here in Karuizawa nobody usually gave these foreigners a second glance, but Alice was another story. She had on a long white dress that seemed to sweep the ground, and a broad-brimmed hat so enormous it looked more like a fluffy parasol. As Saburo walked beside her in his pith helmet—strange headgear for an evening stroll—the brim of his wife's hat would sometimes brush his ear or cheek, making him duck. They were obviously a married couple, and people stared at the unusual combination of a Japanese husband and a Western wife. Alice kept up a stream of conversation in her crisp East Coast English, calling back to her family when they fell behind, and reading out aloud each English shop sign as it came into view. Ken was always popular in Karuizawa, and many people remembered him from years before. The old men who ran the stores nodded at him as they passed, and he stopped to chat with friends.

The Kurushimas had been hoping to find a *bon* dance in progress, but none was to be found. Ordinarily, in mid-August, all the shrines and temples for miles around would echo to the beat of drums. In Karuizawa a stage would be set up in the square next to the tennis courts, and men and women in their summer kimonos would come to dance. But *bon odori*, it seemed, was a peacetime festival. Now that Japan had been at war with China for four years, the shrines refrained from such frivolities, and people stayed away. Tonight the square was dark; no one was around. The group was disappointed. But then Ken had a suggestion: "Ryoichi says there's a *bon odori* at the Jingu Temple. Why don't we have a look?"

So they braced themselves and began climbing the slope that led up to it. They passed the last shop in town and took the dark road further up, until they reached Father Hendersen's little wooden Anglican church. Turning left just before the church, they made their way up a narrow pilgrim's path and into the temple grounds. There they found a *bon* dance in full swing. The organizers had made do with a pile of wooden boxes for a stage. The drums were cheap and tinny, like toys, and instead of the usual small band, the music came from a hand-cranked Victrola. But there was an unexpectedly large crowd, fully half of whom were foreigners. The Western women were dancing in a circle. They were all dressed in summer kimonos, as were their children, who danced in a large circle around them, copying what they did.

Arizumi, in his role as journalist, spoke to a few of the people, and came back to say: "They're German evacuees from enemy territory, the Dutch East Indies, I believe." While he proceeded to interview one of them, Ken jumped into the circle of dancers, followed by Eri, Margaret, and Alice. Saburo, the Hendersens, and Anna watched from the perimeter. Each time a new number began, the old man who was in charge would announce the title of the song through his megaphone, to the cheers of the enthusiastic crowd. The songs were unfamiliar to Anna, but she loved being there. She was reminded of the festivals her father had taken her to see years ago in the traditional districts of Tokyo, in Kanda and Asakusa. They were very Japanese customs—yes, uniquely Japanese—and she realized now how much she'd missed them.

"What's the matter? Why aren't you dancing?" her husband asked her, notebook and pencil in hand.

"I can't, I don't know how."

"Ah, I see. You can do the American jitterbug, but you don't know your own country's dances. Well, don't worry about it, just copy somebody and you'll pick it up naturally. *Bon odori* is a rare sight these days, it's certainly worth an article. I'm going to call it 'Scenes of Solidarity in Karuizawa: Japanese and Germans Join in Healthy Amusements.' "

Saburo glanced at the Germans and asked Arizumi about them. Arizumi, who was delighted to be asked, told him what he'd learned. "The women are evacuees from Dutch Batavia. After the outbreak of war with Russia, they were unable to return to Germany. They're all separated from their husbands. It's a group of wives and children, but they seem to be bearing up pretty well. They chose a leader, and under her direction they work through the day in shifts, from reveille at six to lights out at ten, with a specific time allotted to each task— washing, sewing, knitting, calisthenics, child rearing. The leader seems to be a member of the Nazi party. Her husband was taken prisoner, and she doesn't know if he's dead or alive. I've got an appointment to interview her later on at the Mampei Hotel."

A plump, blond, middle-aged woman wearing a swastika armband on the sleeve of her cotton kimono came up and addressed Arizumi in German. Arizumi, proudly using her language, introduced her to Saburo and Alice. Alice shook hands cordially with the woman and exchanged a few words with her in German, but Saburo merely bowed to her perfunctorily, then turned away. Saburo was himself fluent in the language, having worked without an interpreter when he was Ambassador, but the Nazi woman had put him off. He had seen far too many people like her in Berlin, haughty and self-confident, and he thoroughly disliked them. He started to leave, and Alice and Anna joined him.

When they reached the edge of the temple compound, Eri came running after them. "Papa, what's wrong?" she said. "We came all the way up here, so can't we stay and dance a little?"

Saburo ignored her, walking on. "Papa's not in a good mood right now," Alice explained, and Eri silently seemed to understand. Ken and the Hendersens soon caught up with them, leaving only Arizumi behind. He could be heard talking with the German woman, punctuating the conversation with loud laughs.

That night Anna was unable to fall asleep. She had gotten her husband's bed ready next to hers inside the large mosquito net, but she dreaded his return. Hours passed, the house grew quiet, and still he didn't come back. She opened the window a crack, and the cool night air slipped in, carrying the sound of early autumn insects and making the mosquito net sway slightly. Anna could hear a rooster crowing, and in the distance the barking of dogs; then it was quiet again, so quiet she couldn't bear it. She got up, went to the toilet, and then crept out by the back door into the garden. The insects all began to cry at once. The sound pierced through her. She walked on until she reached the edge of the woods, where she stopped and looked up. Right above her was the Milky Way, awash with stars. The North Star glimmered much further down in the sky than she remembered seeing in Germany. Standing there, she came to a decision: no matter how hard her husband pressed her, she would not give him her body. Until he left that woman, until she had absolute proof that he had left that woman, she would never give in. Her decision made, she felt a deep relief, and went back to her room.

At dawn Arizumi returned, the smell of alcohol strong on his breath. Five or six times he tried to shake her awake, but in the end he gave up and fell into his own bed. The next time he tried to touch her, Anna was wide awake. She hardened her body against him, refusing to respond. In that stiff posture, she fell asleep again.

8

The sound of birdsong seeped into Eri's mind, and she awoke. *That's right*, she thought, *Ken's here today, whoopee!* Bright morning sunlight came through the curtains. It was going to be a fine day. *We can go swimming, or riding, or play tennis. We can hike up to the Mikasa forest or, even better, we can take the railway up to the foothills and climb Mount Asama. If Ken wants to play golf, I wouldn't mind even if I'm not any good at it. Ken looks so manly, so handsome, it's as if he got all the best from Mama and Papa. I was left with the dregs. Sorry, Anna, but you got the dregs too. Ken got everything—he's wonderful. His legs, his chèst, his face . . .* Eri giggled *. . . but that hairstyle's got to go. Poor Ken, having his thick black hair, soft like Mama's and shiny like Papa's, all shaved off. And why does that cropped head look so blue? Waxy, somehow, and slick. But when he puts on his Army cap, he looks fine. A military man, an officer in the Imperial Army. I like the Army uniform. Those blue Navy uniforms make me think of icy water. Yes, okay, they hide the grease, just like those German factory uniforms, but the Army ones are so warm, the color of nice, rich earth. It's like the khaki is reflected in his tan . . . And the smell of him! Wow! It fills his room and it's just Ken's natural smell. Plus his beard. When Ken dances with me he rubs his whiskers against my forehead, and when I say it hurts he does it again—on purpose, I bet—and it makes my forehead burn, it makes me feel like I'm on fire . . . Oh, Ken's such a great dancer. When we went to dance school in Berlin they all used to say how good I was, but it was probably because I was the Ambassador's daughter; the Germans were always flattering me, but I'm nowhere near him. Where did he learn to dance like that? In Japan? . . .*

It's so bright outside. A brand new blue sky. All those shiny golden needles on the larches, shining in the sunlight. Like a scene in a movie I once saw. I know—we'll go on a picnic with Ken, I'll invite Mama and Anna, and of course Maggie too. We'll take the railway up to the foothills, no, we'll get off at the Shiroito Cascade and hike through the forest up to the mountain. I'll make some boxed lunches—I'll have to discuss it with Tanaka first. What kind of food does Ken get in the Army anyway? He said something about Air Corps food, special food that's supposed to be light and good for you. They even have chocolate and candy and liquor. Chocolate! I haven't had any since we were in Berlin. When I came back to Japan—came back? It sure didn't feel like "coming back"—when I came to Japan, when I came to <u>visit</u> Papa's country, anyway, after I arrived here, I couldn't find any chocolate anywhere. They don't sell it. They don't have <u>anything</u> in this country—no cakes, no candy, no chocolate. They have candy stores, but the counters are empty, completely bare! It's not going to be easy putting a boxed lunch together. Tanaka and I will have to use our brains!

Maggie . . . Eri abruptly kicked her legs out and stretched her arms upward. She could see black whorls in the wooden ceiling's wavy grain. *Maggie was really strange yesterday. We were supposed to do our English compositions—she brought her composition book with her. That was the plan. But as soon as she started dancing she forgot all about it (she even forgot her notebook when she went home)! Maggie always said she doesn't like to dance, but as soon as "San Antonio Rose" came on, she grabbed me by the waist and started dancing like she was a prince or something. She never acts like that usually, I'm positive it was all a show for Ken, yes, she was just trying to get Ken's attention. Then, later, I was dancing with Ken. And why not? I wanted to dance with him. I saw Maggie creeping up to him, and I grabbed him before she could get her hands on him, and we started dancing. I gave Maggie a smile and, boy, what a look she gave me! She glared at me. I never saw her look at me like that before. It really scared me. I thought she'd murder me. Then Maggie—what's wrong with her?—she tried to tease <u>Papa</u> into dancing. She's always so reserved around him, when he speaks to her it's all she can do to say a few polite words in*

reply. And then she tried to get Anna's husband to dance with her—
she must have been off her rocker. She'd never even met him before,
and here she was—a girl!—asking <u>*him*</u> *to dance. Well, finally that*
crazy Maggie started dancing with Tanaka. I mean, it's unthinkable,
Tanaka dancing with one of us!

Maggie's in love with Ken . . . Oh God. The thought made Eri feel as
if she'd bitten into a piece of bittersweet chocolate. She couldn't bear
it if Maggie stole Ken from her. But then she also fancied Maggie as a
perfect bride for her brother. So she decided she'd definitely invite
Maggie along today, and the two of them would do everything together
with Ken. In the morning they'd go to church. Afterwards they could
go to the pool by Kumoba Pond, or maybe over to the tennis courts.

Eri was wide awake now. She yawned, stretching her hands as if to
cup the sunlight streaming in through the trees. She changed into her
clothes, and put her hair up in a bun. As the rest of the family still
seemed to be asleep, she stepped lightly through the hall and went
out into the garden. The air felt so cool and light it made her want to
skip about. And suddenly she found herself staring at her brother's
broad shoulders.

"Eri, you up already?"

"You're up early too, Ken."

"It's not early for me. It's already six. That's when we get up in the
Army." Ken stood at attention and gave her a salute.

"The Army . . ." Eri looked sadly at his shaven head. What a pity all
his beautiful hair was gone! Still, as a young Lieutenant, he had a great
future ahead of him.

"Ken, what's it like in the Army?"

"Hard to say. Hard for little girls like you to imagine."

"Don't tease me!"

Ken was wearing a striped summer kimono of Kokura duck cloth.
With his tanned face, and perhaps because his head was shaved like
a middle school student's, he looked very boyish. He certainly didn't
have the authority of an officer in the Imperial Army.

"That reminds me. Eri, you met the Commandant of my school,
didn't you?"

"Who? I don't know what you're talking about."

"You did meet him. This June, right after I entered flying school, I was called in by General Shingo, our Commandant. All of a sudden he asks me, 'Lieutenant, do you have a sister?' 'Yes, sir,' I tell him, and he says, 'Hmm! She speaks remarkably good English.' You met him, didn't you? On the train, this winter."

"Wait a minute, you mean that officer . . . the fat guy with the loud voice and the moustache?"

"Yes, Eri, that 'fat guy' was General Shingo. And you almost had me in trouble with him."

"But how could I know? . . ." Eri burst out laughing, and told him what had happened that day on the train.

It was Foundation Day, commemorating the mythical establishment of Japan in 660 B.C. The schools were closed, and Eri and Margaret decided to slip away from the ceremonies and use this most sacred of national holidays to go skiing at Sugadaira. The train they boarded was almost empty. The two girls sat down and immediately began gossiping about their classmates and teachers. Eri had just transferred to the same Christian school that Margaret went to, and she was hungry for all the information Margaret had stored up. When they began discussing the merits and idiosyncrasies of the various nuns who taught them, they started mixing English words into their conversation, and when they got to the juicy parts, it was English only.

Just then an officer marched in, the tassel of his sword swishing about, and asked in English, in a booming voice, "May I sit down?" The astonished Eri answered, "*Doozo.*" The officer removed his sword and, gripping it between his legs, crammed himself into the seat next to Margaret, nearly crushing her.

"Hmm!" said the officer, stroking his moustache. "Are you Japanese?"

"Yes, sir," Eri replied. The gold stars and bars on the officer's collar shone in the winter light. And here she was, wearing a ski suit in wartime. It made her cringe.

"What's your name, girl?"

"Eri, sir."

"Hmm." The officer gave her a piercing glance. If she had said "Kurushima," the name was rare enough for him to guess who her father was. It wouldn't look good for the former Ambassador's daughter to be out skiing on Foundation Day, especially with a Western friend in tow.

"And your family name?"

"Yes, sir, it's Kuru . . . shima."

"Kurushima! Are you related to Ambassador Kurushima?"

"Yes, sir, I'm his daughter."

"So that's why you're so good at English. Well, this is fortunate. Since we have some time together, you can help me with my English. My pronunciation is awful. You correct it." He obviously meant it as an order. "We'll start with *th*. Go ahead, say it."

"*th*."

"*suu*. Again!"

The other passengers turned and stared, but when they saw he was an Army officer, no one dared speak. The officer was insistent, and they proceeded with the lesson without caring about everyone else. After *th* they tried *r*, and then the difference between *r* and *l*. Eri grew less nervous and began enunciating the words loudly as she corrected his mistakes.

Just as the English lesson was at its most intense, though, the train pulled into the officer's station, and he got up to leave. "Thank you very much," he said in English. "You are a good teacher. I learned very much."

The two girls were relieved—and exhausted. Margaret, who had been squashed in her seat, relaxed, spreading out like a sponge in water, and Eri realized she was bathed in sweat.

"I've never been so scared in my life," she told Ken. "So he's the Commandant of your school. Well, I don't envy you."

"Actually, the General said some very nice things about you. 'Your sister is a brave little girl,' he told me."

"Really? Did he say anything about Maggie?"

"He called her a 'beautiful foreign lady.' He thought she was taking you skiing."

"Maggie was a beautiful lady?"

"And you just a little girl."

"That's unfair!"

Ken laughed, and began imitating the Commandant: his moustache, his paunch, above all the way his round shoulders swayed when he walked. "What's your name, girl? Eri? That's a strange name! What's your family name? Hmm, Kurushima, eh? You mean the Ambassador to . . . Hmm! So the Ambassador's daughter is about to engage in an enemy sport just as the country's preparing for war—that's traitorous! However, in return for an English lesson, I shall give you a special dispensation. How does that suit you, hmmmmm?'"

Eri couldn't stop laughing. She thought her sides would split.

"Ken and Eri!" It was their mother. "You're both very lively for this time of day."

"Ken was so funny. He was imitating a general—perfectly!"

"Breakfast is ready." Alice tapped her son and daughter on the shoulder. "Papa's up too. So is Anna. Everybody's up early today."

After breakfast all the family except Saburo and Arizumi set out together for the Anglican church to attend Sunday services, which began at ten. The simple wooden church stood in a clearing past the last store on the Old Karuizawa Road. It was surrounded by silver firs and zelkovas and huge white birches. To the left of the church was a stone monument commemorating Alexander Shaw, the missionary who had come to Japan from Scotland in 1886. Three years later Shaw had built a simple house there, and that had been the beginning of Karuizawa as an international summer resort. Eri knew she had Scottish blood from her mother, and she felt a particular affection for the Reverend Shaw. She liked taking communion in the little church built in his memory.

Margaret was seated on the left, near the altar, with her mother Audrey sitting facing her at the organ, and the four Kurushimas moved into the same pew. Eri, trying to sit quietly but overjoyed that her brother was with them, peered out of the corners of her eyes and saw Ken's long arms and legs on her right, and Margaret, whose face had immediately turned red, on her left. She began to fidget, smoldering with jealousy, and started knocking her legs together. "Shhh!" her mother scolded her.

People began to arrive, and soon the church was almost full. There were some Japanese there, but three-quarters of the congregation were foreigners. As Japan's relations with Britain and America had deteriorated, many of the nationals of those two countries had left for home. But still a good half of the congregation was either British or American.

Wearing white robes, Father Hendersen walked to the altar and began the service in English. He opened his prayer book and started to read. Then hymn 371 was sung, with Audrey at the organ. The trunks of the white birches were visible through the window, and the chirping of the birds outside could be heard through the thin wooden walls. As the congregation knelt in prayer, a cat meandered past. Eri stared at the red cross woven into Father Hendersen's robes, and thought how unusual it was that Ken had come to church at all. According to their old maid Toku, during Ken's primary and middle school years, when he attended a Catholic mission school, he had gone to an Anglican church for Sunday services out of respect for his mother's wishes. But after he entered the Yokohama High School of Engineering he had stopped going to church altogether.

It was time for communion, and people lined up and knelt at the altar rail. Father Hendersen lifted the Eucharist, and gave the bread and wine to each communicant, among them Margaret, Alice, Anna, Eri . . . and Ken too! *So Ken still believes in God. He still believes.*

After the service the Kurushimas retired to the rectory behind the church, where Audrey served them tea and homemade cookies on the porch. Father Hendersen looked around to make sure they were the only ones there, and then told them hesitantly, in Japanese, "We probably won't be able to use the church after this summer."

The Kurushimas looked at one another. "Why?" asked Anna, as if expressing the whole family's astonishment.

"This has always been a summer church. We close up at the beginning of September. What we don't know is whether I'll still be the pastor here next year . . ." He then switched to English, so as to include Alice. "This June all the Protestant churches in the country were merged into the United Church of Christ in Japan. The idea was to make the Church cooperate in the war effort, in obedience to the Emperor. I told them our Anglican Church could never put Christ below the Emperor in importance, and we refused to join. Since then we've been marked as pro-American, pacifist, anti-Emperor. The authorities have started turning the screws. I don't know how long they'll let me continue doing my mission work."

"But you haven't done anything wrong," said Anna. "You haven't disobeyed the Emperor."

"No . . ." The tall, thin pastor drew a circle on the ground with his feet. "Unfortunately, to be a good Christian in Japan these days, to preach peace on earth to all men, does in fact mean rebelling against the Emperor. The situation isn't easy. The Ministry of Education is trying to dissolve the Anglican Church as a legal entity, and no doubt would like to eradicate our religion itself."

"It's outrageous," cried Anna. "They can't get away with it."

"No, Anna, we're in an age when they *can* get away with it."

"But . . ." Anna looked apprehensive. She was about to say something more, then glanced at Ken, her eyes telling him "*You* say something."

"I don't understand it either," said Ken, "but there seems to be a great deal of misunderstanding in the Army about Christianity. I'm always careful not to let it be known that I'm a Christian. My superiors and my fellow officers wouldn't like it if they ever found out."

"Oh, Ken!" Alice gave her son a worried look.

"It's all right, Mama." Ken laughed. "I'm 'wise as the serpent, harmless as the dove.'"

Back home after church, Eri changed into tennis wear, eager for a game with Ken. But then Ryoichi Koyama suddenly turned up and invited Ken to go riding with him, so Eri had to extract a promise for tennis later. In the meantime, she would play with Margaret.

The tennis courts behind the post office could be rented for two hours. The usual custom among Japanese tennis players was to spend the first thirty minutes practicing smashes and volleys, but at Eri's suggestion they began a proper game right away. Margaret was the better player and Eri invariably lost to her, but today Eri played furiously, racking up point after point. She surprised Margaret by winning three games in a row. "What's happened, Eri? You're fantastic today."

But Margaret won the fourth and fifth games, making it 2–3. Just then Ken and Ryoichi showed up, both wearing white shirts and riding pants. Eri flubbed a simple slice shot, then missed one serve after another. In no time Margaret was ahead, 5–3. Eri grew impatient, started hitting simple returns into the net, and ended up losing the set.

"We've got the court for another forty minutes. Why don't you play us a set?"

"We can't, dressed like this," said Ken, looking down at his riding pants and boots.

"You can borrow some tennis shorts and sneakers at the club."

Ken noticed Margaret looking at him rather intensely, but shrugged it off and headed for the clubhouse.

"Aren't you going to play too?" Eri asked Ryoichi. Even with his bad leg, Ryoichi was known as an excellent volleyer.

"No thanks, I don't want to get smeared by Ken, so I think I'll sit it out. Anyway, I wouldn't want to come between you two girls and the dashing young Lieutenant."

"Oh, don't be silly!"

When Ken came out wearing proper tennis gear, Eri told Margaret to go ahead and play against him; Ryoichi would referee. At first things went in Margaret's favor, but Ken soon rallied, and for a while the match was pretty even. Margaret scored her points with volleys, but she had no answer for Ken's smashes. Eri cheered wildly, though it wasn't clear whom it was for, and people from neighboring courts came to watch the match in progress. The score was three all. The next game went to deuce, then Ken took two points in a row—and soon the set. By the end of it, Margaret was bright red in the face, and so tired she could hardly stand, but she had obviously enjoyed herself.

At the pool Ken dived in first. The girls watched as he plowed through the water. There were other young men in the pool, but none of them had his style or speed. When he climbed out, he flicked drops of water off his chest hair at the girls, making them squeal. Ryoichi then challenged him to a race, which was surprisingly close.

Margaret dived in, her long white body turning golden in the water, with Ken and Eri close on her heels. Ken swam under her, then picked her up and flung her high out of the water. Eri saw a whirl of gold bubbles as she splashed back in.

But, soon enough, it became quite chilly, and they decided to go home. As they were splitting up, Ken took Margaret's outstretched hand to say goodbye. She smiled, shaking her heavy wet hair. It was a lovely, girlish smile, spreading through the freckles below her eyes.

It rained for the next two days. Ken spent the time reading the magazines he'd brought with him and showing the family his photographs from the Kumagaya flying school. There were pictures of the 95-1 trainer, nicknamed the Red Dragonfly, of the Ki-43, of the Hayate fighter. Eri couldn't keep all the names straight, but she liked to go into Ken's room and poke around his desk and bookshelves, poring over the pictures in the foreign magazines he collected: *Aeroplane, Aerodigest, Aero-Science, Aeronautical Journal.* It made her feel proud to know that her brother was an Army engineer who actually built these flying machines.

"Ken, what kind of airplane are you going to make?"

"Well, I don't know. I've only just joined up, and I've no idea what I'll be told to do."

"But there must be some kind of plane you really want to design."

"Well yes, there is. For example . . ." Ken leafed through his notebook, showing her a pencil sketch. "This is my idea of the fighter plane of the future. The engine will develop tremendous power, so you'll get lots of speed. Usually, to get speed the wings have to be small, but then the relative load on the wings increases, which means you lose maneuverability—you can't do loops and things like that. But with this plane you'll get lots of speed *and* maneuverability. You understand what I mean?"

"I don't," said Eri, shrugging her shoulders, "but I can understand why you want to build a plane like that. *You* can do it, Ken, I know you can."

"I wonder," he said, tilting his head and running his fingers over the notebook.

The next morning, just after the rain let up, Ken suddenly asked his little sister to go bird hunting with him. He'd spent the previous evening cleaning his air gun for the occasion.

"You're going to hunt with that?"

"Sure. It's not as good as a real rifle, but you'd be surprised what you can hit with it."

They set out over the soft, damp ground, Ken in knickerbockers and hunting cap, Eri in baggy pants and a scarf.

"What're we hunting for?"

"*Kojukei.*"

She had no idea what kind of a bird a *kojukei* was. She had never known the names of many birds, and the few she did know were English names. The Japanese names had to be translated for her.

"What kind of bird is that?"

"I'll show you."

Ken pushed his way through the stalks of striped bamboo. Eri hurried after him, afraid of getting lost. Then suddenly she heard a gunshot. Something fell from the sky, but she couldn't make out what it was. Ken plunged into the bushes and picked up a large bird. Its eyes were still bright, its black wings still flapping. When he brought it over to Eri, she jumped out of the way.

"Oh, it's bleeding. The poor thing."

"No, that's just its red tail."

"Is that a *kojukei?*"

"No, it's a *yamadori*, a pheasant. This is quite a find, actually. These guys almost never come out except at dawn. And you usually can't hit them with an air gun."

Ken wrung the bird's neck, then unsheathed his knife, sliced its belly open, and removed the innards with a twig. Eri covered her eyes, only peeking through her fingers.

"What're you doing to it?"

"If you don't take the guts out the flesh starts to rot."

"Are we going to eat it?"

"Of course. I killed it so we could eat it."

The pheasant was dappled black and white on its breast and back, its feathers glossy. Eri couldn't forget its shining eyes and flapping wings. There was no way she would ever eat this bird. She had often seen her mother killing a chicken: chopping the head off, then holding the bird upside down and collecting the blood dripping from its neck. Her kindhearted mother didn't think twice about performing such butchery. Ken obviously took after her.

Ken shouldered his rifle again and took aim at a small bird moving through the black clumps of leaves on the whitish water. He fired. The bird took flight. It looked as though it would go on flying, then suddenly dropped as if it had hit an invisible wall. Ken ran over and picked it up. This time the bird was already dead.

"A sparrow."

"Oh no!" Eri sighed at the little bloodstained lump in his palm. "You can't eat them, can you?"

"What do you mean? They're delicious. Especially the ones up here in the mountains. They've got lots of fat, and the meat has a whiff of mountain berries about it."

The basket was gradually filling up. Ken's aim was uncanny. Even when he raised the gun as he walked along and casually pulled the trigger, the lead pellet usually seemed to find its target.

They came out of the forest. A gentle slope spread before them, with trees scattered about a thick carpet of dwarf bamboo. Ken stopped and leveled his air gun, telling Eri to hide behind one of the tree trunks.

"What is it?" she whispered.

"*Kojukei.*"

She couldn't see anything but the bamboo that covered the slope. Nothing moved. Then there was a sharp cry. And, from somewhere else, an answer. And soon all around there came a series of sharp, high-pitched cries: *pyo-pyo-pui.*

"I've heard them before. Sometimes they come near the house."

"That's right. But never in a flock like this."

Ken slowly pushed his way through the bamboo. The clouds parted, and the hilltop filled with sunlight like a sail. When Ken raised his arms, several birds took to the air. There was one, then another muffled report. All around them birds flew up. Ken kept firing. With five shots in a row, he downed several birds—Eri was amazed; it was as if the birds had strings attached to them and the muzzle of his gun was simply reeling them in. Ken gutted each bird before putting it in his basket.

It began to drizzle, and a gauzy mist moved down from the mountains. Ken and Eri hurried off, but halfway down it turned into a driving rain. Neither of them had brought any rainwear, and they were soon soaked to the skin.

"Are you cold?" Ken asked.

"A little. But it's okay as long as we keep moving."

"Let's have Tanaka make us a feast of these birds tonight."

"Good idea. But, Ken, don't you think this rain is sort of a punishment—for all the birds you killed?"

"No. It's the sky weeping because I have to go away again."

Ken's leave, it's true, was almost up. It made Eri feel like crying herself. And, as if in response, by the time they got home it was really pelting down—it was incredible the way it rained—with thunder and lightning, too.

Anna was terrified of storms, and they found her buried in her mosquito net. A bit later, while Ken was helping Tanaka in the kitchen and Eri was doing her best to make Margaret jealous with an exciting account of the hunting trip, they heard a scream: it was Yoshiko, the maid, who wasn't easily upset.

"The stream in front of the house is overflowing. It's about to get into the cellar!"

When everybody rushed out the kitchen door to look, they found the entire field behind the house under water; all the way to the livery stable was now a lake, with sheets of spray gusting across it and even spilling over onto the new highway beyond. It must have been like this during the typhoon in July, and it was a reminder that what was now the town of Karuizawa had once been a riverbed and a marsh.

The water was already lapping at the cellar windows. When the family had reopened the villa, they'd had to drain quite a lot of water from the cellar. Now the cellar was stocked full, not only with wine but all sorts of damageable goods: chests and chairs and books as well. It was too late to carry them out. They simply had to keep the water from getting in through the cellar windows.

Ken's plan was to fill potato sacks with earth and pile them up outside the windows. Inside this makeshift dike they could build a second protective wall by stacking bricks and rocks together. It was a job for the men in the house. Saburo went in to change, and reappeared in raincoat, hat, and boots, but then slipped and fell, his clothes getting smeared with mud. Tanaka reported for duty in a bathing suit, but soon pulled a muscle lugging one of the heavy sacks and also had to be sidelined.

So Ken and Asa ended up doing all the work, Ken stripped down to his loincloth, and Asa in her baggy farmer's pants. Together they filled the sacks with earth and piled them by the windows. This seemed to do the trick, and with the rain now letting up, the water level gradually began to fall. When Ken and Asa came back in, covered with mud, their mission accomplished, the rest of the household applauded. Ken stood there in his loincloth, with Eri too shy to look but noticing that Margaret was even more embarrassed, her eyes glued to the floor. Ken gave Asa a pat on her plump shoulders and said, "Thanks a lot, you really saved the day." Eri, surprised how jealous this made her feel, but making her voice sound as calm as she could, thanked her rather more formally for what she'd done.

9

The next day was beautiful. White smoke from Mount Asama trailed into cobalt skies. The volcano filled the horizon with its ungainly shape. The air was crisp, and swarms of red dragonflies drifted across the cold blue sky. Above the swaying ears of pampas grass, still wet and flushed with color, yellowing leaves trembled in the trees. On the ground, fallen leaves lay stuck in the mud of the lava fields.

It was Ken's last night. He was leaving in the morning, back to the Army. Alice was having a farewell dinner in his honor and had invited the Hendersens, the Wolffs, and the Yoshizawas for a barbecue in the garden. Tanaka had constructed a pit by piling up pieces of lava. He stoked the coals until they were bright red, and laid out skewers of meat and vegetables to grill. Coils of incense to repel the mosquitoes were lit, a dozen red lanterns were strung in the trees, and on the pines Ken had hung Japanese and German flags—talismans, he said, to ward off the Thought Police.

Wolff, a pot-bellied man with a bald, squarish head who owned a trading company, was immediately absorbed in a conversation in German with Arizumi. Beside him was his son Peter, a rather solemn young man sitting bolt upright and eating neatly with his chopsticks.

Saburo was with Kazuo Yoshizawa, the former Ambassador to Great Britain. Yoshizawa was a well-known liberal with Anglo-American sympathies. He had opposed the Anti-Comintern Pact between Japan and Germany, and had been relieved of his duties at his own request. The two diplomats sat away from Wolff, keeping their voices low as they discussed the German invasion of Russia.

"The Soviet Union isn't going to be defeated that easily," said Yoshizawa. "The papers would lead one to think Stalingrad is going to fall any day now, but that's hardly the case . . ."

"There've been reports recently of the Germans preparing for a long battle."

"And they're right. Even Hitler has begun to realize he can't defeat Russia with one of his blitzkriegs. Of course it'll be a long battle. But what will happen if it runs on into winter? I doubt if the Germans are really prepared to fight through a Russian winter. The climax of the war on the Russian front will come before the winter's over." Yoshizawa glanced sharply at the swastika emblazoned on Wolff's sleeve. He hadn't been able to suppress a frown when Alice introduced Wolff to him, and had turned away from the German's effusive greeting, quickly moving to the other side of the garden. This might have led to an unpleasant scene had Arizumi not quickly addressed Wolff in German and diverted his attention.

"What worries me," said Saburo, "is that shipboard conference between Churchill and Roosevelt. I wonder what sort of agreement they came to. According to our cables, they discussed not only the war against Germany but a strategic blockade of Japan in the Far East . . ."

"That man Churchill is a formidable politician." Yoshizawa flicked ash from the cigar he'd just lit. "Britain's situation is desperate, and Churchill wants the U.S. to restrain Hitler indirectly by giving military assistance to Russia. He's waiting for a chance to get America to declare war on Germany. Churchill's diplomacy is brilliant. I'm just frightened that Japan will get sucked in."

"How do you think they view Japan?"

"Well, Churchill has got to be worried that we'll attack India. Just as the defeat of France and Holland got them worrying about Indochina and the East Indies falling into German hands, now with this Axis pact Japan has emerged as another threat. They're afraid India is next."

"As far as India is concerned, Churchill is a colonialist to the core."

"You can see he's trying to link up his colonialism with Roosevelt's defense of democracy. And Roosevelt certainly doesn't want to lose the Philippines."

"And that's what makes them such hypocrites." This came from

Arizumi, who was suddenly standing beside Saburo. "Roosevelt talks about the defense of democracy, but all he cares about is protecting the Western colonies. That's why he's putting economic pressure on Japan, trying to break our nerve. It's a filthy trick."

Yoshizawa irritably flicked the ash off his cigar again, obviously displeased that Arizumi had butted in. "And what do you suggest we do about it?"

"Japan should take a resolute stand, and make them renounce colonialism."

"Empty threats don't work with the Americans. Matsuoka already tried that."

"But if we just stand back like this, what will happen to Indochina and the East Indies? They'll remain colonies forever. And what about India? India deserves to get its freedom too. That's our mission, surely—to help Asia throw off the yoke of the Western powers."

"We can go on and on about our sacred 'mission,' but it's not going to fool the Americans. The Americans believe that Japan wants to wrest control of Asia in order to replace the European empires with its own rule. Of course they'll oppose it. Opposition backed by force leads to war. War will mean a great loss of life—a staggering loss—for Japan, and for the United States as well."

"But our armed forces are unbeatable—we're strong enough to defeat the United States!"

"I wouldn't count on it." Yoshizawa waved his little pink hand dismissively, a gesture saying he didn't want to discuss it and he particularly didn't want to discuss it with the likes of Arizumi. He took one puff after another on his cigar, and closed his eyes in a cloud of smoke. Flecks of ash fell on his shirt.

Arizumi could have had Yoshizawa arrested for his remark. He was about to respond, but the look in Saburo's eyes stopped him, and he returned to his seat next to Wolff. Alice could make out bits and pieces of their conversation—something about the former Ambassador to Britain . . . a rigid mind . . . still wants a reconciliation with Britain and America . . . tiresome old liberal.

Laughter arose from the direction of Ken and Eri, who had built another barbecue pit of their own and were roasting skewers of meat on it. Ryoichi and Peter were there, along with Margaret and Wakako Yoshizawa. And Anna, too. The aging housewife of a week ago, anguished over her husband's adultery, had been transformed into a young woman again. Her hair was up, and she was wearing the same kind of sage blue dress her little sister had on.

"Mama, come over here!" shouted Eri. "The birds that Ken shot are delicious."

"This one's ready," said Anna, placing a skewer on her mother's plate. Ken gave her a chair.

"Ken's been doing imitations of all the famous comedians. Now he's going to do His Excellency General Shingo, Commandant of the Kumagaya flying school." Eri burst out laughing.

"Eri, he hasn't even begun yet," said Anna, laughing herself.

Ken drew an upturned Kaiser moustache with his finger and made a gesture suggesting a huge beer belly. Then his voice boomed across the garden. Yoshizawa and Father Hendersen turned around to look.

"We of the great nation of Yamato are deficient in foreign languages, especially English! We shall therefore engage in some pronunciation drill. You there, that teacher over there, we shall begin with you. Now —harumph—enunciate! 'Breathe' . . . 'Breeze' . . . 'I lead' . . . 'I read' . . . 'I love you' . . . 'I rub you'!? Hmm. These foreign tongues are difficult!"

Twirling his moustache, he struggled out of his chair, using his sword as the General's cane. Eri was in stitches, Anna laughing alongside, stroking her sister's back.

Alice suggested they take their dessert and coffee in the parlor, as it had gotten chilly and a mist had risen.

Wolff sat down at the piano and began to play. His thick fingers moved lightly over the keyboard, his plump red cheeks and double chin drooping expressively. Then he begun to sing, in a superb tenor, the Schubert lieder "Der Leiermann" and "Der Lindenbaum." Tears were soon streaming down his face. In the middle of one song, however, Arizumi joined in, and the sad strains of Schubert were ruined by this off-key voice.

Manche Trän' aus meinen Augen
Ist gefallen in den Schnee . . .

Arizumi stumbled loudly across the floor and sat down beside
Anna. "Well, who could this lady be?" he said, turning to her in mock
surprise. "Could it be Meine Frau? I hardly recognized you. Sie sind
sehr schön!"

Anna backed away from his boozy breath, moving nearer Ken.

"Well, *excuse me!*" Arizumi staggered to his feet and bowed to her.
"How rude of me to have spoken to the wife of a Lieutenant in the
Imperial Army!"

Eri glared at him. "You're drunk, aren't you, Mr. Arizumi?"

"I'm drunk. Yes, I'm drunk!" He then staggered over to Peter Wolff
and mumbled something to him. Peter dutifully stood up and, to his
father's accompaniment on the piano, began to sing with Arizumi:

Die Fahne hoch! die Reihen dicht geschlossen!
SA marchiert mit ruhig festem Schritt.
Kameraden die Rotfront und Reaktion erschossen
Marchiern im Geist in unsern Reihen mit.

"What's that they're singing?" Yoshizawa asked Saburo.

"It's the Horst Wessel Song. It's a Nazi party favorite, very popular
these days."

"Oh, I see, 'SA marchiert,' is it? But I thought Röhm, the chief of
the SA, was purged by Hitler. I thought the 'defenders of the German
state' these days weren't the SA but the SS and the Gestapo."

"That's correct. You're very well informed." The two singers made
Saburo visibly wince.

"Of course, Hitler's ultimate goal is German domination of the
world. Our own admiration for *Mein Kampf* is so misguided it makes
one want to laugh. Have you ever read it?"

"Yes, I have."

"He has some pretty nasty things to say about the Japanese in
there."

"I know. They were deliberately cut out of the Japanese translation by that rightist Murobuse."

"Of course they were. If he'd published it with those passages intact, it would have been banned. They merely translated what suits the present regime and left out the rest. As a result, the Japanese would happily lay down their own lives for that noble ally of ours. But Germany's aggression serves only Germans. As far as they're concerned, the more Japanese blood spilled the better." Yoshizawa flung the butt of his cigar into the ashtray, then pulled out another and bit the tip off.

The duet ended to scattered applause. Next, Ryoichi slid onto the piano bench and began to play "Let Me Go, Lover," which prompted Ken and Margaret to get up to dance. This led Father Hendersen to invite Wakako onto the floor, and even Mr. Wolff, his pot belly heaving, bowed to Eri and asked her for the pleasure. The three couples moved around the floor in a circle, waltzing. After the Schubert lieder and the Nazi anthem, this New Orleans-style tune seemed to bring everyone to life.

Yoshizawa turned again to Saburo and said, "That boy's performance would put a professional pianist to shame."

Ryoichi then launched into "San Antonio Rose," which brought on three different partners—Father Hendersen with Eri, Ken with Wakako, and Wolff with Margaret. Peter, Arizumi, and Anna remained seated, as if abandoned by the others. The German youth, with a lock of brown hair draped over his forehead, turned a cold, sarcastic eye on his father's clumsy steps and exchanged winks with Arizumi.

"Why aren't you dancing?" Saburo asked Alice.

She shook her head. "I can't, not now. Ken's leaving tomorrow morning. I just don't feel like it."

"Your son's a splendid fellow," said Yoshizawa, joining their conversation in English. Then, angrily, he added, "All the young men like that are becoming soldiers these days. What a waste!"

"But Mr. Yoshizawa," Alice protested, "we're very proud that our son is a soldier."

"Madam," he replied, pointing the lighted tip of his cigar directly at her chest, "I can't believe you really mean that."

Alice gave him an enigmatic smile, the kind a Japanese might give a foreigner. Their diplomatic friend saw through everything, she thought. Ken wasn't in the Imperial Army because he wanted to be, but simply because he had been drafted. And the only reason he was an Air Corps officer was that the authorities wanted to exploit his talents as an engineer.

"Still," said Yoshizawa encouragingly, "I'm sure Ken will a first-rate pilot. He's an excellent athlete, and he has good reflexes. And a really first-rate pilot is never in danger."

"Are you sure?" Alice looked at her son's radiant face as he was dancing.

"Yes, I'm positive. A pilot is like a diplomat. A really expert diplomat will never make the kind of blunder that would put his country in jeopardy."

"But Mr. Yoshizawa," she objected, her cheeks puffed out like a sulky girl arguing with her father, "no matter how good a diplomat is, there will be times when the problems are simply too big for anyone to solve, and he can't help putting his country in danger."

"I think what you mean is that there are limits to what even the best person can accomplish," said Saburo, eager to mediate.

"About those limits," said Yoshizawa, as he watched with obvious pleasure the sight of his daughter Wakako dancing with Ken. "Those limits, madam, can be infinitely stretched. And that is the greatest mystery about human beings."

Alice didn't get up to dance. She was worried about Anna, who sat with her eyes on the floor. Arizumi either hadn't noticed her or was deliberately ignoring her, as he engaged in a lively conversation with Peter. The young German was standing perfectly straight with his back to the dancers, as if to show his displeasure with their "decadent" music.

II

THE RED DRAGONFLY

1

The seagulls flew in a single column like a long, long row of kites tied together with an invisible string. One after another they came, barely moving their wings as they rode the ocean breeze. From time to time a gust of wind would cause a break in their ranks, but soon enough the column would reform and their buoyant procession moved on.

He was lying on a beach, watching the seagulls in the glow of sunset. Their yellow necks were bent downward, their wings gray silhouettes against the orange clouds in a limitless expanse of sky. The rhythm of the waves matched the rhythm of the birds. It was a beach on Long Island, a white gleam of sand.

I'd like to fly like that. To fly naturally, without the slightest fear or tension.

"Lauren," he called out in English, "I'd like to become one of those seagulls. To have the soul of those seagulls."

"You already *do*."

"I wish it were true."

"Look at the sunset."

The sun was sinking between the distant skyscrapers of Manhattan, turning one side of the buildings gold and the other black. Lauren's soft hair curled in the wind and twisted around his fingers. Her perfume mingled with the smells of the beach. He felt desire rise in him as if rising from the sea.

"Lauren." He embraced the girl, and their bodies were soon smeared with sand.

The seagulls continued their flight, becoming black dots in the distance. His desire rose, hot and insistent . . . then suddenly he awoke.

He wasn't on Long Island. Here the ceiling was low, and men were sleeping on plain straw mats on wooden beds. This was his room in the officers' barracks, and it felt like another dream, this one even more unreal. He turned in his bed and faced the dim light from the window. The dawn breeze blowing through the pines rustled like the sound of waves. It was clear outside, a good day for flying. Suddenly he noticed the bed next to his was empty. Where was Haniyu? Probably in the john.

He must have fallen asleep again. Now it was bright outside. 5:27. The next bed was still empty. Thirty minutes must have gone by. Where the hell was Haniyu?

Ken sat up and looked around the room. There were five beds. On the other side were Yamada, Sugi, and Hanazono. On this side were Haniyu and himself. The snores, and the prominent mound of flesh, were unmistakably Yamada's. The surface of the desks lined against the windows gleamed in the morning sun. On Haniyu's desk lay a violin case. Ken stepped into the corridor. There was nobody there.

Just then Hanazono whispered to him, "Haniyu's been gone two hours."

"That's strange."

"I looked all over the barracks, but there's no sign of him. I'm worried."

"Did you go over to the airfield?"

"Not yet."

"Let's go there." The two of them quickly changed into their uniforms. Walking briskly, they passed the pine grove, heading for the airfield.

"Kurushima, you got some idea where he is?"

"No, but I know he likes to go behind the shooting range to play his violin. I've got a feeling he's back there."

"What the hell's he doing there now?"

"That's what I can't figure out."

Hanazono stopped in his tracks. "I bet he's *not* there. Playing the violin at this hour of the morning? No, I think the guy's deserted."

"Deserted?" Ken was stunned. The possibility had never entered his mind. That an officer in the Imperial Army might desert, might run away from flying school—it was just unthinkable.

"For a whole week now," said Hanazono, "Haniyu's been depressed. The guy's convinced he can't fly. He acts demoralized, as if he's lost all his confidence. He doesn't finish his dinner, he's always sighing, he can't sleep. When he finally knocks off, he's mumbling in his sleep. You haven't noticed?"

"Yeah, I've noticed . . ." Ken was well aware that Haniyu had been depressed lately. He had always been a quiet fellow, but recently he looked pale and numb. When Ken asked if something was wrong, Haniyu had replied weakly, "No, nothing."

Haniyu was a young man with a small build, a fair complexion, and clean-cut features. He looked a lot younger than his age and was often mistaken for one of the teenage cadets enrolled at the school. Like Ken, he had entered the flying school directly after finishing his civilian education and had been commissioned a lieutenant after serving as an apprentice flight engineer.

Hanazono had little respect for him. For Lieutenant Hanazono—a regular soldier who had been to the Junior Army Academy, making his way up from a lowly infantryman to be an officer in the Air Corps—it was hard to accept that this weakling with his wishy-washy attitudes was an officer. Two months earlier, Hanazono had bawled him out for not jumping out of bed at reveille. And just two nights ago, when Haniyu was setting off with his violin to practice in his free time, he had bawled him out again, this time about his "unmilitary" attitude. "You're a slob. If you've got time to go play that instrument of yours, you can damn well come and do some judo with me." So, head drooping, Haniyu followed him to the judo hall, where they spent about an hour working out together.

"How was he?" Ken had asked.

"Hopeless. Out of breath after a few throws. When I pinned him with a four-corner hold, he just gave up."

"Gave up?"

"That's the trouble with Haniyu. He won't give it all he's got. He doesn't have the fight-to-the-death approach that a real soldier needs.

The way he gives in—starts whimpering 'That's enough! That's enough!'
—he's got no right to be treated the same as people like us."

"He's got bad reflexes, and he's not that strong. Don't bully him."

"*Bully* him?" Hanazono looked indignant. "I want to teach that kid
what fighting spirit is all about!"

Ken didn't argue any further. You could get in trouble if you
crossed Hanazono. Behind him stood a hundred Army Academy graduates. Among the flight officers here, engineers like Ken, Haniyu, and
Sugi or doctors like Yamada were in the minority, coming from civilian schools. In Ken's squad, though, Hanazono was the only real soldier, which led Ken to suspect he was there to monitor their behavior
and lead them "in the right direction." The slightest deviation in behavior would immediately elicit a reprimand from him.

At the edge of the airfield was the shooting range, surrounded by
earthen walls. Haniyu was to be found there almost every day at
dusk, playing his violin, but now, as Hanazono predicted, there was
no sign of him. They climbed up the banks, which were thick with
pampas grass, and looked out over the shuttered hangars, the wind
socks puffed out with wind, the airfield lined with a dozen trainer
planes. There was no sign of anyone. Smoke trailed from the chimney
of the cookhouse, and around it they could see soldiers milling about.
But no Haniyu.

"Ten minutes to reveille. Damn!" Hanazono rubbed the palm of his
hand against his rough moustache. Right after reveille there was
inspection. For officers the inspection was a simple business, a perfunctory round of all the rooms by the officer of the week. But if
someone was not in his room at that moment it was a very serious
matter. And if their superiors decided the missing man had deserted,
not only the deserter himself but his entire squad would be held
responsible.

As they were passing one of the hangars, Ken noticed the door
was slightly ajar. There was no fighter squadron at this base, and the
only aircraft were trainers, so the hangars weren't strictly secured. Also,
ground crews went in and out of the hangars all the time, so it wasn't
that unusual to see a door left open. Still, it bothered Ken.

"Hey," he said, "let's take a look inside."

From a window near the ceiling a shaft of sunlight gleamed on the rudder and tail of a 95-1 trainer, the two-seater biplane everyone called the Red Dragonfly. Beside the airplane stood the casual figure of Haniyu in his white sleeping robe.

"Haniyu! What's going on? What're you doing?" the two of them shouted simultaneously.

A tremor seemed to pass through his shoulders as he turned around. His face didn't register surprise so much as doubt that they were really there. "What're you guys doing here?"

"What're *we* doing here? You shithead, it's almost reveille!" Hanazono shouted. "What the hell are *you* doing here?"

"I just couldn't grasp . . . ," he said, taking a deep breath, "how the flaps work on the tail. So I'm studying it."

"At this hour? Damn, we've only got five minutes. Come on! We'll be in big trouble if they spot us on the way back."

But Haniyu kept gazing at the tail of the airplane, and the other two almost had to drag him out of the hangar. As they ran through the pine grove, they could see the bugler coming out onto the tree-lined road leading to the front gate. The bugler positioned himself, the red tassel dangling from his shiny instrument, and blared out the call. Soon from all the surrounding buildings came the cry "*Kisho.*" The three men dashed into their room, covered with sweat.

Sugi and Yamada ran up to them. "Where have you been?" cried Sugi. "We thought you'd disappeared."

"Out for a morning jog, gentlemen? How elegant." Yamada's fat body shook with laughter.

"Hurry *up!*" Ken and Hanazono shouted at Haniyu. They made him strip from his sleeping robe and jump naked into his uniform, then told him to quickly make his bed. But their urging only seemed to make him clumsier, so finally Hanazono shouted, "Consider this an emergency! The enemy's coming!" And this seemed to do the trick.

"All five present and accounted for, sir," Hanazono barked to the inspecting officer. With a brief nod, the officer continued down the corridor. Hanazono gave Haniyu a long, loaded look.

All five of them proceeded to the washroom and started shaving. Ken used the electric razor his father had given him as a souvenir from America. By now his roommates were used to it, but at first it had been the object of considerable curiosity.

The face in the mirror showed an odd sort of shading. The parts that were always covered by his flying helmet and goggles were white, while the rest of his face was tanned from exposure to the strong infrared light of high altitudes, from his sepia chin to his even darker cheeks. All the faces around him looked basically the same, but the whiteness around his eyes and the blueness of his shaved head stood out more starkly than the others.

When Ken had gone to Karuizawa on leave the month before, his sisters had been startled by the change in his appearance. He remembered how Eri had almost been in tears as she stared at him, and how she came over and embraced him with a look of pity, planting her soft lips on his cheek.

The face in the mirror wasn't Japanese; it was unmistakably a foreigner's, with Yankee blood running in his veins. Ken remembered an episode at the induction center last spring. After having his head shaved for the first time in his life, he lined up with other young men with cropped skulls, standing in their loincloths waiting for a physical. The Army medics weighed him, measured the circumference of his chest, and took X-rays. At some point he was ordered to remove his loincloth. His foreskin was pulled back, and his testicles were squeezed. He was told to get down on all fours, and a finger in a rubber glove was inserted into his anus. The other draftees were undergoing the same humiliating procedure as if it was all perfectly natural, and Ken himself wasn't particularly embarrassed, until the medical officer stared him hard in the face and asked skeptically:

"Are you Japanese?"

"Yes, sir."

He then examined Ken's documents as if something was missing, and examined his naked body in the same way, from head to toe.

Once this was over, Ken's name was called out by an elderly medical officer and he was told, "You passed, you're strong enough to serve the nation." The doctor paused. "Your mother a Caucasian?"

"Yes, sir."

"A half-breed, are you? What about your fighting spirit? You have enough of that?"

"Yes, sir."

"Half of *that* won't be enough. Watch out for yourself."

In January Ken had joined the 8th Air Squadron in Yokaichi as a private second class. His training there began with the same basic drill he had learned at high school in Yokohama: "Attention!" "Shoulder arms!" "Fix bayonets!" "Forward march!" The camp at Yokaichi was exposed to the cold winds that blew down from Lake Biwa, but initially things weren't any tougher than his rugby training had been. Doing laps around the airfield, even at double time, was no real problem. Physically strong recruits were respected in the Army, and as a result his squad leader and the older NCOs generally left him alone.

But then his turn came on the food detail. "Here to receive the food for the 3rd Squad, 1st Company, sir," he reported.

The Sergeant, a squat but overbearing little man, squared his shoulders and shouted in his face, "Huh? What language you speaking? Say it again, in Japanese this time."

Ken repeated the request, the Sergeant still trying to stare him down.

"Hey, you're not Japanese. No wonder you can't speak our language. Say it again!"

Ken repeated his request, speaking more quickly. This seemed to goad the Sergeant all the more.

"What? Deliberately speaking English at me! What's that look on your face? Eh? You got some beef about the Imperial Army? You got some complaint about serving His Majesty the Emperor?"

"No, sir."

"No? Then what's that look on your face? What's your name, eh? Kurushima? You foreign bastard, I'm gonna knock the foreigner right out of you!" The Sergeant made a fist and hit Ken on the chin. Ken stood there at attention, taking the punch without flinching. The second punch was stronger, but still Ken didn't register much pain. When a third punch didn't cause any reaction, the Sergeant grabbed a huge ladle that was leaning against a cauldron of boiling water and whacked it across his buttocks. This time the pain was considerable, and at the second blow he fell forward on his hands and knees. The Sergeant struck him two or three more times.

"You understand now, you *keto*?" The word meant "hairy barbarian."

The Sergeant finally let up, and Ken staggered back to his squad shouldering a bamboo pole with a bucket of soup on one end and a tub of steaming rice on the other. The moment he returned, one of the soldiers shouted, "You're late! Built like an ape but can't even carry a bamboo pole!" and pushed him to the ground.

Ken would come to hear a lot of "*ketos*." Rumors about him swept through the camp, and epithets seemed to fly at him from every direction: "*keto*," "foreign bastard," even "Russian spy." The latter was typical of the Army tendency always to regard the Soviet Union as the enemy. The Army was as pro-German as it was anti-Russian and anti-American, but no one knew that Ken was the son of the Ambassador who had signed the Axis pact. And Ken kept that fact to himself.

After the first stage of basic drill, the training suddenly turned brutal. On days when a north wind grazed the surface of the lake with powdery snow, recruits would be ordered to assemble without jackets or shirts. The half-naked soldiers would then be taken to pull out weeds in a field where the runway was to be extended. In the most severe February weather, this task would go on for days at a time. Ken's skin seemed to shrivel in the cold, and his stomach was so badly chapped that it hurt when he laughed.

If anyone made the slightest mistake—if any of them failed to remember a single line of the Imperial Rescript for Soldiers, or was late for inspection, or showed a bayonet with a drop of spindle oil on its tip, or a crease in his leggings that wasn't properly aligned—the infraction of one person would bring punishment on the whole squad. The men would have to do a full lap around the airfield at the double, then line up in the order they finished in. This was easy for Ken, but after he'd come in first twice in a row a couple of recruits said to him, "You're too fast. You're making everyone else sweat." After that, he slackened his pace.

Following basic training, Ken passed the examination for junior flight officer, and four months later he was commissioned a lieutenant in the Air Corps. This quick promotion was the result of the Army's special treatment of engineers, of which it was desperately short. The NCOs who had been taking it out on him until the day before weren't too happy to see this "hairy barbarian" suddenly moved up to a higher rank.

This resentment of technical officers was shared by the Army Academy graduates. Hanazono was one of them. Having gone through a decade of training before he finally made lieutenant, he was quick to complain that technical officers were a bunch of weaklings lacking in fighting spirit and military discipline.

When Ken returned from the washroom, he found Yamada and Sugi lecturing Haniyu. Sugi turned and gave Ken a wink.

"What're you doing?" Ken asked.

"We're trying to teach Haniyu how to get a plane out of a tailspin, but he just doesn't seem to get it. Can't understand my explanations. Maybe I'm no good at explaining something I know too well. Dr. Yamada here can't get it through to him either."

"I know the theory behind it," said Yamada, straightening his uniform jacket, which looked as if it was about to burst at the seams. "I just can't explain the damn thing!"

"So . . . unh . . . ," Haniyu said slowly, as if half asleep, "a tailspin happens . . . when you're in a stall. So you shift to the other pedal . . . Why do you do that?"

"Because," Ken laughed, "when you're in a stall the only thing that works is your rudder. Your ailerons aren't working."

"Why not?"

"Because you're in a stall."

"That's what I don't understand."

Sugi and Yamada looked at each other and sighed.

"Okay, let me draw you a diagram." Ken led Haniyu over to his desk.

There was some yellowish muck in the corners of Haniyu's eyes, and he had a three-day beard. The way he looked worried Ken. Their Squadron Leader, Otani, was a fanatic about appearance. Otani kept reminding them that, as members of the Air Corps, they must always be prepared for death, and preparation for death included cleanliness. He therefore insisted that they always wash "down below" and wear fresh loincloths, keep their bodies clean and their heads clean-shaven.

Hanazono came in, dressed in his uniform jacket and a formal pleated *hakama*. In his right hand he held the *Collected Imperial Rescripts*.

"Hey, you guys, don't you ever attend the reading of the Imperial Rescripts?"

"Yeah, we do," said Sugi, "but we're boning up on aviation theory right now." Sugi had been commissioned a year before the others, which made him their senior, and even Hanazono had to pay him due respect. Disappointed, the latter turned, his epaulets flashing at them, and left the room.

"That guy's really getting obnoxious. They're such damned fanatics, those Academy graduates. Look, they're at it now."

Through the window they could see a group of men on the crest of a low hill. In unison, they made two deep bows, first toward the Imperial Palace, then toward the Holy Shrine of Ise. Removing their caps, they bent their bodies forward forty-five degrees, then jerked back like mechanical toys and, holding their books of Imperial Rescripts in front of them, began to intone each ponderous syllable, like monks chanting a sutra. The wind carried their voices as far as the barracks.

"They're really going at it today," said Sugi. "Hanazono's so damned insistent I suppose we ought to go sometime. What do you say?"

Yamada shook his head. "I get out of breath climbing that hill. It affects my flying, and flying is my service to His Majesty. So you can count me out."

"I'm going," said Haniyu. The gloomy young man of a moment ago suddenly looked enthusiastic. Moving briskly, he grabbed a copy of the Imperial Rescripts, rammed his cap on, and ran out with Sugi.

Yamada shook his head. "What a funny guy."

"What do you think of him—from a medical point of view?"

"What do you mean?"

"Well, he's been pretty depressed lately. But then suddenly he'll be cheerful again. Or, when he's up in a plane he panics and starts mumbling about how he wasn't meant to fly—but the next minute he grabs the control stick and he's flying like a pro."

"That's it, that's him exactly." Yamada squirmed about in his tight uniform. "My back's itching like crazy. Where's my back scratcher? I thought I put it . . ."

"Here it is." Ken picked up the little wooden claw, which had fallen between their beds, and handed it over.

"Okay, I know I'm a doctor, but my original specialty was internal medicine, and now I'm supposed to be a specialist in aviation medicine. In other words, I don't know much about psychiatry. But Haniyu does seem to have some kind of psychological problem."

"You mean what they call a 'neurosis'?"

"Well, I don't know how he'd be diagnosed, but he's certainly unstable."

"What can we do to help? I've known him since our student days. He's never been an athlete, but he always had a good clear mind. After graduation he joined Tachikawa Aircraft, and I heard he came up with some blueprints for a new engine with incredible performance."

"That kind of guy shouldn't be flying at all. He ought to be kept on the ground where his technical skills can be used."

"But an engineer has to be able to fly himself. Only when he's up there piloting a plane can he get a real grasp of the technology. That's Air Corps policy."

"Yes, okay, they have a point. But look at doctors, if you're trying to invent a new medicine you give the job to a specialist in pharmacology, not a GP."

"I think I've got an inkling of what's bothering the guy." Ken smiled, but only because Yamada's double chin and pudgy shoulders looked funny somehow. "He's self-conscious about being the son of a general, who used to be in charge of the Air Corps. Haniyu's pushing himself because it wouldn't look good for a general's son to be afraid of flying."

"You probably have similar feelings yourself."

"I probably do. Somewhere inside me I'm aware that the son of Ambassador Kurushima can't ever allow himself to be a coward."

"But fortunately, you bastard, you're a good pilot. So good you make me sick. Somehow I just can't bring myself to like that control stick. The only kind of stick I like has got a fried potato or a sausage on it. That reminds me, I'm famished! Can you believe it? They've got me looking forward to that slop they serve up."

Ken began to lay out his flying suit and cap, and the harness for his parachute, on the bed. He then started polishing his boots with whale oil. Everything had to be ready for his training flight at eight o'clock.

"Oh yes, Haniyu almost made me forget. I've got to go feed the rabbit." Yamada ambled out with a basket full of carrot leaves. Sugi and Haniyu almost bumped into him as they came running in.

"Big news! For Air Corps Day they're sending a squadron of Red Dragonflies to Tokyo."

Yamada came back in. "Who's going to pilot them?"

"We are."

"But we haven't even started solo flying yet. Surely they're not going to have us fly to the air show with our instructors on board?"

"Of course not. So we're going solo soon."

"How soon?" asked Haniyu, looking serious.

"I don't know. Maybe today or tomorrow. Probably tomorrow."

"That's crazy!" The basket of carrot leaves made a shuffling sound in Yamada's agitated hands. "I'm not ready at all. I can barely manage the control stick with the instructor behind me."

"We only have twenty planes, so not everyone's going to be involved," said Ken. "Out of a hundred flight officers and sixty cadets, only twenty will fly. Even if they put two in each plane, that still only makes forty."

Sugi seemed enthusiastic. "They'll probably have a test to select the pilots. Hey, I'd love to fly in the air show. Imagine flying at really low altitude, right over the heads of that crowd at Haneda airfield!"

"No thanks," said Yamada.

"If there's a selection," said Haniyu, "I'm sure they'll play favorites with the Academy graduates."

Just at that point, Hanazono appeared. He had probably been eavesdropping on them from the corridor. Haniyu's face turned red with embarrassment, while the other three assumed an innocent look.

2

September 20th had been designated Air Corps Day. From early morning on, the radio repeated the schedule of the various events slated to take place in Tokyo and eleven other big cities across the country. There would be ceremonies where fighter planes purchased with public contributions would be unveiled. There would be lectures on aviation and civil defense, film showings, concerts, and exhibitions. There would be flights in a DC-3 for four hundred widows and children of fallen soldiers to view the capital from the air. And there would be a grand air show at Haneda airfield.

The unsettled weather of the past few days finally cleared. Beneath a crisp autumn sky, people thronged to the airfield; by midday the police estimated the crowd at more than 300,000. The bleachers were packed, and spectators spilled out onto the surrounding roads and rice fields. Yoshiaki Arizumi was there to cover the event with a photographer in tow.

Fifty-one Army and Navy fighters were due to be dedicated and given names such as "Serve the Nation" and "Patriot." The planes lined the runway, their silver duralumin wings gleaming in the sun, a pilot in a flying suit standing in front of each. The spectators applauded as girls in kimonos, trying to keep their long sleeves from flapping in the wind, stepped up to hand each man a bouquet of flowers.

After a speech by a representative of the citizens whose contributions had paid for them, Army Minister Tojo mounted the platform to express the country's gratitude. Even from a distance Tojo's black moustache and yellow medals stood out, and a stir passed through the crowd. Arizumi had heard Tojo's speeches many times before. He always read from a handwritten text, speaking slowly and crisply with the emphasis on the last syllable of each word, building up the crowd's emotion. Among the ministers in Prince Konoe's Cabinet, Hideki Tojo was a rising star. Konoe himself was of aristocratic birth, but his stated positions were never clear and there was something effete about him. People worried that Konoe might even yield a step or two to Roosevelt, and newspaper editorials often sounded the alarm, encouraging the idea that entrusting the future of Japan to this irresolute fop of a Prime Minister would lead to its downfall. By contrast, the manly, decisive Tojo seemed to have the will necessary to cut the Gordian knot. Tojo had risen from the infantry. He had served as Commandant of the Army Air Corps, and he realized, early on, the importance of an air force in modern warfare. He was widely regarded as a man who combined Hitler's resolve with Goering's vision, and the young men of the Iron Cross, for example, believed that he could save Japan.

The savior began to speak:

> On this occasion, graced with the august presence of an Imperial Prince, it gives me great pleasure to witness the splendid ceremony to dedicate these airplanes contributed through the fervent patriotism of all of you assembled here today, and of the people of the entire nation.
>
> Our situation is filled with tension, both at home and abroad. At such a time, it is with profound gratitude that the Army receives these advanced instruments of war, symbols of the people's sincere support. I am certain that those who pilot these patriotic aircraft, and the officers and soldiers who gaze up at them from the battlefields, will repay your gift and illuminate the fields of war with brilliant feats of military prowess . . .

The speech was met with tumultuous applause. An address by Navy Minister Oikawa followed, but the reception to it was clearly less enthusiastic. Rumor had it that the weak-willed Navy Minister, unnerved by the prospect of war with Britain and America, was conspiring with Konoe to bring about a peaceful compromise. It was also said that the government's stance toward the United States had been discussed at a secret conference in the Emperor's presence on September 6th, and that a momentous decision had been reached: that if efforts to find a diplomatic solution were unsuccessful, Japan would use military force to break the siege of the Western powers.

The blue sky was filled with the roar of engines. Above the upturned faces of the crowd, sixteen carrier-based fighters and attack planes glinted in the sun as the whole formation executed a loop. Applause rose from the crowd. Then the planes came swooping down, closer and closer, engines screaming, silver wings slicing the air right above people's heads as they swerved away to bomb a mock target beyond the airfield. The ground shook. White smoke rose. Somewhere in the crowd a baby's cry was swallowed up in the applause.

After the Navy came the Army. First was a great formation of fighters, reconnaissance planes, light bombers, and transport planes. Then, from far out to sea, came the deep roar of heavy bombers flying toward them in groups of three. Fighter planes went after the bombers, circling the massive aircraft in an aerial battle. But the bombers evaded the smaller planes, droning in low over the airfield and dropping real bombs on a makeshift target, which burst into flying shards of wood. The boom from the explosions echoed through the crowd, ringing in their stomachs. Little girls buried their faces in their mothers' chests. Old men in the ancient uniforms of the Meiji period let out sighs of admiration. In their excitement a mass of spectators pushed against the police lines, jostling and shouting in an attempt to get onto the airfield. Several dozen people broke through. The police yelled through megaphones, immediately moving in and grabbing the offenders.

Arizumi, wearing his Tokyo News Agency armband, pushed his way through the crowd. There were parents with their children and teachers with flocks of elementary and middle school students. The Naval Defense Boys' Club was there, as was the Greater Japan Women's Patriotic League and the Provincial Veterans' Association. Clusters of university students in uniforms and spats raised their school colors. Banners rippled in the wind: "The Gliders Club," "The Aviation Club."

But most conspicuous of all were the young members of the Iron Cross, dressed in khaki uniforms with swastikas emblazoned on their sleeves and imitation Army caps that could have passed for the real thing. Arizumi proudly acknowledged the bows of several students in the group. A couple of dozen of them had formed a circle, at the center of which a law student stood making a speech. He stood perfectly straight, shaking his clenched right fist, screaming out the words:

> Our ally Germany has risen, risen in glory! With unstoppable force Germany has gone from victory to victory on its march to build a new world order. The hero of the century, Adolf Hitler, has made substantial gains, a great expansion of his realm. Brussels, Dunkirk, Paris have fallen, and now the German Army sweeps on like an angry wave from Smolensk to Moscow. Any day now the Soviet Union will surrender. Britain has had its day. The Aryan people have risen in a massive display of solidarity, and a Great Co-Prosperity Sphere is emerging in Europe. Gentlemen, at a time like this, what is the task we face ourselves? The answer is obvious. We must respond to the great achievements of Hitler, the hero of the West, and bring about a new order in East Asia. To expel the Soviet Union, to liberate the colonies of England, America, France, and Holland, to establish a Greater East Asia Co-Prosperity Sphere of true freedom and peace—this is the urgent task before us!

The speaker pressed his clenched fist against his chest, then shook it in the air, in a perfect imitation of the Fuehrer.

> Now is the moment to put the Axis pact into action. The time has come to reveal our true selves to the world. Attack the Soviet Union! Destroy the United States and Britain! Smash the siege surrounding us! Now is the moment for us students to give our lives for the Imperial nation, for a new order in the East, for the peoples of Greater East Asia! Respond to the call of the spirits of our fallen heroes and enlist forthwith! At this urgent moment of history, we have no time to indulge in leisurely stud-

ies contaminated by foreign learning. Throw away your books! Throw away your books, and pick up the sword!

In the applause that followed, members of the Iron Cross raised both arms and shouted, three times in succession, "*Banzai* to His Majesty the Emperor!" Then with right arm extended they shouted, "Heil Hitler!" There followed a series of alternating "*Banzais*" and "Heil Hitlers," each shout joined in by more students.

But the sound of engines soon drowned them out. Flying toward them was a formation of trainer biplanes. When someone announced that the pilots were former students like themselves, the others on the ground began jumping around with excitement. There were fourteen groups of three planes each. Each group passed directly over the heads of the crowd, and each proceeded to circle the airfield.

Compared to the aircraft they had seen so far, the little trainer planes were pitifully slow. The engines of the Red Dragonflies purred as they passed over the crowd. It was like watching a children's class after a display of acrobatics by Olympic gymnasts. But there was something endearing about the sight, and the students in the crowd waved in solidarity. These were members of their own generation who had seen far enough into the future to know that Japan would need their particular skills.

The formation came in extra low, almost skimming the ground. When the planes got down to about ten meters, the students could see the pilots' faces and waved frenziedly at them. Hats were tossed in the air, flags and banners fluttered in salute.

Anna had told Arizumi that Ken would be flying a Red Dragonfly, and he found himself checking for his brother-in-law in each plane that flew by. In the second plane of the fourth flight he saw a face that looked like Ken's. The pilot had a larger than average build and was leaning out of his seat, waving his long arms. "Go, Ken!" Arizumi suddenly shouted. For a moment he was embarrassed at having displayed such childish enthusiasm.

It was at the moment when the sea abruptly ended and the airfield began that Ken realized that what looked like a layer of black sesame seeds covering the airfield was a great crowd of people. Passing over the airfield once, he banked to the left and came in again at ultra low altitude from the sea. He had been practicing this maneuver for a week. He was so low he could almost feel his wheels grazing the ground. The instructor in the lead plane raised his hand. Ken, behind him on the left, exchanged a glance with Yamada, who was on his right. Then he saw the main section of the airfield and the crowd coming at him like a surging wave.

He saw the Haneda terminal. *Somewhere on that roof is the Prince,* he thought. *Now wouldn't it be an almighty scandal if I crashed into His Highness? But I can go in real close and scare him out of His Imperial Wits.* The first plane was heading straight for the viewing seats on the roof. Ken's formation zoomed in, buzzing the roof at ten meters, close enough for him to see the expressions on the dignitaries' faces as they gasped and ducked their heads. *The Prince must have gotten the fright of his life. They could arrest us for lèse majesté. But at least His Highness got a chance to appreciate our airmanship!*

They were now directly above the crowd. Ken could see thousands of agitated white specks—hands waving at him. They were groups of students. Ken waved back. The lead plane was now starting a rapid climb. Ken pulled the control stick with all his might. Blue sky, wind, sun, and light. *Climb, climb!* 100, 200, 400 meters. *Now reduce speed and go into a roll. Bank to the left, and swoop down again. Where the hell is Yamada? Come on, get behind me. Okay, there you are. Now one final loop.* The airfield—the sea—blue sky—the airfield—the sea. *That's it, mission accomplished.* Their orders were to break formation at this point, and for each of them to return solo to the school by visual navigation. Ken went up to 500 meters. Following the coastline of Tokyo Bay, he headed north.

He passed over the docks at Shibaura, crowded with freighters. From the park at Hamamatsu-cho, at the northern end of the bay, he turned to fly over the city streets. Suddenly he had a mischievous urge to fly over his family's house in Nagata-cho. Of course Air Corps pilots were absolutely forbidden to make any detours, but since he'd be flying over the vicinity anyway it wouldn't really be a detour, would it? He could see the tall buildings of the bustling entertainment districts, Shimbashi and Ginza. It was a Saturday afternoon, the streets crawling with people and automobiles, in a city of a million little houses jammed together, where the spirits of the dwellers seemed almost to be squeezed out into the air.

Beyond the bright crimson halls of the Hie Shrine and the chalky white of the Diet Building, there it was, a distinctive two-story Western-style house near the Mexican Embassy. It resembled their villa in Karuizawa, with its red roof and whitewashed walls. It reflected Alice's tastes—a Connecticut country house in the middle of Tokyo.

Someone was in the garden. Was it his mother? He passed over. He tried to go back for another look, but the turn was tricky here. On his right was the Imperial Palace, on his left the residence of the Crown Prince. Nobody intruded into these skies, not with all those grand inhabitants. He flew up to Akasaka, turned around, and began his descent. He saw the Sanno Hotel and, there on the bluff behind it, the family house and . . . it wasn't his mother, it was Eri! Ken waved, and Eri saw him. She was waving back. She was running into the house to tell everyone. He wanted to make one more pass over the house, but the Military Police would be suspicious if he flew over the same place twice at this low altitude. He could see the Diet Building, the government ministries at Kasumigaseki, the various foreign embassies. He was flying over the nerve center of the Japanese Empire. Ken saluted his family with a wave of his wings and headed due north.

His mother was probably watching. He could hear her saying, "Isn't this exciting, Ken dropping in like this—from the sky! Let's call Anna and tell her. Oh look, isn't he flying well! What a pity, Papa would have *so* enjoyed seeing him!"

Ken hadn't written his family a single letter since their reunion in Karuizawa in the middle of August. Every day had been taken up with intensive training, and he had hardly had time to catch his breath. He had had to digest in six months what would normally have taken a year. In the third month of his training, solo flights had begun. As soon as he'd mastered the special techniques involved—

loops, rolls, reverse turns while climbing—they had started him on
formation flying (it had actually been too early for Ken's squadron to
start this, but instruction had been speeded up for the air show). He
had been busy not only with this cockpit training but with classroom
studies as well: aeronautics, engines, meteorology, navigation, piloting
. . . The classes filled all his afternoons, the subjects pounded into his
head through one test after another.

But he wanted to go back to his home in Nagata-cho at least once.
He wanted to see his father and mother and Eri, and he missed
Tanaka and the maids too. More than anything else he just wanted to
see the house again, the garden, his own room.

A broad field opened up below him: the Toyama parade ground.
Right beside it stood the Army hospital where Haniyu, who had never
been confident about his flying, had been taken a week before, after
crash-landing his trainer. Ken promptly veered to the east, beginning
a sharp descent. Over the Army Middle School and the Toyama Military Academy, he approached the wooden barracks-like wards of the
Army hospital. He made full speed for the window of Haniyu's room,
the second from the right, and passed by so close he almost touched
the eaves. Had Haniyu noticed him? Once again, he did a right turn
over Waseda University and came down over the hospital grounds.
He was sure he could make out the form of someone lying on the
bed inside. Did Haniyu realize it was him?

Ken had to get back. He picked up altitude. 500, 700, 1,000 meters.
In the suburbs of Tokyo the rice fields were turning yellow.

The previous Sunday Ken had gone to visit Haniyu in the hospital.
Haniyu had broken his left thighbone and his right fibula. He was
unable to move, with casts on his leg and torso. He had also suffered
a superficial laceration of his scalp, and his head was wrapped in
bandages. As he lay there he didn't look like a wounded soldier at all,
but more like the handsome male lead in a play who had been
injured in a scuffle over a woman. Any military impression was further weakened by the presence of the beautiful young woman nursing him. As she placed the flowers from Ken in a vase, he noticed the
slender hand that emerged from her kimono sleeve. It was small,

white, and delicate, unlike Eri's plump hands or Margaret's long, slim ones. Ken didn't know a thing about kimonos, but he realized that the girl was wearing one in the finest taste. This had to be Haniyu's sister, for she had his features, the same eyes and nose, and especially the slight upturn of the narrow chin.

"Toshiko," Ken whispered to himself in the air. The thought that it might have been her at the hospital window filled him with happiness as he flew back to base.

3

As the streetcar passed the bright red halls of the Hie Shrine, Ken could see, ahead in the distance, the forested precincts of Prince Fushimi's and Prince Kan'in's palaces. He felt a surge of nostalgia for the Sanno Hotel and the streets of Akasaka surrounding it. *This is my hometown*, Ken thought, as he stepped down from the streetcar and gazed across the avenue. Everything looked the same, the flower shop, the vegetable store, the pharmacy, the rice dealer, the photographer's studio, the barbershop—even down to the doctors' advertisements pasted on the telephone poles. The only thing different was all the rising sun flags hanging at the entrances of houses and festooning the buses and streetcars. Today was the Meiji Festival, commemorating Japan's first modern emperor. The autumn sky was cloudless, and the wind was cool and refreshing. Ken walked along with large strides, until he came across a crowd of people standing not only on the sidewalk but in the road as well. There were several banners hung on a nearby building with large slogans on them: "CONGRATULATIONS ON YOUR DEPARTURE FOR THE FRONT." Smaller flags waved in the crowd. Someone was speaking in a gruff voice, making congratulatory remarks. Because of his height Ken could easily see over the heads of the crowd. He saw a young man, about his own age, standing nervously on the stage with a rising sun banner draped around his neck. The youth apparently wasn't used to having a shaven head, for as he listened to the speech he occasionally reached up and scratched himself. His bewildered eyes wandered over the crowd, the children in their school caps, the housewives of the Women's Patriotic League in their aprons, the white-haired old man in a civil defense uniform standing next to him giving his speech.

Suddenly the young man noticed Ken. A look of surprise crossed his face, and he gave Ken a deep bow. The bow was so deferential that people turned around to look. But Ken couldn't recall ever having seen him before. Since the "celebration" was taking place in front of a dry goods store the Kurushimas had patronized since Ken was a little boy, he decided the young man must have remembered him as an old customer. The bluff was lined with mansions, including the Kurushimas', but below it was a street of little shops, and Ken was often greeted by people he couldn't recall as he strolled by.

He slowly climbed the narrow road to the bluff. The alley was lined on both sides with tall stone walls. It was dark in this alley, with a damp, moldy smell. The smell was always a reminder that he was home. Everything was the same here, down to the dark gleam of damp moss and the crack in the wall where, as a boy, he had inserted a bottle with a secret message in it.

A group of boys came running up the slope. They were students of the Municipal Middle School, dressed in khaki uniforms and wearing military-style caps. They probably had just been let out of the Meiji Festival ceremonies at school. Compared to Ken's officer's uniform, made of pure wool, their shiny rayon uniforms looked cheap and shabby. Ken felt sorry for them. It was the same pity he felt for the young draftee in the street below who was about to be shipped off to the front in China. The feeling included a sense of embarrassment at his own privileged position as a member of the Army elite.

"Attention!" he heard one of them shout, the command echoing in the narrow street. The boys halted, doffed their little caps, and gave Ken a salute. At first he thought it was a joke, but when he crisply saluted back the boys swarmed around him. There was a solemn look on their faces.

"Lieutenant, sir," one of them spoke up. He was a skinny boy with a high-pitched voice, who could have been a primary school student. But there was nothing timid about his attitude. "Sir, are you in the Air Corps?"

"That's right," said Ken with a grin.

"We really hope you'll give 'em hell, sir—those Americans!"

"All right," Ken nodded gravely.

"Really give it to them, sir, wipe them out!" the boy said, lowering his head as a sign of embarrassment at having been so outspoken.

Ken felt as if the little voice were a needle poking him in the heart. As long as he was in uniform, wearing his cap low over his tanned face, no one took him for a half-breed whose other half was American. Standing among the boys was not a "foreign bastard," but a tall Imperial officer who happened to have sharp-etched features, in whom a boy had placed his trust.

"Giving 'em hell" had become the fervent hope of a majority of the Japanese, a desire expressed in newspaper editorials and in daily conversation at the flying school. Why was America picking on them? Japan had never done anything to America, so why was it squeezing the lifeblood out of them? Ken remembered his surprise at first learning that the United States had embargoed the light metals—aluminum, molybdenum, etc.—used in manufacturing aircraft and, shortly afterwards, made it illegal for American companies to sell Japan the equipment to produce aviation fuel. Then in January the quota for exports of tin and scrap iron to Japan was cut in half, and the list of embargoed items kept increasing, until it included all strategic materials —copper, nickel, and lumber—and, by June, all petroleum products. At the end of July, Roosevelt had frozen all Japanese financial assets in the United States. It was tantamount to declaring economic war. By this time public opinion in Japan had reached boiling point: "Attack America!" one read in the papers, and "Crush Roosevelt's schemes for world domination!"

Ken could never bring himself to like Roosevelt, but he was also troubled by the journalists like Arizumi and intellectuals and military officers like Hanazono who pounced on Roosevelt's every act to stir up fanatic passions. If Japan started a war it wouldn't have a chance. It was obvious from the difference in aircraft production alone. America's immense industrial output, which Ken had seen with his own eyes not long before, and its ingenuity in developing new aircraft were awesome. What a wonderful collection of planes they had in the Air Force Museum at Wright Field—why, Japan didn't even have an air museum! But, above all, there was the toughmindedness of America, of which his mother was a good example. Look at Ambassador Grew, or Lauren, for that matter—they had such strength of character, Americans. When you added it all up, Japan's going to war with America would be an act of national suicide.

At heart, though, Ken simply hated the idea of going to war with his mother's country. The little boy's words—"Give 'em hell"—went on hurting in his chest.

When he reached the top of the slope, he looked back. Beneath the cloudless autumn sky, beyond where the roof tiles of the Akasaka quarter shone dully, Mount Fuji urged its pure form upon the city. There was more snow on the mountain than two months ago, when he had seen it from the seat of his Red Dragonfly, and against the blue sky this almost perfect cone was a quite improbable white.

Looking from the top of this slope to see whether Fuji was visible was a habit developed over many years, something one did unconsciously. Ken quickly regained his spirits, and when, across from the exotic yellow buildings of the Mexican Embassy, he saw his own house, he stamped his boots on the ground with pleasure. He'd been away for ages.

The room at the corner of the second floor belonged to Eri, but it had been Anna's before she got married. They had playfully called it "the observation post," for it commanded a view of both the Mexican Embassy and the Municipal Middle School, and was an excellent place to spy on diplomats and other schoolchildren. Now Ken could see the curtains with their red and yellow stripes, a leftover from Anna's days.

The white picket fence (Connecticut-style, his mother said) was lined in front with azaleas (this, she claimed, was Edo-style), which blossomed all at once in the spring. The house was known as the "Azalea Palace" in the neighborhood, and every spring people would come to admire the flowers.

The iron front gate was shut. Ken was about to ring the doorbell, then stopped and went to try the kitchen door instead. This wasn't locked, and, opening it, he could hear the sound of running water, and Tanaka's voice along with someone else, probably Yoshiko. Stepping lightly, he walked around to the garden behind, peered under the fence, and saw his mother talking with the gardener in the bright morning sunshine. The old gardener's face was a familiar one.

The garden was about six hundred square meters in size. Along the wall they had planted cherry trees, persimmon trees, and zelkovas. But not that many, for there was a lawn in the center, with a ping-pong table set up on it. Beyond the wall was Prince Konoe's estate, whose dark, luxuriant foliage growing over hedges in the Kennin Temple style made an elegant backdrop to their own patch. Indeed, the entire garden seemed like a clearing in the surrounding woods. Around the lawn was a small greenhouse, a flower bed, and a pond. The pond was shallow, designed as a pool for the birds, with a feed stand on an island in the middle.

The gardener and Alice were arguing about something.

"*So-ko da-me!*" she shouted, in less than perfect Japanese. "Not there! Over this way!"

"It's better here, madam. Much better. There's nothing wrong with my eyes."

"That rock isn't straight."

"It is."

But Alice insisted, and the old man, with a sweatband on his crew-cut head, gave in, shifting the position of the rock he had just placed on the ground. There were several other rocks lying there ready to be set out.

"No, that's not right!" said Alice, flapping her arms about. "It's even worse now." It was characteristic of her that, once she realized she'd made a mistake, she immediately corrected it. "No, no, *so-re da-me*. Put the rock back where you had it before. It looked better then. I was wrong."

But the old gardener either didn't understand her English or was exasperated with this woman's constantly changing demands, for he stood up straight and refused to answer her.

"Do you see? Put the rock back where you had it before. You were right, I admit it."

There was no response from the old man. Ken judged this a good moment to put in an appearance. Like an actor making a dramatic entrance, he leapt onto the terrace with a thud of his boots, pressed his cap to his chest, and bowed.

"Ken!" his mother shrieked. In her excitement she kicked away the disputed rock. She looked at it for an instant, then broke into a huge smile and ran toward him. Ken met her halfway and threw his arms around her.

"Oh Ken, what a sight I must be. I'm all covered with dirt."

"Mama." He ignored the dirt and kissed her on both cheeks.

Alice slapped the earth from her hands. "This is so sudden, you startled me. If you had told me you were coming, I would've had a big meal waiting."

"It wasn't easy getting leave. In fact . . ."

Alice immediately understood, and cut her son off in mid-sentence. "You look wonderful. You've gotten such a tan. Oh, this is terrific! Anna's coming over today, so we'll have the whole family together for dinner." She looked at her son uneasily. "You're not going back right away, are you?"

"No, I've got two full days. I can stay till the morning the day after tomorrow. Unless, of course, there's an emergency."

"An emergency?" Her bright eyes clouded over again.

The conditions under which Ken worked had become particularly strict recently, and officers would often find themselves called back in the middle of a furlough. It was explained to them that this was just one more part of their training, and soldiers had to steel themselves for the sudden returns to camp that wartime conditions might dictate.

Ken quickly changed the subject. "Where's Papa?"

"He's upstairs." The smile returned to Alice's face. "He's probably reading now. Since he went into semi-retirement he's had time on his hands, as you know. He only visits the ministry occasionally, and spends most of the day with his head in a book. Eri was right here a minute ago, playing ping-pong with Maggie. If Anna gets here early, we can all have lunch together."

"Incidentally, what are you doing with those rocks?"

"Making a Kyoto garden."

"A Kyoto garden?"

"Yes, dear, a *Kyoto garden*." Alice began enthusiastically explaining her plans. She wanted to arrange eight rocks in the form of the Chinese character for "rice," and make flower beds in the center and around the edges. This, she said, would be in the "Zen style" of Kyoto.

"You understand, don't you, Ken?"

"Nope." He smiled. "It doesn't make a bit of sense."

"Show more respect, my boy." She waved her finger at him. "You know the garden like this in Kyoto. The Something-or-Other Zen Temple—you know, the rock garden. We went there together."

"Oh, that." Ken nodded, not having any idea which one she meant.

"Yes, that one." She nodded back with a look of satisfaction. "That's the garden I want."

"So what're you going to do about this rock?" Ken pointed to the rock at his feet.

"Tell this man," said Alice, "that he was right, it looks better where it was. Tell him to put it back there."

Ken conveyed her instructions to the gardener. The old man rubbed his palm over his chin.

"I guessed that's what she was saying in English," he said, "but now I think the rock looks a hundred times better in the position she wanted it. See, it's in perfect balance with the rock on the other side. Just right. I was only stuck because I didn't know how to tell her in English."

When Ken interpreted this, his mother clicked her tongue in annoyance and shrugged her shoulders. "What a stubborn old man!"

"But Mama, he's admitting you were right. He's complimenting you on your aesthetic sense."

"Oh yes, my aesthetic sense. Tell him I like the rock where it is, and to start working on the next one."

The old gardener picked up another rock. "Please tell your mother I understand exactly what she wants. Ask her just to leave the rest to me, and I'll do it all her way."

Ken gave the man a wink and said to Alice, "Am I *hungry*!"

"What time is it?"

"It's past eleven-thirty."

"Good heavens!" Suddenly Alice was in a flurry. She ran into the house shouting, "Tanaka! Yoshiko!"

Ken nodded to the old man, then went around to the front entrance. Yoshiko was waiting for him there. She looked delighted as she took his Army sword. Tanaka, in his chef's hat, stuck his head out from the kitchen and bowed, twisting his hips in a sort of curtsy. Behind him was Asa, with the usual rather sullen look on her face. She gave Ken a perfunctory nod. Alice, who had slipped on an apron, was busy at the sink.

When Ken entered the house, he first went into the parlor across from the dining room. This was their family room. At its center was a stove surrounded by chairs, with an ornamental chest of Peruvian mahogany to one side that was crammed with family photographs.

The old photograph in a silver frame was of his parents at their wedding. The young bride, wearing a lace chapeau and holding a bouquet of carnations, was seated, with the groom standing beside her in a tuxedo. There was a photograph of Anna on her first birthday, which showed the happy parents holding up their baby daughter between them. And there were snapshots of the family through the years in their different residences as they moved from Chicago to Lima to Rome, then from Tokyo on to Brussels and Berlin. There was a photo of Ken just before he was drafted, in a suit, with his hair parted at the side. One photograph caught his attention, and he picked it up. It had been taken on his last visit to Chicago. It showed Lauren standing between Ken and George, the two young men pressing their smiling faces against hers. Ken and George looked like brothers, and Lauren was strikingly similar to Alice in her youth. Ken knew that George was in the U.S. Army Air Corps now. Was he already flying? Someday Ken wanted to co-pilot a plane with him, and take their family on a trip somewhere. He hadn't heard from his American cousins for a long time. Since the embargo began, letters to and from the U.S. didn't always get through.

He couldn't make up his mind where to go first, his father's study or Eri's room. Then he heard music and bright, laughing voices coming from behind Eri's door. He stood in the hallway, listening. When he heard Count Basie's "One O'Clock Jump," he knocked.

"Who is it?" It was Eri's voice.

"It's me," he said, imitating his father's voice.

"Papa? Wait a minute!" The music stopped. Ken could hear the clatter of things being hurriedly put away. He tried the knob. The door was locked. Finally it eased open from the other side.

Expecting her diminutive father, Eri was startled to find herself looking straight at the imposing uniform of her tall brother. "Ken! What a dirty trick to play on me! You're horrible!" And she flew at him with her fists. But as soon as she seized her brother by the front of his jacket, she kissed him on both cheeks. Along with the scent of her hair, he could smell perfume, and noticed she had quite a lot of lipstick on.

Margaret was there too, and another girl he didn't know, both also wearing makeup, which made their school uniforms look more than usually childish on them. When Ken nodded hello to Margaret, it seemed to make her dizzy with embarrassment. Her face flushed, as if someone had put a match to her. Ken could almost see the red reflected in her flaxen hair.

"Just what have you girls been up to?" Ken demanded, deliberately putting on a disapproving tone as he stared around the room. On the bed lay his mother's wedding dress and veil. A cosmetics case had been hastily stuffed under the bed.

"Aha," said Ken with a faint smile.

"Don't tell Mama!" Eri pleaded.

"If you don't want her to find out, you'd better take that makeup off." Ken got some tissue and helped rub the rouge off Eri's cheeks. This made Margaret burst out laughing. Her laughter then spread to Eri and the other girl, whose name apparently was Keiko. Eri was soon doubled up.

"Eri, get hold of yourself!" said Margaret. "Ken, Eri's a real whiz with makeup. Just before you came in she was showing us how to put it on."

"I was not. We were having a 'wedding rehearsal,'" said Eri. "Maggie was the bride, and Keiko was the groom. But who do you think Maggie's real groom is?"

"Eri, don't say it, don't you dare!" Margaret put her hand over Eri's mouth.

"Lieutenant Ken Kurushima!" squealed Keiko. "Maggie said she wants to be your bride!"

"You . . ." Margaret sprang at her. Eri jumped in between them and pulled the two apart.

Out in the hallway again, Ken smoothed the wrinkles in his uniform and put on a sober face before knocking on the door to his father's study.

"Come in." Saburo calmly inserted a bookmark into the middle of the book he'd been reading, and turned around. "Oh, Ken, welcome back. Did you get leave?" He had put on some weight, and there was more white in his moustache.

"Yes, sir, I'm back for two days." Ken bowed, then sat down on the sofa. "Am I bothering you?"

"Of course not. I wasn't doing any work. Not having an occupation these days has left me with plenty of time on my hands. I was bored, so I started reading this." He took the book off his desk and handed it to Ken. It was in English: *The Role of the Fighter in Aerial Warfare*.

"Hey, this is . . ."

"That's right, I borrowed it from your room. It's quite interesting, actually. It gives one a good idea of the status of military aircraft production around the world."

"I bought it in America the year before last. But most of it's already dated. The progress in aircraft design the last couple of years has been amazing. The planes with upper wings and the biplanes in the pictures here are already obsolete. Lower wings are common now, and the engines have twice the horsepower."

"I see." Saburo looked at his son, impressed. "And what about your own progress?"

"I've come on quite a bit. I'm already doing long-distance solo flights and I can do special maneuvers like loops. Right now we're doing formation drills. I flew in a formation at the air show at Haneda."

"I thought so." Saburo slapped himself on the knee. "Young Arizumi was there covering the show. He told us he saw somebody who looked like you flying at low altitude."

"That's right. I buzzed the terminal. And right after the show I flew over this house. Didn't Eri say anything about it?"

"No."

"Really? That's funny. I'm sure I saw her waving at me. I was flying so low I could make out the trees in the garden."

"Well, if she had seen you she certainly wouldn't have kept it secret. Are you sure you didn't imagine it? People have a tendency to see what they want to see."

Ken thought it over. He was sure it had been Eri waving at him. But then maybe it *had* been an illusion.

A gong rang out downstairs. It was a ship's gong that had been in Saburo's family home in Yokohama, and the Kurushimas had always used it to announce meals.

There was a knock. Eri poked her head in.

"Lunch is ready."

"We heard," replied Ken. He motioned his sister in. "Incidentally, did you notice when I flew over the house in my trainer plane on the day of the air show?"

"When was that?"

"September 20th, a Saturday, in the afternoon."

"No," she said, shaking her head, "I didn't see anything."

"Really?" Ken looked disappointed. He had wanted to give them all a surprise. Instead he had just been fooling himself. At this rate Haniyu and his sister probably hadn't noticed him either.

"Ken," said Saburo, "let's go for a walk together after lunch. It's a nice day outside. How about a stroll over to the Meiji Shrine?"

"Yes, sir." Ken came to rigid attention. With his eyes fixed on his father, he bent his torso forward exactly fifteen degrees in a military bow.

4

He couldn't get used to the sensation of his high Army boots constricting his shins. It made his legs feel as if they belonged, not to his own body, but to some crustacean covered in a hard shell, picking its way over the gravel. The boots weren't the only thing he couldn't get used to, either. With every step he took, the sword attached to his waist swayed this way and that, as if with a will of its own. At least the samurai of the past could secure the hilt of their swords in their belt. Ken felt that nothing he wore looked right on him—not his uniform, nor his cap, nor his officer's stripes. He was only a Lieutenant in the Army Air Corps on the outside. The soft body inside had nothing to do with soldiering.

Soldiers saluted him as they passed, and he returned the salute each time. What a bother it all was, this constant reminding of one's rank. At the same time, he had to keep an eye out for officers above him in rank, for he was obliged to notice them before they noticed him and to salute them first. As long as he occupied this particular niche in the strictly hierarchical society called the Japanese Army, there was nothing he could do about it. But he just couldn't get used to all the saluting—he was only a brand-new Lieutenant, after all, commissioned just this June. Yet if he ever failed to salute a senior officer, there were endless repercussions, particularly if someone like Hanazono, a spit-and-polish soldier with a monomaniacal regard for the Code of Military Courtesy, got to hear about it.

Even when he broke no regulations, Ken's height brought him unwanted attention. From a distance he was taken for a Japanese, but when people looked at him close up they would suddenly realize they were looking at a foreign face. The fact was, the Japanese military uniform seemed to have been tailored so as never to fit a long-legged Westerner. Some clever fellow had designed it to make a race of short men look impressive.

Maybe he just wasn't cut out to be a soldier. He remembered his first days in the Army, last January, when he joined the 8th Air Squadron in Yokaichi. How cold his shaven head had felt. He'd always been sensitive to the cold, but there it seemed to seep into his skull, and he shivered constantly. Private Second Class, a single star on his collar, the lowest of the low. That was how it all began.

As they now approached the Meiji Shrine, Ken looked down at his father's head and shoulders alongside him. He was trying to walk slowly, but still his father was bustling along just to keep up with him. Few would have taken this plump, aging figure in a black overcoat and felt hat, tapping the gravel with his walking stick, for the father of the officer walking beside him.

Back in January, Ken had been surprised when his parents had shown up one Sunday during visiting hours. It seemed out of character for his father, who never liked going out and who had been a virtual recluse since returning to Japan, to come all the way out to Yokaichi, a remote town north of Kyoto, ten hours away by train from Tokyo. But it was a cause of even greater astonishment, to him and to the entire camp, that the Army, which had become a hotbed of hostility to the United States, and the Air Corps, which had shifted the emphasis of its training from a hypothetical war with the Soviet Union to one with the United States, should suddenly find an American woman in their midst.

I remember the way people crowding the visiting room stared at her suspiciously. There she stood, among the women in their farmer's trousers and gray kimonos, wearing a loud red dress with bright yellow lace trimmings! Not only that, but when she spotted me she ran over and flung her arms around my neck and kissed me on the cheek. You could hear people snickering, making snide remarks. Didn't Mama realize what a shocking sight it made—a woman kissing a man in public, even if it was her own son? I guess it's because she didn't realize it that she's Mama . . . Later, when I got back to my barracks,

*the older soldiers were waiting. "So your old lady's an American, eh?
Speaks funny, eh? And you're half one yourself. So they were right
when they said you're a spy." The rumors spread through the whole
regiment. I became known as the "half-American." And soon the "half"
came off, and everyone called me "the American."*

*I remember the Sergeant in the cookhouse cornering me. "Hey, Yan-
kee! Let's fix that Yankee face of yours—show you some real 'fighting
spirit.' Stand over there." And that ladle he'd already used on my ass
now came flying in my face. It was an unspoken rule in the Army that
you didn't touch a soldier's face when he was getting a whipping. Even
a buck private was still "a son of the Emperor," and the older NCOs
tried not to leave any signs of violence on you. But not with me. My
face became a target—this foreign bastard's face, filthy Yankee face,
un-Land-of-the-Rising-Sun face—yes, this face, this face! And they
threw fists and ladles, boots, curses and gobs of spit at this face. My
white, American, half-breed face puffed up, and my eyelids swelled up
like almonds, and the result, surprisingly, was that my eyes became
Oriental eyes with tiny folds—their eyes.*

*I swear to God (O God, let me swear before you!) that I bore the
pain without complaining. When they thumped me I didn't even flinch.
When they saw I was taking it all in silence they said I was being
"cocky," and redoubled their efforts. "How dare you!" they screamed at
me. "Think you can keep your trap shut, do you?!" And they came at
me with their fists flying.*

*Yes, I was "cocky." The beatings were worse than anything I'd ever
experienced before, but I had reserves of strength in me. Did they think
a few punches would make me cry? I'd been in training for this since I
was just a kid. When I was eight my family left me on my own in
Tokyo so that I should get a Japanese education. I started school two
years later than the other children. The first day of school I could
hardly understand a thing the teacher was saying. When the other kids
spoke to me I couldn't answer. We always spoke English in America,
and Papa was always too busy to teach me Japanese. The only Japanese I heard was a few broken phrases that my sister Anna, who was
three years older than me, had managed to pick up. My classmates*

took my inability to speak as a sign of stupidity, and poked fun at me.

Then one day I ran into an ambush. Three nasty little kids shouting "Hey, Yankee!" "White pig!" attacked me and threw me to the ground, kicked dirt in my eyes and punched me. I closed my eyes. The blood from my lips tasted like sea salt. I held my breath and pretended I was dead. The moment they stopped, scared that they might have killed me, I kicked one of them in the balls and knocked another one down with an uppercut. The other one tried to run away, but I tackled him from behind and held him down. They began crying, moaning, screaming for help. I kept hitting each one in turn, till some adults came running over. I yelled at them in English, I worked up such a storm of English that it made them flinch. I clenched my fists in front of my chest and spat at them. "Damn you all! I hate you, you Japs, you filthy Japs! Go to hell!" I yelled at them.

That word—"Japs"—it set me apart, made me feel Caucasian. I wasn't one, of course. I had lived in the Japanese Consulate in Chicago, I'd been raised a Japanese and continually reminded that I was Japanese. But when I found myself surrounded by Japanese children, and saw their flat yellow faces, and heard them jeer at me in their mushy-sounding language, I considered myself Caucasian. I fought them as a foreigner, with my foreign face and language, and I won. Yes, the moment I turned white even the adults left me alone. I caught a glimpse of how cowardly Japanese adults are, shrinking back from a foreigner, even a little boy.

When a Japanese becomes conscious of himself as an Oriental, he feels awkward and inferior toward Caucasians—this was my discovery. It was the other side of the contempt and superiority the average Caucasian felt toward an Oriental. Often I'd seen the children of Japanese officials at the Consulate in Chicago being spat on, or tripped up, or sworn at by white children, simply because they looked Asian. It was a time of intense anti-Japanese prejudice, a time when the papers were full of "the Yellow Peril," when laws were passed prohibiting Japanese immigration. Where white children were in charge, Asian children had no choice but to run and hide. And since the white child retained his superiority even in Japan, Japanese children when they were out to get him did it by ganging up on him, envy and resentment mixed in with their fear, and only attacked him with superior numbers. But as soon as their victim fought back, they burst into tears and ran away, shouting for help.

I had to make myself strong. I never knew when I'd suddenly be branded "white." I threw myself into sports, not because I particularly enjoyed it, but to make my body strong. In primary school I did boxing, in middle school sailing, riding, and judo. Then in my last year of middle school I discovered rugby, and in high school I became a pretty good fly half. I had clout. As long as I was a better athlete than my classmates, nobody bothered me.

But all this changed in the Army. I was a bare-assed private. The abuse began again, I found myself subjected to the same kind of violence. The primary school bullies now wore sergeants' uniforms. But after fourteen years of training, I was strong enough to take it. Their punches couldn't break me. Ever. Beaten and laughed at, I never lost my composure. I honestly didn't flinch. And I got on with my work in preparation for the officer candidate exam. When I passed, I was promoted to junior flight officer. When the Sergeant in the cookhouse saw me in my new uniform, he couldn't hide the look of shock and alarm as he bowed to me. But I had no wish to get revenge. He was just one small-minded Japanese out of millions, who saw me as a foreigner and reacted with automatic resentment and bigotry. It would have done no good to single him out for blame.

Ken and his father walked through the archway into the precincts of the Meiji Shrine. Pausing at the fountain to wash their hands and mouths with holy water, they climbed the steps to the shrine hall and stood side by side, clapping their hands in prayer. When they turned around, they saw an immense crowd below, spilling over both sides of the wide approach to the shrine. Most of them were soldiers and sailors. Conspicuous among them were young fathers with their wives and offspring, paying a round of visits for the Children's Festival. In an ordinary year the little girls would have been dressed in bright, colorful kimonos, but now they were in subdued robes, somber hand-me-downs from their mothers and older sisters, or even in gray farmer's trousers. Overwhelmingly, the boys wore military uniforms: little generals and admirals—even, to Ken's surprise, little pilots in flying suits. He saw a mother alone with her son, the boy in a black ceremonial kimono with pleated trousers. His father was probably at the front in China.

Parents and children had formed a line to one side of the shrine hall, where a sign read "Special Prayers for the Children's Festival." The crowd swarmed up the steps, their faces puffed up with a more-Japanese-than-thou sort of pride, serenely confident in their roles as mothers, fathers, and children of the mighty Japanese Empire. The many military men present, apparently on leave from their regiments and ships, moved about in groups of fifty or so. One saw Navy uniforms, Army uniforms, civil defense uniforms, farmer's trousers, middle school student uniforms. There were national flags, Imperial Navy flags with the blood-red rays of the morning sun, banners with slogans: "PRAY FOR VICTORY!" "DOWN WITH CHIANG KAI-SHEK!" "ENGLAND, GET OUT OF ASIA!" "CONGRATULATIONS TO OUR ALLY GERMANY ON ITS GREAT VICTO-RIES," "CELEBRATE THE MEIJI FESTIVAL" . . .

The crowd advanced toward Ken and his father in an undulating wave. Soon people would notice that Ken wasn't . . . but no, there were so many visitors that Ken attracted no attention. The clouds of dust kicked up by the surging crowd swirled in the wind and flew in the faces of the fathers and sons who followed behind.

Saburo closed his eyes and said, "Let's go somewhere quiet." They left the crowds, turning onto a side path, and from there into the surrounding woods. Signs of the season were everywhere. The light of the low-hanging autumn sun lay on leaves of various colors: the brown and crimson of zelkovas and paulownias, the scarlet of Yoshino maples, the yellow of ginkgos. From clumps of high grass came the wan cries of dying insects. Trampling the leaves that covered the gravel path, father and son made their way to a bench and sat down.

"It's warm here," said Saburo, lighting his pipe. "In Berlin it would already be winter. Remember how cold November was in New York and Chicago? It makes you realize Japan's a southern country."

Bluish wisps of smoke drifted up from his pipe and, when they reached a certain height, were carried away by the wind. Ken could remember Europe in September when the leaves were already beginning to change color. The year before last, he had used his high school summer vacation to visit his family in Europe, and on September 1st was in France just as Germany was invading Poland. There was chaos. He quickly made his way to Liverpool, where Japanese evacuees from all over the Continent had gathered, and returned to Japan via the United States.

Ken sighed. "We're living in a pretty extraordinary time."

"We certainly are. In the last two years the world's gone mad." Ken noticed the sadness in his face.

A leaf brushed against his pipe. Ken pulled out a Golden Pheasant cigarette, and his father lit it for him with his lighter. There was nobody near them. Each gust of wind brought down a shower of leaves, which crackled against each other as they fell.

"Papa," Ken said quietly, "a lot of people in the Army are saying we should attack America. Until recently they were saying 'Attack Russia. Go to our ally Germany's aid.' But now it's shifted to 'Attack America.'"

"I imagine so," his father nodded.

"What do you think, as a diplomat? Do you think there'll be war between Japan and America?"

"Hmm." He looked right and left, to make sure nobody could hear, before speaking. "It's reached a very dangerous point. Unfortunately there are people in both countries who would like to start a war. Especially in the military." He looked around again.

"Papa," said Ken, "let's look over each other's shoulders as we talk. If we see anyone, we'll signal by turning to the front."

"All right," he agreed with a smile. "The Japanese military, especially the Army, seriously underestimate the power of the United States. And not only the material power. A lot of people here have fooled themselves into believing we have a monopoly on spiritual power. They think that America will just give up. Blindly they're going ahead, making threats to invade Indochina, for example, which can only provoke the United States. The upshot of it all is that America has frozen our financial assets and embargoed oil exports to us. Without oil Japan is helpless. Hence the emergence of the pro-war faction arguing that we should jump-start a war before supplies run out."

"Do you think it's only the Army?"

"Oh no, there's a pro-war faction in the Navy too—mainly, I think, among the general staff. Most of the upper ranks of the Navy are extremely hesitant about starting a war, but they're not in a position to oppose it because of Army pressure and popular sentiment. They don't want to appear weak-kneed or cowardly. And the Army's using that as a way of dragging them into war."

"Even at flying school, you know, you often hear talk about 'our timid Navy.' But I can tell you this: there are certainly no extremists in the Air Corps shouting for an immediate attack on England and America. Everyone realizes the gap between us and them in aircraft production is huge."

"What about in aircraft performance?"

"I'd say it's neck and neck right now. The 97s that the Army used against the Russians in Manchuria are probably superior in maneuverability to anything Lockheed or Curtiss have developed. And the Ki-43 and the 1 Fighter chosen to be the main attack plane this April are even more advanced. But the problem is, what happens in the future? Aerial warfare won't be a matter of a simple one-on-one duel; it'll be a contest of speed, high-altitude performance, and sophisticated weaponry. If all we make are highly maneuverable planes, we'll fall behind."

"Are there any new planes in development?"

"They're in the planning stage. I'll probably be working on the designs for some new aircraft myself. But we need time. If someone starts a war now, it'll be too early."

"No, we mustn't start a war under any circumstances."

"The trouble is, fighting is what being a soldier is all about."

"I wanted to ask you about that." He looked Ken directly in the face, as if gazing at a statue. "How do you feel about being a soldier now?"

Ken bit his lip and remained silent.

"I meant to ask when we were all up in Karuizawa, but I didn't get a chance. You know, when your mother and I went to visit you at that camp in Yokaichi we were worried about you, you looked so depressed."

"I was in basic training then, and I was pretty worn out by all the drilling."

"Your mother noticed bruises on your face."

"Oh, did she? I was . . . slapped around a bit. It was nothing, it happens all the time in the Army."

"It must have hurt, though."

"It didn't hurt at all when they hit me. What was hard, Papa, and still is, is that I just can't get used to what they call 'Japanese fighting spirit.' For them the Imperial Rescript for Soldiers is the absolute truth. You're not allowed to deviate an inch from it. In flying school now there are a lot of former Army Academy cadets who think of nothing but the Imperial Rescripts. It's 'the august words of His Majesty' from morning till night."

"I imagine they're pretty fanatic."

"Yes. They're a completely different breed from us graduates from civilian schools. They're fanatics who believe the Emperor is literally a living god."

"Are all the cadets like that?"

"Those who aren't have to pretend to be. They're always picking fights with us, attacking us for being 'lacking in fighting spirit.' " Ken stopped. He realized there was no way he could make him understand the sheer ferocity that Hanazono and other men like him brought to their Emperor-worship.

From a path in the shadow of the trees a young man and his father emerged. The boy, in student uniform, bowed to Ken before nudging his father toward a stretch of grass, where they sat down and opened a wooden lunchbox containing a few balls of rice mixed with wheat.

It was a meager-looking meal.

"You can't win a war on fighting spirit alone," Saburo continued.

"I agree. The officers in the Air Corps, of all people, should realize that. But unfortunately even among them there are some who say we can make up for our backwardness in technology with our warrior spirit. I just can't accept that kind of thinking."

"A conflict simply has to be stopped, especially one with the United States. It's madness. Japan would be utterly defeated."

"Utterly?" Ken raised his eyebrows and looked at him directly. His father returned his stare.

"Yes. The power balance is too unequal. Why, even in strategic materials we don't even come close. They have ten times more coal than us, five hundred times more petroleum, ten times more iron. If one looks at industrial production, they produce six hundred times the oil we do, eleven times the steel. It should be obvious even to a child! There's no way to fight a giant like that and win. The Army thinks they can make up for it with their 'fighting spirit' and surprise attacks. But they forget that the United States has its own patriotic spirit. Its sense of justice—what the Americans call 'fair play'—is particularly strong. And they would take the kind of surprise attack that's been Japan's specialty as an act of cowardice, and react with fury. Japan can't fight a war with them, it's impossible . . ." He abruptly stopped speaking and turned to the front. Ken looked back the other way. A dozen burly-looking men dressed in black crested samurai robes, their high wooden clogs clacking loudly on the ground, were coming toward them. They were rightists. Forming a circle on the grass, they began arguing about something in loud voices. The father and son eating their lunch glanced uneasily at them and quickly got up and left.

"Shall we go too?" Saburo stood up and stretched. "I haven't been to the Ginza in a long time."

Making their way out of the shrine, they got on a train for Yuraku-cho, where the Ginza district began. The first thing that met their eyes when they got there was a huge poster:

PARAMOUNT PRESENTS WILLIAM HOLDEN

IN

I WANTED WINGS

Surrounding the words were crudely drawn pictures of B-29s and B-17s.

FEATURING THREE THOUSAND OF THE LATEST AMERICAN BOMBERS!

As if to apologize for the ostentatious display of American war power, the poster included a tiny disclaimer: "Presented as valuable material for studying present trends in a hostile country." Another poster advertised the film *Mr. Smith Goes to Washington*, with the likenesses of Jean Arthur and James Stewart done quite artistically. There was also a poster for *Edison, the Man*, featuring Spencer Tracy.

"Well, what a scandal! They're all American movies!" Ken remarked, a smile rising to his lips. To someone who had been subjected to a frenzied anti-Americanism day and night at the flying school, the sight of people swarming to see these foreign films, without a trace of hostility on their faces, actually seemed subversive.

Ginza was packed with people leisurely enjoying their holiday. What a contrast they made to the military uniforms, the black samurai robes, and the farmer's trousers on display in the Meiji Shrine. Here women were strolling along in colorful kimonos splashed with flower and bird designs. In front of every movie theater and restaurant, lines of people waited to get in. The sidewalks and street corners where the blue city buses stopped were overflowing. At the main Ginza intersection huge banners hung from the roof of the Mitsukoshi department store telling passersby to "SEND A GIFT TO A SOLDIER AT THE FRONT." It was having a sale of comfort bags.

Saburo and Ken turned down a side street and came to a Western-style restaurant. Years before, when Saburo had been Director of the Trade Bureau and Ken was in middle school, they had often eaten there. The restaurant specialized in French cooking, and served an excellent duck with lemon sauce, meat pies in Provençal style, and bouillabaisse. The waiters, in identical white jackets and black trousers, moved about with a practiced grace as they served these elegant dishes on gilt-edged plates.

Today, however, there was a notice posted on the door: "Due to instructions from the authorities, we are unable to serve dinner. The café is open." For over a year now, restaurants had been forbidden to serve rice; only potatoes, wheat, and bean flour were allowed. But now even supplies of these rice substitutes were running low, and many establishments had had to close. It had become something of a triumph in the Ginza just to keep a café going.

Ken's father put his forehead to the glass door and peered in. When he recognized the gray-haired owner sitting at the counter, he pushed the door open.

"Ambassador!" The old man stood up and greeted him. "It's been a long time."

"Are you serving anything today?"

"We aren't able to do any meals these days . . ."

"That's all right, we already ate, but do you think we could get something to drink?"

With a sidelong glance at the dozen customers in the café, the proprietor whispered, "Go upstairs. This must be your son. He was just this high the last time you were here. What a splendid young man he's become."

There was no one on the second floor. Rosewood tables with silver vases were arranged on a thick red carpet beneath chandeliers. Nothing seemed to have changed from years before.

Bending his stooped body forward, the old man told them: "We have some rice-cake soup and coffee. We only make them for a few special patrons."

"Well, they're both rarities these days."

"The soup is even sweet," he said proudly. "Of course there's no sugar available, but we use potato sugar and honey, and it tastes just like the real thing. As for the coffee, we use genuine Brazilian coffee beans. We have a secret stock."

"Good. Let's try it."

"The soup, or the . . . ?"

"We'll have both."

"Thank you, sir." The old man rubbed his hands together gleefully, bowed again, and left the room.

"Coffee's a treat nowadays," said Saburo as he took out his pipe. "Even at home we've run out of it, and have to use substitutes."

From where he sat, Ken could see into the department store across the street. People were rummaging through the counters filled with comfort bags. Posted on the walls was a series of forlorn advertisements: "STEEL-PLATED HAND MIRRORS FOR PROTECTION AGAINST GRENADES," "PUMPS FOR PURIFYING WATER," "SOAP SUBSTITUTES," "RUBBER WORKING SHOES." Suddenly he noticed a foreigner among the pedestrians in a side street. It was a young Caucasian man, walking with a Japanese woman in Western dress. The two seemed to be talking quite intimately. Could they be husband and wife? Whatever they were, they presented quite a rare sight.

"Papa," Ken said in a slightly childish tone of voice, "may I ask you something?"

"What?" Saburo asked, with the wary smile he put on when his children were about to talk him into something.

"Why did you marry Mama?"

"There's no simple reason. Anyway, you know the circumstances in which we got together, don't you?"

"Yes, I do, but . . ."

It seemed Ken was after something else, but Saburo told the story anyway. Alice had been born in Washington Square in New York City. Her parents, who had met when they both happened to be traveling in America, were Scottish, the father a Protestant minister. It was through Alice's brother Norman, who was a member of the America-Japan Society in Chicago, that Alice met the young Japanese Consul in that city. Saburo was a frequent visitor to Norman's house, and his friendship with her blossomed there. They were engaged on March 25th, 1914, and on October 3rd of that year they were married in the New York townhouse that had been Alice's childhood home.

"It must have been unusual for a Japanese to marry an American back then."

"Yes, I suppose it was."

"Weren't there any barriers?"

"Barriers?"

"Prejudice against mixed marriages. For example, from Mama's parents."

"Oh, I don't know . . . well, to tell you the truth, there was some resistance. Your mother's family were a bit opposed at first, but Alice was so determined that they finally gave in. As you know, the Littles were quite keen on Japan. Starting with Norman, who first became aware of it during the Russo-Japanese War, the family took a certain interest in this country, which for most Americans at that time was still an obscure archipelago at the far end of the Far East. I'd gotten to know Alice's parents, too. They sometimes invited me to their parties. So when I asked for their daughter's hand, well, I suppose it was a surprise, but they had already accepted me as a person. No, I don't think they were prejudiced, just a little uneasy about our prospects."

"What about your parents, Papa?"

"Oh, there was no objection at all. My father was from Yokohama, as you know. He'd started up a shipbuilding company in the Meiji period, and had dealings with quite a lot of foreigners. Actually, the biggest barrier was the Foreign Ministry. A diplomat quite often has to deal with state secrets, so the ministry rather frowns on its people bringing foreigners into the family. In the case of marriage one has to make a formal request and obtain their permission."

"Was there any problem getting permission?"

"Not really. You see, the Great War had just broken out, and Japan and America were allies against Germany."

"So it was thanks to a war that you and Mama were able to get together," Ken laughed.

"That's right." Saburo laughed too, but the laughter quickly died away. Both seemed to have had the same thought flicker at the back of their minds, and when they looked at each other Ken caught the foreboding in his eyes.

"If there's a war now . . . ," he started to say.

"It'll be hard on your mother. And on you and your sisters too." His father looked away.

"Have you ever thought about what *would* happen if war broke out?"

"No, I haven't. I don't allow myself even to consider it. A diplomat's job is to stop war by all means possible. I don't think about the alternative. That's the difference between a diplomat and a soldier."

"Okay, but about you and Mama . . . ," Ken pressed on. "What I wanted to ask you was, when you got married did you give any thought to the children you'd have? I mean, did you ever consider what kind of life they'd lead—as half-Japanese and half-American? I realize that's a hard question to answer, but I really would like to know."

"Of course we thought about it. And your mother and I agreed on one point: that we would raise our children as Japanese. The only life I could live was as a Japanese diplomat. Your mother accepted that when she married me."

"Then why did you leave me on my own in Japan, while you took Anna and Eri with you overseas?"

"I . . ."

Just then, the proprietor came shuffling in with their trays. "I'm sorry to have kept you waiting. Our cooks and waiters are all in the Army, and I have to run the place myself."

Saburo removed the lid from the porcelain bowl. "Ah!" he said admiringly. "There's a real rice cake in it."

"Yes, sir." It was an extravagant gesture, and the old man was obviously proud of it. "It's illegal, but I wouldn't think of serving Your Excellency a rice-cake soup without the rice cake."

"Delicious," said Saburo, taking a bite. "The taste of Japan at peace."

"Indeed, sir. I look forward to the day when we're free to eat things like this again."

Some customers were calling from downstairs. The old man was about to leave when Saburo stopped him and asked, "Do you know what's on in the way of Kabuki now?"

"Well, they're doing *Chushingura* at the Tokyo Theater, and *The*

Lions at the Kabuki-za—they say Ennosuke is absolutely brilliant in it."

"Ah, that sounds good. If we go now we can make the evening show."

"Shall I order some tickets for you?"

"No, that's all right. We'll just catch one act, so we won't need reservations. We've got to get home for dinner. My wife's waiting for us."

When they were alone again, Saburo explained how when he was a student, he and the restaurant proprietor often went to the Kabuki together. "He's a great fan. You've probably never seen *The Lions*, have you?"

"No, I don't know much about Kabuki."

"That's because you spent all your time playing rugby. Well, you should see it at least once. Now, what were we talking about . . . yes, the reason we left you in Japan. It was because you were a boy. I wanted you to be brought up as a Japanese, to become the best of Japanese men. As you know, a diplomat's family wanders from country to country like a ship without an anchor. I wanted you to feel you *belonged* here."

"Did Mama agree to that?"

"She was against it at first. But in the end she, too, agreed. Her opposition was based on her love for you as a mother—quite naturally, she wanted to have you with her while you were growing up."

"Was that the only reason?" Ken asked suspiciously.

"What do you mean?" He raised his thick eyebrows. A tiny piece of food was clinging to the edge of his mouth.

"Didn't Mama want to raise me in America? Anyone can see I have Western features. I would have easily fitted in as an American. But here I was always seen as a foreigner. I could never have become completely Japanese. Mama must have sensed that; she must have gone through the same thing herself when she first came here. She knows what it's like . . ."

"Have you been unhappy in Japan?"

"Unhappy . . . ?" Ken thought about it. "It wasn't that I was unhappy, it's just that they never *allowed* me to be Japanese."

"And could you become an American?"

"Not now. It's probably too late. But before . . ."

"No, Ken, even if we had raised you in America you could never have become completely American. Half your blood is mine. It's Japanese blood."

"I know that, but still . . ."

"Ken." He looked at his son, and spoke slowly and deliberately. "Was it because of your foreign looks that you were ill treated in the Army?"

"Yes, sir, I think it was."

"And do you hate me for it?"

"No!" He shook his head, astonished at his father's question. "I don't hate anyone. I realize it was probably inevitable that you should leave me here. But Papa, I just wanted you to know what it was like for me, how I've been treated. I'm more confident now. I feel I can overcome any problems I'm faced with. But I just wanted you to know."

"I'm glad you feel confident. But you've got more than your usual share of problems, and it's going to be tough."

"Maybe I'll fail. Then it'll really be tough."

"Shall we go?" He stood up.

"Papa, you've got some food on your lip."

When they arrived at the Kabuki-za, Saburo, who was familiar with the layout of the theater, led his son up a side stairway and into the upstairs gallery. The climb made him start sweating, and he was breathing heavily. Ken grew concerned, but after a bit he seemed to be all right.

Ken looked down at the front rows, which were nearly full. Most of the audience seemed to be young women in kimonos. It soon struck him that there wasn't a single soldier in the place. *How interesting*, he thought—*it might be the only place in all Japan without any*.

The clappers were struck. The curtain opened.

A lion and its cub, red and white manes swaying in their hands, began to dance. They were traveling through a landscape dominated by a high peak and a deep valley. Ken smiled. The narrator began to chant:

> From the towering mountaintop
> the lion kicks his son
> into a deep ravine—
> as deep as his paternal love—
> and watches as the cub
> tumbles, rolling helpless,
> but then turns itself around
> and claws its way back up—
> to be thrust down and down again.

His father had brought him here specifically for this scene. *When he left me on my own in Japan, wasn't he kicking* me *into a ravine? Maybe I should be grateful to him,* he wondered; *I certainly don't resent him, or anyone else for that matter. It made me look out for myself. The only thing is, did he ever understand what it felt like to be tumbling helplessly to the bottom? He's never had to take that kind of fall himself. He doesn't know what it's like down there. But yes, I can be grateful, I can take it as an act of kindness, the opportunity he gave me to forge an inner strength.*

The scene was followed by a comic interlude. The lions, father and son, began to dance again as a classical *naga-uta* was sung. The tempo quickened, the lions now prancing about among peonies and butterflies.

As the applause died down and they stood up to leave, Ken told his father: "It's the best thing I've seen in a long time. Thank you very much, Papa."

"Was it really that good?" Saburo looked up at Ken, taken aback by his son's sudden formality.

They grabbed a taxi in front of the theater. It was a charcoal-burning car, driven by a wrinkled old man. Every time he pressed his foot on the accelerator there was a deafening roar, and white smoke trailed behind them. Just before the Akasaka intersection, Saburo ordered the driver to stop. Ken thought his father must have realized the car would never make it up the slope to their house, so he was surprised when he started walking back toward the Sanno Hotel, which they had just passed.

"I just had an idea," Saburo told him. "I noticed a photographer's studio was open, so I thought we might go and have our picture taken."

"Our picture?" Ken looked at him, wide-eyed. His father had always acted on sudden impulses.

When they went inside, they found yet another old man attending to them. From the proprietor of the French restaurant to the taxi driver, and even the Kabuki actors, it seemed the only men left in the city were old.

"Here for a commemorative photograph, sir? Ah, I remember, I took the young man's photograph to commemorate his promotion to lieutenant. Congratulations again! Fortunately I have some dry plates, so I can take care of you right away . . . Just take a seat over there . . ."

5

Someone was knocking. It sounded like the front door. A man was calling out. Who could it be in the middle of the night?

Ken reached for the switch on his bedside lamp. Then he thought about who might be lurking outside. Tokyo was full of fanatics. Someone might just be waiting for a light to come on up here on the second floor. He squinted at the luminous dial on his wristwatch. Two-thirty. The knocks continued; it sounded like a machine gun. Then came a young man's voice shouting, "Is anyone there?"

Was it a soldier come to order him back to base? His mother had said the telephone wasn't working properly; in the middle of a conversation it would suddenly go dead. Maybe the flying school wanted him back but had been unable to get through to him on the phone.

Ken jumped out of bed and quickly put on his uniform. He walked down the stairs in his slippers, trying not to make any noise. At the foot of the stairs he found Yoshiko dealing with the sudden visitor.

"Who is it, please?"

"A courier from the Foreign Ministry."

"Please wait a minute."

When Ken appeared in the hallway, Yoshiko, embarrassed at being seen in her long silk under-kimono, quickly hid behind a folding screen.

"I'll see who's there," said Ken, unlocking the door. Outside, illuminated in relief by the porch light, were two men. One was a policeman in uniform, the other a young man in a black suit, who introduced himself again as a courier from the Foreign Ministry and stated, in a smooth, well-rehearsed sentence, that the Foreign Minister had an urgent matter to discuss with Ambassador Kurushima, and asked if His Excellency would be so kind as to accompany him to the ministry at once. The man stood there shivering, and his breath was white in the freezing air.

"Come in. I'll call my father right away."

The light in Saburo's study was already on. When he knocked, he was immediately told to come in, as if he had been expected. His father was putting on his morning suit.

"Were you up, Papa?"

"Yes." He pulled the bottom of the vest over his protruding stomach. The seat of his striped trousers looked as if it was going to split. "I've let myself get so fat my clothes don't fit any more," he said.

Ken didn't have to tell him about the courier; obviously he had heard everything from upstairs.

"What could it be, at this hour of the night?" asked Ken.

"Must be something important."

Ken straightened up. "Shall I go wake Mama?"

"No, let her sleep. I won't know for sure what it's all about until I get there anyway. Oh yes, remember that picture we took yesterday? I'd like to see how it turns out."

Saburo left his study and went downstairs, where he showed the courier into the parlor. Ken followed, but went into the dining room across the hall. Yoshiko poked her face in.

"Do you want something to drink?" she asked.

"No, no thanks." Ken stood leaning against the back of a chair, waiting for his father's meeting to end. This sudden summons at the dead of night—what could it mean? It had to have something to do with the negotiations between the U.S. and Japan that had begun that spring. There had been reports in the newspapers about Ambassador Tonomura's talks with President Roosevelt and Secretary of State Hull. Yet his father had kept any opinions he had about it to himself, even though he must have had more than a passing interest in the subject. After all, if the United States remained suspicious of Japan's motives and was digging its heels in, it was because of the Axis pact that Saburo himself had signed.

The Kurushima family usually avoided any discussion of diplomatic subjects. Of course that didn't stop them from gossiping about the various dignitaries and their families in their acquaintance. In Berlin they had often amused each other with tales of the various eccentricities of Hitler, Goering, and Ribbentrop, and after returning to Japan the doings of Ambassador Grew's family provided grist for the gossip mill. But they strictly avoided any talk of the roles their acquaintances were playing in the various international issues of the day. The one exception was Yosuke Matsuoka, the pro-Nazi Foreign Minister in Prince Konoe's Cabinet, whom Saburo couldn't bring himself to like. This was the only time the family ever heard negative comments about a colleague escape his lips: "Matsuoka's not quite up to the task, is he?" "With Matsuoka in charge, things are shakier than ever." "Matsuoka's policies must seem absolutely bewildering to Roosevelt." When the Konoe Cabinet had resigned and the Tojo Cabinet took its place, with Matsuoka being replaced as Foreign Minister by Shigetoku Togo, Saburo was heard to mutter, "That man was about to get us into a war through sheer incompetence . . . Things should get a bit better now."

Before long, Saburo emerged from the parlor and told Yoshiko: "I need a bag right away. Where's the large briefcase I bought in Germany?"

"It's on top of the safe in the storeroom, sir."

"I'll go get it." Ken kicked off his slippers and ran swiftly up the stairs. He found the briefcase and was downstairs with it in no time at all.

There was the sound of an automobile pulling up in front of the house, and after scooping up some documents, his father was gone.

Ken went back to his bedroom on the second floor and changed into his sleeping robe again. Then, as if he'd suddenly remembered, he walked along the corridor to the bedroom at the far end, gently pushed the door open a little, and peered in.

A narrow beam of light shone in from outside, and he could dimly make out the bed. His mother's face loomed white in the darkness, lightly rising and falling with the quiet rhythm of her breathing. It was a peaceful face, the sleeper unaware that her husband had just been summoned on the most urgent business.

Back in the stillness of his own room, Ken could sense the gravity of the moment. By now his father must have arrived at the Foreign Ministry. Here his mother was asleep. The whole house was asleep. Outside, all of Japan was asleep.

He remembered a river in winter, in Connecticut, and the sound of cracking ice. The water had streamed over the half-frozen banks, where icicles, like little rakes, had formed. He reached out to break one off. "No, Ken, don't—it's dangerous!" His mother was holding him back. "But Mama, the icicles, they're so pretty." "No, you mustn't. You'll fall in the river. You'll freeze to death." His mother's clear voice echoed gently in his ears, and he fell asleep.

6

Alice woke up with the feeling that something heavy was pressing down on her. There was a bright edge to the darkness. The door was open, and someone was standing there. It was her husband. He was wearing morning dress.

"Saburo? Are you going out?"

"I'm not going out—I've just come back."

Startled, Alice jumped out of bed. What was going on, in the middle of the night? For an instant, she thought it was one of Saburo's jokes. She turned on the light. Her husband's face was pale and drawn. She had never seen him look so tense. No, it wasn't a joke.

"Alice," he began, his voice low but quite firm, "I have to go to Washington."

She nodded without a word, just staring at his face. She was completely awake now.

"Earlier this morning a courier came asking me to go the Foreign Minister's residence. When I arrived, Togo explained that negotiations with the United States have reached a very dangerous impasse. Then he asked me to go to Washington as a Special Envoy to take charge of the talks. The mission is of crucial importance. I accepted." Before Alice could say anything, he continued. "We have to prevent a war, at all costs. For the sake of Japan, and for America too, for the lives of millions of young men and for their parents in both countries. I'm only a small man, of limited ability, one infinitely small being before God. But when so many lives are at stake, I have to use every ounce of strength that I have."

"Saburo," Alice murmured faintly, "I understand."

"Alice," Saburo said, putting his arms around her. "This will be the biggest event in our lives."

"I *understand*." She shut her eyes and pressed her face against her husband's chest. "May God protect you. When do you have to go?"

"Probably tomorrow morning. The Foreign Minister said he'd ask Ambassador Grew to get me a seat on the Pan American Clipper."

"Tomorrow? . . . So soon?"

"Yes." He kissed her on the lips. He embraced her once more, then released her. "Now, please help me get ready. I've got to read through all these documents. The next twenty-four hours are going to be the busiest in my life."

Saburo removed one thick sheaf of documents after another from his briefcase and laid them out on his desk, then tossed off his morning coat and sat down to read. Alice quickly changed from her nightgown into a black satin dress, in case they had any official visitors. *Oh yes*, she thought, *the first thing is coffee. Saburo will want lots of coffee.* The lights were on in the stairway and in the hall downstairs, but the house was still perfectly quiet. Nobody else was awake. In the kitchen, pale and gleaming, was the gas range she was so proud of, the one they had bought in Sweden. She looked up at the sky from the window. The full moon hung low in the west, and trees swayed white in the moonlight. There were wisps of grayish white cloud in the deep indigo sky. Dawn was near. The clock said a few minutes after five.

Alice prepared a pot of coffee, not too strong, the way Saburo liked it. She poured a cup, added milk, and went up to their bedroom. She was about to speak when she was startled into silence by his concentration. He was reading furiously, his whole being focused on the mountain of material in English and Japanese, handwritten and typed, before him.

Alice sat quietly as far away from him as possible, giving an occasional glance in his direction. Mingling with the rustle of the trees outside was the crisp sound of pages being turned. She could see the early light of dawn, and feel a chill in her feet from the floor. She stood up and laid a blanket over her husband's lap. Then she took out her notebook and began jotting down the things he would need for his journey. It was probably already winter in Washington, so she would have to pack lots of warm clothes. She could hear the sparrows now. Saburo sat in the same posture, with a pile of documents already scanned on the left side of the table.

There was a light knock on the door. Ken peeked in. Alice went out into the corridor to talk to him.

"Ken, you're up early."

"What do you mean? It's already six-thirty. In the Army we'd already be hard at work." He was wearing a sweater his mother had knitted for him. "So what's happening with Papa?"

"Oh yes, I have to tell you . . . he has to go overseas, on a very important mission."

"I know. He's going to America, isn't he?"

"How did you know?"

"Well, there was someone from the Foreign Ministry here at two in the morning. I figured it must be something like this. After all, Papa's the only diplomat in Japan who can express himself easily in English and negotiate with the American President and Secretary of State on an equal footing."

"Oh Ken, you make me feel ashamed. I should have been up to take care of him. Instead I slept through the whole thing!"

"I was going to wake you up, but Papa said not to." Ken leaned over and kissed his mother on the cheek. "When's he leaving?"

"Probably tomorrow morning."

"Then I'll try to get my leave extended. I definitely want to see him off."

"But you can't mention it to anyone. The mission is top-secret. The Army mustn't know . . ."

"I understand. I'll make up a good excuse."

Yoshiko had just lit the stove in the parlor, and the coal crackled over the flames rising from the kindling. Anna stood watching the fire vacantly. She had on the light green housedress she used to wear in her teens, which looked incongruous with her disheveled hair and tired eyes. She had come home the evening before just as the family had begun dinner. She sat through dinner without saying a word, and then hurriedly withdrew to her old room on the second floor. Alice had followed her upstairs, and there Anna, in tears, reported that her marriage with Arizumi was near the breaking point.

Now, lifting her heavy eyelids, she greeted her mother and asked, "What are you going out so early in the morning for?"

"I have a couple of errands to do." Alice wasn't more forthcoming. "Were you able to sleep last night?"

"Yes, strangely enough." Anna gave her a plaintive smile. "I always sleep well here. It's the first time in a long while that I slept so well, but it still doesn't seem enough."

"You needn't stay up, dear—why don't you go back to bed?"

"Yes, but . . . Ken's going back to camp this morning, isn't he?"

"It seems he's getting a one-day extension."

"Oh, good. I can hear all about his life in the Army."

Eri came in with Ken. She was dressed in her girls' school uniform. She had evidently caught the end of the others' conversation in English, and she asked Ken, "*Honto na no?* Is it true? Are you going to be here till tomorrow?"

"That's right," said Ken.

"Oh, Anna's so lucky! She gets to be with Ken for a whole day. I have to go to school. It's not fair! Ken went out with Papa all day yesterday. I never get a single moment with him."

"School's out at three, isn't it?" said Anna.

"*So, so,*" said Alice, joining their conversation in Japanese. "Just make sure you come straight home."

"Don't worry, Eri," said Anna. "I'll let you know *everything* he tells me."

"Oh, Anna! *You're* the one who wants to know everything. I don't care. I'm just interested for Maggie's sake. Maggie's the one who was sad when Ken went out with Papa yesterday." Eri's eyes were round and bright. She was obviously thinking up some extravagant notion to draw attention to herself. "Ken, you've got to promise me something. Promise you won't marry Lauren."

"Wow." Ken looked genuinely astonished. "That's a bit sudden."

"But Ken, Maggie loves you more than Lauren does."

"Hey!" Ken and Anna said in a chorus of disapproval.

"Eri!" her mother joined in.

"What's wrong?" She took a step back. "Did I say something I wasn't supposed to? Don't look at me like that. Stop it, please!"

"Eri," said Anna, with a hint of condescension, "people's feelings aren't that simple. How so-and-so feels about Ken is that person's private business and not something you would understand."

"But I *do* understand it!" She was getting desperate. "I understand it very well. You know it too, but you won't say it. You're such a coward, Anna!"

"It's not a question of understanding or not understanding." Her tone was still condescending. "It's a serious matter, and maybe a little too subtle for you."

"How can you . . . ?"

"Now stop it, girls!" said their mother. Yoshiko brought in the morning paper. Anna and Eri stood there, refusing to look at each other. Ken scanned the front page.

Yoshiko then announced that breakfast was ready, and Alice, after sending her off to call her husband, stepped forward to address her children.

"There's something I have to tell you." She nodded at Ken, then looked at the girls. "Ken already knows about it. Tomorrow morning your father is leaving for America on a mission of the utmost importance—to prevent a war with the United States. Papa says he wants to devote all the strength he has to doing that."

"If anybody can do it, *he* can," Anna said, nodding, as if trying to convince herself. But then a shadow of unease passed across her face. "But what happens to him if war does break out?"

"If that happens, I'm afraid Papa won't be able to return until the war is over. But don't worry, America is a civilized country. It's not the kind of place that would mistreat an enemy's ambassador."

"But there won't ever be a war, will there?" Eri searched her mother's face for affirmation. Alice looked at Ken.

"Frankly, we're now on the verge of war, the situation's critical."

Ken tapped with his right index finger at the newspaper spread open on the table. "Just look at these articles. A majority of people here are eager for war. Everyone's shouting that we've got to do something before our supplies run out and the oil runs dry or we'll be ruined."

"Anyway," said Alice, "we've got to believe in Papa, and pray for peace. Now, tonight, I'd like to have a farewell dinner, with just us present. Anna, you help out. And Eri, you make sure you come straight home from school."

The two sisters nodded in agreement.

"And one more thing. Don't breathe a word about Papa's trip to *anyone*."

"Keep your eyes open," said Ken.

"And your lips sealed," the sisters chorused in response.

"If word gets out, it could be dangerous for him. There are a lot of people around who don't like the idea of someone being sent to America to sue for peace. A Special Envoy would be a natural target for them."

"What do you mean?" Eri sounded puzzled.

"She means," Anna explained, "that there's a danger he might be assassinated."

"As-sas-sinated. Oh no!" Eri exclaimed and, in a gesture unique to Japanese schoolgirls, fanned air into her mouth with both hands, as if to retrieve the words she'd just let out.

On hearing from the maid that Saburo had come downstairs, they all moved into the dining room.

"Oh." Saburo blinked at the sight of his assembled family. "You're all here." His bloodshot eyes showed his tension and exhaustion. The trousers of his morning suit stuck out from under his bathrobe, and his moustache was untidy, one side out of alignment with the other.

Alice sat across from him, with the children ranged between them. Tanaka and Yoshiko served breakfast. Tanaka customarily hid himself in the kitchen, but he seemed to realize that today was a special day, and he insisted on personally serving Saburo the substitute oatmeal made from barley—his own creation—and the ersatz coffee made from chicory roots.

"Sa-bu-ro." The children stopped eating when their mother spoke, and looked attentively at their father. "How's your work coming along?"

"I'm managing to get through it."

"Tonight I'd like to have a farewell dinner, with just us and the children."

"That's a nice idea, but I'm going to be running around the entire day without a moment's rest. I've got to make dozens of calls, starting with the Prime Minister and the Foreign Minister."

"But you'll be back tonight, won't you?"

"Probably."

"We'll all be waiting for you, no matter how late you get back."

Saburo's silence affected the rest of them, and they got through breakfast without another word. When Yoshiko came to tell Eri it was time to set out for school, she bowed and said goodbye to her father with reluctance, and left. When Ken announced that he had gotten his leave extended until the next day, Saburo nodded, but after a few moments asked, "What did you say just now?" When Anna told him she too would be staying an extra night, Saburo nodded again, then, as proof that this time he understood, he asked her, "Is it all right for you to leave Arizumi on his own for so long?"

"It doesn't matter," she answered.

"It doesn't, eh?" he muttered, and then fell silent again. He had another cup of coffee, roused himself, shaking his head vigorously, and stood up. Alice, Ken, and Anna rose too, and watched him as he walked back in silence to his study.

Alice called the cook. "Tanaka, we're counting on you tonight."

"C'est entendu, madame. Laissez-moi faire." Tanaka nodded proudly, puffing his chest out like a pigeon.

7

It wasn't till well after midnight that Ken caught the sound of a car approaching and ran out to the front entrance. His mother, Anna, and Yoshiko followed after him.

Saburo was speaking to the young courier who had driven him home: "Then I'll see you tomorrow, I mean later today."

"I'll be here at four-thirty, sir."

"Welcome back," Alice said, as they all greeted him with a bow. They could tell at a glance he was totally exhausted. Yoshiko took his shoes, and he stepped up over the threshold. He staggered, and Ken held him up. Even so, he didn't forget the kiss he always gave his wife on returning home.

"What did you do about my luggage?" he asked her impatiently.

"It's all right, dear," she smiled. "Everything's ready."

"Really? Thank you. I don't have much time. I have to leave from the naval air base at Oppama later this morning. A ministry person—Yoshimoto—is going with me, and I have to meet him at Tokyo Station at 5:00 A.M. They're sending a car at four-thirty."

"Four-thirty? Then you've still got two and a half hours. I'll bet you haven't eaten dinner."

"Dinner? I completely forgot about it."

"First you should take a bath," said Alice in a soothing voice, "then have something to eat. Then try to catch a little sleep."

"Whatever you say, ma'am." The tension in his face relaxed a bit. He rubbed her shoulders.

When he emerged from his bath and came into the dining room wearing a casual kimono, his wife and children were standing at the table waiting for him. Ken was in his Army uniform, Eri in her school uniform. Anna and her mother were both dressed in kimonos.

"*Ho!*" he exclaimed in a Japanese grunt of surprise as he took in the unfamiliar sight of his wife in a kimono.

He nodded to the children, then to Tanaka, Yoshiko, and Asa, who were lined up behind the family. "What a feast! It's too bad I won't have time to really enjoy it."

Alice, who understood every word of his Japanese, answered in English, "You have more than enough time, dear. The way you gobble down your food, the whole meal won't take you more than thirty minutes."

Saburo gave another grunt, scratching his head. He was famous for eating quickly, and was known to finish off a meal before everyone else was halfway through.

"Tanaka has outdone himself getting all our favorite things ready. Anna and Eri helped too."

"But Mama did the most," said Anna.

The meal was a blend of Japanese food—a whole sea bream, the traditional dish for special occasions, along with sashimi, tempura, and rice with red beans—and French dishes: pâté de foie gras, roast lamb, and salad. There was both *sake* and wine. The table was covered with things it was usually impossible to obtain at this time. As they began to eat, Tanaka brought out a bottle of red wine in a little basket, moving slowly so as not to disturb the sediment at the bottom. "A 1914 Saint Emilion," he announced.

"1914. That's the year of the Great War," muttered Ken.

"No, dear," said Alice. "1914 was the year of our marriage, a year of peace."

Saburo examined the bottle closely. "I remember. This is one of a dozen Saint Emilions we bought then."

"Yes, it is."

"Exactly twenty-seven years ago," said Anna, with a sense of awe.

"Papa," said Eri, "when you go to America, you'll be seeing George and Lauren, won't you?"

"I don't think I'll have time to."

"Papa is a Special Envoy," her sister explained. "He won't be free to act as a private individual."

"But he can at least see them, can't he?"

"He's going to Washington. They live in Chicago."

"Well then, they can go to Washington to see him."

"Come on, now, don't start fighting again," Ken told them.

"Ken," said his father, "you know, today was one of the most incredibly busy days of my life. But it goes to show that if a person really puts his mind to it, he can accomplish anything."

"Yes, sir." Ken took this to be his way of encouraging him.

"The problem is," Saburo went on in English, for Alice's benefit, "there's a powerful mood of opposition in this country to any diplomatic negotiations. My mission to America is being kept top-secret, but someone already seems to have guessed that something's going on. Today there were a bunch of fanatics outside the Foreign Ministry screaming, 'Break off relations with the U.S. immediately!' 'Answer Roosevelt with an ultimatum!' The reason that tomorrow—I mean this morning—I'll be taking a train from Tokyo Station is to throw any possible terrorists off the scent. But I'm still worried because my face is fairly well known from the newspapers."

"Why don't you have Ken go with you in his Army uniform?" said Alice. "You can pretend you're a father sending his son off to the front. That way you won't be conspicuous. Oh yes, we've got an old Inverness and a felt hat you could put on. People will take you for a country gentleman. Maybe you'd better not shave those whiskers, after all."

Saburo rubbed his cheeks and chin, and everyone laughed.

"A country gentleman, eh? Not bad."

"Sa-bu-ro," she continued, "there's one more thing. While you're over there make sure you buy me a new handle for the vacuum cleaner."

"The vacuum cleaner?"

"Yes, ours is a GE. I can't get any parts for it here."

"Okay, if I don't forget I'll get one."

"You'd better not forget! We'll be in big trouble without it."

Alice had Yoshiko bring the vacuum cleaner in, and showed him the broken part. Saburo burst out laughing, scratching his head in bemusement.

"I see I'm charged with a mission of the utmost gravity! This is a tougher demand than anything I anticipate from President Roosevelt."

"Come on, dear, you've got to get a little sleep," she said, giving him a gentle nudge. It was shortly before three.

After his parents withdrew to the master bedroom, Ken went into the parlor to wait. Anna and Eri slept uncomfortably under blankets there. Beside them was the large steamer trunk that Alice had packed as full as possible, and the clothes meant to disguise Saburo as a country gentleman. Ken suddenly had an inspiration. On scraps of rice paper he wrote the popular slogans of the time: "PRAY FOR SUCCESS ON THE BATTLEFIELD," "CONGRATULATIONS ON YOUR DEPARTURE FOR THE FRONT," "GIVE SEVEN LIVES FOR YOUR COUNTRY." Then he pasted them all over the trunk in a haphazard manner suggestive of a rustic hand. He used only tiny drops of paste, so that they could easily be removed later with a little water. Then he checked the railway timetable, to make sure the first train of the day on the Yokosuka Line left at 5:12.

By four o'clock Saburo had yet to emerge, but ten minutes later he came downstairs with Alice on his arm. While he was changing into his country gentleman disguise, the car arrived. Ken slipped the lunchbox Tanaka had prepared into his leather officer's pouch, and picked up the trunk. Saburo embraced Alice. He shook hands with his daughters and exchanged polite bows with Tanaka, Yoshiko, and Asa. When the door slammed shut, Eri burst into tears and buried her face in her mother's chest. Alice smiled as she waved him goodbye.

The streets were dark and deserted. There were no other cars about. Even so, as a precaution they didn't take the direct route but made a detour, heading toward Akasaka at full speed, then, from the Hanzomon gate, driving on around the walls of the Imperial Palace. As they passed Nijubashi, the Double Bridge that led into the Imperial precincts, Saburo and Ken both bowed their heads deeply.

They reached Tokyo Station at 5:05. The train was leaving in seven minutes. They rushed up to the platform, where they found the first train of the day ready to depart. They entered one of the third-class carriages. As they sat down on the hard wooden benches, two young men entered and casually took seats not far from theirs. The young gentleman in a suit carrying a large bag was the ministry official, Yoshimoto; the other, in a civil defense uniform, was a clerk named Shimazu. They both looked like ordinary office workers on their way to work.

In the last few moments before the train pulled out, Ken carefully looked around. But there was no one on the platform, and there were no other passengers except a couple of sailors and a civilian presumably employed at the naval base in Yokosuka, plus an old woman in a tattered kimono. Even the most alert of spies would surely fail to recognize the provincial gentleman accompanying his officer son as Saburo Kurushima, Special Envoy to the United States. The thought made Ken chuckle to himself.

When the train started moving, Saburo leaned against the window and fell asleep. He didn't wake up until they reached Yokosuka. Ken resisted sleep in order to keep watch; he was his father's guardian now. When his drowsiness became overwhelming he stood up and walked up and down the aisle. Around the time they passed Zushi dawn broke, and Ken could see the waves in Tokyo Bay gleaming red. It was a clear autumn day.

At Yokosuka Station a Navy limousine was waiting for them. They drove at high speed and, like a runner sliding into base, raced onto the naval airfield at Oppama, right up to the side of a 96 Continental Raider with its propellers already turning. Ken had once made models of this plane. It was the best intermediate bomber in the Japanese fleet, capable of speeds up to 400 kilometers per hour, with a cruising range of 6,000 kilometers. It had achieved sudden fame during the invasion of China in 1937. Ken had never seen the real thing before, and he looked it over quickly. It was a superb airplane. His father would be safe in it.

"All right, Ken," said Saburo, "thanks for everything."

"Take care, Papa," Ken said cheerfully. He took the lunchbox from his pouch and handed it over.

"I'll do my duty," his father said in English, raising his voice against the roar of the propellers, "you do yours."

"Yes, sir."

Yoshimoto and his father were almost blown down by the slipstream as they climbed the unsteady ladder. Somehow they managed to clamber inside.

The plane took off smoothly, climbing into the sunrise and then heading west. It didn't look like the departure of an aircraft carrying men on a vital diplomatic mission, but like a bomber setting out on one of its morning practice runs.

III

THE MISSION

1

Saburo gave a sigh as he put down his fountain pen. He wanted to record all the details of his mission in his journal, but he was tired of writing now. He changed into his sleeping robe and lay down on the hotel bed. Although he was exhausted, his nervous excitement kept him from falling asleep. He began rearranging the things in his trunk, and as he did so his fingers touched a bottle of aspirin and a small vial wrapped in paper. The white powder in the vial was cyanide. He'd obtained it on the day of his departure from a professor of medicine he knew, in case he failed to find a peaceful solution to the crisis. He hoped he wouldn't have to use it. He hid it between two shirts and shut the trunk. When he lay down on the bed again, memories of that last day in Tokyo came flooding back.

He remembered waiting for Tojo in the unheated parlor of the Prime Minister's official residence. When Tojo finally appeared, he was wearing an everyday kimono. Since Saburo had come on an official visit, he'd expected to be received by him in his general's uniform. He took Tojo's casual dress as a mark of condescension: neither Saburo himself, nor his mission, were perhaps all that important to him. This may have accounted for the disappointment he felt at the size of Tojo's shaven head, and his uneasy feeling that the complex issues on which the fate of Japan rested couldn't possibly fit into that little cranium.

Tojo silently looked over the detailed memo in his hand, then began speaking, with sudden solemnity. "When I mentioned your mission to the Emperor, His Majesty graciously said, 'I heard Kurushima was ill. Has he recovered?'"

Saburo bowed. "I am deeply honored by his concern." The Emperor must have remembered that he had turned down the post of Vice-Minister in the previous Cabinet for reasons of health.

"You've taken on a tough job, Kurushima," said Tojo. "I'd give you maybe a thirty percent chance of success."

"Thirty percent . . . you think it's that high?"

"It's up to you. If you take a resolute stand, and if you push them hard, we'll succeed."

"But . . ." Given the crisis, he felt that Tojo was being rather optimistic.

"The United States isn't ready for war yet," Tojo went on. "They don't have the ability to fight a war in both the Atlantic and the Pacific. They can't fight Germany and Japan at the same time. And the American public doesn't want to go to war. If you exploit these weaknesses—and keep pushing them—you might get them to compromise."

"But we can't just push them. Diplomacy is a matter of give-and-take. We won't reach a compromise unless we make some concessions as well. It seems to me the most effective concession at this point would be Japan's military withdrawal from China."

"No! Absolutely not!" The voice was suddenly much louder, his moustache quivering. He spoke to him as if he were scolding a schoolboy. "Now get this straight. China is off limits. China is territory wrested with the blood of the Imperial Army—lots of it. If I were to yield to American pressure and withdraw from China, I could never show my face at the Shrine of the War Dead again."

Saburo was speechless. Plan A, which had already been outlined to him by the Foreign Minister, called for concessions from the United States in exchange for a Japanese withdrawal from China after a set number of years. But now Tojo was insisting on permanent occupation.

After discussing some of the other details of Saburo's trip, Tojo glanced at the memo he was holding, written in small, neat handwriting, then made what seemed a very strange statement. "Kurushima, I want you to wrap up the negotiations by the end of November."

Saburo was startled for a second time. Complex negotiations had been going on for half a year with no success, and now Tojo was telling him to finish the talks in less than a month. In fact, if he arrived in Washington in the middle of November, it only gave him a little over two weeks.

"It can't be done."

"It can't? Listen, Kurushima, it must be done. The end of November is the absolute deadline, which even His Majesty has approved."

"Yes, sir." Saburo nodded at the mention of the Emperor. Tojo had direct access to His Majesty, so what Tojo reported him as saying was not to be questioned. All the same, Saburo mustered the courage to ask another question. "If the negotiations don't succeed by the end of November, will you resort to military force?"

"I can't say at present."

"But . . ." It was unbelievable. Here he was, the newly appointed envoy, and Tojo wasn't telling him their anticipated course of action. It was downright insulting. Yet it might have been expected, given the notorious arrogance of the military. Shortly after the invasion of China, at a Cabinet meeting with the Prime Minister, the military command had been asked how far it intended to go. When the Navy Minister actually gave an answer, the Army Minister blew up, shouting, "How can you discuss such a matter in front of civilians!"

Tojo was both Army Minister and Prime Minister, and he wasn't about to let a diplomat, a mere civilian, in on any military secrets. Nor could Saburo do much about it, insulting though it was. He couldn't argue with Tojo. And he couldn't back out either, having already promised to undertake the mission. Checking his emotions, he looked Tojo straight in the eye and said:

"If the negotiations do succeed, I imagine there will be vehement opposition from certain quarters in Japan, especially within the Army. If I do manage to reach a compromise with the United States, can I have your assurance that you will support it, even if it means restraining domestic opposition?"

"If you can achieve a compromise acceptable to us, of course. I promise there will be no use of military force in that event."

Saburo suspected that the Emperor and the Army leadership had already made the decision to go to war if negotiations failed. But he also sensed that Tojo genuinely wanted to avoid war if at all possible. Tojo would at least give the negotiations a chance. Saburo was slightly relieved.

The open window let in the sound of the sea. It was almost dawn on Midway Island. Near the horizon, red stripes ran across a pure blue sky, and the beam of a distant lighthouse was now barely visible. Would the Pan American Clipper make it out this morning, or would they be laid up here another day? It was already the eleventh of November. There was no way he could keep to his scheduled arrival in Washington on the thirteenth. November would be half gone. Day by day, precious, irretrievable time was slipping away. He tried to sleep. But when he closed his eyes this time, his farewell meeting with Ambassador Grew at the American Embassy came back in vivid detail.

Grew had been a friend of Saburo's for more than ten years. They knew each other's character well, and it was Grew who understood better than anyone how pro-American he was. Also, Grew's daughter Elsie was a close friend of Anna's.

"Are you taking any new proposals with you?" Grew asked.

"No, I don't have anything new," Saburo said, speaking loudly, as Grew was hard of hearing.

"That's a pity." He frowned, stroking his white moustache. "Then I'm afraid there won't be much point in your going. There won't be any compromise as long as the two sides keep repeating the same old positions."

"But I still feel I have to go."

"Do you foresee any new developments?"

"The only new development is me. For the last six months negotiations have been stuck on the same rigid course. I might be able to loosen things up a bit. And, fortunately, I'm at ease in the language of your country."

"I see, instead of a new proposal they're sending a new man. It might just work. Your English *is* superb. There are a lot of Americans who can't use the language with the same scope and precision."

"The only trouble with the new man," Saburo said, in a serious tone of voice, "is that he doesn't know the people on the other side. I've read the biographies of Roosevelt, and I think I have a pretty good grasp of his personality. But I've only met Cordell Hull once, and there are no biographies of him . . . What kind of man is he?"

"I'm afraid I don't know him either." Grew was silent for a few moments, as if searching his memory, and then said, "I've only met him once myself. It was in the summer of 1935, when I was back in Washington on home leave. It's hard to describe Hull in a single word. In the case of the President, you can say he's a great optimist, a man of extraordinary vigor. But the Secretary of State is so cautious, so understated, it's hard to catch a glimpse of the real man inside."

"You'd say he's practical and businesslike? . . ."

"On the contrary, I'd say he's an idealist. He's a man of lofty vision, and his idealism can make him inflexible at times. He hates getting entangled in trivial details. He prefers to decide things on principle."

"That's going to be a problem." Saburo gave a long sigh. "What I'm going to propose is that we put our principles aside for the moment, and come to an agreement through reciprocal concessions on details."

"That's exactly the sort of thing the Secretary of State is least comfortable with."

"I understand Hull is from Tennessee."

"That's right. He has quite an accent. His speech may be more difficult for you to understand than my own Bostonian English. Curiously, his rural origins seem to reinforce his internationalist views. Just as a conservative isolationism is often born in big international cities, so the reverse can happen."

"I understand that the isolationists hold the upper hand in Congress, and that they're vehemently opposed to America's entry in the war."

"That's correct. On this issue, the supporters of Roosevelt and Hull are definitely in the minority in Congress. Therefore, in order to maintain the peace, it would be best for Japan to refrain from acts that would provoke Congress."

"Such as . . ."

"Such as invading French Indochina, or hitting the headlines with anti-American speeches by your leaders, or making preemptive strikes."

"Preemptive strikes?"

"Surprise attacks, the kind the Japanese Army is so fond of. If that happens, then all the isolationists in Congress will turn into internationalists overnight. And you can be sure the President would get his majority then."

"A surprise attack would be outrageous," said Saburo emphatically. "But the Japanese military do worry me. They're so ignorant of public sentiment in America. All they think of is the glory of the moment, never the long-term consequences."

"You're right. The young officers who attempted the coup d'état in 1936 were just like that."

"The Japanese tend to make heroes of those who carry the day but fail in the long run. The young officers in 1936 were like that, and so were the great samurai heroes of the past—Yoshitsune and the Shogun Nobunaga. But in America the true heroes are those who *prevail.*"

In 1936, during what was called the February 26th Incident, the rebel army had occupied the Sanno Hotel near Saburo's home, and Alice, mistaking them for soldiers on maneuvers, had taken some soup down to them as they stood there shivering in the snow. Grew had been rather touched by the story, and had told him it was the right thing to do, that most of the men were just ordinary soldiers and weren't to blame for the mutiny.

As if reading his thoughts, Grew now asked, "How is your wife?"

"Fine, thank you. And the children are well too."

"Good." Knowing his own wife would want to say goodbye, he picked up the phone and gave her a call. A few minutes later she appeared, and Saburo quickly told her about his impending trip.

"Why, it's so sudden!" she exclaimed.

"He's just been given the most important mission in the world," said her husband, "and the most difficult."

"Do, please, take care of yourself. For your country's sake."

"And for yours, too," Saburo added. As he shook her hand, saying *"Gokigenyo"* in farewell, he noticed tears shining in her eyes.

"Alice," he murmured to himself, and turned in his bed. He almost never found himself thinking of his wife's naked body, but now the memory of their lovemaking on the morning of his departure, as the children waited for them downstairs, was vivid, almost palpable . . . Then sleep drew over him like a heavy curtain.

Some time later, he woke to the sound of someone knocking. His young assistant, Yoshimoto, walked in and told him briskly: "They've repaired the plane. We'll be taking off in an hour."

"Thank heavens."

The hotel was stirring to life. Dawn had broken, but traces of darkness remained in the sky. The bus to the airport was already full of American military officers. Saburo managed to get a seat only because one had been saved for him in the back.

On board the Clipper, Yoshimoto turned to him and said, "There was a telegram early this morning from the Consul in Honolulu. He said to expect a crowd of reporters at the airport."

"What a bother. But from here on the American press is going to be watching every move we make."

"Will you want to prepare a statement to read at the airport?"

"I don't think it's necessary. I'll field the questions as they come."

"I spent yesterday making a chart of all the points of disagreement between Japan and the United States. You can look at it later."

"Thank you . . . Well, Yoshimoto, you're finally going to America. You probably don't have any clothes, do you?"

"That's all right, I can buy some there. I wanted to have a new suit made anyway." He laughed, revealing a set of healthy white teeth. His face was tanned, like Ken's. Unsure whether he could get a seat on the Clipper, he had planned to accompany Saburo only as far as Hong Kong, and all he had with him were the clothes on his back. He was from Fukushima prefecture, and he spoke with a strong provincial accent. But he was a serious young man, determined to give Saburo all the help he could.

"Did you get enough sleep?"

"Yes, sir, I slept very well."

"That's good."

Below them, all the way to the horizon, was a clear, peaceful sea, with small waves reddened by the rising sun like shoals of fish. Would this sea become a battlefield one day? That mustn't happen. With this thought Saburo closed his eyes and let a pleasant languor spread through his body. He would write up his journal after they arrived in Pearl Harbor.

2

November 12th, Wednesday, Honolulu

We left Midway Island at dawn and touched down on the waters of Pearl Harbor in the afternoon. As we approached land, we were ordered to pull the window shades down. It made us realize we were coming into an important military base.

As soon as we set foot on shore, just as we expected, there was a barrage of questions and flashbulbs popping as newspaper reporters swarmed around us. I was afraid any casual comments might influence Washington one way or the other, so I just smiled and gave the briefest of replies. I was careful not to say anything about the possible outcome of the negotiations.

November 14th, Friday, en route from San Francisco to New York by air

From Honolulu we boarded the California Clipper—a much larger plane than the China Clipper—and after an overnight flight arrived in San Francisco. There was an enormous crowd of reporters. Honolulu was nothing by comparison. "What did you think of Churchill's speech?" they asked. "What are the chances of the negotiations succeeding?" "Why did they send you when you're the one who signed the Axis pact?" . . . I finally got away from them, and after a short rest at the Consul's house we boarded this Stratoliner for New York.

These first-class seats are reclining. Very comfortable. Maybe I can get some sleep. I'm tired, very tired. It's all I can do to scribble these notes.

J just came over and told me something a bit alarming. It seems that G, who has been making a nuisance of himself since we left Manila, was interviewed by a reporter at San Francisco Airport and said, "I've been riding with Ambassador Kurushima, and he told me he's pessimistic about the negotiations. He says he doesn't think there's even a one percent chance of success." J suggested I reply to this when we reach New York. G's damaging remark is a major nuisance, but I'm reluctant to reply to it at all. It would be unbecoming for the ambassador of an independent nation to get upset at every piece of gossipy journalism.

November 15th, Saturday evening, in my room at the Japanese Embassy in Washington

We experienced little turbulence on the flight to New York, probably because the Stratoliner flies at such a high altitude. (It's quite a plane. If Ken had been along, he could have explained it all for me.) I finally got some real sleep. Shortly after noon we landed at LaGuardia. After a brief rest we took off again for Washington and arrived here this afternoon.

From the airplane window I could see an enormous crowd waiting for us: Ambassador Tonomura, Embassy officials, various Japanese citizens in the U.S., officials from the American State Department, reporters, movie cameramen, radio announcers, and hordes of curious onlookers. I stepped down from the ramp and walked into an impenetrable wall of microphones. I bowed to this person and shook hands with that, and ran a gauntlet of photographers and radio announcers and reporters asking for interviews. Finally I stepped into the limousine, and a short while later arrived here at the Embassy on Massachusetts Avenue.

I'm in a room on the second floor. Tomorrow is Sunday, thank God, and my meeting with the President and the Secretary of State has been scheduled for Monday. I'm so tired. My inability to sleep at Midway seems unimaginable now. I've been sleeping like a baby the last two days. Perhaps my insomnia has been overwhelmed by sheer exhaustion.

It was shortly before ten when Saburo awoke. Having slept on airplanes the past two nights, he found the comfort of a proper bed a real luxury, and he had overslept. But since he wasn't due to meet the Ambassador until after noon, there was no need to rush.

The room was nice and warm, heated by a steam radiator, but outside was a winter landscape. From the window he could see the bare branches of the trees lining the broad avenue, and in the Embassy garden the cypresses seemed to be twisting in the cold.

This being Sunday, there was less traffic on Massachusetts Avenue than the day before, but there was still a steady stream of huge American cars, their polished hoods gleaming in the morning sun. The rattling charcoal-burning jalopies of Tokyo bore no comparison with them at all. It was a land of plenty: from the moment he entered American territory in Manila, every single meal had been a feast of meat and vegetables. What a painful contrast with Japan, where it was a struggle to get one's daily piece of fish! The pedestrians on Massachusetts Avenue were dressed in a variety of colorful styles, so different from the drab gray kimonos and military uniforms on Japanese streets. A land not at war, a land that knew no want, a country of peace and prosperity—the great, immense nation of America. What in God's name was Japan, a little string of islands in the Far East, doing taking on a giant like this? Again Saburo felt the misery of the position he found himself in.

He went downstairs to look around. Only a few of the Embassy staff had shown up for work; they bowed politely when they recognized him. Yoshimoto had been waiting for him in the lobby and handed him a newspaper.

"Are you having any breakfast, sir? It's ready in the dining room."

"I overslept. I'll be having lunch soon, so I'll wait till then."

"The Ambassador says he'd like to have lunch with you."

Saburo laid the thick, heavy newspaper on the table. The Sunday *New York Times* must have come to a hundred pages; this too was unimaginable in Japan, where paper was rationed and the pages were thin. Saburo didn't know where to start. Yoshimoto pointed to an article at the bottom of the front page under the headline "Envoy Kurushima Arrives." His picture was there, along with a quote saying that he hoped for peace. But the article was much smaller than he'd expected, and quite inconspicuous. He flipped through the pages with news articles and advertisements, thinking there had to be more about his mission, but he couldn't find a thing. Maybe there *was* nothing else. A tax increase, inflation, new automobiles, fur coats, movies, actresses, football, baseball, society gossip—they were all more important than negotiations with Japan. The only big war news was a special report on the battles between German and Russian forces, with a detailed analysis of how the German Army's siege of Moscow had bogged down.

Ambassador Tonomura greeted Saburo in the lobby, and together they walked into the dining room. Yesterday they had been with a crowd of other people, and Tonomura wanted to use this day for a quiet, leisurely conversation between just the two of them.

The Ambassador had spent much of his life in the Navy, and even now the tall, broad-shouldered diplomat looked every inch an admiral. He had a glass eye, which never moved, the result of what was known as the "Shanghai Incident" nine years ago. He had been sitting on the reviewing stand with Minister Shigemitsu in a park in Shanghai, watching Japanese troops go by in celebration of the Emperor's birthday, when a bomb placed by a Chinese nationalist exploded, killing several officials and blinding him in the right eye.

Saburo had first gotten to know Tonomura in Chicago, when the latter was the Naval Attaché at the Embassy. He went on to become Foreign Minister eventually, and it was he who had asked a reluctant Saburo to go to Berlin as Ambassador. When Saburo visited him in Washington at the beginning of the year on his way back to Japan, Tonomura had told him about the negotiations which had just begun. But now was the first time the two of them would actually be working together.

"Did you have a good sleep?" Tonomura asked as he eased himself into his chair. "Your trip must have been exhausting. I'm afraid your work here is going to be even more tiring."

The food arrived. It was a Japanese lunch in a tiered lacquer box, along with a boiled fish soup. After eating Western food, all that meat and fat, for the last three days, Saburo was grateful.

The two men exchanged news of their families, and then Tono-mura said: "I paid a visit to Cordell Hull yesterday morning. He's a rather severe man, you know. I tried to draw him out by suggesting we at least try to come to an agreement on the proposal to reduce trade restrictions in Plan A. But he brushed me off, saying he'd have to negotiate similar agreements with England and Holland as well, that it would be out of order to make a deal only with Japan. When I argued this was a special case, and it would advance our negotiations a step if we could find at least one specific point to agree on, he told me I was being 'importunate,' and became quite irritated."

"Does Hull get irritated often?"

"It's a strange sort of irritation. He seems to withdraw into himself. He never raises his voice or allows his displeasure to show. Instead he becomes expressionless—and thoroughly stubborn. He's like a thick steel wall then. You can push against it, hit it, but you won't get any response. It can drive you mad."

"I gather the internationalists like Hull are having a tough time in Congress."

"Yes, he's a Wilsonian interventionist trying to deal with a Congress where the isolationists are in the majority. He and Roosevelt are especially having trouble with the House of Representatives. But it's also a fact that Cordell Hull has had a long career in both the House and the Senate, and he commands a good deal of respect as an elder states-man. You have to remember he's eleven years older than Roosevelt. He's seventy now. But he has extraordinary vitality for a man his age. He goes to his office on Sundays, while Roosevelt's taking the day off. He never appears in Washington society circles, saying he can't spare the time. And if you ask for an appointment with him, you can usu-ally get it on the same day."

"Even Roosevelt must defer to him."

"Yes. Of course the President himself makes all the final decisions. But if Hull was absolutely opposed to something, I'm sure Roosevelt would think twice about it. I've heard that when Roosevelt first ran for president, Hull, who was an important lawyer in Tennessee, was responsible for a good part of his financial backing."

"Oh yes, I remember reading the same thing in a biography of Roosevelt."

"Hull is his horse. A powerful horse. Yes, the President rides a thoroughbred."

"You mean, 'If you want to get the Shogun . . .'"

"Exactly. 'You aim for his horse.' Speaking of shoguns, what did you make of Tojo? I don't know him at all. All of a sudden in July this nobody becomes the Army Minister, then in October, just as suddenly, he's Prime Minister."

"I don't know much about him myself. I met him for the first time just before I left Japan."

"Since he'd been Commandant of the Air Corps, I assumed he was some sort of aviation specialist. But it turns out he rose through the ranks, from a corporal. You know, it worries me. The Americans have a two-ocean strategy now, covering both the Atlantic and the Pacific. I wonder whether it isn't all a bit too much for a corporal to comprehend!"

"It worries me too," said Saburo, laying down his chopsticks. "Tojo told me the Americans are unprepared for war in both areas, so I should push them in the negotiations. Use the Axis pact, use the German victories, and 'push them hard,' he said."

"That's ridiculous! The man is reckless. Doesn't he realize that 'pushing hard' isn't going to bring down the steel wall that Cordell Hull sets up?" His false eye gleamed as if it were alive.

"He said something even more reckless. When I suggested that the withdrawal of our Army from China, as set forth in Plan A, would be the best way to achieve a compromise, he blew up. He said if that happened he wouldn't ever be able to show his face at the Shrine of the War Dead again."

"Those Army people never tell us what's going on. You don't suppose he's having us negotiate while he secretly prepares for war, do you?"

"I'm sure he's making some kind of preparations. No doubt the Americans are doing the same. However, he did promise me that if our negotiations succeed, he would restrain the pro-war factions at home."

"Well, I'm glad to hear that." Tonomura finished his lunch and began to sip his tea. "We can't go on with this rigid policy where every dispute leads us one step nearer the brink."

Saburo looked around to make sure they were the only ones in the room. "There's one more thing that disturbs me. His ordering us to conclude the negotiations by the end of this month could mean there is a firm plan to attack at the beginning of December. Here he thrusts these impossible problems on us, gives us half a month to solve them, and while we're floundering around looking for a solution he completes his preparations . . . You could interpret it that way."

"Let's try not to. It would mean all our efforts are in vain. Let's do our best for peace. War would be a disaster for Japan, for the United States, for all humanity."

"Yes." Saburo gazed with affection at the old Admiral, nine years his senior. Before leaving on this trip he'd heard that the old man had at first refused the ambassadorship, saying it would be extremely difficult to bring about a reconciliation with the U.S. while Japan was a member of the Axis pact. He had told the Foreign Minister he was "shamefully inadequate for such a grave responsibility at a time of national emergency, with little prospect of success." His conscience wouldn't allow it. But eventually he yielded to his colleagues' entreaties and accepted a mission he knew was almost certainly doomed to failure. His situation was painfully similar to Saburo's.

"Let's not give up hope until the very end. What do you say, Kurushima-san?"

"I agree."

"As for me, I'm an old man, not long for this world. I'd like to bring these talks to a successful conclusion as my final act of public service."

"But if we do succeed, the pro-war factions at home will be after us, waving their swords."

"In that case I'll still go home. I don't mind getting assassinated. I was almost blown up in China anyway."

"No, no. *I'll* go first. It's only natural for the Special Envoy to return first."

"No, I won't allow it. You're still young. I can't let you die."

"No, really, I insist."

The two diplomats realized they were arguing like little boys and burst out laughing. But both of them were probably thinking of the terrible treatment Japan's representative at the talks in Portsmouth had received at the end of the Russo-Japanese War, when he returned home carrying a compromise treaty to a people drunk with victory.

3

November 17th, Monday evening

This morning at ten-thirty, along with Ambassador Tonomura, I called on Secretary of State Cordell Hull in his office at the State Department. After a short discussion, he took us over to the White House, where we met with President Roosevelt at eleven. Afterwards the Secretary of State proposed we continue our discussion with him in his office, but we excused ourselves, saying we'd prefer to talk about details tomorrow.

When I was first introduced, Hull had a somewhat rigid expression on his face as he shook hands with me. It didn't strike me as the tension a person often shows on meeting someone for the first time, so much as a sort of condescending brusqueness, as if shaking my hand was something of an obligation. Actually, it wasn't our first encounter. I had met him in 1936, on my way to Belgium. I remember asking his opinion on the subject of free trade.

He's certainly aged in the last five years. He seems to have lost some of his hearing, and his manner of speaking shows the repetitiousness and stubbornness characteristic of old men. Rather than what Tonomura called a "steel wall," I got the impression of a "corridor of stone," narrow and perhaps impassable.

Instead of immediately addressing the problems at hand, Hull seemed to be suggesting we discuss the details only after establishing some basic principles. He gave us a preamble. "The lack of wisdom shown by men in the aftermath of the Great War"—he might just as well have been reading us a formal document—"has brought the present crisis upon us. It is our strong desire to save the world from a repetition of that tragedy." I admit I was genuinely moved by this honest assertion of his beliefs, and I in turn stated clearly why I was sent here by our government.

And so we proceeded to the White House, the three of us walking past a crowd of reporters and cameramen. Hull is even taller than Tonomura, and I felt like a dwarf as we went past all those Americans staring at us. Tonomura and I must have looked curious, two Orientals, members of an alien race, walking into the White House. When we lived in Chicago, I was often reminded of my race in the most unpleasant ways. I had stones thrown at me when walking through a local neighborhood, and once on the lakeshore someone came up and spat right in my face. This time too, at the airport in Washington, a woman reporter asked me rudely, "I understand your wife is a white woman, an American. Tell me, is she taller than you?"

It was my very first meeting with President Roosevelt. His large face, familiar from a hundred photographs, was an intricate web of wrinkles. Indeed, Hull, though older, has a smoother and more youthful face. And their voices are so different! Whereas Hull speaks in a low monotone, almost without intonation, Roosevelt's voice is rich with accent and emphasis, and, yes, "polyphonic." One moment he gives you a cheerful laugh, the next his face assumes the gravest expression as he urges some crucial point on you. You can usually guess somehow what's on Hull's mind from his simple expressionless features, but Roosevelt's thoughts seem to be dispersed among that rich and subtle play of expressions, and his innermost thoughts aren't easily discerned there. When people speak of truly great men, it must be this sort of man they have in mind. There I was, face to face with a patrician as dignified as our own Prince Konoe, but with a vigor and intensity seldom to be found among Japanese aristocrats. No tricks or artifices could have any effect on this man. All I could do was state my thoughts exactly as they came to me. Fortunately my English, the English I've used in conversing with Alice over many years, is similar to Roosevelt's own speech, a New Yorker's English, and I was able to speak without hesitation.

Yesterday a cable came from the Foreign Minister insisting that we conclude and sign an agreement by November 25th. I was looking for an appropriate moment, and an appropriate way, to bring this up with the President. But I realized I would have to mention it right at the start.

"We will have to consider the time element here," I told him. "If the situation continues as it is, the conditions for Japan's national defense, especially its economic conditions, will worsen. Japan is under tremendous economic pressure because of the American boycott, and to give in without doing anything would be intolerable for a sovereign nation with any self-respect. We must get a move on if we are to reach an agreement."

But the way I put this only seemed to play into Roosevelt's hands. I got the impression he wanted to draw the negotiations out in order to gain time to expand his own Navy in the Pacific. The President wound up his answer with the comment: "Secretary of State Bryan once said, 'There is no last word between friends.' We are friends."

"Yes, of course we are . . ." That was it. There was to be no more discussion of the time element. The President, it seemed to me, had adroitly turned the question of the deadline into one of friendship. Obviously the Americans were in no hurry to finish the negotiations. I regretted having mentioned it, and turned to another subject. "The American side has asked for a complete withdrawal of Japanese forces from China. Although this may sound good to your people, such a withdrawal would be virtually impossible for us."

"Concerning the China problem, I realize a withdrawal would be difficult for your country. The United States has no intention of intervening or mediating between Japan and China. I don't know if this word exists in the diplomatic vocabulary, but we would like to serve as an 'introducer.' "

When Roosevelt said this, the Secretary of State visibly stirred in his seat, expressing his dissatisfaction with a slight pursing of his lips, and I realized that this offer to help was not something the President and Hull had agreed on beforehand, but a sudden inspiration on the part of Roosevelt alone. Later I asked Tonomura about this, but he'd been unaware of any change in Hull's demeanor. Our good-hearted Admiral also took the President's statement about there being no last word between friends as a simple expression of friendship and goodwill, *and found it "moving."*

While Roosevelt was talking with me, Hull kept silent, apparently out of deference to the President's initiative. But whenever he disagreed with something the President said, he would show it with a slight movement of his body or a tightening of the lips. How could I find out what he was really thinking? I supposed he would finally say something when he was really displeased. I wanted to draw him out, and I realized the only way would be to bring up the major point of contention in the negotiations so far: the Axis pact. What an ironic situation it was for me to have to justify to a man vociferously opposed to it a pact that had led to my own resignation! For a moment I felt the pathos and humiliation of my own position as a diplomat. It struck me that this was the price I had to pay for signing that treaty against my own instincts, that retribution had finally come. It was that treaty that had brought us to this crisis, and all I could do was cover the situation with a smoke screen of words. At times like this a diplomat's words float away from reality and hang there in the air—mere words.

"Japan's intentions on joining the Tripartite Alliance were to prevent an expansion of warfare and to secure peace." I couldn't believe I was saying this, but I went on. "In the event of one of the other signatories going to war, the obligation to enter the war on that ally's behalf is one that Japan is free to fulfill or refuse according to its own sovereign interpretation of the treaty. I understand that one sector of American opinion interprets this to mean that Japan is waiting for the right moment to attack America from behind. This is a grave misunderstanding of our intentions. By Japan's 'own sovereign interpretation of the treaty,' I wish to make it clear that our country is not a tool or a pawn of Germany, that in the event of an agreement between the United States and Japan, such an agreement would"—and I chose the best English word I could think of—"outshine the Axis pact. Japan's purely formal obligation to enter the war on Germany's behalf would then no longer constitute any threat to the United States . . ."

Suddenly Cordell Hull cut into my insincere harangue. His entire face was shadowed with loathing for me. "Any kind of peace settlement for the Pacific, with Japan still clinging to its Axis pact with Germany, would cause the President and me to be violently denounced. Such a peace arrangement would not be taken seriously for a moment, and all the countries interested in the Pacific would redouble their efforts to arm against Japan's aggression."

The Secretary of State, in other words, was going to stick to the moral high ground. He was saying that as long as Japan refused to dissolve the Axis pact the United States would regard Japan as an enemy, and increase its military preparations accordingly. Tojo, however, would never accept an abrogation of the Axis pact. For all my insincerity, my suggestion that an agreement with the United States would "outshine" the Axis pact was the only practical solution that could be implemented before our time ran out. It was an "Oriental" solution that would save face for Japan and just might be accepted by our military. But Hull wouldn't hear of it, for it went against all his principles. Any nation that belonged to the Axis pact was automatically an accomplice in Hitler's aggression—and an enemy of humanity.

Hull went on: *"When Hitler started on a march of invasion across the earth with ten million soldiers and thirty thousand airplanes, and with an official announcement that he was out for unlimited invasion objectives, the United States from then on was in danger, and that danger has grown each week until this minute. This country has recognized the danger and has proceeded thus far to defend itself before it is too late."* He added that the United States would spend *"ten, twenty-five, or fifty billion dollars"* to defend itself.

It almost sounded like a threat, to which I responded, *"At this point Germany has not demanded that Japan enter the war on its behalf, and Japan hopes that will not happen . . ."* My voice weakened, and I fell silent. If I expressed a desire for peace in the face of Hull's fifty-billion-dollar defense budget, it would seem as if I were backing down in the face of American pressure because Japan's military preparations were inadequate. Tojo certainly wouldn't be pleased. But if I took the forceful stance Tojo wanted, and countered Hull with a threat from our side, well, it was obvious this wasn't an opponent to be silenced with a threat. I could see the talks breaking down right here. If I boasted of our military power and pushed Hull into a confrontation, it *would look good to Tojo and make me a hero in Japan. I chose restraint instead. I told myself to be patient, and made my way back to the Embassy.*

Saburo inhaled deeply on his pipe and watched the parade of headlights as the cars streamed down Massachusetts Avenue. Out there Washington was on the move, oblivious to his thoughts and hopes. All the efforts of the Foreign Minister, creating Plan A, then the backup Plan B, in the face of intense military opposition, all his ingenious ideas for somehow preventing war, to the point even of sending a Special Envoy to the negotiating table—all seemed to dissolve in the Washington air, useless and irrelevant.

For one country to demand that another abrogate a treaty it had signed by its own sovereign will was just unreasonable. After all that had happened, for Japan now to withdraw from the Axis pact was impossible, given the situation in Tokyo. But Cordell Hull was deficient in knowledge or sympathy regarding Japan's domestic situation. No, maybe he did know something about it, but for him the only important thing was his principle of opposition to Germany. Nothing else mattered. Just as Tojo couldn't care less about America's fears of Hitler, so Hull couldn't care less about what was going on in Japan.

There was a knock on the door. It was the Ambassador.

"I've just cabled Tokyo about our discussions today," he said.

'You must be tired. It's been a long day."

"It certainly has. What did you think of Hull?"

"He's pretty stubborn, isn't he? His mind is completely fixed on Germany and Hitler. I can understand his concern, but when he starts preaching in that high-handed way, as if Japan didn't exist as an independent nation, I find myself getting annoyed. You have to have a lot of patience to keep on smiling through all that. I've got a short temper, you know."

"You must never lose your temper with him. I can't count the number of times he's made me angry, but I've always borne it in silence."

"Don't worry, I've ordered myself never to show it. And to tell you the truth, I happen to agree with much of what he says. Especially about Germany. Hitler *is* a dangerous aggressor. But I wish he would stop lumping us together with him, as if we were just an appendage of Germany. Japan doesn't have the slightest designs on Europe or America. The only issue for us is East Asia."

"But it's precisely East Asia that America is worried about. Ever since the Axis pact, they've been afraid of Germany's ally taking over the Far East."

Saburo nodded. "Again, I understand their concern. But just what is this East Asia they're worried about? The American Philippines, French Indochina, the Dutch East Indies, British India? Apart from Japan, China, and Thailand, they're all colonies. If the American idea of peace is merely to protect the colonies . . ."

"Yes, you're right. The American presence in the Philippines makes them vulnerable to that argument; it's their blind spot. But from their perspective, Japan simply wants to grab all the colonies to establish its own empire."

"You know, Tonomura-san, the two of them keep talking about American public opinion, but do they realize how overwhelmingly opposed to these negotiations Japanese public opinion is?"

"We're in a very tough position."

As Saburo and Tonomura continued their conversation, they realized they had been standing the whole time. But when they sat down on the sofa, they had nothing much more to say to each other.

November 18th, Tuesday evening

This morning at ten o'clock, the Ambassador and I visited Hull at the State Department and spoke with him for approximately three hours. As in our previous meeting, Hull expounded on his opposition to Hitler, on the barbaric cruelty of the Nazis, and on the lies and betrayals of German diplomacy. He told us again that Japan's alliance with Germany was the greatest stumbling block in his negotiations with us. Then he said (almost as if he had eavesdropped on my conversation with Tonomura last night) that the U.S. intended to grant independence to the Philippines in 1946. He added that the U.S. Navy was pulling out of China and that, far from intervening in East Asia, they were making efforts toward achieving peace in the world. I stated clearly that it would be impossible for Japan to withdraw from the Axis pact, and that for us the treaty did not have military expansion as its goal. We were getting bogged down in the same old arguments. Unable to remain silent, Tonomura intervened with a new idea: he suggested we try to go back to the situation that existed before the United States froze our financial assets; Japan would withdraw its troops from southern Indochina, the U.S. would rescind the order freezing our assets, and thus we could lessen the tension between the two countries. Hull reluctantly agreed to consider it.

According to the newspapers, yesterday Congress passed an amendment to the Neutrality Act. It passed in the Senate by an overwhelming majority—50-7—but it was much closer in the House: 212-194. Despite Roosevelt's efforts to bring the United States into the European war, there is still strong resistance to it. The American people still don't want war—that gives us some hope. While Hull is still interested in peace with Japan, we've got to move the negotiations forward, even if only a single step, even if only a __half__ step. We can't go to war. War would be an unparalleled disaster for both countries.

I thought Tonomura's proposal, focusing on one single point of Plan B, an excellent idea for breaking the deadlock. The absurd demand from Tokyo that we sign an agreement by the twenty-fifth doesn't give us enough time to negotiate all of Plan B with the United States. To get the intractable Cordell Hull to say he would consider rescinding the freeze, i.e. restoring the situation to what it was before July—with the condition that he discuss it with Britain and Holland first—was a small victory. On returning to the Embassy, I cabled a report to the Foreign Minister in Tokyo.

OUR MINIMUM CONDITIONS FOR ENDING THE STALEMATE IN THE NEGOTIATIONS ARE A RESCINDING OF THE ORDER FREEZING JAPAN'S FINANCIAL ASSETS AND A GUARANTEE OF A CERTAIN AMOUNT OF OIL. AT OUR MEETING ON THE EIGHTEENTH WE SUGGESTED RESTORING THE SITUATION TO THAT EXISTING PRIOR TO JULY TWENTY-FOURTH. JUDGING FROM THE AMERICAN ATTITUDE SO FAR, THE UNITED STATES WILL PROBABLY NOT

AGREE TO THIS ONLY ON THE BASIS OF VAGUE PROMISES OF WITHDRAWAL FROM SOUTHERN INDOCHINA. THEREFORE IN THIS CASE I STRONGLY URGE YOU TO INDICATE TO THE UNITED STATES THAT JAPAN IS WILLING TO BEGIN A WITHDRAWAL OF FORCES FROM SOUTHERN INDOCHINA FIRST.

In other words, whereas Plan B called for Japanese withdrawal from southern Indochina after the United States had lifted the freeze on Japan's assets and had given formal assurances that it would not intervene in China or prevent Japan from keeping its material gains in the Dutch East Indies, I was now advocating that Japan withdraw from Indochina in exchange only for the unfreezing of our assets, forgetting about the other conditions, and that Japan withdraw first. I remembered my misgivings when I read Plan B in Tokyo, and I put everything I had into the composition of this all-important cable. I wrote it out with fixed intensity, and when I was done I grabbed Tonomura's hand and we looked at each other, nodding. This cable was our only hope.

November 20th, Thursday evening

Tonomura's face was white when he brought me the reply from the Foreign Minister this morning. "It's just not going to work. Tokyo has no idea of the situation here. Look at this. Just look at the tone of this. They're about to destroy everything."

The tone was cold and inflexible, with a scathing reference to our "private" proposals.

GIVEN THE TENSE DOMESTIC SITUATION IN JAPAN, THE PRESENT CRISIS CANNOT BE RESOLVED THROUGH PROMISES FROM THE UNITED STATES TO RESTORE THE SITUATION TO THAT BEFORE THE FREEZE ON OUR FINANCIAL ASSETS. WITHDRAWAL FROM SOUTHERN INDOCHINA ON THE MERE BASIS OF SUCH PROMISES IS IMPOSSIBLE. WE DO NOT HAVE THE LUXURY TO CONSIDER PRIVATE PROPOSALS SUCH AS THE ONE YOU SENT US. YOU ARE TO PRESENT PLAN B TO THE AMERICAN GOVERNMENT. THIS IS THE FINAL PROPOSAL OF THE IMPERIAL JAPANESE GOVERNMENT. THERE MUST BE ABSOLUTELY NO FURTHER CONCESSIONS. IF THE AMERICAN SIDE WILL NOT ACCEPT PLAN B AS IT IS WE HAVE NO CHOICE BUT TO END THE NEGOTIATIONS. IF THE NEGOTIATIONS BREAK DOWN, SO BE IT.

I could picture the expression on Togo's large, boorish face. When I met him that last day in Tokyo he had expressed his dissatisfaction with Tonomura's less than fluent English and less than competent handling of the talks, and he had complained that the Ambassador was coming up with too many initiatives of his own without first clearing them with Tokyo. But I knew what was really bothering the Foreign Minister. Plan B was a compromise he had managed to hammer out only after long and vehement arguments with the Army. The slightest modification of it would force him to go back for another furious debate with them. But I still hoped—almost prayed—that Togo would try once more, would make one more effort to convince the Army.

This very minute the United States and Britain are preparing their defenses against Japan, in Hong Kong, Manila, Guam, Wake Island, Hawaii. Every port is filled with battleships. Bombers and fighters are crisscrossing the Pacific skies. If I could I would go back to Tokyo right now and tell them about the situation here in Washington. Someone's got to tell them what can't be conveyed in the rigid prose of cablegrams: the atmosphere in the White House, the tone of the newspapers, the feelings of the American people.

"We've no choice but to present the original Plan B," I said to Tonomura. There was nothing else to say.

"I suppose you're right," he replied with a forlorn shrug of his broad shoulders. "But you and I both know Hull will never accept it."

"Let's give it a try anyway."

The Congress was still opposed to war, and Hull himself supposedly wanted the negotiations to continue. I felt there was still a glimmer of hope left as we set out for the State Department.

As Hull began to read the English translation of Plan B that our Ambassador had handed him, I noticed something curious. Despite his solemn demeanor and his apparent interest in the proposal, he merely glanced over the pages with a speed I found surprising. Instead of reading every word, it seemed as if he was scanning material he already knew. It was at that moment that I began to suspect they were intercepting our messages. *Have the Americans broken our code?*

Plan A and Plan B were originally cabled from the Foreign Minister to Tonomura on November 4th, Washington time, the day I left Tokyo. Following that a great many telegraphic requests and instructions have been traveling back and forth across the Pacific. They were all in code, and if the code has been broken, and they've all been read, it means that Hull and Roosevelt have known everything we were going to say before we even opened our mouths. Come to think of it, from the very first day Hull has adopted a strangely condescending attitude toward me. It's been especially obvious whenever I present him with a new proposal.

It was on November 7th that Tonomura delivered Plan A to the Secretary of State. Hull apparently showed little interest in this crucial document, and merely gave Tonomura a speech about America's peaceful intentions. If Hull already knew the contents of Plan B—the backup proposal we were going to present if he rejected Plan A—his behavior would make perfect sense.

And on November 9th, Secretary Walker made a curious statement to Tonomura, saying that "both the President and Mr. Hull already have proof that Japan is going to resort to military force." Where did they get their "proof"? An extraordinary thought crossed my mind. Could it be they are reading the military messages as well? Could it be the Americans know more about the intentions of the Japanese Army than the representatives of the Japanese government themselves, who know next to nothing?

Gentle as a dove on the outside, crafty as a snake inside: that's how Hull came across when I studied him carefully. As if he had prepared his answers beforehand, as if he and the President had agreed on what he would say, he confidently refuted the proposals in Plan B one by one: for the United States to cut off assistance to Chiang Kai-shek was no more possible, given the context of Hitler's aggression, than for them to cease assisting Britain. Even if we did withdraw from southern Indochina, we could invade again from the north a few days later. Therefore our offer was meaningless. And so forth.

At that point I brought up Roosevelt's previous offer to serve as what the President called "an introducer" between Japan and China. I said an "introducer" has to be neutral, and if the President really meant what he said, shouldn't the United States first stop assisting Chiang Kai-shek? Hull brought up the belligerent speech Tojo had made on the seventeenth, and said he found it very difficult to see any shift by Japan toward a peaceful policy, and that when the President offered to serve as "introducer" he of course based it on the presumption that our government would first adopt a less hostile policy. Hull was putting his own spin on Roosevelt's statement. Our proposal to stop the coming war through reciprocal concessions was again being buried under Hull's insistence on principles.

Then he said that, in any case, American assistance to Chiang Kai-shek was not as significant as it was advertised to be.

Who are you trying to fool, I thought. Your country has already extended enormous loans to him, and is providing him with American pilots and a massive stockpile of weapons and ammunition. This is clear from reports made by our own people in China, but it's even listed in the American military budget.

When Tonomura, speaking as a military officer, said that the withdrawal of our forces from southern Indochina was a concession of crucial military value, the Secretary of State merely inclined his head in doubt and didn't respond.

Tojo isn't helping us at all. Every word of his speeches gets translated. His last one was more bombastic than ever—he was obviously playing to the gallery—and I found it sickening. The moment he sends me off to Washington, he turns around and makes inflammatory speeches about America. Of course I can see what he is up to: by taking a hard line in public, he thinks he can force Washington to compromise. But it all comes across as empty and contemptible bluster here.

It's not only Tojo: the Finance Minister and the Director of the Planning Agency have also been throwing around too many strong adjectives in public. Which is not to say that the hard-liners on the American side haven't been stirring things up as well. Secretary of the Navy Knox declared recently that the Navy is now ready for war and could respond to an attack on any front. And the newspapers are full *of hostile editorials. But Hull and Roosevelt have been cautious in their public statements. Theirs is a class act compared to Tojo's.*

I'm beginning to feel that Tonomura and I are caught between the hard-liners of both countries, trying somehow to pacify both sides and floundering about.

Hull was rejecting Plan B knowing full well—knowing, I'm convinced, from reading our cables—that to bury it means war. I can't escape the conclusion that the man wants war. His stubbornness, and his narrowness, are a danger for both Japan and America. I've got to do something. I think I'll try talking to him one more time, this time alone.

November 21st, Friday evening

I went by myself to see Cordell Hull. We spoke for about thirty minutes, in an unexpectedly friendly atmosphere. (Rather than "friendly," perhaps I should say "pleasant," so pleasant it made me a little uncomfortable. If anything, it showed his indifference to my role here as a Special Envoy.)

I started by saying: "Previously I said that any agreement we reach with the United States would 'outshine' the Tripartite Pact. As the man who signed the pact, I'd like to explain what I meant. You have stated again and again that the main obstacle to an agreement between us is this alliance. I'd like to explain why I think it doesn't have to be an obstacle."

"Certainly. Go ahead."

"I can assure you there are no secret agreements attached to the Tripartite Pact. I give you my solemn promise that this is true."

"I believe you."

"Thank you. So Japan's only obligations are those specifically outlined in the text of the pact. For example, if the United States and Germany were to go to war, Japan's position would be determined according to Japan's own choice. We are not bound by any interpretations the other signatories might have. We do not take orders from Germany."

"Yes, I see."

"I have brought with me a document to that effect. If you wish, I can sign it in your presence and give it to you."

"All right, I'll accept it. There are some other people I'd like to discuss it with."

"Do you mean the President?"

"No, not the President." He abruptly changed the subject. "Since you've come all the way to Washington, I really should invite you to dinner. Unfortunately, I've been terribly busy. Do you play golf, by any chance?"

"No, I'm hopeless at it."

"Actually, I am too. Golf takes up so much time, you just can't indulge in it when you're conducting affairs of state. And affairs of state are certainly not good for one's health either. I've had this cold recently—I just can't seem to shake it off."

"I hope you take good care of yourself."

"Thank you. By the way, I wanted to tell you how much I admire your English; it really is first-rate. I understand your wife is an American. She was your secretary . . ."

"No, she was my English teacher when I was Consul in Chicago."

"Oh, so she was your teacher? Well, it's obvious she was a very good one. Thanks to her, the negotiations have gone much more smoothly than before. Your knowledge of the language has enabled our two countries to make a great deal of progress in mutual understanding."

"Mister Secretary," I said, deciding to cut through this banter, "whatever happens, I want to prevent a war between us. Is there no way that you could possibly accept this proposal from our government?"

"Well, this sort of thing can't be hurried. Let's give it the time it deserves."

"We don't <u>have</u> any time. The Japanese government is in a hurry. As I told you before, there's a time limit to my mission."

"The Japanese government is in a hurry, but the American government isn't. A difference in national character, perhaps?"

"I don't think so."

"I had the feeling the last proposal you gave me was Japan's ultimatum."

"No, absolutely not. It's just a proposal, not an ultimatum."

"Well, if it's only a proposal, let's take the time to consider it."

"But we don't have any time."

"Why not?" A smile played in the corners of his piercing gray eyes. I had the feeling he was mocking me. His smile seemed to say, "I can see right through you."

"I think you understand the situation we're in. We're trying to find a peaceful solution while restraining the hard-liners at home, especially in the military."

"Of course I understand. We have hard-liners here as well. Believe me, it's difficult for me too."

With that he rose from his chair and extended his hand. His hand felt hot as I shook it. Apparently he really did have a cold. I told him again to take care of himself and left his office.

November 22nd, Saturday

At 8:00 P.M. Ambassador Tonomura and I visited Secretary Hull in his suite at the Waldman Park Hotel. We conferred with him for three hours.

The friendliness Hull had shown me yesterday was completely gone. He seemed profoundly irritated as he told us he was "discouraged" by the Japanese government's insistence on a hurried solution and by our coercive "demands."

I realized that Hull's smiling face of yesterday was nothing but a mask. Unlike the naturally cheerful Roosevelt, who always seems to enjoy a joke, Cordell Hull seems capable only of an aristocratic calm or profound irritation. Nothing in between. A gentleman one day, a bully the next.

A cable came today from the Foreign Minister to the Ambassador:

I THINK YOU ARE AWARE HOW DIFFICULT IT IS FOR US TO EXTEND THE DEADLINE FOR

THE NEGOTIATIONS. HOWEVER, SINCE THE IMPERIAL GOVERNMENT WISHES TO DO EVERYTHING POSSIBLE TO REASON WITH THE UNITED STATES AND RESOLVE THE CRISIS WITHOUT COMPROMISING FUNDAMENTAL NATIONAL POLICY, AND SINCE YOU ARE DOING YOUR UTMOST UNDER DIFFICULT CONDITIONS, WE ARE EXTENDING YOUR DEADLINE. YOUR NEW INSTRUCTIONS ARE TO CONCLUDE THE TALKS BY THE TWENTY-NINTH. IN ADDITION, ANY AGREEMENT MUST INCLUDE AN EXCHANGE OF INSTRUMENTS OF AGREEMENT WITH BRITAIN AND THE NETHERLANDS SECURING THEIR CONSENT. WE WILL HOLD OFF UNTIL THAT DATE. HOWEVER, THIS DEADLINE IS THE FINAL ONE. THERE CAN BE ABSOLUTELY NO POSTPONEMENTS. PLEASE MAKE ALL POSSIBLE EFFORTS TO CONCLUDE THE NEGOTIATIONS SATISFACTORILY BY THEN. AFTER THAT DATE EVENTS WILL PROCEED AUTOMATICALLY.

So they've extended our deadline a little, but what can we achieve in four extra days? Tokyo is completely misjudging the mood in Washington. On my departure, Tojo told me I had until the end of November. Then after I arrived in Washington this was shortened to the twenty-fifth, and now it's been pushed back again to the twenty-ninth. It doesn't help our bargaining position to have the government arbitrarily moving the deadline back and forth like this. I can't help feeling that our government has given up on the negotiations. And I get the same impression of the American side too. But Tonomura and I will not abandon hope. We'll stick it out to the very end.

November 23rd, Sunday
America and Japan lie under dark thunderclouds, wondering when lightning will strike. But not the Sunday Times. It's as thick as ever, crammed with news about football, films, society gossip.

In the afternoon I received an unexpected visit from the Little family. Alice's brother Norman came with his son George and his daughter Lauren.

When Saburo had finished the newspaper he had handed it to Yoshimoto, telling him to cut out the articles circled in red. He then went out through the deserted lobby onto the veranda. The sun was dazzling when it shone between the clouds, but there was a chill wind that cut through his clothing and made him shiver; at least the lobby had been heated.

It seemed peculiar, very peculiar, that almost none of the Embassy staff had shown up for work, while over at the State Department all the important officials were apparently hard at it, despite its being a Sunday. It disturbed him, particularly as the two countries were nearing the point of no return. Plan B was the last proposal. Japan had nothing new to offer after it. Hull had called the plan an "ultimatum." Of course strictly speaking it wasn't one, but if it were rejected, and the deadline passed, it could only mean war.

Something else bothered him. It seemed to take the Embassy staff an inordinate amount of time to encode and decode the official cables. He had hoped a strict chain of command could be set up, so that a message would reach the code specialists in the communications room as quickly as possible. When he arrived in Washington he had asked Yoshimoto to take charge. But he soon realized that any requests made by a young Foreign Ministry official, an outsider to the Embassy staff, would have no effect at all. Things began to run a little more smoothly after he got the Ambassador to issue some orders. But even then there was a limit, for Tonomura had the opposite problem; he was originally from the Navy, and thus wasn't a ministry insider. In addition, he wasn't familiar with the process of composing and receiving official cables and, more importantly, he didn't have a team of his own among the staff. He didn't have those personal ties, formed at the beginning of a career, which are crucial to the functioning of any Japanese group, especially a group of bureaucrats. In that respect Saburo, who had spent his whole life in the Foreign Ministry, was able to communicate with the staff better than the Ambassador. But Saburo was a Special Envoy, and the Embassy staff were not officially his subordinates.

These subtle bureaucratic distinctions resulted in a needless delay in the chain of command. Nobody jumped when he or Tonomura spoke, and if an emergency ever did arise, they would be in trouble. But professional sensitivities were involved, and there was nothing he could do to reform the system. He let it go, but he could never shake off a sense of anxiety about it.

It was icy cold. But Saburo stood on the veranda bearing it, and gazed at the thorny branches of the bare black trees as they poked up into the pale sky. Each tree was sturdy and tall, growing thick on the rich soil, so different from the scrawny trees around Tokyo. Clinging to the branches were strands of what looked like ice, as though the trees were hung with jewels. Suddenly he found himself smiling: he was thinking about Alice. He had dreamed about her this morning. She had been in her nightgown, the one she wore on the morning of his departure. In the dream she had sternly reminded him of his promise—to get a new vacuum cleaner handle!

Alice, Ken, Anna, Eri . . . memories of his family had become faint and distant. Ever since his arrival he had been commuting by limousine between the Embassy and the State Department; he hadn't taken a single step outside the Embassy grounds apart from that. But now that his government's final proposal had been submitted, he had time to kill, waiting for the American response. He had done everything he could to make Hull agree. He had no new ideas.

On a sudden impulse he went inside to put on his overcoat and muffler and felt hat, and set out for a walk. He walked around the Embassy to the south and proceeded slowly down the slope into Rock Creek Park. He walked into the woods, and after a while came to the riding grounds, where he saw a young woman leading a horse. The horse's breath left a white trail in the cold air, and the sweat on its flanks looked slick in the dim winter sun. As Saburo tramped over the fallen leaves glittering with frost, they crackled like pieces of glass. There was nobody out on the golf course or the tennis courts, but the ranks of winter trees seemed to be watching over him like wooden guardsmen.

He turned around. The Embassy was no longer in sight. He realized it might be dangerous to go too deep into the woods alone. There were strong anti-Japanese passions loose in this country, and America had its share of extremists who weren't pleased with the idea of a mission for peace. But Saburo was alone now for the first time since his arrival and, rather than unease, he felt a powerful sense of relief. Subject of the Japanese Empire, Special Envoy—for a while he could cast off these titles, these uniforms, and become a plain human being again. But how helpless this human being was, he thought. Airplanes and tanks, cannons and battleships were being mobilized for mutual destruction. With a single word from the Emperor, with a single command from the President, several million young men would set out to murder each other. And that immense force had to be stopped by this one, helpless man. Saburo was overcome with a sense of doom. Hanging his head, he began to climb the steep hill back to the Embassy. He was out of shape. The muscles in his legs seemed to have atrophied. He was breathing heavily by the time he reached the top.

When he entered the lobby, three Americans rose to greet him. Norman Little smiled as he opened his arms to embrace him. Beside Norman was George, who was in uniform, and Lauren, who was wearing the casual clothes of a college coed. Each of them embraced Saburo in turn, and then the four sat down around a table.

"You've certainly got quite a job to do this time," said Norman. "We read about your mission in the newspaper. They had your picture in it several times as well. We were waiting for an opportunity to come and see you, then George got a furlough, so we decided to fly up here last night."

"George, I understand you've become an airman," Saburo said.

"Yes, sir, I'm in the Army Air Corps."

"Then you're the same as Ken."

"Oh, is Ken in the AAC too?"

Saburo laughed. "Well, we don't call it that, but yes. He was drafted at the beginning of the year. I only found out about it when I was posted back to Japan."

"Is he a pilot?"

"No, up to now he's been a technical officer working on aircraft design. But he does fly for testing."

"So he's a test pilot." There was a glimmer in his blue eyes (only the color was different from Ken's). "I'm still in flight training. We do basic and intermediate training for ten weeks each, and then move on to the advanced stuff. I'd like to pilot a fighter, but I don't know if I'll qualify . . ."

"Ken wants to do the same." A shadow passed across Saburo's face. Monstrous though the idea was, it was always possible that George and Ken might have to fight each other.

"And Lauren has started Japanese at the University of Chicago," her father went on.

"*Konnichiwa*," said Lauren in greeting. "*Gokigen ikaga desu ka?*"

"Very good. When did you begin?"

"This April. My teacher is a nisei. But what I really want to do is Japanese art."

Their talk quickly moved on to more serious things, with Saburo saying he hoped to see them in Chicago "if and when an agreement is signed." To cheer him up, Norman took a small package out of his briefcase. It was a little toy horse, a wooden Pegasus. Its white paint had peeled off in spots.

"Do you recognize it?" Norman poked at it, and it began to sway in a see-saw motion.

"Let me think . . ."

"It was Ken's," said George, smiling. "We found it when we were cleaning out the basement this spring. Neither Mom nor I knew what it was, but Lauren remembered because she'd given it to Ken for Christmas years ago. He forgot it when you went back to Japan. Oh, and we also found one of Anna's old dolls, but the cloth had rotted away and we couldn't fix it."

"And then Dad said he wanted to paint it with fresh white paint," added Lauren. "But I told him we should leave it as it is. Do you think Ken will remember it?"

Saburo poked at the horse. Moving its wings, the little Pegasus swayed back and forth as if flying slowly through the air.

Norman took out three more packages which his wife Aileen, who was ill with asthma, had contributed. "This is for Alice—a pair of lace gloves Aileen made for her. And these are dolls for Anna and Eri. I know they're both a bit old for dolls, but Aileen insisted on making them herself. And this is a tiepin for you, with the Little family crest on it."

"Thank you," said Saburo. "I'm afraid I don't have anything for you. My departure was so sudden . . ."

"That's all right." Norman smiled. "It's nice just to be able to see you."

They talked for a while more, then the three of them left. The moment they were gone, Yoshimoto, who seemed to have been waiting, came up.

"There's a cable from the Foreign Minister."

It was a reconfirmation of the new deadline. The twenty-ninth. Six days left.

"Yoshimoto," said Saburo, "I have a favor to ask you. You can do it tomorrow if you want, but I'd like you to get me a handle for a General Electric vacuum cleaner. I've got the specifications written down here."

"Did you say a vacuum cleaner?" Yoshimoto looked surprised, but he accepted the order without asking further about it.

November 24th, Monday

There are signs that Cordell Hull has gone into action. According to reports from the man we posted in front of the State Department, there's been a steady stream of visitors: the Dutch Minister, the British Ambassador, the Australian Chargé d'Affaires, the Chinese Ambassador. Some of them have been there more than once. Evidently the Secretary of State has been holding some important meetings with his allies. I'd like to think all this activity means he has accepted our plan, and is rushing to formulate a response to meet our deadline. But, judging from Hull's displeasure at our meeting on Saturday, I find it hard to believe his response will be favorable. The hour of truth is pressing closer, minute by minute.

The papers are full of rumors—that Hull is going to offer us a temporary agreement to keep the peace for another three months, that Roosevelt wants this extended to six months, etc. Some of the articles stress the government's efforts at finding a peaceful solution, but I've seen ones bragging that once a war starts Japan will be a "pushover," and others clamoring for a crusade to stop the Japs from taking over the world.

Tonomura was upset about my going out alone yesterday, and warned me to be cautious. "There are a lot of people around who would like to see you dead," he said.

"You mean American extremists?"

"No, the Americans would never do anything so stupid."

"Then who would want to kill me?"

"First of all, the Nazis. Then, young Japanese Army officers."

"You mean our side is more dangerous?"

"Exactly. If you were assassinated it would give them a perfect excuse to start a war. Just between the two of us, I wouldn't be surprised if Tojo wanted you out of the way."

"You're joking!"

"No, I'm not. Take a look at this." He handed me a handwritten document. "This just came in from the military attaché's office. It's Tojo's speech opening the new session of the Diet on November 17th, the speech that caused such a stir in the American press here—the one Hull was so angry about. How can the man be so stupid as to make these idiotic threats at a time like this? I was furious when I read it!"

I could just imagine the bald Prime Minister throwing out his chest and addressing the parliament. I could almost hear that bizarre intonation as his words echoed around the chamber.

> *On the basis of an agreement with the Vichy government, we decided this July to strengthen our presence in southern Indochina. But the United States, Britain, and Holland responded to this entirely natural defensive measure with suspicion and jealousy, and froze our financial assets. Along with what amounts to a total ban on exports, they have attacked our Empire with an economic blockade, and have rapidly increased the military menace they pose to us . . .*

How could he come out with extreme statements like this after approving an eventual withdrawal from southern Indochina in Plan B?

Needless to say, an economic blockade by a power which we are not at war with is no less a hostile act than war itself!

Applause. Applause from the Diet members, applause from the public, applause from the journalists. I suddenly thought of Arizumi. He was sure to have been there listening to every word of Tojo's speech. Arizumi never missed any of Hitler's speeches while he was in Berlin, and he was now no doubt following Tojo around with the same enthusiasm.

Since the founding of our Empire, the national policy has been based upon a peace-loving spirit. In order to ensure the survival, and the authority, of our Empire, and to establish a new order in Greater East Asia, we have made, and are continuing to make, the utmost effort to achieve a diplomatic solution. However, judging from the negotiations to date, the outcome of this diplomatic effort is difficult to foresee. Consequently the government, anticipating all possible obstacles in our path, is taking every necessary step in preparation. We are prepared for any eventuality . . .

More applause. What does he mean by "any eventuality"? Was that what the Foreign Minister meant in his cable: "After that date events will proceed automatically"? If Tojo is planning a surprise attack, a Hitler-style blitzkrieg, it will be extremely dangerous. The Americans always talk about Hitler's sudden moves as cowardly acts, as stabs in the back. If Tojo tries something like that in Asia, it will turn the American public pro-war in a flash.

"What do you think?" Tonomura asked me.

"I think he's deliberately pulling the rug out from under us."

"And look at this. A speech by Toshio Shimada supporting Tojo in the Diet." The ultranationalist Shimada was famous for his booming voice and his radical opinions.

We know full well that the greatest obstacle to a successful conclusion of the China problem is the hostility of certain Western pow-

ers, led by the United States. But how can they find any aggressive purpose in our perfectly right and proper position, whereby we are actively contributing to the maintenance of peace in the world? How dare the United States persist in blocking us in this? We must respond to talk with talk, to action with action. At this point our only choice can be war. The whole nation is agreed on this.

"God, this is horrible," I muttered. Here they were announcing to the Americans that they were about to attack them, while making us continue to sue for peace. It was totally irrational.

"Awful, isn't it?" Tonomura agreed. "That's why I said the people who would really like to see you dead are Tojo and his cohorts."

"I'd rather die than destroy the negotiations and become a national hero."

"I feel exactly the same way."

November 26th, Wednesday evening

Everything has ground to a halt. All the work we've been doing has abruptly stopped. We are back where we began. And the deadline is almost upon us. There are no more cards to play. But I must do something. Young men are about to start killing each other. I must do something.

Yesterday I asked for a meeting with Cordell Hull, but I was refused. There has been some strange and hectic activity on the American side, centered on the White House. Our observer reports that shortly before noon the President had a meeting with Hull, Secretary of the Army Stimson, Secretary of the Navy Knox, Army Chief of Staff Marshall, and Navy Chief of Staff Stark. It was obviously to discuss the "Japanese problem." Hull has had repeated contacts with the Ambassadors of Britain, China, and Holland over the last three days, and no doubt has made some sort of proposal to their military people. But I find it impossible to believe all this activity is only the result of our Plan B. There must be another reason for it.

(Perhaps they _have_ broken the Japanese code. In that case they *themselves must be wondering about the significance of the November 29th deadline—November 30th in Washington. Could it be they're afraid Japan is going to make some sort of military move on December 1st?)*

We finally managed to obtain a meeting with Hull today. We asked for one in the morning but were kept waiting until close to five o'clock in the afternoon. Hull abruptly handed us a single sheet of paper—the "Hull Note." My heart sank when I read it. It said our latest proposal was completely unacceptable, and went on to restate the principles of the American position. But not only did it ignore all the points I've tried to raise so far, it went further than anything he has said before, pressing for a complete withdrawal from both China and French Indochina, and demanding that we abrogate the Axis pact immediately.

I was shocked. I told him it was impossible, it just took us back to where we were at the start of negotiations six months ago. But Hull, without explaining, without raising his voice or arguing, calmly said: "This is the reply of the United States government. Here you will find all our demands, a thorough accounting of our position." He said this with a firmness and composure that allowed for no debate.

Before I came to Washington, I had assumed that two countries with differing national convictions could not engage in a real dialogue simply by asserting those convictions. How could they possibly accomplish anything unless they put aside their principles or ideology and found a middle ground by agreeing on specific, separate concessions? This is what we placed our hopes on, and what Plan B represented for us. But Hull merely reaffirmed his way of thinking and refused to reply to any of my questions. There would be no concessions, no compromises.

I didn't have the heart to transmit the Hull Note to our government immediately, and I said I would like to go back to the Embassy and study it carefully. Then Tonomura asked, in a voice that was close to a groan, "Does the American side have no reply to our proposal other than this note?"

"Oh no," Hull said, "but this is our position."

"The last time we met we presented our final proposal. We would like your reply to it."

"This *is* the reply."

"Then are you saying this is your government's final word?"

"No, it's just our position."

"I would like to ask you one last favor. The other day the President said 'There is no last word between friends.' Could we possibly talk to the President again?"

"But that's between friends."

"Then we are not friends?"

"Well, we are. But the President is very busy at present." Hull thought for a moment, then picked up the telephone and called the White House. Roosevelt was willing to see us tomorrow.

It seemed to me Hull had suddenly given up on the negotiations. This man, from whose manner one could usually tell at a glance whether he was pleased or displeased, today seemed to be neither. He was calm but he was cold; he was polite but he was expressionless. Above all, he was indifferent to us both. He couldn't care less about Japan's position. There was a strange serenity in him as he effectively foreclosed the negotiations, a self-assurance which said, "The position of the American government is the only valid one in the world."

When we got back to the Embassy, Tonomura and I just looked at each other and, involuntarily, sighed. Our sighs said it all, a mixture of dejection and exhaustion. There was nothing more to say. It was unbearable that the talks should come to an end like this, and that the situation should now move "automatically" to war. Tonomura's face was empty as he tapped out the cable to the Foreign Minister. I could see my own despondence reflected in his.

It was then that I hit on the idea of asking President Roosevelt to send a personal cable to the Emperor.

Directly after my arrival in Washington, the First Secretary, Terasaki, told me about an influential Christian minister named Stanley Jones. Jones was a friend of the President, and he had suggested to Terasaki some time ago that it might help to break the deadlock in *negotiations if Roosevelt and the Emperor could communicate directly. Terasaki had an American wife named Gwen. The young diplomat was fluent in English, had many American friends, and was on close terms with Dr. Jones. Perhaps he could ask Jones to suggest to the President that he write a personal message to the Emperor.*

As a first step, I immediately wrote out a cable asking the government to inquire if the Emperor would be willing to accept such a message. It would be an extraordinary measure, but it was the only way to go over Tojo's head. The Emperor was the only one who could stop the coming tragedy. But as I was about to send my cable, I realized just how serious the implications of this were. Even if the Emperor were willing, the President might refuse. If Roosevelt were willing, but said anything in his message to offend the dignity of its recipient, I as the go-between would be disgraced for life. But when I discussed the matter with Tonomura, he said without any hesitation, "Let's do it. I'll share the responsibility with you. Let's both sign the cable."

Thus, shortly after we cabled the Hull Note to Tokyo, we sent another message proposing that His Majesty himself intervene.

Ambassador Tonomura and I talked late into the night about our upcoming meeting with President Roosevelt. Both of us were acutely aware of the fact that this would be our last meeting with him; we also realized that, given the Secretary of State's attitude, even a meeting with the President couldn't save the situation. We imagined the reaction to the Hull Note in Tokyo. No doubt they would hold a joint conference of the government and the military. I could just see their faces as they read the new American proposal which ignored all our discussions to date and in effect demanded total Japanese submission. War was unavoidable now. The only person who could stop it was the Emperor.

The Americans probably won't strike first. The Japanese Army, with its fondness for surprise, will probably attack in Thailand or the Dutch East Indies. But if they do strike first, it will give the American government, which has been stymied so far by the isolationists, the perfect excuse to enter the war. Please, let it be the Americans who start it! The only thing we can do now is urge the Army to rise above its traditions and restrain itself.

November 27th, Thursday evening

Looking through the American newspapers today, I see the Hull Note is the leading headline everywhere. "U.S.-Japan Negotiations Reach Final Impasse"; "American Conditions Delivered to Japanese. Hull Refuses to Budge"; "War and Peace Hang in the Balance"; "Final Proposal to Japanese Envoys." None of the papers report the Hull Note as merely a "position"; they all see it as the government's formal response, and recognize that the talks have reached breaking point. It's perfectly obvious that even the Americans don't expect the Japanese government to swallow the Hull Note.

UPI has a piece saying that Secretary Hull had intended to propose a temporary agreement lasting six months, but when he met the representatives of the Chinese government yesterday afternoon, the Chungking delegation expressed vehement opposition, and Hull dropped the plan. Hull was also reported as having finally bowed to public opinion, which is overwhelmingly opposed to any concessions to Japan. (Hull himself is always bringing up "public opinion." Nothing unusual about that—a strong stance is always a hit with the public in any country. But my being in Washington looking for a peaceful solution is in direct opposition to Japanese public opinion. The very fact that the talks are being held in Washington and not in Tokyo represents a concession by the Japanese government. But such points count for nothing with Cordell Hull.) Anyway, the result was a hard-line response.

Hull was present at the last-ditch meeting Tonomura and I had at two-thirty this afternoon with the President. The conversation lasted an hour.

We were braced for a tense confrontation, so we were a little surprised when we were led into the President's own office—the previous time we had talked in a formal meeting room. This was his private working area. The desk was a jumble of papers, and as we spoke we were interrupted several times by the telephone. We were catching a glimpse of the President's everyday life.

The President offered us cigarettes. Tonomura put one between his lips and the President lit a match for him. But with his glass eye the Ambassador was unable to align his cigarette with Roosevelt's match. Roosevelt chuckled and lit another one for him.

"Usually at this time," said the President, "I'm taking my vacation in the country. But this year Mr. Kurushima is here, and Mr. Lewis of the United Mine Workers has been causing trouble, so I haven't been able to get away."

"I'm sorry," I said, laughing. "But which one is causing more trouble, Mr. Lewis or me?"

"Why, Mr. Lewis, of course."

Everyone laughed. But Hull merely let a tiny smile crease the corners of his eyes and soon resumed his mask.

"In the last war," said Roosevelt, "Japan and the United States both suffered from the self-righteous attitude taken by Germany, a nation blind to the sentiments of other nations. But since the start of the negotiations between our two countries, I've been delighted to find that there are people in Japan too who cherish peace. The vast majority of the American people hope for a peaceful solution in the Pacific. No matter how serious the crisis has become, I want you to know I am not giving up."

"But Mr. President," Tonomura interrupted, "the response made by the American government yesterday was bitterly disappointing to our side."

"Yes," replied Roosevelt, "I too am disappointed that the situation has reached this impasse. But in the period since the talks began, the Japanese Army's occupation of southern Indochina has been a serious setback, and recently we have reason to fear more of the same."

"What do you mean, sir?"

"Your Army has started to move. We have definite information about military movements in French Indochina and along the Chinese coast."

Tonomura and I looked at each other. When I left Tokyo, the Foreign Minister had expressed concern that the military might go ahead and do something that would provoke the United States. And now it had happened. The Americans were probably worried about an alliance between Japan and Thailand, and an eventual takeover of all Southeast Asia.

"I fully realize," said Roosevelt, with a smile, "that we cannot judge the attitude of the Japanese people, who have been at war with China for four years, by the yardstick of American experience, which has been one of peace. But during your talks with the Secretary of State, not once have we heard the leaders of Japan express a desire for peace, and this has made the talks extremely difficult from our point of view. If we go on in this manner, any temporary agreement we reach with you would only gain us a few months' time. It seems to me we cannot achieve anything without some agreement on basic principles between our two countries. As you know, in my shipboard conference with Prime Minister Churchill this August we first came to an agreement on our basic policies, and only then did we set down the agenda for our discussions."

The smile never left his lips as he continued his eloquent argument. Unlike Hull, he always showed concern for our standpoint as he spoke. I was favorably impressed. Where Hull was elderly and repetitious, Roosevelt's manner of speaking was vigorous and versatile. But he too argued, finally, on the basis of his moral principles. How very American he is.

Just two months ago Prime Minister Konoe also proposed, through our Ambassador, a shipboard conference with President Roosevelt. Although the President himself apparently showed some interest in the idea, it was soon dropped when Hull objected that it would be too risky. Lord Kido, the Keeper of the Privy Seal, described the episode allegorically. Japan had invited America up to the second floor of a house to admire the scenery. America demanded to know what kind of scenery it was before it would go up. Japan refused to answer, telling America it had to come up itself and take a look. Thus nothing came of the initiative. But it seemed to me the United States was worried that once it got up there Japan would kick away the ladder leading down again. The Japanese side had proposed holding a summit and then taking

*care of the details. The American side suspected that Japan would
merely exploit any joint U.S.-Japanese statement to its own advantage.*

*Our conversation with Roosevelt continued for a while until Tono-
mura, in a tone that could only be called imploring, asked the President to use his statesmanship to resolve the deadlock. Roosevelt just
smiled and shook hands with us. He didn't answer.*

*The meeting was a failure. Roosevelt supports the Hull Note. Of
course he does. So we're heading for war. Is there <u>nothing</u> I can do? . . .*

November 27th, still Thursday evening
*I placed an international telephone call to Yamamoto, Director of the
American Affairs Bureau at the Foreign Ministry in Tokyo. Assuming
our call was being intercepted, we spoke in a code we had agreed on
beforehand.*

KURUSHIMA: *Hello. It's Kurushima here.*

YAMAMOTO: *Hello. How's the marriage question [the negotiations]?*

KURUSHIMA: *The same as before. The southern thing is the biggest problem.*

YAMAMOTO: *The southern thing?*

KURUSHIMA: *Yes, the whole marriage depends on it. I'll give you the
details in writing. How are things over there? Is the baby
on its way [is the crisis coming]?*

YAMAMOTO: *Yes, it seems to be due soon.*

KURUSHIMA (surprised): *But it hasn't been born yet, has it?*

YAMAMOTO: *Did you keep them posted [talk to the press] about your
meeting with Kimiko [the President] today?*

KURUSHIMA: *No, I just said we met. There's nothing more we can do
here. I don't see any chance of their marrying, actually.*

YAMAMOTO: *I'll cable you about that. The situation does look pretty
bad.*

KURUSHIMA: *Yes . . . but they do want to go on discussing a possible
marriage. At the same time they're very concerned about
the baby. I imagine Tokugawa [the Army] is champing at
the bit.*

YAMAMOTO:	Well, no more than before, really.
KURUSHIMA:	Kimiko's leaving town tomorrow and will be at her place in the country until Wednesday.
YAMAMOTO:	Please do what you can.
KURUSHIMA:	I'll do my best. Tonomura is working on it with me.
YAMAMOTO:	Is there anything else?
KURUSHIMA:	No, nothing. Just that everything depends on the southern thing, that's all.

November 28th, Friday morning

I've just had a quick look at the morning papers. After our talk with Roosevelt yesterday, Hull held a press conference at which he said that the situation had become very dangerous, with "Japanese military extremists effectively in charge," and that he was "moving heaven and earth" to work out an arrangement with Japan before the situation "got out of hand," but that reinforcements were pouring into Indo-china and "a Japanese attack might come within a few days."

The Hull Note almost seems designed to provoke our forces into attacking first. And in his statement to the press Hull deliberately used language that will infuriate the Japanese military. I'm very frightened. The Army is full of wild men, quick to indignation and ready to rush blindly ahead, just itching for a quick, decisive strike. If those fanatics respond to Hull's provocations and attack first, it will be a disaster. Japan will taste the full fury of an America united against it. The country will be destroyed.

November 28th, Friday evening

A cable came from Tokyo. Not surprisingly, the government is in an uproar over the Hull Note.

THE AMERICAN PROPOSAL IS ASTONISHING AND MOST REGRETTABLE. WE CANNOT NEGOTIATE ON THE BASIS OF SUCH A PROPOSAL. THE IMPERIAL GOVERNMENT WILL PRESENT ITS OWN RESPONSE WHICH WILL BE CABLED TO YOU IN TWO OR THREE DAYS.

*ALTHOUGH IN SUBSTANCE THE TALKS HAVE COME TO AN END YOU ARE TO AVOID
GIVING THE IMPRESSION THAT THE NEGOTIATIONS HAVE BROKEN DOWN.*

*What on earth are they saying? That in fact the negotiations have
broken down, but for strategic reasons we're to continue talking as if
they haven't? Just what does Tokyo have in mind? And now that our
code has probably been broken, what possible good can that kind of
pretense do? Who are they trying to fool? They're mad if they think I'm
going to put on an act for them.*

*And to declare that our negotiations "have come to an end"—I
refuse to accept that. Hull and Roosevelt may clamor that war is coming, Tojo may rant and rave, but as far as I'm concerned the diplomatic endeavor is <u>not</u> over, and won't be until one side or the other has
delivered its ultimatum.*

*A personal communication between Roosevelt and the Emperor, the
last possible measure to stop the war, has been turned down by Tokyo.*

*CONCERNING YOUR PROPOSAL: WE HAVE RELAYED IT TO THE RESPONSIBLE PARTIES,
BUT ALL ARE OF THE OPINION SUCH A MEASURE WOULD BE INAPPROPRIATE AT THIS
TIME. WE HOPE YOU UNDERSTAND.*

Understand?! That was my last move. Now nothing remains.

*I thought about it until late into the night. In spite of the Foreign
Minister's refusal, a personal cable from the President to the Emperor
was the only hope left. The American side probably won't strike first.
The only person capable of ordering the Army not to launch a surprise
attack is the Emperor. If His Majesty, the Commander in Chief, issues a
command not to attack first, the military must obey it. His Majesty is
beyond the counsel of ordinary mortals. Only one man on earth can
move him to act—President Roosevelt. To hell with government instructions!*

*I telephoned Terasaki, the First Secretary. He came to my room at
once, without first asking why.*

*I told him, "I just received a cable from the Foreign Minister, an out-
right rejection of the plan we talked about; he called it 'inappropriate
at this time.' But I want to try it anyway. Terasaki, I must emphasize*

that this is strictly between the two of us. I haven't even told Ambassador Tonomura. I don't want to get him involved."

"I understand," he said, nodding. I have a lot of faith in Terasaki. When I asked him to have Dr. Jones approach the President, the large forehead below his receding hairline seemed to gleam with enthusiasm.

"Just remember," I warned him, "the whole thing is fraught with danger. The Foreign Minister is against it, so obviously we can't go through our own government. I'd like you to make sure the President's cable is sent to Ambassador Grew, and that he hands it over personally at the Palace. That way the government can't intercept it. You realize it would be the end of our careers if anyone found out what we're doing. And if the Army officers swaggering all over Tokyo with their dreams of attacking America got wind of it, they'd cut us to pieces."

"Yes, I'm fully aware of that. I'll work in the utmost secrecy."

"If anything does happen, you can put all the blame on me."

"No, sir, I'll share the responsibility. Actually, when I met Dr. Jones the day before yesterday I brought up the idea of a personal message to the Emperor then, and he promised he would raise it at his next meeting with the President."

"Very good. Then as soon as you can, tell Jones to have any cable the President sends transmitted through Grew in Tokyo."

"Yes, sir."

As I watched Terasaki walk away, I thought, this is one man I can depend on.

November 29th, Saturday

The local newspapers are full of loathing for the Japanese. If our side won't accept their just and law-abiding demands, any war that results will be entirely our responsibility. America can do no wrong.

It is now 10:00 A.M. In Tokyo, fourteen hours ahead, it's midnight, November 30th. The deadline has passed.

Mere diplomacy can do nothing now. If the President is willing to send a personal cable, and if his message manages to get through to the Emperor, and if His Majesty takes it upon himself to . . . but these are now faint hopes.

November 30th, Sunday night

A thick bundle of newspapers sits in front of me. And what do I see on the front page under banner headlines but a speech by Tojo: "The exploitation of the people of Asia by the British and Americans must be stamped out. Britain and America, get out of Asia!" This masterpiece of Japanese arrogance has further enraged the American public. There are calls for war to protect American and British interests in Asia. Hull has telephoned the President at his retreat in Warm Springs to report on this new development. Roosevelt will interrupt his vacation and return to Washington on the morning of December 1st.

I discussed the matter with Ambassador Tonomura, and we decided to ask for clarification from Tokyo. An explanatory cable soon arrived from the Foreign Minister. Something apparently went very wrong; there seems to have been a colossal misunderstanding.

THE SPEECH THAT WAS REPORTED AS PRIME MINISTER TOJO'S WAS ACTUALLY WRITTEN BY AN ORGANIZATION CALLED THE ASIAN DEVELOPMENT LEAGUE FOR THE PRIME MINISTER TO DELIVER AT A MEETING HELD BY THE LEAGUE ON THE THIRTIETH. SINCE THE THIRTIETH WAS A SUNDAY AND NO AFTERNOON PAPERS ARE PUBLISHED ON SUNDAY, THE CHAIRMAN OF THE LEAGUE, ENTIRELY ON HIS OWN INITIATIVE AND WITHOUT THE APPROVAL OF THE PRIME MINISTER, GAVE THE DOCUMENT TO THE PRESS, WHO WERE EAGER TO HAVE MATERIAL TO PRINT IN THEIR SATURDAY AFTERNOON EDITIONS.

THE SPEECH WAS THEN PRINTED AS IT IS, WITHOUT THE PRIME MINISTER'S KNOWLEDGE OR APPROVAL, AND WITHOUT PASSING GOVERNMENT CENSORSHIP. IN FACT THE PRIME MINISTER HIMSELF GAVE NO SPEECH AT ALL ON SUNDAY, BEING OTHERWISE OCCUPIED, AND NEITHER HE NOR ANYONE ELSE IN THE GOVERNMENT KNEW OF OR APPROVED THE SPEECH.

REST ASSURED THAT APPROPRIATE MEASURES WILL BE TAKEN AGAINST THE ASIAN DEVELOPMENT LEAGUE.

I was flabbergasted. The crassness of some wretched patriotic organization, the crassness of the newspapers in publishing such a speech, the incompetence of a government that can't control something as important as this—it's all beyond belief!

December 1st, Monday

Shortly after ten this morning Tonomura and I paid a call on Cordell Hull at the State Department. The Secretary was livid on the subject of "Tojo's speech." I tried to explain what had happened, and asked for his understanding of a situation that would be unimaginable in the American press. It turned into an argument.

There were no new solutions for breaking the deadlock.

December 5th, Friday

A cable suddenly arrived from Tokyo ordering the transfer of the First Secretary, Terasaki, and three other Embassy officials to South America within two days.

This is a bewildering order, and an extraordinary inconvenience, coming just when Terasaki is running around trying to arrange Roosevelt's cable to the Emperor. I sent a reply in my own name:

GIVEN THE PRESENT SITUATION TERASAKI'S ABRUPT TRANSFER WOULD CAUSE GREAT DIFFICULTIES FOR ME. I WOULD LIKE HIM TO BE KEPT HERE UNTIL THE END OF THE NEGOTIATIONS.

What is Tokyo up to? It makes no sense. Two days from now is December 7th. That's a Sunday. Why would they want him transferred by a Sunday?

I can't afford to lose Terasaki right now. But the Embassy staff seem to be taking the transfers as some kind of promotion—they're even planning a farewell party for them.

4

Two clerks at the Embassy were talking.

"Hey, guess what! I managed to sell my car. They really took advantage of me but at least I sold it."

"You think it's better to sell it now?"

"Of course, the sooner the better. War's inevitable now. Didn't you see the paper this morning? Someone at the State Department said it'll happen in the next couple of weeks. Can't sell your car once the war starts, you know!"

"You think we'll all be evacuated?"

"Naturally. Enemy diplomats can't just hang around as if nothing had happened. We'll probably be moved out just before they issue the ultimatum. Some of the guys are already packed and ready to go—they've asked their landlords if they can pay the rest of their rent by the day."

"But how're we going to get home? There aren't any ships from the U.S. to Japan any more."

"Didn't you hear? The *Tatsuta-maru* left Yokohama on December 2nd. It'll be docking in L.A. on the fourteenth, then returning via Panama to Yokohama on January 15th."

"That's the first I heard of it."

"Hey, wake up! All the senior staff are booked on it. It's only people like us who aren't supposed to know what's going on."

". . . So we're actually going to be evacuated."

"You better sell *your* car too. Listen, I can get you a good price. I know a dealer."

"Okay, thanks. I guess it'd be pretty useless to keep a car here."

Saburo had heard snatches of their conversation from where he stood in the garden. His legs had begun to shiver in the cold, and he stamped his feet, kicking the gravel on the path. The moon had just begun to wane, though it was still as bright as a full moon. Exactly a month before, when he had been summoned by the Foreign Minister in the middle of the night, the moon had shone like this. What a strange and frenzied month it had been, and yet throughout it all the same moon had risen and set.

He thought of the beach on Midway Island, how the waves had washed away the words he'd scrawled in the sand. He had written so many words, but now all had been washed away. There must be many futile jobs in this world, but none where more words were squandered than in his own profession. All the treaties one drew up, the sincere and elegant expressions of goodwill, all were wiped out without a trace by the waves that surge up when the interests of nations clash. Saburo had said as much to his son the year before last. And Ken had answered that, rather than spend his life doing things like that, he wanted to build something that would last, anything—a bridge, a machine. Ken turned to designing airplanes because he knew the nature of his father's work only too well.

The Embassy roof was white in the moonlight. The branches of the bare trees gleamed like needles of ice. Saburo was the only person likely to be out taking a walk in the garden on a night as cold as this. Trailing a line of breath behind him, he reached the edge of the pond and gazed up at the moon again. The patterns on its surface made him think of a corpse. He had the vial of cyanide in his pocket. Ever since he'd been given the Hull Note, he had carried the little tube about with him. He had made up his mind to swallow the poison on the day war broke out between Japan and America, when it was clear that all his efforts at peacemaking had been in vain. He would not be dying to spite anyone or to prove anything. He bore no resentment toward Tojo and the Foreign Minister, or toward Hull and Roosevelt, or even those people, soldiers and civilians, in both countries who seemed so eager for war. They had all merely acted the way they had to, given their respective positions. Especially Cordell Hull. He was a rigid, puritanical old man, yet an idealist who was absolutely dedicated to his own principles and those of his country, who had stood, a tower of inflexibility, against every endeavor of Saburo's over the last two weeks. He couldn't bring himself to hate the man. If anything, Hull had been a magnificent opponent. How could one feel resentment when losing to someone like that? No, if Saburo chose death it would be out of remorse at his own poor judgment in accepting responsibility for so great a task, one that he knew was hopeless. On that moonlit night in Tokyo he had known, deep down, that the task was beyond him, that no matter what effort he made he was doomed to failure, and that if he failed he would be responsible in part for the deaths of millions of people. It wasn't that he was "prepared" for death so much as that, at the moment he told the Foreign Minister "All right, I'll go," his own death had already become essentially a *fait accompli.* The Americans probably wouldn't understand it. The Japanese would. But would Alice? . . .

Saburo shivered. It was, in fact, bone-chillingly cold out in the garden, but it was the thought that Alice would never be able to understand his death that made him shiver.

When he returned to the lobby, Yoshimoto was waiting for him. "You're back. I was looking for you, sir."

"Has something happened?"

"The State Department just announced on the radio that Roosevelt has sent a personal cable to the Emperor."

"Really? I'm very glad to hear it."

"But there's another thing . . ." Yoshimoto hesitated. "They also reported that 125,000 Japanese troops have assembled in Indochina, and that in addition to a convoy of battleships, two divisions are moving toward the Gulf of Siam."

It was the worst possible news.

"If it's true, we're in big trouble. Does the Ambassador know this?"

"Yes, sir, he called and asked me to inform you."

"Thank you. By the way, that memorandum for the U.S. government that started coming in from Tokyo this morning—are they making any headway on it?"

"I think so." From the tone of his voice Yoshimoto didn't seem quite sure. The only ones with direct access to cables were Iguchi, the Counselor in charge of the communications room, and the code specialists—bureaucrats who weren't likely to share the contents of secret messages with Yoshimoto, an outsider as far as they were concerned.

"I want to see Terasaki," Saburo said.

"I think he's at the farewell party."

"Farewell party?"

"Yes, sir. Since Terasaki and three others are being transferred to South America, they . . ."

"I've heard. There's work to do. Tell them to cancel it or at least break it up early. That memorandum could be crucially important."

"But, sir, we couldn't do that." There was a hint of sarcasm in his voice. "*Everyone* is there except Counselor Iguchi, who's in the code room. Terasaki is pretty popular."

"For God's sake!" shouted Saburo. How could they waste precious time like that, when those cables were probably their government's ultimatum to the United States? And yet he knew the sort of petty bureaucratic jealousies that probably lay behind it. Iguchi, aware that he was participating in historic events, had made it clear that he, and he alone, was responsible for dealing with the incoming document; and his colleagues, showing their resentment at the way he was monopolizing it, had all gone off to the party.

That morning, a telegram had arrived from Tokyo saying that a memorandum in English would be cabled for delivery to the U.S. government. It would be a long document—the government's full reply to the Hull Note of November 26th—and it would probably take until the next day to receive and decode the entire thing. The document was to be readied for delivery at any time. Saburo didn't exclude the possibility of a declaration of war.

A follow-up cable arrived with instructions to treat the memorandum as top-secret, and to ensure that no typists or other unauthorized personnel were involved in any way.

All through the morning the key Embassy staff had crammed into the communications room, awaiting its arrival. Just as they got tired of waiting and started leaving for lunch in groups of two or three, the cables began to come in. A code specialist set to work, but because the decoding machine had been destroyed on the orders of the Foreign Minister five days earlier, and most of the code books had been burned, this was a long, painstaking process. Before the specialist could finish decoding one cable, the next one arrived, and the next, until the table was piled high with telegraphic paper. Saburo suggested that each page should be typed up as soon as it was deciphered, but Iguchi, who was in charge of the operation, disagreed. "Since we're not allowed to use any typists, one of our staff—Okumura—will have to do the typing," he said. "It'll be easier if we have the whole thing decoded first."

By the end of the afternoon the decoding was still not finished. Saburo picked up the pages that were done. What he saw was a review of the U.S.-Japan negotiations to date, with a point-by-point refutation, in strong language, of the demands made in the Hull Note. It also seemed that the government had abandoned all the compromise proposals it had made in Plan B.

Saburo turned to the Ambassador. "It looks like an ultimatum."

Tonomura nodded.

Later that evening, one by one the Embassy people wandered off. Saburo assumed they were going out for dinner and would soon be back, and it was only after his walk in the garden that he found, to his astonishment, that they were all at Terasaki's party.

Saburo now quickly made his way to the communications room. "How's the decoding going?" he asked Iguchi.

"We're up to the tenth cable." Iguchi looked annoyed at the way he had burst in without knocking.

"Will we make it in time?"

"What do you mean, 'in time'?"

"I mean, will we be finished with all the decoding and typing by the time we have to deliver the memorandum?"

"But," the Counselor laughed, "we haven't even been told *when* we're to deliver it!"

"Yes, I know. But it's important that we be ready to hand it over at the exact hour that's specified. It's quite clear this is an ultimatum. I'm afraid it means war."

"Well, I wouldn't jump to conclusions," said Iguchi, with the faintly contemptuous tone of a seasoned bureaucrat. "Just to make sure, I had the last cable, part thirteen, decoded first. It certainly doesn't sound like an ultimatum to *me*. Here."

Saburo read the sheet he handed him. It was a denunciation of the "siege" mounted against Japan by the "ABCD" powers—the Americans, the British, the Chinese, and the Dutch. The last sentence read:

IT MUST BE CONCLUDED THAT ALL THESE COUNTRIES ARE AT ONE WITH THE UNITED STATES IN IGNORING JAPAN'S POSITION.

"It sounds to me as if there should be something more," Saburo said.

"No, that's it. That's the whole thing. The cables came in from noon till 2:00 P.M., but there's been nothing else for a long time. Tomorrow's Sunday, and they're very unlikely to send any cables on a Sunday."

Saburo said nothing.

"In my reading this is not an 'ultimatum,'" Iguchi went on. "The war's still a way off. After all, the *Tatsuta-maru* hasn't even arrived yet."

"What's the *Tatsuta-maru* got to do with it?"

"Well, it's the ship coming to pick up Japanese evacuees, isn't it? It's not due in Los Angeles until December 14th, so even our trigger-happy military will presumably have to wait until after that date to start the war."

Saburo felt deep misgivings, and they weren't limited merely to the memorandum. Why had the President waited until now to send his cable? Was this a ploy—so they could say the President had sent a personal message, but the Emperor ignored it, thus making war inevitable? He'd thought that, at the very least, the cable would force Japan to put off any plans for war for a few days; after all, the Emperor had to answer it. But now he wasn't so sure. Perhaps it wasn't the conciliatory message he had hoped for. And why did the State

Department choose this particular moment to make its announcement about Japanese troops in Indochina?

"Anyway," he told Iguchi, "let me know as soon as you finish the decoding. I want to look over the whole document." With that he went up to his room.

The treetops in Rock Creek Park swayed back and forth in the moonlight. The branches looked like fish swimming, dim and ominous, at the bottom of the night. Facing his desk, Saburo held his head in his hands. He realized he had forgotten to take his overcoat off, but all the strength was gone from his shoulders and legs, and he couldn't be bothered. He started to doze off, then suddenly roused himself and called Yoshimoto, telling him he wanted to discuss Roosevelt's cable with Terasaki as soon as he got back from the party.

It was after 11:00 P.M. when he was woken by a telephone call from Counselor Iguchi. The decoding was finished, and the whole memorandum was being brought up to him. Saburo had just removed his overcoat and was smoothing his rumpled clothes when Iguchi knocked.

The Counselor had a confident smile on his face. "I read the whole thing through carefully. It says absolutely nothing about the negotiations being over." He gave him a handwritten draft.

"I'll read it right away."

"All right, I'll leave it with you till tomorrow."

"But you have to get it typed up, don't you?"

"Okumura is the only one of us who can type English. I believe he's still at Terasaki's party. I'll have him do it all tomorrow."

As soon as he left, Saburo started to read. Iguchi was right: it looked like a recounting of the course of the negotiations so far. There was nothing new in it. He began to feel drowsy again and, deciding to leave it all until the morning, collapsed onto his bed.

He slept through until nine. He was woken this time by the Naval Attaché calling to say, in his husky voice: "When I got in this morning, sir, I found a whole stack of telegrams. I took them over to the communications room, but nobody was on duty. I thought you should know because it might be important."

"Thank you."

Saburo immediately called Counselor Iguchi at his home number. Iguchi's confident voice assured him: "Yes, yes, I know about them. Don't worry, I called the code specialist and told him to get over to the Embassy right away."

Saburo then rang the Ambassador at the Residence and told him about the telegrams. A "stack" of them sounded ominous.

It was a beautiful day. The clear blue sky looked almost autumnal. Cars glinted in the sunlight on Massachusetts Avenue, and even the bare trees lining the boulevard seemed to glisten. Saburo put on his black silk suit as he did every morning now, so as to be ready to set out for the State Department at any time, then went down to the lobby.

The two military attachés were reading the *New York Times* there. "This paper's so damned thick," one of them was complaining, "you get tired just reading all the headlines."

"Did you see that Roosevelt sent a personal cable to the Emperor? Those Americans certainly come up with some fantastic schemes!"

Saburo thanked the Naval Attaché for calling him, adding "I don't see any of the rest of the staff here yet."

"No, sir, nobody's shown up for work yet. Perhaps I shouldn't say this, sir, but frankly the discipline in this Embassy is a bit slack. They'd never permit it in the Navy."

Just then someone pushed open the front door and ran in; it was one of the code specialists. Counselor Iguchi soon followed. Saburo asked him if he knew where Terasaki was.

"I tried to call him several times, but he's not at home. He often spends his Sundays taking his family for a drive in the country. Maybe that's where he is."

"*On a drive?*" Here, where every second counted, the man responsible for Roosevelt's cable—without even checking to see if Grew had safely delivered it or not—was *out for a drive!* "I want these new cables processed at top speed," he told Iguchi firmly.

"All right, all right." The Counselor looked irritated. "I've asked Okumura to do the typing, so it should be done by tonight."

"Tonight?" Saburo shouted. He had never raised his voice with any member of the staff before. "That's far too late. I need it sooner."

"Why?" Iguchi's frown became more pronounced, as if he found the other man's behavior uncivilized.

"Because we've reached a critical stage. There's something extraordinary going on, judging from all the activity on their side since last night."

"But the memorandum is just a repetition of all the arguments to date."

"What about the part that came in this morning? We won't know until we decode that, will we?"

Iguchi fell silent, his eyes smoldering with resentment that this visiting official—this outsider—should order him around.

Ambassador Tonomura now appeared and watched as the laborious business of decoding and typing proceeded. Okumura could type, but his typing was of the hunt-and-peck variety. Nervous working under the scrutiny of the senior diplomats standing behind him, he started making mistakes, skipping lines.

Only one code specialist had shown up. At eleven another appeared, yawning and hung over from the previous night's party, but even so it helped to have two men working on the task.

The first cable they decoded was a thank-you note from the Foreign Minister to the two Ambassadors and the Embassy staff for their work. Then, a few minutes later, an important sentence emerged:

THE TWO AMBASSADORS ARE TO DELIVER THE MEMORANDUM PERSONALLY TO THE AMERICAN SIDE (IF AT ALL POSSIBLE TO THE SECRETARY OF STATE HIMSELF) AT PRECISELY ONE P.M., DECEMBER SEVENTH, WASHINGTON TIME.

"We've got less than two hours," Saburo groaned. "It's all got to be finished by 12:30 at the latest. Will we make it, Iguchi?"

"Well, we haven't decoded the last part yet. By 12:30? That's a bit much to ask . . ."

"We *must* get it done in time. This is our ultimatum."

"Allow me to correct you," Iguchi replied sullenly. "We have received nothing suggesting an ultimatum."

"It will be in *the last sentence!*" Saburo yelled, slapping the table with his hand. The men sitting there looked up in astonishment. "Now look." His voice boomed across the room. "We are living a moment of history. If we fail to deliver Japan's ultimatum to the United States before the opening of hostilities, we will bear the stigma of shame until the end of time . . ."

Iguchi's shrill voice cut him off. "We're doing the best we can. Spare us your speeches."

"How dare you . . ." He was choking with fury.

"Gentlemen!" Tonomura stepped between them.

"Contact the State Department," Saburo ordered another counselor, "and ask for an appointment with Secretary Hull at one o'clock."

The State Department informed them that Hull had a lunch engagement and suggested they speak to Undersecretary of State Wells. Just as Saburo was objecting that this important document could not be delivered to an undersecretary, there was another phone call, to say that the Secretary of State would see them at one o'clock.

Okumura got one of the translators to help, and both started typing furiously. But the faster they worked the more mistakes they made. Then one of the decoded cables instructed them to insert several new lines into the document, which meant that all the pages that came after the revision had to be retyped.

At twelve-thirty the last two sentences were finally decoded:

THUS THE EARNEST HOPES OF THE JAPANESE GOVERNMENT TO ADJUST JAPANESE-AMERICAN RELATIONS AND TO PRESERVE AND PROMOTE PEACE IN THE PACIFIC REGION THROUGH COOPERATION WITH THE AMERICAN GOVERNMENT HAVE FINALLY BEEN THWARTED.

THE JAPANESE GOVERNMENT REGRETS HAVING TO NOTIFY THE AMERICAN GOVERNMENT HEREBY THAT, IN VIEW OF THE LATTER'S ATTITUDE, IT CANNOT BUT CONCLUDE THAT TO REACH AN AGREEMENT THROUGH FURTHER NEGOTIATIONS WOULD BE IMPOSSIBLE.

There it was: an ultimatum. Saburo stared at Iguchi. The Counselor hung his head, looking devastated.

"I'm very sorry," Iguchi gasped.

Saburo nodded, and asked Okumura how long the rest of the typing would take.

Another hour, was the reply. If they left the Embassy at 1:30, they would reach the State Department fifteen minutes later. Saburo reluctantly had someone telephone them to ask for a postponement until 1:45.

"It's done."

At the sound of Okumura's constricted voice Saburo grabbed the document and ran with Ambassador Tonomura to the front entrance. Massachusetts Avenue was crowded with motorists setting out for a drive on a beautiful Sunday afternoon. The traffic was slow. Squares, vistas of monuments, crisp silhouettes of bare trees that looked polished under the bright blue sky . . . and it was already after two o'clock. At 2:05 their limousine slid into the State Department driveway. They were twenty minutes late, but when they reached the reception room on the third floor Cordell Hull wasn't there. They waited.

At 2:20, they were called in. Hull stood stiffly, his chest stuck out, like a prosecutor awaiting two defendants. He did not extend his hand. Saburo and Tonomura remained standing.

Tonomura was sweating heavily. Stumbling over his words, he began to say: "We received instructions from our government to deliver this document to you at one o'clock, but we were delayed because of problems in decoding the cables . . ." He handed Hull the memorandum. The document was smudged in places and covered with erasures. Hull held it by the tips of his fingers, as if it were a filthy thing, and began to turn the pages.

"Why," demanded Hull with a severe expression, "did you first specify an appointment at one o'clock?" His forehead was creased with anger, twitching uncontrollably as he spoke.

"Those were our government's orders."

As always with documents from the Japanese side, Hull read

through it at abnormal speed, as if assuring himself of something he already knew. After reading two or three pages, he asked, "Is this being presented under instructions from your government?"

"Yes, it is."

Hull glanced indifferently through the rest of the document, then looked directly at Saburo and Tonomura and said: "In all my fifty years of public service I have never seen a document that was more crowded with infamous falsehoods and distortions—infamous falsehoods and distortions on a scale so huge that I never imagined until today that any government on this planet was capable of uttering them."

Saburo could not understand why Hull was so furious. When the Hull Note had been handed to them on November 26th, he and Tonomura had expressed more astonishment than anger. They had behaved like gentlemen, hadn't they? How could Hull be so rude now that they were presenting their government's reply? Tonomura started to say something, but Hull waved his hand at him, as if chasing a dog away, and indicated the door with a motion of his chin. Tonomura nodded to Saburo. The two men left the room without another word.

There was a commotion outside in the corridor: a crowd of newspaper reporters, flashbulbs popping. Several ran up to them, but the two diplomats shook their heads and hurried into the elevator.

At the entrance to the Japanese Embassy was an even greater crowd of reporters. Counselor Iguchi, who met them at the door, stepped up to Saburo and whispered, "Aerial forces of the Imperial Navy have attacked Pearl Harbor. It's reported they inflicted heavy losses on the American side." He hesitated for a second, then said, "It happened at 1:25 our time."

5

It was just before dawn. Ken was flying a Red Dragonfly across the skies north of Tokyo. He was on a night training flight, taking advantage of the moonlight. He had flown about a hundred kilometers east, to a village on the Pacific Coast called Oarai, and he was on his way back to the flying school. They called this "night flying," but actually the ground was quite bright. The Tone River, Kasumi Cove, and, especially, the ocean itself gleamed in the moonlight like bronze burnished white. The lights were clear in the towns and villages below, and he had no problem finding his position.

Ken had flown exactly according to schedule, and he was happy to be almost there. His eyes had become accustomed to the dark, and now, growing brighter moment by moment, he saw the mountains of Inner Chichibu and Yatsugatake protruding above the clouds. Stretching above the peaks was a whitish ring of morning light. Finally he was able to make out Mount Asama, dyed red in the rising sun, and he knew the base wasn't far away. The sunlight streaming from behind flared on the edges of his windshield. Soon the rice fields would begin to sparkle.

All at once the earth below began to awaken. The long shadows of forests and houses stretched distinctly across the ground. Then directly under him he spotted the runway. His orders were to fly twenty kilometers ahead to the village of Nagatoro, and not to come back to the base until dawn had completely broken and it was bright enough to land. As he passed over the runway, he suddenly noticed two signal cloths on the ground. Normally there was one large T-shaped cloth to indicate the direction planes were to land in; when there were two, it meant an emergency order to land immediately. Ken executed a quick turn and, as soon as he was properly aligned, headed for the runway. He landed safely in the lingering darkness.

"It's war!" someone yelled.

"Oooaaah!" The cry rose from Ken's throat, a sound that wasn't human.

"With America and Britain!" said Yamada. "A *big* war against two big countries."

"Where? In Thailand? In Indochina?"

"No, in the Pacific. But it'll spread to Thailand and Indochina, and everywhere else."

Ken was unable to think. He started running. When he reached the Flight Assignment office he reported in. "Training flight completed as scheduled, sir!" he told Wing Commander Otani.

"Kurushima, you know that war's broken out?" the normally close-mouthed officer said.

"Yes, sir, I just heard."

"That's why we ordered all the planes to make emergency land-ings. Your father was handling the negotiations with America, wasn't he?"

"Yes, sir."

"You must feel . . ." He thought for a moment, but was unable to summon the words. Then, twisting his mouth in that strange way of his, he said, "All right, get out of here."

Ken proceeded to the storage room, where he dumped his para-chute, flying cap, and goggles. When he came out Sugi and Yamada were waiting for him. There was the sound of cheering from what seemed to be quite a large crowd, and they led him in that direction.

"It's the cadets," said Sugi. "Hanazono came to get us, to go to the hill. He said the whole corps was assembling to pray to the Imperial family and recite the Imperial Rescripts and then, as he put it, 'give three cheers for the Emperor to help him wipe England and America off the map.' We begged off, saying we had to go meet you. Look, they're really going wild today."

Standing on the sidelines, they could see a circle of teenage cadets gathered reverently around the flight officers, with one lieutenant making an impassioned speech: "We face the formidable air power of two powerful nations. But the fliers of the Imperial Army are *invincible*! At this very moment, over the Pacific, our planes are falling like eagles on their prey. With them in the lead we shall conquer the Pacific, then attack the American mainland, then sweep on to attack the British Isles! *Banzai* for His Majesty the Emperor! *Banzai* for the eagles of the Empire! *Banzai* for the Army of Japan!"

Ken, Sugi, and Yamada, who had hoped to remain onlookers and then just slip away, began to draw disapproving attention from the crowd: "We'll have to join them," Ken whispered, and the three of them walked over and took their place beside the cadets. These were just children, with runny noses and cheeks reddened by the cold wind, but they had been well drilled at the Junior Army Academy and stood rigidly at attention while the young officer harangued them, urging them to acts of bravery, asking them to lay their lives down for their country. The same slogans were repeated over and over again, like a hammer banging on steel: "Liberate the people of Asia!" "A new order in the East!" "Become the shield of His Majesty!" . . .

Ken remembered the last words his father had spoken to him at the naval air station before boarding his plane for America. He had been surprised to hear him say, in English, "Do your duty." Not "*Ninmu wo mattoseyo*," where *ninmu* had the sense of "obligation," something you did because a superior ordered you to, but the English "duty," meaning something you took upon yourself. "Duty" was a word his mother often used. When the Foreign Minister had asked Saburo to become the Special Envoy to the United States, he had accepted it as his personal "duty." Ken had chosen to be a pilot in the Imperial Army, and the duty he had accepted included doing battle with America. But as he stood there with those teenage cadets on the morning after the bombing of Pearl Harbor, the words he heard, the shrill voice urging them to fulfill their "obligations," had no effect on him at all. The enthusiasm of the others only depressed him. If fighting America was now part of his "duty," he would fight. But deep in his heart he knew he would never be able to go into battle with the zeal he saw in the cadets around him. This wasn't because he was afraid of the immense air power of the awakening giant, America: it was because of Alice, and Lauren, and George, and because he was loath to kill that half of himself which was American.

Alice was having a cup of coffee. She had just told Eri, who was in her school uniform, "Don't forget anything," and Eri had grumbled, "Oh Mama, you always say the same thing!" Yoshiko poured her another cup. None of them had heard the news bulletin that had just been broadcast. No one in the Kurushima household was the sort of person who would leave the radio on all morning . . .

Saburo gazed at the moonlit sky over Rock Creek Park. Everything looked the same as the night before. Only one thing was different: he was now in an enemy city. The faint hope he had kept until yesterday had frozen over, and all around him was a frigid landscape. FBI agents were positioned among the hedges in the garden. An angry crowd had gathered in front of the main gate, restrained by a line of policemen. All contact with the outside was cut off. The diplomats were prisoners in their own Embassy.

Turning from the window, Saburo saw the Embassy staff gathered in the lobby. Too restless to stay in their own rooms, some sat on sofas, some paced aimlessly. They looked depressed. No one spoke.

In his coat pocket, his fingers touched the vial of cyanide. One thing was clear—his mission had been a failure. All his efforts had come to nothing. And in the end his own government had betrayed him. He was prepared to make the ultimate apology for having failed to prevent the war. To choose death now, to apologize to the Emperor and the people of Japan, would be the appropriate course. But to *choose* wasn't what men in his profession did. To change the course of things wasn't in their power. He was an intermediary, nothing more. The war had started without him, and would go on without him. So he would wait; he would wait and see . . .

Alice and Anna were walking in Ginza toward Sukiya Bridge. They had gone to a theater in Asakusa to see a revue, and afterwards had taken the subway to the Mitsukoshi department store in Nihonbashi. But they had forgotten that the store was closed on Mondays, and so decided to walk to Ginza and do their shopping there instead. They still hadn't heard the news. It was a clear day, and they felt quite carefree as they strolled along in the winter sunlight. Alice was wearing a white fox coat. Anna was much less conspicuous, with a black coat over a dark blue kimono; the colors were so somber she might have been going to a funeral, and the sight of the two of them together drew more than a few stares.

Bells were ringing. A crowd had gathered, hovering near a newspaper stand. Alice, curious as to what the excitement was about, asked her daughter to buy a paper, but Anna was reluctant, not wanting to push her way through all those people. Alice, however, had no such qualms. Shouting "*Sumimasen! Sumimasen!*" she waded in. People, astonished to see this tall foreign woman in a white fur coat saying "Excuse me" loudly, stepped out of her way, and she soon returned with a newspaper.

Alice smiled and asked, "Well, what does it say, dear?"

Anna looked shocked and didn't answer.

Alice tapped her daughter on the shoulder. "What is it, Anna?"

"Mama, Japan has attacked America. It's war!"

"Oh!" Her body jerked back. She didn't understand. She had decided long ago that war just wasn't possible. She believed in Saburo. Saburo would take care of it. Saburo would surely make the negotiations work.

"Oh!" Alice said again. "What are we going to do?"

"Mama," Anna said gently, "let's go home." She noticed that the blood had drained from her mother's face; she looked as if she might faint. They ought to sit down, but there were no benches in sight and no cafés nearby. Anna steered her toward Yurakucho Station, but by now people were pouring out of the station, spilling from the sidewalks onto the street. There were excited cries, flags waving in people's hands. The crowds were surging toward the Imperial Palace.

"Mama! Are you all right?" Anna managed to squeeze her into the space between the pillars of a building. The two women caught their breath.

Suddenly a man in a tattered civil defense uniform approached them. He wore a white headband with blood-red characters on it saying "GIVE SEVEN LIVES FOR YOUR COUNTRY." He walked up to Alice and stared her in the face.

"Hey! You're an American, aren't you?"

Anna stepped between the man and her mother and said "No, she's not. This lady is German."

"Yeah? What's a German doing speaking English?"

"She's doing it because *I* don't speak German—which is nice of her."

The man grunted, and turned back to a gang of men with similar headbands. "Hey boys! She says she's German!"

The men stared at Alice. All at once they raised their right arms and cried "*HAIRU HITORAH!*"

6

It was June of the following year, 1942.

The sun set, and the river winds lost some of their heat. The passengers, liberated from their hot and stuffy cabins, came out on deck to get some of the breeze.

Unfortunately, the breeze was hardly cool at all. The heat of the summer city seemed to pour out onto the river, and the air was filled with the stench of rubber and exhaust fumes. People walked the narrow passageways, their sweaty faces brushing close to each other. There were people everywhere. The repatriation ship held a thousand Japanese, three times the normal number of passengers.

Avoiding those who recognized him as the Special Envoy and tried to talk to him, Saburo stood in one corner of the deck, gazing at the Manhattan skyline. Beneath the darkening evening sky rose the even darker skyscrapers. The city was under blackout orders, and there were no lights in any of the windows. A year and a half ago Saburo had arrived here from pitch-dark Europe and, seeing the brilliantly illuminated skyscrapers, had marveled at the sheer beauty of peace. And now this country too had sunk into the darkness of war. A war against his own mother country.

An enemy country. Yes, New York was now a metropolis in an enemy country. The city he'd been so enamored of in his youth, Alice's hometown, the place where he had been married—how far off it all seemed now. He and the others were prisoners. Enemy aliens confined in this ship.

The Coast Guard launches loudly blew their whistles as they sailed alongside. No other ships came near them. From the day the war began they had all been cut off from the outside world. The confinement had in fact protected them from harm from the local population. Saburo tried to repress the memories of the hatred he'd encountered on American faces these past six months. He winced, trying to think about something else. But still the memories floated there, unsinkable, deep inside him.

He had been detained, but still was allowed access to the radio and to newspapers, so he knew what the Americans were thinking, and he had a grasp of how the war was turning out. One day the newspaper carried a special section on Pearl Harbor. The article stated that Ambassador Kurushima had been sent to the United States under secret orders from Emperor Hirohito and Tojo to deceive the Americans while they planned the attack. The same newspaper carried a quote from Secretary of State Hull in which he said that of course Kurushima had come to buy time as his government made preparations for the sneak attack. Hull said that from the very first day of their negotiations he had seen through this man as a liar whose smile hid his true intentions. Saburo had been carrying on diplomatic talks with a man who, the whole time, assumed that his every word was false. Yet the truth of the matter was that no one—not the Prime Minister, nor the Foreign Minister—had told him a thing about any planned attack on Pearl Harbor, so if the object of his mission had been to disguise such an attack, he was one of the first victims of the exercise.

But the American people believed he was the key figure in the treachery. The newspapers and the radio repeated again and again that the great losses the United States suffered at Pearl Harbor were the result of the military's being lulled into a false sense of security by Japan's diplomatic efforts, which continued almost to the last minute before the attack. In his speech to Congress even the President had spoken of their having been tricked by Japan's deceitful diplomacy. It was the President himself who had as a result fixed in the minds of his people the image of Ambassador Kurushima as an evil and cunning man.

After a journey halfway around a world that was at war, docking at

Axis and neutral ports, the repatriation ship finally reached Singapore on the morning of August 9th. Awaiting them at the entrance to the harbor were thirty small boats, each flying a rising sun ensign. As they sailed in, whistles blew from all the ships, and people lined up on board waving at them. The docks, shadowless beneath the tropical sun, were also jammed with well-wishers. Prominent in the crowd were soldiers and reporters.

"You've finally reached Japan," said the young naval officer who greeted them at the top of the gangway. Turning to the crowd below on the dock, he suddenly shouted *"Banzai!"* and a thousand *"Banzais!"* echoed in response.

As Saburo disembarked, the young officer told him that Singapore had been renamed "Shonan," with the first character of Emperor Showa's name followed by the character for "south." "This is our new territory," he said proudly.

The military men there to welcome him were eager to show him the sites of recent battles. As they drove through the city the officers pointed out the skeletal remains of British aircraft and the forts that lay in ruins, and each time they passed the temporary graves of Japanese soldiers they bowed. Saburo was taken to see the Army commander and given a tour of the new naval base, but all the formal greetings and ceremonies made him ill at ease. Each time he was introduced as "the man who faced down Roosevelt and Hull, and bought time for our secret attack," he felt an inner pain that he couldn't admit to anyone. After the day's tour he shut himself up in his cabin, and did his best to avoid going out.

It was in his cabin that he received a sudden visit from his son-in-law, Yoshiaki Arizumi. Arizumi was dressed in a short-sleeved khaki shirt and Army shorts. His skin was deeply tanned, his head shaved, and he had grown a beard. But the way he moved his thin lips and shook his head as he spoke was the same as before.

"This must come as a surprise," he said. "I've been posted here in Shonan as a special correspondent since May. I wanted to see you, but you were surrounded by all those Army and Navy bigwigs and I couldn't get close." He told Saburo that Alice and the family were fine, and that Ken, having graduated from flying school, would soon be assigned to a technical division where he would be working on aircraft design.

"And how's Anna?"

"Oh, she's fine," he nodded, but a shadow crossed his face and he said, "You know, war is especially hard on women." Saburo was about to ask if they had any children yet but something about his silence held him back.

Switching the conversation from his wife and promptly assuming the tone of a newspaper reporter, Arizumi began to ask him questions about the recent negotiations. Since Saburo had expected to answer questions of this sort at a news conference after his return, this abrupt turn in the conversation annoyed him. But he couldn't just ignore him, so he kept his answers as brief as possible.

"What was Hull's expresssion when he handed you that note on November 26th?"

". . . Hmm. I'd call it dissatisfied."

"What about on December 8th—the seventh over there?"

"Well, he looked angry."

"Angry? . . . Didn't he seem astonished or shocked?"

"No . . . just angry."

"What are your present feelings about the negotiations?"

". . . I wasn't up to the task. My mission was a failure. I feel unhappy about it." He hung his head.

"Oh, but you're wrong there, Father. You carried out your task magnificently. It was the American side that provoked the conflict— without a doubt. Japan endured all their unreasonable demands and only acted as a last resort. The result was that you, sir, prevented them from anticipating the attack. You were absolutely splendid."

"Wait a minute! I didn't have the slightest intention of concealing any secret military plans when I set out for Washington."

"But the *result* is that you did. We're well on the way to winning the war now, and your work, Father, helped provide the thrust for victory. Your diplomatic success has made you a hero of the Empire!"

"Stop it, will you!" Saburo shouted. "I don't want to talk about it any more."

"Why not?" Arizumi put down his pencil, looking puzzled.

"I'm a diplomat who botched his mission. I failed." Saburo felt a black rage in his belly. He managed to repress it, and sighed instead. "Don't you understand? For me to admit my failure is the very *least* I can do now."

"Ah, but the public doesn't see it that way. For them, Ambassador Kurushima is a national hero on a par with Admiral Yamamoto, who planned the attack."

Arizumi wouldn't leave, and continued with his questions. Saburo, wiping the sweat from his face, felt too weak to be able to get rid of him. The sight of the blinding tropical landscape outside the porthole made his head spin.

Early on the morning of August 20th Saburo returned to the house in Nagata-cho. The family was waiting for him at the entrance. Alice ran to embrace him, and he warmly greeted his children and Yoshiko the maid. He was home. And for the first time in almost a year he felt human again. To his eyes, which had become accustomed to American dimensions, the house seemed rather meager: the ceilings were low, the rooms were small, the windows let in too little light. But the cypress pillars and the paper screens with the garden beyond brought comfort to his eyes, and when he stepped over the slatted wooden floor in the bathroom and allowed his body to sink into the overflowing water of the wooden tub, the sheer warmth of it made him feel he had indeed come back to his own land. Everything—the smell of the tub, the green branches of the trees trimmed with such precision by the gardener, the rasping of the cicadas, the clear water that soaked him to the core—brought back the reality of his own country. And the most joyous thing of all was the sense of the season's subtle changing, the red dragonflies that seemed to flit about in rhythm with the cicadas, the shadows of autumn that he could see gathering over the new ears of pampas grass.

He changed into a yukata, thinking how natural this informal summer kimono felt, and made his way to the dining room. There the entire family was waiting for him. At the center of the dining table, resting on a scarlet cloth, was a black-lacquered layered box and a bottle of *sake*. When he noticed the golden chrysanthemum seal glittering on the box, Saburo was startled, and stood as if at attention.

"It's a gift of food and *sake* from the Emperor," Ken explained. "Yesterday a courier came from the Palace. He said it's in appreciation of your 'special service to the country.'"

"I'm overwhelmed. But how can I do it justice dressed like this? . . ." He glanced at the sleeves of his yukata.

"Are you going to put on your morning suit, sir?" Ken asked mischievously.

Everyone was dressed casually, in short sleeves. It was hot and humid. No wind came through the window.

"It's all right, Saburo. It may be a gift from the Emperor, but Eri couldn't resist taking a snack from it last night." Alice was teasing, too.

"No! I just took a little bite," Eri protested.

"It wasn't so little," said Ken. "She helped herself to a big spoonful of the chestnut dessert, three pieces of the bamboo shoots, a whole sweetfish, and even some of the ceremonial red rice."

"Eri, how could you!" Her mother glared at her. "The Emperor will be mad at you!"

"Well, I was hungry."

"All right, all right!" Saburo laughed, and took his seat.

Alice distributed portions of the food onto everyone's plates. Yoshiko, of course, got her share, too. Shortly after the war broke out their cook Tanaka had been drafted; he was now in the Philippines. Their younger maid Asa had returned to her home in Chiba to help her mother after her father and older brother joined the Army. So Yoshiko was left to take care of the house by herself, with Alice helping with the cooking and cleaning. As Alice related all this to Saburo her joy at his return was obvious from her bright tone of voice.

She seemed to have lost some weight. She had more wrinkles than before, and there was some gray in her hair now. Since there was no

postal service any longer between Japan and the United States, and
international telephone calls were out, the only communication between them had been a brief message she asked the Foreign Ministry
to convey just before the war broke out, telling him that everyone was
all right.

"It must have been hard for you," Saburo said to her.

"No, no," she replied. *"You're* the one who had a bad time, living
like a prisoner all those months."

"But I was in American hands. Even though we were enemy aliens
they treated us courteously. I was in a first-class hotel while I waited
for the repatriation ship."

When Ken thanked him for the presents he'd brought with him, all
the others began expressing their thanks at once.

"Actually, I'd thought buying any presents would be impossible,
but it turned out there were shops right next to the hotel, and I was
allowed to get a few things. That radio's really something, isn't it?
Japan couldn't make anything that intricate yet."

"And that automatic phonograph you brought us last year is terrific,
too," said Anna.

"Eri's monopolized it. She won't let us near it," said Ken.

"That's not true! Everybody plays it."

"I was looking for it everywhere yesterday, and sure enough it was
in your room."

"I just borrowed it for a bit."

"Your 'bit' is all year."

"By the way," said Saburo, slapping his knee as if he'd just remembered something. "While I was in Washington, Norman, George, and
Lauren came to see me."

Since this was a matter of great interest to the family, he recounted
his reunion with the Littles in detail. There were sighs of admiration
when they heard that Lauren had started learning Japanese. Then
Saburo remembered the gifts he'd received from Norman. These had
arrived separately in a package from the ship, which he now proceeded to open. There was a pair of lace gloves for Alice, dolls for
Anna and Eri, and a wooden toy for Ken.

As he handed Ken the little flying horse he asked him: "Do you recognize it?"

"Wait a minute. This is . . ."

"Alice? Anna? Do you remember this?"

"It's an antique. A long time ago children in America used to play with this kind of thing." Alice poked at it with her finger. The horse's wings began to move in a see-saw motion.

"Ah!" Ken and Anna cried at once. "This was my toy when I was a kid!" "That's right. It was a Christmas present from Aunt Aileen."

"I'm amazed you remember," said Saburo.

Alice's face brightened. "I remember it too! Ken used to love this toy. Why did we ever leave it when we moved?"

Ken turned the Pegasus over and held its wings in his fingers. Placing it on the table, he set it in motion. With his chin on his hands he gazed at the little horse flapping its wings, his expression the same as when he'd been a boy. His parents looked at each other.

"Ken loved this toy," said Anna. "He wouldn't let anyone else touch it. He used to get mad if I tried to play with it. The only one allowed to touch it was Lauren. I used to get so jealous."

"Oh, so even back then Lauren was special." Eri nodded, as if deeply impressed.

"What do you mean!" Ken glared at her.

Ignoring the look, Eri went on, "But if George is now a pilot, does it mean he'll have to fight Ken?"

They were all disconcerted by the question. In the past the possibility that Ken and George might fight as enemies had been talked about, but it had seemed a harmless fantasy. Now it had turned into a very real possibility, something that might actually take place in the not so distant future. Saburo was appalled at the very idea of two cousins who had been as close as twins trying to murder each other in the sky. There was a cross, brooding look on his face.

Eri was shocked at the sudden silence around her. In a tearful voice she asked, "What's wrong? Why did you all stop talking?"

Ken managed to assume a cheerful expresssion as he broke the silence. "We're at war. It can't be helped. If George comes flying in I'll just have to shoot him down. Papa, did you know that American planes bombed Tokyo this spring?"

"Oh, yes, Captain Doolittle's raid. I read about it. There were banner headlines in the American newspapers." Saburo had switched from English to Japanese. "It seems we couldn't down a single one of them."

"That's right. Most of our advanced planes, the Hayabusas and the Shokis, had gone to the South Pacific, and the older 97s we sent up were no match for their B-25s."

"I read that they put the B-25s on an aircraft carrier, which got to within 1,200 kilometers of Tokyo, then after the raid the planes landed at a base in China."

"Yes. It was a pretty daring plan. But I figure the Navy is now carefully monitoring the seas to make sure it won't happen again, so another raid like that isn't likely."

"But what about the Battle of Midway?"

"Oh, that was a big victory for us."

"Really? . . ." The American newspapers had reported that the Japanese had lost four aircraft carriers at Midway while they lost only one. The fact that Ken believed it was a victory suggested that the authorities had lied about the results. Deciding to check on the matter later, Saburo changed the subject. "I understand you'll be joining a research division this fall, working on designing new planes."

"How did you know that, Papa?"

His father turned to Anna. "I met young Arizumi in Singapore, I mean in Shonan. Busy with his reporting, as usual."

"Oh? . . ." Anna looked down.

"Asked me some thoroughly improper questions. He suggested that I conducted the talks knowing that Pearl Harbor was going to be attacked. I had to tell him off."

Anna raised her head. "Did you have a fight?"

"It wasn't really a fight, I just told him not to make any stupid insinuations. Look, I didn't know a thing about Pearl Harbor. I would never accept a mission whose only goal was to deceive the other side."

Alice couldn't follow their conversation in Japanese. "What are you talking about?"

"I'm sorry." He switched back to English. "I was telling them about meeting Arizumi in Singapore."

"Anna and Arizumi are no longer together," she explained matter-of-factly. "They've been divorced."

"What!" He was astonished. "Why?"

"I wanted to tell you the details later. In the end their personalities just weren't compatible."

"But Arizumi didn't even mention it."

"He probably didn't think he had to. That's the kind of man he is. Or maybe he thought that concealing the fact would get him a better story."

"I see . . ." He remembered Arizumi calling him "Father" with those thin lips of his curling as he spoke. For some time he had been aware of trouble between Anna and him, and he had certainly noticed his daughter's gloomy silences. But the divorce still took him by surprise. Divorce was a serious business.

"When did it happen?"

"This spring," Anna said in a listless voice, "just before he left for Shonan. I'll tell you all about it later."

Suddenly her mother clapped her hands. "Sa-bu-ro," she said cheerfully, "did you remember the vacuum cleaner?"

"Oh!" he said, pressing his hand to his chest. "You mean the handle? Of course I did."

"So you didn't forget."

Since everyone wanted to see it right away, Saburo went and got it from the trunk. When Alice attached the new handle to the old cleaner, it fitted perfectly.

The entire family burst into applause, for Saburo and for GE.

IV

THE HAYATE

1

He could see across the runway to the mulberry fields that spread beyond it. In front of the hangars were assembled various airplanes old and new; the scene resembled an aircraft museum. Along with the well-established and battle-proven Ki-43 (known as the Hayabusa) and Ki-44 (the Shoki) were the water-cooled, single-seat fighters still undergoing inspection: the Ki-61 and three of the experimental Ki-84s recently acquired from Nakajima Aircraft. Standing by the three experimental planes was the maintenance crew, listening to instructions from the new chief maintenance officer, Major Nakada.

First Lieutenant Ken Kurushima peered over the edge of his newspaper at the cowling of the Ki-84, which brightly reflected the sun. He had been meaning to read the news about the death of Admiral Yamamoto, his final promotion and state funeral, but his attention had drifted. Lighting a Golden Pheasant cigarette with his Dunhill, he gazed at the flowing lines of the brand-new duraluminum frame. "Nice shape," he said to himself as he slowly blew out the smoke.

He had already heard rumors that this new fighter was under development when, last year, in the fall of 1942, he was posted here to the Aircraft Inspection Department at Fussa. Each time Major Iwama, head of the fighter inspection section, went to check up on the new plane under manufacture at the factory, he would return with glowing reports about it. Iwama was responsible not only for basic design decisions but negotiations with the design team at Nakajima Aircraft, discussions about the manufacturing process, and getting approval at each step from the top brass. And his obsession with the Ki-84 had spread to all the members of his team including Ken and his fellow technical officers Sugi, whose background was in mechanical engineering, and Yamada, who had studied aviation medicine.

Iwama, opening a thick binder of blueprints for the new plane, had turned to Ken and the others one day and said, "Unlike you technical people, I've been a fighter pilot from the word go. I've seen so much combat I can't count the missions I've flown—in China and the South Pacific. And, boys, what I learned in all those shows is that, for a fighter plane, combat performance is everything. In Manchuria the maneuverability of our 97s overwhelmed the Soviet E-16s. Our 97s moved so lightly, twisting this way and that, we blew those highly touted E-16s out of the sky. And when this Pacific War began, the enemy's Hurricanes, Buffaloes, Republic P-43s, and Curtiss P-40s were no match for our Army Hayabusas and our Navy Zeros. From all this experience, I decided the key to victory lay in combat performance and maneuverability, and that was my philosophy when I started working here. But . . ." The Major stopped. There was a twisted smile on his face. "I was wrong. And it was the technical folks who taught me that. I realized that it was speed that would decide the day from here on out. The Germans had their high-speed fighters, the Me-109 and the He-110, and the enemy was coming out with one high-performance fighter after another, like the Grumman F-6-F Hellcat and the P-51 Mustang. This was bad news for us. But that's when I heard about the Ki-84. And let me tell you, this is it. This is the fighter we've been waiting for."

It had been only a month since the prototype of the Ki-84 had taken its maiden flight, and they were now being told to speed up testing. Their boss had asked for one hundred of these experimental aircraft to be made ready for combat, giving them six months at most to complete the trials.

As he sat in the cockpit, Ken strained to hear the instructions Major Iwama was barking at him from where he stood on the wing.

"Once again, Lieutenant, when you get up to 7,000 meters, make a quick and sudden descent. When you reach 4,000 meters, your speed will be around 700 kph. You sit there and wait. When you're down to

3,000 meters, come back slowly. If there's any flutter, immediately flatten out. Got it?"

"Yes, sir."

"One other thing. The flaps. Especially at high speed they might not work right. Be careful."

"Yes, sir."

"Okay, you're off."

Iwama jumped down from the wing. Ken opened the throttle. The engine sounded good. He waved his hand left and right. The maintenance crew removed the chocks. As he was about to close the canopy, one of the soldiers guarding the plane signaled to him. There was a fat man in white medical garb running out from the hangar. It was Yamada. He was carrying something. Stumbling into the propeller's draft, he grabbed the wing but was unable to climb up. The soldier pushed him from behind, and he finally clambered onto the wing.

"Here, take this with you."

"What the hell is it?"

"It's a rabbit. I want to do a G-force test on it."

"Where am I supposed to put it?"

"I thought about that. Move forward a bit," he said, as he placed the rabbit cage in a cranny under the bulletproof plate behind the pilot's seat, and fastened it with wire.

"You could have told me a little sooner," said Ken, aware that Iwama was watching them.

"I didn't get it ready in time. I came up with a device to monitor the rabbit's pulse and breathing, but I had to rig up the batteries in a hurry. It's not going to interfere with your flying, is it?"

"Of course it is. But I can put up with it."

"The rabbit's name is Lauren, same as that foreign girl you once told me about. I'm sure the two of you'll get along."

Yamada jumped down, and Ken pulled the canopy shut. Yamada, Sugi, and one of the technicians called Aoyagi were watching as he taxied to the edge of the airfield. Once more he checked his instruments—compass, altimeter, tachometer . . . There were about twenty gauges, along with more than forty levers and switches. All in order. He pressed on the brake and opened the throttle to full power. Two thousand horsepower. The dust was swirling outside. He began his run. Takeoff.

Ken savored the sense of liberation he always felt at the moment he left the earth. He rose up and up. The plane climbed beautifully. The blue sky filled the windshield, and the few clouds offered no resistance. His eardrums began to swell, and he swallowed hard. The temperature had fallen. He touched the air duct directly in front of the pilot's seat—the outside air was icy. There were no more clouds now, and the sun shone naked on the wings. The sound of the engine was sucked into the emptiness around him. His altimeter was above 5,000 now. It was hard to breathe. His head began to ache slightly and he put on the oxygen mask. There was nothing, no one, around—utter emptiness. 6,000, 6,500, 7,000. *Okay, flatten out, increase speed. Then, push hard on the stick and head down!* He could see the ground, the airfield, way below him. Just then he remembered the rabbit and shouted in English, "Lauren, we're going down!" Gravity disappeared and his body seemed to float. He kept his eyes fixed on the air-speed indicator. 400 kph, 500, 550, 600. The airfield spread out huge below him. The fuselage was wrapped in the roar of the wind. The control stick shook furiously. Would this throw him off? At full throttle now. 650, 655, 660. But the gauge wouldn't budge beyond that. 4,000 meters, 3,500. His ears hurt. Suddenly it was warm. He was sweating. 660 kph . . . 3,200, 3,000. Time to get back. But the stick wouldn't move. He pulled with all his might. Finally, movement. He was pushed back hard in his seat. G had hit him. All around it was suddenly dark. Sky and ground had turned to night, with a single round spot of brightness, like peering through a narrow pipe. Within that pinhole he could make out the horizon. He seemed to have leveled out. His altimeter showed 50. 50? *Must be a mistake, surely it's 500.* But no, right below him were pine forests, farmhouses. A hill coming at him. He shifted the controls, and there it was—the airfield, flooded with sunlight.

After landing and taxiing to the maintenance hangar, he saw the

Major running over. "What happened, Kurushima? Did you black out?"

Ken shut down the engine and climbed out. The parachute was heavy on his back, his footing uncertain.

"I'm sorry, sir. I couldn't get 700 kph out of it."

"How much speed did you get?"

"660."

"You did? Well, that's something."

"There was no flutter."

"Okay. What did you do at the start of your descent?"

"Level out, then dive, sir."

"That's what was wrong—that's why you didn't get 700. First you turn, or else you lose some initial speed. Then you descend at full throttle."

"Yes, sir."

"Well, we'll overlook it this time."

"Let me take it up again, sir. I'm sure I can make it to 700."

"You don't want to overdo it today. We've got to check the plane anyway."

Yamada was standing on the wing with the cage in his hand, giving the rabbit a "physiological checkup." "Hey, Lauren, you made it!" he shouted. "You shat all over the place, but you lived through the trip, and all the electrical connections are still in place."

Iwama was told by maintenance that the plane only needed a quick once-over before being ready to fly again. He had somebody wipe the oil stains off the exhaust ports, then clambered up and peered at the engine himself.

"All right, Kurushima. Let's try it again. But no fuckups this time. You're flying valuable property."

"Yes, sir, don't worry." Ken was aware of the excitement in his own voice.

Yamada tied the rabbit cage on board. "Okay, Lauren, here you go again. Be nice to your boyfriend and don't shit so much."

In six minutes Ken was up to 5,000 meters. When he got to 7,000, he went into a large turn so as not to lose speed. In the thin air a perfect turn was impossible. Just as Iwama had warned him, you got blown about at that altitude. The glare of the sun sank below him, the flat ground tilted up overhead. Now upside down, he started his descent. He kept his eyes fixed on the instruments. His eardrums were bursting, his head throbbed, but he paid no attention to the pain. At 5,000 meters he passed 670 kph. Then 680. *I want more.* 690 . . . then, finally, 700, 705. He'd made it! At that point the control stick began to move violently on its own. Vibrations shook the plane. It felt as if all the instruments would fly off the panel, the levers and pedals disintegrate. With all his strength he held on to the control stick. Altitude 3,000. *It's going to be okay.* He tried to slowly raise the nose, but the shaking was worse than before. His body felt as though it was being crushed; his vision darkened to a tiny point of light again. *If this light goes out, I'll faint.* He stared desperately at it. All the blood in his body was rushing to his feet like mercury. The vibrations eased. The light grew wider. He was still in one piece. Before he realized it he was down to 1,000 meters. He could make out the airfield, smiling up at him.

But when he turned for his final approach he found he was still in trouble. The plane wouldn't stay level. Suddenly the nose dropped. He brought it up, only to have it tilt further up again. There was something wrong with the rudder. Somehow he managed to keep the plane flying, and decided to try for a landing. Countering the constant pitching movement, he headed in. He lowered the wheels. He could see the runway. *Flaps down and reduce speed.* But the flaps wouldn't budge. Furiously he worked the control stick. There was a fierce jolt as he touched down. Had the propeller hit the ground? No, it was all right, it was only his rear wheel.

Major Iwama, with the maintenance chief, Nakada, and Aoyagi the technician, came running over.

"What happened?" asked Iwama, a tremor in his voice.

"Sir, the rudder wouldn't work. And the flaps wouldn't go down."

"How about the speed?"

"I got it up to 705. But flutter began right after that."

"So there was flutter." Iwama turned to Aoyagi, who began checking the rudder, while the crew and Major Nakada took a look at the flaps.

"Part of the rudder's fallen off," Aoyagi reported.

"So the flutter was that bad? He could have crashed. How are the flaps?"

"On the surface they look okay," Nakada answered.

"I had trouble getting the flaps down when I tried it out myself," Iwama said. "That time the problem was oil pressure. But we solved that problem before today's flight."

"Kurushima," Nakada shouted, "try getting those flaps out again."

"Sir, the lever won't move."

"Then we'll have to take it apart. Looks like a mechanical fault."

At a command from Nakada the crew quickly set to work. After a couple of hours it was established that flutter had caused a rupture in the oil pressure cylinder and oil had leaked. But they couldn't figure out why the flutter started when the plane reached a speed of 700 kph.

The Ki-84 was fitted with a lightweight, high-performance engine developed by the technical team at Nakajima Aircraft. This had enabled them to keep the fuselage narrow and streamlined, but the complexity of the engine had led to continual problems. First, the drive shaft, which transmitted power to the propeller, tended to wear out the bearings. Also, the plugs had to be replaced every ten hours or so, and since there were a total of thirty-six plugs for the eighteen cylinders, this was time-consuming. Even one overlooked plug meant that the engine wouldn't start. And then there was the insulating rubber between the tightly packed cylinders. The rubber was of inferior quality, burning easily when overheated, and so had to be constantly replaced.

Major Nakada and his team had struggled to keep these problems under control. Whenever there was a test flight, they would be up before dawn working. Any major malfunction would keep them up all night. But all their careful effort and attention to detail couldn't keep the flutter from occurring. Nor did an afternoon meeting to analyze Ken's test flight produce any conclusion. Was it unusual air turbulence? Instability in the propeller rotations?

Several days later the same phenomenon occurred. A Ki-84 with 20-mm. machine guns in the wings was chasing an old Hayabusa piloted by Lieutenant Sugi over the sea. Flutter started as the guns were being fired during a rapid descent. The vibrations affected the pilot's aim, and he accidentally fired a burst into the fuselage of the Hayabusa. Fortunately nobody was hurt, and Sugi managed to land safely, but the episode served to confirm that this experimental plane would be dangerous in actual combat.

Discussions were held between the Inspection Department and Nakajima Aircraft, and together they were able to ascertain that the problem lay with a part of the propeller known as the governor. This device, operating through a direct-current motor in the shaft of the propeller, adjusted the pitch of the propeller's four blades. Under certain flight conditions, a malfunction in the governor was causing unsynchronized rotations—the "hunting" that shook the aircraft from nose to tail. Ken had a hunch that it was something very simple—a faulty electrical connection, perhaps—that was to blame, but it wasn't until he shared this hunch with the technical whiz, Aoyagi, that the exact problem was isolated. Some days afterwards, Ken had a call asking him to go to the hangar. There he found Aoyagi in grimy overalls standing by a disassembled, oil-smeared propeller shaft.

"Take a look at this. It's a connection in the governor; the current isn't strong enough, so the motor that trims the pitch isn't coming on in time. When we change the connection, I guarantee you won't see any more flutter. You were right—it's so simple it's almost stupid."

The adjustment worked, and from then on things moved fast. At the end of December, a new 22nd Air Squadron using the Ki-84 was formed. Major Iwama was appointed Squadron Leader, with Lieutenants Sugi and Hanazono among the pilots. Lieutenants Kurushima, Haniyu, and Yamada were chosen for the final inspection team of the remodeled 84; their team leader would be a Major Wakana, a graduate of Tokyo Imperial University.

Cold weather and rough combat practice combined to create new problems—ignition failure, fuel leaks, unretracted landing gear, canopies refusing to close—but by spring in the following year, 1944, the Ki-84 was officially commissioned for combat and given the name Hayate—"Swift Wind"—and the 22nd Squadron moved to another airfield, at Nakatsu.

2

There was a small wood Ken sometimes used to go to during his lunch breaks and on Sundays; it was a ten-minute walk from the rear gate of the Inspection Department. The ground formed a gentle slope. As one climbed, the runways and buildings of the air base passed from sight and in their place appeared a view of rice fields and straw-thatched huts. Where the wood ended was a twisting stream, over which lay a half-rotted log bridge. The sun-dappled water and the murmuring of the stream were soothing, and Ken would often lie down there.

From autumn through the winter he had been too busy to come, but now that the Ki-84 had been officially designated for production, and the scent of spring was in the air, he had suddenly decided to make his way here again during one afternoon break. Thinking that he might even do some bird hunting, he had brought his air gun with him.

Because there was more than one top-secret military aircraft at the Inspection Department, the area was under heavy surveillance. Several guards patrolled the barbed wire that formed the perimeter; there were even guards who slept in the surrounding farmhouses. Almost every day some child would be scolded for trying to draw pictures of the airfield, or someone who had lost his way and wandered in would be taken away for interrogation. Ken always wore his uniform when he went out, but even then, with his foreign face, he had once been followed by a member of the local Military Police and had been stopped just at he entered the wood.

Today, however, there were no inquisitive policemen about, and Ken felt good as he walked through the fields, heading for the grove of trees. Soft buds had formed on the mulberry branches, and there was the smell of blossom in the warm wind. By the farmhouses the ground was covered with cherry petals, and the azaleas were in full bloom, their red and white flowers massed together.

Ken stepped over the brambles on his way to his old spot by the stream, where he lay down on a bed of dry leaves. The wind came through the branches of the trees, swaying first one branch then another, the sound merging with the cries of birds and the murmur of the water. Ken closed his eyes and tilted his cap to shade his face from the sun. His everyday life—of oil and engines and mechanical noise—faded away like a distant dream. Even the war seemed like a dream. And yet a sense of unease remained in his chest.

The war. Japan was smack in the middle of it. And there was no way he could escape it.

The enemy's massive counterattack had begun. Japan's line of defense was being pushed back day by day. Last April, after the death of Admiral Yamamoto, the garrisons on Attu Island had committed mass suicide. The Army had lost New Guinea, then Guadalcanal, and after defeats on Makin and Tarawa, it was clear that the Marianas would fall next. The enemy wanted airfields, airfields from which to attack Japan.

The Allies' great advantage was their control of the skies. Dogfighters like the Zero and the Hayabusa were shot down one after another by the Grumman F-6-F and the P-51 Mustang, with their high-speed and high-altitude capacities. The long-distance bombers—the B-24 and now the B-29, sighted recently over China—were making Japan's military inferiority all too clear. Japan had developed the Hayate at last, but its production wasn't going well at all. And it wasn't enough to bridge the gap. Some day probably not too far away, this peaceful countryside would also become a battlefield. They were developing aircraft here, so it was a sure thing the enemy would target the area. *And I too will have to fight. At twenty-five . . .*

The character for "death" flitted across his mind like a ragged bird. Ken jerked upright, so that his cap fell off, and the sunlight struck at his eyes. He felt hungry. Even though he had just eaten lunch, he still felt hungry. The Inspection Department was often visited by planes from China and the South Pacific, which brought them more sugar and rice and barley than other units, but even so their rations had decreased recently. Their usual fare now was potatoes, rice mixed with bits of squash, and half a dried fish. Beef and pork they had once a week, if at all. There were times when he had to shoot birds to get enough to eat.

It had been over two and a half years ago, just before the Pacific War began, that he'd last been bird hunting in Karuizawa. This spring the Kurushima family had moved from Tokyo to Karuizawa for safety. His mother and sisters were all there now; only his father, with his occasional work for the Foreign Ministry, commuted between the Tokyo house and the country villa.

The shadow of a real bird flew past him. Ken raised his rifle and fired. It was a casual, reflexive gesture, but his aim was good. Several more small birds were added to it later, as well as one larger bird, a pheasant of some kind, plump and meaty.

He gutted them, tied them roughly to his waist, and set off through the shade of the wood again. At the foot of a downward slope he found a pond with a little waterfall leading down to a brook. He peered into the pond. His military cap swayed about as fragments of his face came together to form an image. No wonder that military policeman had got suspicious: it was a very foreign face. He raised his gun and shot at his own reflection. The face shattered.

In the shade of a hangar Ken skinned the birds. As he was pushing the feathers into a bag for disposal, he heard the roar of an engine, but from an aircraft he didn't know, even though he thought he knew them all. It was a clear, metallic sound, peculiar to water-cooled engines, but it was sharper than that of the Hien. He looked up as a black point in the sky grew larger. Its shape became apparent, then unmistakable—a P-51 Mustang.

"Enemy attack!" he yelled.

He tossed the birds aside and ran toward headquarters, only to encounter men running out, making for the runway. Yamada, his fat body lurching from side to side, came with his puppy Momotaro, dressed in a sweater, chasing after him. Also among them were Major

Wakana, Warrant Officer Mitsuda, Ken's friend Haniyu, and their boss, Colonel Imamura.

"That's a Mustang," Ken said to Mitsuda.

"Yes. We captured it in China." Mitsuda was small and stocky, the son of a fisherman. Five years older than Ken, he had worked his way up from private.

"Ah. Now this is interesting." Ken pounded his fists together in excitement.

The Mustang landed, kicking up dust on the runway. It was painted green, with a shark's-teeth design under its nose.

"How crude—just what you'd expect of the Yankees," said Haniyu of the paintwork.

"But it's the mark of the Flying Tigers, based in China."

"You were in China, weren't you, Mitsuda?"

"Yes, but this is the first time I've seen a Mustang."

The plane came to a halt in front of them. The bulbous canopy opened and Major Kurokawa from the 22nd Squadron emerged, jumping to the ground. He saluted Colonel Imamura, then nodded to the rest of them. Three days earlier Kurokawa had set out for China on a mission to ferry some redesigned Hiens to the front.

"That was a quick trip," said Imamura.

"Yes, sir. The others are scheduled to come back in transport planes, but they just happened to bag this Mustang, so I thought I'd ride it back. They only had time to paint the rising sun over the American stars, and when I stopped for refueling at one of our bases they loosed off a few rounds at me."

"No test flight—just straight off?" said Mitsuda.

"It was no sweat. The Americans build planes that even an idiot could fly. You could take this thing straight into combat."

"Really?" Mitsuda stroked the fuselage of the unfamiliar aircraft. "Hey, there's something written on it."

"Alina," Ken read aloud. "It's a girl's name."

"Must have been the guy's sweetheart."

Ken walked to the front of the plane. Its wings were similar to the Hayate's, but significantly larger in both length and breadth. To turn a propeller like this, you needed a powerful engine. The jutting nose of the propeller gave the plane an aggressive look, and the overall impression was of great confidence. Ken followed Haniyu and Mitsuda up onto the wing for a look at the cockpit, but was called back by Major Wakana below.

Wakana, his new commanding officer, was a nervous, demanding man with a high-pitched voice. Members of the Inspection Department were under constant pressure to fulfill several orders simultaneously, but Wakana always insisted that his commands take first priority.

"Kurushima, do you notice anything about this?" He had removed the cover on the exhaust port and was peering inside.

"Well, it's a water-cooled engine, six cylinders on each side."

"Yes, but do you notice anything unusual?"

Ken examined each part of the engine carefully. "It's obviously very well constructed."

"No! Look at this." Wakana, frowning, pointed at the exhaust port. "There's absolutely no oil leakage. You can't tell it was flown here all the way from China."

Oil leaks were one of the biggest defects of Japanese planes. The fuel itself was of low quality, but even with the new Hayate, the ports were black after every flight.

"What model is this Mustang?" Wakana asked.

"Do they have different models?"

"Of course they do. You're technical officers, aren't you? Didn't they teach you that at flying school? Lieutenant Haniyu, what model is this?"

"I don't know, sir." Haniyu nervously shifted away from his staring eyes.

Wakana had his group gather around him and, nodding to emphasize almost every word, told them: "The boss's orders are to make a thorough investigation of this plane. For those not familiar with the Mustang: it's a new version of the fighter made by North American which has already seen action in Europe. The earliest version, Model A, used an Allison engine, but Model B had a Rolls-Royce. Now what we have here is Model D, with its canopy redesigned in the shape of an air bubble."

Mitsuda, impressed, couldn't help asking where all this information came from.

"A German submarine," he was told. "It docked at Yokosuka recently. It had data on the Mustangs used in the European theater."

"I see, I see," Mitsuda said. "So this is the P-51-D."

Ken was then told to get into the cockpit and describe what he found. "Steel bulletproof plates behind the seat, thirty millimeters thick," he reported in a loud voice.

"Those Yankees sure hate to die," said Mitsuda. "As soon as they're in danger, they bail out!"

"The perspex is solid. Maybe twenty millimeters thick."

Ken shut the canopy. Suddenly he couldn't hear anything—it was amazing—and he could see everything around him with no distortion. It was clearer than the view from Japanese fighters, whose canopies were an assembly of flat glass.

He pushed it open and reported, "The visibility is excellent."

"Start the engine," Wakana ordered.

The crew brought up an ignition vehicle to the front of the plane.

"Lieutenant, we can't find the switch."

Ken looked at the words on the various dials: AIR SPEED, ALTIMETER, OIL PRESS., OIL TEMP., EX. TEMP., GYROSCOPE . . . STARTER. Before he pressed the STARTER switch, he yelled, "Get back, this might be automatic."

He closed the throttle and hit the switch. There was a light response, then the engine roared into life. Japan had nothing as advanced as this: to start the engine involved either using a mechanical starter, where a rotator shaft was attached to a groove in the front part of the propeller, or having someone turn the propeller by hand. The 22nd Squadron, which used the Hayate, encountered ignition difficulties daily. The head of the crew would signal with hand-held flags as three men, one in the cockpit and two by the propeller, went through their routine. Compared to that, this automatic starter was simplicity itself.

Major Wakana climbed up. "Pretty impressive. How's the other equipment?"

"Everything's automatic."

"Then they've beaten us. We've lost."

Ken looked at him in astonishment. No Japanese soldier ever said that sort of thing. But he went on: "The cockpit seems to be pressurized. I couldn't hear any outside sounds at all. Let me just look for a pressure switch."

He closed the canopy. Even the engine vibrations seemed muffled, it was so quiet. As he was searching the controls, he happened to find the radio switch and turned it on. There was a burst of Glenn Miller; a little static, but he could clearly hear the music, along with a woman's voice, perhaps a broadcast from Hawaii. He remembered a dance party in Chicago where he'd jitterbugged with Lauren. George was there, along with Uncle Norman and Aunt Aileen. He'd been completely American then, while it lasted. Long ago. An eon ago.

Wakana was tapping on the glass. "Are you all right?"

Ken was about to answer in English, but caught himself in time and switched the radio off.

Next to Wakana was Major Kurokawa, still wearing his flying helmet. "Look, there's the pressure switch. Over there—no, there. And another switch, to turn on the oxygen. Talk about luxury! I tried taking it up to 10,000 meters—no problem at all."

"Did the supercharger work all right?" asked Wakana.

"Perfectly. It even responds automatically to the air pressure."

"Automatic, automatic. Everything's automatic!" they heard Mitsuda say.

"That's right," said Kurokawa with a loud laugh. "It's so simple even *you* could fly it."

Major Wakana decided that Ken should give the Mustang a performance test. Since it would take several hours for the maintenance crew to get the plane ready, Ken returned to the hangar where he'd been plucking the birds. But when he got there he found the bag had been ripped open and feathers scattered all over the ground. The birds themselves were gone, with the exception of the pheasant, lying out on the grass with its head torn off. Ken wondered what on earth had done it. A stray dog?

To kill time, he decided to give Yamada at the Aviation Medicine Institute a visit. The wooden two-story building was, on the outside, no different from headquarters, but inside was the usual jumble of machines and instruments lying in the corridors and in the various rooms. No one seemed to be around, and Ken walked on down the corridor until he reached the animal huts at the back. In cages were rabbits, hamsters, and dogs, with tags indicating the date and type of various experiments. A puppy came sniffing at him. It was Momotaro. Yamada was squatting by a sink, in a cloud of steam and yapping puppies.

"What are you doing?"

"As you can see, I'm giving the kids a bath."

From a clump of soap bubbles, young Hanako emerged, looking quite happy. He poured a can of water over it, then shook the little gray animal dry. Water splashed right in Yamada's face, but he barely noticed. He too seemed happy.

Next it was Kintaro's turn, who had been yelping all this time. The puppy tried to run away, but Yamada grabbed it and dunked its skinny, brown-spotted body in the bubbles.

"I had some birds I shot stolen by a stray dog."

"A stray dog?" Yamada took Kintaro out. "There aren't any around here."

"Really?"

"If there were I would have found them and brought them in. These guys were originally wild. In fact all the dogs in the cages were strays when I caught them."

"If it wasn't a dog, then what was it?"

"Maybe a cat." He dunked Kintaro in the sink again, then let it loose. Ken gave him a hand as he struggled to stand up. "These days I've put on so much weight that when I bend down my waist gives up on me and I have a hard time getting up. God, I've gotten heavy."

Yamada shook his huge bottom and put on his white doctor's coat.

The sleeves were yellowed from animal droppings, and all the buttons were gone. The filthy uniform flapped as he walked, making him look like a tramp. There was an open space outside where they found a dozen cats poring over the remains of Ken's birds. Bits of sparrow lay scattered about.

"So these are the culprits!"

"I'm sorry," said Yamada, putting his hands together in a gesture of apology. "These are all my cats. Since there isn't enough to feed them on, I let them loose to scavenge for themselves. I'm afraid your birds became their dinner."

"It can't be helped. By the way," he added, "I'm about to give the Mustang a performance test. Is there anything I can do to counter the G-force problem? According to Major Kurokawa, the plane can fly straight at 9,000 meters at a speed of 700, so in a dive you'll obviously get more out of it. When I got to 700 in the Hayate and the G hit me, I almost fainted, and with the Mustang the effect's going to be even fiercer."

Yamada stepped in among the gang of cats and picked three of them up. "Dealing with G-force is our biggest headache right now. All of a sudden we have a plane like the Hayate, and we're supposed to come up with a solution. When a pilot is hit with G, all the blood rushes down to his lower body, leaving his skull empty—that's why he faints. So we need to come up with a kind of air cushion around his middle to stop the flow of blood. For now all we can do is wind loincloths around his belly and legs."

"What a lousy solution!"

"Well, that's all there is, though. They say the Yankees have come up with an anti-G suit, but I'm making my own and it should be ready by this fall. Come into the lab, I'll show you the design."

Yamada led Ken upstairs. He opened a door which led into a bright room on the southern side of the building. To Ken's surprise Haniyu was sitting there listening to a record.

"What are you doing here? You certainly look cozy. What's the music?"

"Beethoven. The Violin Sonata in F Major."

Ken took a seat at a desk and lit up a Golden Pheasant. "It's hard to relax in that junior officers' room of ours, isn't it? You never know when a superior is going to burst in, and you're completely visible from the airfield."

"Hey, Kurushima," said Yamada. "As a way of apologizing for my little subordinates' stealing your precious birds let me give you a treat—some pilots' rations we invented recently." He handed him a plate with several pill-like objects on it. "This one is pilots' chocolate. These are pilots' vitamins. Oh yes, and we even have pilots' coffee to keep you awake."

"Give me some of that." Ken pointed to a brown bottle on the shelf, marked "Pilots' Good Health."

"No, you can't have that. They'll notice it's missing. And I can't send you back to headquarters drunk."

"What about the chocolate—won't that be missing too?"

"Well, yeah, but I can claim I gave it to you to help your 'physiological adjustment' before you test the Mustang."

"So you've been pilfering food all year in the name of 'physiological adjustment.' That's why you're so fat. Well, okay, I'm hungry, so thank you." Ken shoved half a dozen of the little pills into his mouth. He gagged slightly on the mixture, which tasted unlike anything he could identify, but then gulped it down.

"Delicious, isn't it?"

"Bit of an acquired taste, I'd say. Sort of like a newly invented airplane engine."

"Here, wash it down with some tea," Haniyu said, flipping the record over.

"Chocolate, tea, and music. What luxury!" said Ken. "Hey, Haniyu, I haven't heard you play your fiddle in a while."

Haniyu glanced at Yamada and, with a wink to Ken, brought a violin case down from the shelf.

"You mean you actually play it *here*?"

"Well, sometimes." There was a sly smile on his face. Normally it was hard to tell what he was thinking, but when he smiled one saw a real warmth there. And there was a certain delicacy in the way he poured the tea.

"Give us a tune, then."

Haniyu casually opened the case and, after tuning the violin, began to play. Was it Bach? Ken soon found himself again remembering the past: Eri at the piano in the house in Nagata-cho or the villa in Karuizawa, his mother nodding to the music. He thought of his father, and Anna, and Lauren . . . Particularly Lauren. *If there hadn't been a war I would have proposed to her*, he thought, remembering kissing her in the dark on the way back from church.

The two listeners applauded when the piece came to an end. Yamada's thick hands made quite a powerful sound.

"Haniyu, you should have become a professional," said Ken.

"Everybody tells me I should become something else. Become a poet. Become an artist. But I happen to be a soldier, a soldier in the Imperial Army."

"Of course. What was that thing you just played, soldier?"

"Tartini's 'The Devil's Trill,'" Yamada answered.

"I'm amazed you know."

"What do you mean? That piece is Haniyu's specialty, he plays it all the time."

Ken looked at his watch. "Well, I've got to go test the Mustang. Thanks for the food."

"But it's almost evening," said Haniyu, sounding concerned.

"It's okay. The days are pretty long now."

"I don't know how you can fly an unfamiliar plane without practicing. And an enemy plane to boot."

"I'll be okay. They say even an idiot can fly it."

"Well, you're certainly the best we've got," said Yamada. "It must be the rugby player in you. They never let me near a cockpit any more."

"Your job's important too. Keep some of that 'health drink' for me."

As Ken approached the Mustang, he was met by Colonel Imamura,

Majors Wakana and Kurokawa, and Warrant Officer Mitsuda, in addition to men from the 22nd Squadron—Major Iwama, Lieutenant Sugi, and Lieutenant Hanazono.

"Hey, Kurushima, it's been a while!" Sugi greeted him.

"Hey!" Ken responded, nodding also to Hanazono.

"We flew right over from Nakatsu. Couldn't wait to see this enemy plane." Hanazono's moustache was thicker than before.

"Where the hell were you hiding, Kurushima?" asked Wakana. "Maintenance was finished with it an hour ago. We've all been waiting for the test to start. Even the Colonel's here."

"Sorry, sir."

"Go easy on him," Iwama put in. "We wouldn't have made it in time otherwise." He was suntanned and unshaven, looking every inch the commander of a combat squadron. Only Sugi had the same clean-shaven face as before.

Frowning at the way a fellow officer of the same rank but from a different command was interfering with his treatment of his subordinates, Wakana gave Ken the flight plan. First he was to circle the airfield at 500 meters, and then go up to 3,000, where he would do a speed test, followed by another one at 5,000 meters, after which he was to descend at a 60° angle.

"You don't want me to try a high-altitude flight?"

"Not today. We just want some basic data."

"Oh, come on, Major Wakana," said Iwama. "We came all the way out here to see this. We need to know as soon as possible how the Mustang performs in turns, sudden climbs and dives. Let him try some tricks in it."

"I'm sorry, Major," said Wakana, with the politeness due to the other officer, yet firmly all the same. "Today's aim is to observe basic flight performance. It's a valuable aircraft for us and we can't afford to have an accident. If its turning ability is to be tested, Major Kurokawa should do it. He brought the plane here all the way from China, so he should be used to it."

"No, no, not me," said Kurokawa, with a large shrug of his shoulders. "Just transferred the thing, didn't try any high-level stuff in it."

Ken boarded the plane. With the push of a button he started the engine. The chocks were pulled away. With only the slightest twist of the throttle, the engine responded with instant power. He heard that high-pitched metallic sound peculiar to water-cooled engines. Once again he looked over the unfamiliar instrument panel, checking the positions of all the levers he would need. Everything seemed different, but in fact the basic things, the control stick and pedals and throttle, were the same. Everything was in order. He started down the runway and then smoothly took off.

As he proceeded with the basic flight plan, he relaxed and enjoyed the view from the wide, curved windshield. The Chichibu Mountains, dyed in the reds and purples of dusk, seemed to smile at him. Beyond the clear shape of Mount Fuji, the quietly glowing sun was about to set, but the sky still retained the blueness of day. He climbed to 5,000 meters. What an enjoyable plane this was. When he opened the throttle it thrust forward with wonderful speed, pushing his body back into the pilot's seat. With ease he crossed the speed barrier of 650 kph, the point where the Hayate seemed to hit a solid wall. "They've beaten us. We've lost," he mumbled to himself, without noticing that he was repeating what Major Wakana had said.

Suddenly he felt the urge for a little mischief. He descended from 5,000 meters to 3,000, and at a speed of 500 kph he flew over the air base at Fussa, then headed north. When he'd ascertained that the airfield was out of sight he started doing turns, then somersaults. He could feel the plane's sure response in the control stick and the foot pedals; a sensitive but confident response. It executed the complex movements like a well-trained athlete. Ken felt the joy of being one with this marvelous machine—just him and the plane in the blue sky—and was certain it could outfox any Japanese fighter put up against it. It was only a momentary fantasy, but for a little while he felt as if he were an American pilot engaged in aerial combat with a Japanese plane: he zoomed up and dived and did one last terrific turn, before leveling off and, with a look of resignation on his face, returning to the airfield.

After he had reported to Major Wakana on the basic maneuvers he'd been ordered to do, Sugi approached.

"How was it?"

"Terrific. Terrifying, if you like—as an enemy plane. It felt like it was part of me."

"How does it compare with our Hayate?"

"Well, I'm not sure. Maybe I'd put them at fifty-fifty. The Mustang's got greater speed and better high-altitude capacity. But the maneuverability is similar."

Maneuverability? So you put it through its paces, did you? This was the look on Sugi's face. When he saw that Wakana was out of hearing, he gave Ken a wink.

"It's been a while," said Ken. "Why don't you come over to my lodgings? We can have a drink."

"Hanazono's with me." They were staying, apparently, for three days to check out the Mustang.

"That's okay. Bring him along."

Hanazono agreed. The three of them first went to the junior officers' room. Warrant Officer Mitsuda was there, heating up some dried cuttlefish. He poured some cold *sake* for them.

"Well, Kurushima," said Hanazono, "how is the enemy plane? Does it measure up to our Hayate?"

"It's fast, and it climbs well. At 5,000 meters I got up to a speed of 650 with no problem at all. It remains to be seen how it turns and shoots."

"I'm looking forward to the tests tomorrow," said Mitsuda.

"Actually," said Ken, scratching his head, "I secretly tried a few turns. It was quite impressive. Maybe even better than our Hayate."

"That's impossible," said Hanazono. "The Hayate was recently improved. It's a hell of a plane. The P-40s can't touch it. Even the Mustang is no match for it."

"Yes, but it's still pretty impressive. The real problem is that it's been thoroughly bulletproofed. There's a thirty-millimeter steel shield all around the pilot's seat. Bullets won't worry him."

"Just what you'd expect of them—no guts."

"No," Ken said, "if the pilot's killed you lose the fight. It's not a question of guts. Even the Hayate has a bulletproof plate behind the pilot. The important thing is, the American plane has enough power to ensure that all that steel plating doesn't affect its handling at all."

"Yes, but the correct way to fight is to get rid of as much of the protective armor as possible, then beat them with superior technique. Those gutless wonders only care about machinery. Whereas we're developing mechanical capabilities to match our guts."

"Sure. But with any amount of guts you still need a superior machine to back you up."

"You're wrong!" said Hanazono, his face darkening and his moustache trembling. "We don't have time to worry about that—superior and inferior machines . . . that's enemy thinking. When the hell did you turn into one of *them?*"

"What are you talking about?"

"All we have is the Hayate. That's our point of departure. It's our only weapon. That's why we're practicing in it day and night. We win in the Hayate, we die in the Hayate. You in your nice safe job get to test-pilot the Mustang. You can play around in it and fall for the enemy's technology. But we combat pilots don't have that choice!"

"Hey, you guys, stop it." Sugi tried to intervene.

"If you're so in love with machines, then build us a machine better than the Hayate. If you can't, then shut up!"

"Hanazono, you've gone too far." Sugi gave Ken a smile. "Kurushima, don't take it to heart. The Iwama squad is on a crazy schedule. Hanazono is their ace fighter. He's confident about licking these Yankees, but if you hurt his confidence, it makes him boil. So don't get angry with him."

"I'm not angry," Ken muttered, "it's just that . . ."

"Don't you have any women in Nakatsu?" Mitsuda asked suddenly.

"Women?" Sugi asked back.

"I heard that there's only one bus every two hours to the nearest town."

"Yeah, you're right about that. It's a real hick place. Just one little seafood restaurant in the village, always packed with so many customers you can't get in."

"Why don't we go get some women tonight? I know a place in Shinjuku."

"You really serious?" Hanazono looked a little worried, which didn't quite fit with his moustache.

"Yeah, let's go," said Sugi. "I'm tired of living like a monk. Didn't *you* tell me recently you wanted a woman?"

"I did, but . . ." Hanazono seemed embarrassed.

"Ha! Still a virgin—is that it? Come on, why not try it?"

"I'm on," announced Ken. "I'll get Yamada and Haniyu to come along. Why don't we all go to a farmhouse near my place for some food and drink first? I've got some special *sake*—in fact it's from the Imperial Palace. We can drink it and then go to Shinjuku."

"*Sake* from the Imperial Palace?" Sugi asked dubiously. "You mean a cup or two?"

"No, a liter."

"That's unbelievable."

"I've got a whole heap of dried fish from home," said Mitsuda, the fisherman's son. "Why don't I bring it along?"

The group left from the main gate on the stroke of five and went to the farmhouse. Ken brought out the bottle of *sake* his father had received from the Emperor on his return from Washington. Mitsuda grilled some fish, and Yamada broiled some vegetables, also from Mitsuda's family, on a hibachi borrowed from the farmer's family. It was a warm spring evening. All present, except for Mitsuda, had been classmates at the Kumagaya flying school, and the conversation naturally turned to their time there, now already three years ago. Their Squadron Leader at the time, Otani, had become a fighter ace in Burma but had then been killed in combat, and their chief instructor had died on the Chinese front.

"They all die eventually, don't they?"

"Yes, they do. And so will we."

"Among us the only one who's had real combat experience is you, Mitsuda."

"The planes I flew are ancient now. My experience doesn't really count. By the way, I heard a rumor that the 22nd Squadron is going to the Philippines."

"Apparently a directive has actually gone out," Sugi said. "That's why there've been all these practice flights over forests recently. It's for aerial combat over jungle."

Mitsuda told them about the time he'd been escorting some heavy bombers over Burma and had run out of fuel and crashlanded in the jungle; he had wandered about in enemy territory for three days before meeting up with friendly forces. "Compared to that, combat over home ground is easy. If you bail out you're okay, and you can always belly-land in a rice field. All that mud makes for a nice soft landing."

"I can't wait to go," Hanazono said, rubbing his arms. He wasn't playing the hero, just genuinely eager to go. Ken began to feel he could forgive him for his rudeness earlier.

Before long, they were slightly drunk, and they started singing. First Hanazono, who had had marching songs drummed into him at the Junior Army Academy, stood up and sang one march after another. Yamada, who was tone deaf and unfamiliar with the words, pretended to sing along. Then Mitsuda belted out all the popular songs of the day. After Haniyu gave a recital of folk songs and Schubert lieder, Ken, instead of singing, did his imitations—of Colonel Imamura, Major Iwama, and Major Wakana. Each one was greeted with a burst of laughter and applause.

By the time they arrived in Shinjuku by train it was already midnight. The city was under blackout orders, and Shinjuku was pitch dark. Mitsuda, who knew his way around, led them to a place in the pleasure quarters in 3-chome.

As the lattice door was opened Hanazono hesitated. "I'm not drunk enough yet. I'll go get something to drink at a bar first."

"There're no bars open at this time of night. Go on, go inside." Mitsuda tried to push him, but Hanazono refused and left.

"Our hero is still pure as snow," Sugi laughed.

They were served tea in a tatami room by the entrance. Then the madam of the house appeared. When Mitsuda handed her some packages of seafood, a luxury at that time, and told her they were all Army officers, she became quite welcoming and called for the best girls in the house.

This was Ken's first visit to a place like this. He envied Hanazono for having had the courage to leave at the last moment, and began to regret coming here. When the woman asked him which girl he liked, he shrank back uncomfortably. With wide eyes he watched Mitsuda and Sugi talking familiarly with the girls, and was surprised to see the innocent, aristocratic-looking Haniyu and clumsy old Yamada make their choice with little fuss or embarrassment. Before he knew it, they had all disappeared, and he was left alone with the madam.

"You don't fancy any of the girls, sir?" Her manner was apologetic as she served him a freshly brewed cup of tea. "A lot of them have gone to be of service at the front, and we're in short supply here . . ." Apart from being the madam, she seemed like any ordinary old woman. "We're grateful to you soldiers, for what you're doing for the country. Are you sure there isn't one you like?" The old woman coughed as she drank her tea, and gave her thin chest a quick pat.

When he noticed her stealing glances at him, Ken grew even more uncomfortable. "Is there something sticking to my face?" he asked.

"No, sir." The woman looked away.

"I'm of mixed blood. My mother's a foreigner."

"Oh, no wonder you're so handsome . . ."

"But I'm Japanese through and through. Serving in the Imperial Army."

"Of course, of course."

"All right. Since I'm tall, get me a tall girl."

She immediately assumed a professional air and disappeared inside, reemerging with a young woman in tow.

"How's this one?"

She was a large girl, with dark features. Ken was led down a dim corridor lined on both sides with rows of small, identical rooms. He was shown into one of these cave-like spaces. Under the wan lamp, hung with a blackout cloth, the red coverings over the mirror stand

and the chest of drawers loomed erotically. The bedding was laid out, with two pillows.

"Will you change out of your clothes, sir?" The girl spoke in a rather refined voice which belied her coarse looks.

"No . . ." Ken sat down, shaking his head. "Most yukatas are too small for me. That one looks small too."

"Then will you have a bath?"

"A bath? No, actually I'd like a drink. Do you have any *sake*?"

The woman tilted her head to one side and asked, "Sir, is it your first time in a place like this?"

"Yes, it is," he answered. Telling her this had the effect of putting him at ease. "So I don't know what I'm supposed to do. Don't you have any *sake*?"

"No, we don't. They don't distribute liquor rations to establishments like ours."

The woman wasn't smiling. Ken liked that.

"All right, then let's talk. Where are you from?"

"Asakusa."

"Oh good. I'm from Tokyo myself."

Ken looked the girl straight in the face. Until that moment he had been too embarrassed, and had only been vaguely aware of her looks. She was possibly still in her teens. She wasn't wearing any makeup, which made her dark features somehow endearing. He felt desire for the girl. But his reluctance was even stronger than that desire. He remembered the night he'd spent with Lauren in the room where he had been staying, at the Drake Hotel in Chicago. The memory was a secret shared only by the two of them.

"I'm leaving," Ken said as he rose to his feet.

"Are you upset about something?" The girl seemed astonished. "Did I say something wrong?"

"No, not at all. I'm glad to have met you."

Ken handed the girl a ten-yen note. Mitsuda had already paid the fees for the whole group, so this was a tip.

Ken walked the dark streets alone. The effect of the drink had worn off, and he walked with large strides, sure of his footing. From

Shinjuku to Yotsuya there was not a single light to be seen, but he knew the streets quite well. As he passed in front of the police box at Yotsuya-mitsuke he was sure he would be taken in for questioning, walking around out of uniform at this time of night. But the patrolmen didn't seem to notice. He half ran down the slope that led to Akasaka-mitsuke, and by the time he reached his family's house in Nagata-cho he was sweating, his heart pounding.

The house was quite dark, its occupants asleep. But then he saw a dim light on in the dining room. Somebody was still awake. He jumped lightly over the gate and tried to open the latticed door, but it was locked. Fortunately he had a key to the house on his key chain and, fumbling with it, he managed to open the door and quietly stepped inside. As he was taking his shoes off he heard the dining room door open and Yoshiko's voice cry out: "Who's there?"

Ken hid behind the staircase, making quite a lot of noise as he did so.

"Who is it?" she cried, with fear in her voice.

He could see the tip of her broom. Brave Yoshiko was going to chase the intruder out with a broom.

When he heard her pick up the telephone and say, "Hello, police? . . ." he quickly appeared in front of her.

"Master Ken!" she shrieked. Her face was suffused with both anger and joy. When the joy won out, she gave him a huge smile. "You scared the life out of me. What are you doing here at this hour of the night? Did something happen?"

"No, I was drinking in Shinjuku."

"Well, that's a relief. You look fine."

"Where's my father?"

"He went out this evening. He called and said he'd be staying over at the Yoshizawas' house."

"And you're still up?"

"Yes. Somehow I couldn't get to sleep."

Ken went into the dining room, where he found the table strewn with letters and photographs. He picked one up.

"Why, it's Tanaka!" he exclaimed.

"Yes, it's when he left for the front."

Their lighthearted fop of a cook was in uniform with his head shaved—a souvenir of basic training—looking frail and overage. Sadly, he'd been killed on the battlefield only a few months after being sent overseas. During his tours of duty around the country Ken had often encountered middle-aged or elderly draftees being abused by NCOs, and it was these older conscripts who were the first to fall in the front line.

"I want to tell you a secret," Yoshiko said. "Before he left we became engaged."

"Really!" He realized immediately why her eyelids were red and swollen: she had obviously been looking through Tanaka's letters and photographs. They would have been well suited to each other. Yoshiko had outgrown the "appropriate age for a bride" during her service with the Kurushimas. There had been occasional proposals, but she had turned them all down, saying that the family needed her —something which Ken's parents had felt guilty about.

"How old are you, Yoshiko?"

Her face reddened with embarrassment. "You're not supposed to ask a woman her age." Then, quietly, she added, "I'm in my mid-thirties."

When Ken had first come to Japan he had been put in the care of old Toku in Ueda. Toku's daughter Yoshiko had been about seventeen at the time. Apart from some of the family's foreign tours, she had been with him his entire life. They had been so close that he'd never really thought of her as a member of the opposite sex, but now suddenly he noticed her well-fleshed neck and bosom, and it unnerved him. Was the liquor still affecting him?

"I'd like to take a bath. I'm all sweaty."

"It's already warm. I got it ready for your father, before I knew he'd be staying out. I'll just go and heat it up."

"Thank you."

Ken wandered into the parlor, glancing at the shelves and feeling disappointed that there wasn't a single photograph of the family there. They must have been removed to Karuizawa for safekeeping. He realized that what he'd really wanted to see was a picture of Lauren. He felt listless, and lay down on the sofa, and soon dozed off. When Yoshiko returned to tell him the bath was ready, there were already wisps of dawn in the sky. From the bathroom window he could see the contours of his mother's "Kyoto garden" gradually becoming clearer. In his own home for the first time in ages, he wished he could stay longer, but he had to submit a report on the Mustang to Major Wakana that morning, which meant taking the first train back. He slid down into the hot water with its smell of cypress wood and let out several deep breaths which could have been either yawns or sighs.

3

Beyond the dark green range of the Chichibu Mountains, Fuji stood languidly, its white peak touched with light blue.

On the Fussa airfield was a group of men that included generals from Air Command, senior officers from the Air Technical Institute, the technical staff from Nakajima Aircraft, officers from the Inspection Department, and members of the 22nd Squadron. There was a relaxed atmosphere, as if everyone had gathered to watch a sports event. While there was no liquor, food and tea were passed around, and laughter came easily.

In front of the assembled guests were four airplanes: a Hayate, an older Hien, the P-51 Mustang, and a German fighter, the FW-190. The maintenance crew had attended to the planes with even greater care than usual. The Hayate had a chrysanthemum emblem on its tail, and the Hien the red star of the Chofu Air Training Squadron; the Mustang still had its Flying Tigers shark's teeth and the name Alina inscribed on it, and the German plane had a design of black clouds.

The appointed hour of nine o'clock arrived. The four pilots stood in front of Colonel Imamura and saluted: Major Kurokawa, Major Iwama, Lieutenant Kurushima, and Warrant Officer Mitsuda. The Colonel returned their salutes and announced: "As previously decided, you're to climb to 8,000 meters above Oshima Island and begin your race at a speed of 350 kph. Head due north, and above Hiratsuka switch to horizontal flight at 3,000 meters, then check your speed above the airfield at Fussa. The Hien and Focke-Wulf will then land, and there'll be a mock dogfight between the Mustang and the Hayate. The purpose of this exercise is a comparison of the performance of each plane in combat."

The four men climbed into the cockpits. Iwama was in the Hayate, Kurokawa in the Mustang, with Ken in the Hien and Mitsuda in the Focke-Wulf. The Mustang started up at the push of a button, but it wasn't long before the other three planes, aided by ignition vehicles, were going full blast.

Iwama, Kurokawa, and Mitsuda were all veterans of real combat, and Ken felt a keen sense of pride to be in their company. He had flown the Hien on more than just trial flights, but he wasn't as familiar with it as he was with the Hayate.

The four planes proceeded to the runway and one after another took off into a southerly wind. They flew in a line, climbing quickly, with Iwama in the lead. *Just don't get out of line, and don't fall behind,* Ken told himself as he held the control stick. Fortunately the engine of the Hien, which was prone to problems, had been checked and double-checked by the ground staff, and was working smoothly.

Mount Fuji stood due west, and where the plain casually ended the sea spread out, immense. The Izu Peninsula to the west and the Miura Peninsula to the east were exactly as if drawn on a map, and Suruga Bay glimmered with a bronze tinge. He could see Oshima Island. Altitude 7,000 meters. When he was just above the smoke-spewing volcano on the island, he had reached 8,000. Iwama's plane flipped its wings. Turn due north, speed 350. Again the Hayate flipped its wings. It was the start of the aerial race. At full throttle the four planes began their descent. The land rose toward them. The Mustang zoomed out in front, followed by the Hayate and the Focke-Wulf, with Ken's Hien trailing behind. It was no match for the others. Still Ken hung on as best he could.

The German plane landed first, then the Hien. After making his performance report, Ken went over to where Yamada and Sugi were standing.

"What was the result?"

Yamada, his voice full of excitement, said: "The Mustang was first, with the Hayate three seconds behind. Then, one second later, the Focke-Wulf. Your Hien wasn't in the race—it's already an antique."

"That Mustang's a terrifying plane, all right," Sugi sighed. "It's going to be hell fighting against it."

"Hey, there it is!" shouted Yamada.

Bursting out of the sun it came and with one sweep of a blade cut clean across the base and the fields around and was off into the sky. High up, waiting for it, was the Hayate. The Hayate closed in, the other trying to escape, but the Hayate got right behind it. With its speed advantage, the Mustang drew away, and flipped into a somersault. The two planes wheeled together, looking for their chance. Abruptly the Mustang turned again, leveled off, and raced away. The Hayate went chasing after it.

"Go get him, Iwama!" Sugi stamped on the ground. "Get that Yankee bastard!"

A dogfight ensued, the planes coming together, drawing apart, turning one somersault after another. Iwama, the veteran, was putting up a hell of a fight; maybe his actually *was* the better plane. Just when he'd managed to tuck in behind the Mustang, though—quick as a flash his target did a tight little loop and, before he knew it, was now sitting on *his* tail.

"What happened?" Yamada shook his head.

"That must be the Kurokawa magic," said Sugi. "I've never seen flying like that."

"It's the combat flaps," Ken explained. "The Mustang is equipped with special flaps that allow it to maneuver like that."

Now the Mustang was in pursuit. The Hayate swept up and down trying to get away, but it just couldn't shake it off. The fight was apparently over. The Mustang closed in for the kill. In real combat the Hayate would have taken a burst of machine-gun fire and would be spewing smoke. But then it jinked to one side, the Mustang flew out in front, and Iwama slipped in behind it again.

"He did it!" Sugi leaped in the air. "It's his *hinerikomi*—Iwama's special move."

"What's a *hinerikomi*?" asked Ken.

"It's from judo. Using the opponent's strength to your advantage. We've all been practicing the technique. When an enemy plane is behind you, you make a little jink, so small he doesn't realize, then let him get ahead—and *pow!*"

Ken and Yamada nodded.

"The Hayate's like the Hayabusa in that the rudder is especially sensitive. Other planes probably couldn't do it."

The Mustang tried to wriggle out of it, but the Hayate stuck on its tail for a full ten seconds at close range—long enough for the Mustang to be shot down. The fight was over, and the two planes landed in close succession.

Iwama and Kurokawa—one short, one tall—ran together to where the Colonel stood, and made their reports. Then, laughing, they came over to Ken and his group.

"You got me," Kurokawa said. "I was no match for you." Iwama had been his senior at the Army Academy, and in Kurokawa's voice was both the intimacy of a schoolmate and the politeness of a junior officer,

"Wrong. I just barely managed to tip the balance. Your combat skills are damned good, and that Mustang is a heck of a plane. A real adversary."

"It sure has the speed."

"Not only that, those combat flaps can operate at that speed. And the armor around the pilot—it's going to be one hell of a job bringing it down."

"Your *hinerikomi* move, though—that's what made the difference."

"I agree. But it takes a lot of practice before a pilot can get the hang of it. The real question is whether we have that kind of time left."

4

The dismal rainy season was the wrong time for testing new aircraft, but the war situation was pressing and there was no time to relax. Flight performance, shooting angles, engine details, fuselage endurance, all had to be checked, with medical research being stepped up as well. Inevitably the training schedule of the 22nd Squadron only became more intense. Airplanes constantly took off and landed, churning up mud on the unpaved runways.

Ken was almost finished with the model airplane he was making; all he had left to do was the painting and lacquering.

"Now that's an advanced-looking plane," said Yamada, who was knitting. Yes, Yamada's latest passion was knitting. Whenever he had a moment to spare he would unwind the wool and ply his needles. "But it's got a funny shape. Who's the maker? Nakajima?"

"Yes, it's the Ki-94. It's being designed by Aoyagi, who did the Hayate. It'll have a pressurized cabin and an engine with a special supercharger."

"Same as the Mustang." Yamada glanced at the scale model of the Mustang on Ken's desk. His boyhood passion for making model airplanes had revived recently. The extraordinary accuracy of the details had impressed everyone in the junior officers' room, and word had gotten around. Even Colonel Imamura had come to see the models, and the 22nd Squadron had asked him to make extra editions for their training classes. Making model airplanes wasn't his job, Ken complained, but he obviously enjoyed it, and in no time he had completed models of all the major aircraft on both the American and Japanese sides.

"That's right, exactly the same as the Mustang." Ken was trimming it with his pocket knife. "We're in the age of ultra high-altitude flight now. The age of the stratosphere."

Yamada dropped one of his balls of wool, and the puppy Momotaro picked it up in its mouth. "Thanks," he said, patting it on the head.

There was a roar of engines as a squadron of Hayates flew past at low altitude.

"Look, that's Iwama's plane in the lead," said Ken. "Didn't one of the planes malfunction again?"

"Yes, but they're all flying okay now," said Yamada.

"The maintenance crew's superb, but they do have their hands full."

Again there was the roar of engines. This time it was a formation of Hiens, the shriller sound of the water-cooled engines making the windows vibrate.

"The stratosphere. Is that where that new enemy plane, the B-29, flies?"

"Yes. At least according to my research."

There was a diagram of the B-29 pasted on the wall. It had been made by the Bomber Inspection Division, which had investigated a B-29 shot down during the recent bombing of Kyushu. On June 16th, sixty of these planes had set out from Chengdu in China to bomb the city of Yahata. Seven had been shot down. Major Wakana and Ken had been part of the investigation team. They had been astonished by the sheer size of the plane, with its 43-meter span; it was twice as large as the biggest Japanese bomber, the Hiryu. Its estimated capacities were:

Weight empty: 30 tons
Weight equipped: 50 tons
Top speed: 600 kph at 8,000 meters
Operating ceiling: 12,500 meters
Flying range: 9,000 kilometers
Bomb tonnage: 10 tons

The B-29 made every bomber in history obsolete, especially with its operating ceiling of 12,500 meters—a place where no Japanese air-plane had ever been. Their own reconnaissance planes had a limit of 11,000 meters, while the Hayabusa and the Hayate could only reach 10,500 and the Hien 11,600. It had therefore become absolutely essential to develop a new fighter to counter the B-29, but the work wasn't going at all well. When Ken thought about all the difficulties they were having getting the Hayates out of the factories, the task of producing the next generation of planes seemed an unattainable dream.

"And yet we *have* to produce the Ki-94," Aoyagi, its designer, had said a week ago, pounding the air with his bony fist. "If we don't, we'll be helpless when the B-29s start bombing."

Ken too was a technician, and as a technician he had a firsthand sense of the precarious situation Japan was now in. The more he studied the Mustang and the B-29, the more he realized how ad-vanced the enemy's technology and manufacturing were. It was a feature of American manufacturing that the parts were precision made, so that spares would fit perfectly in their place. In Japan main-tenance crews had to shave and pound the parts to make them go in. When the remains of the downed B-29s' engines were hauled in, they were almost able to reconstruct a single engine from the fragments of many.

The machinery used in the aircraft factories was getting worn down. But even worse was the fact that the best factory workers had been drafted and sent off to the front, leaving students and part-timers in their place. There was no way these people could build the com-plicated engine of the Hayate properly. The ground staff had to work around the clock to make up for all the defects the factories were turning out. Yes, they were heading into the age of the stratosphere, but Japan didn't have the technology or the manufacturing prowess to keep up.

Recently, a German submarine which had docked at the Yokosuka naval base had brought with it blueprints and a model of the Me-262. The new German plane dispensed with propellers altogether and instead used a kind of rocket for propulsion. The very thought of such a plane, using what was called a "jet engine," gave Ken both a sense of excitement and alarm. At this point the Germans were ahead of the Americans. But it was clear that the age of the jet was on hand. What the propeller-driven plane couldn't do, the jet aircraft could do with ease. The "advanced" Ki-94 they had been placing their hopes on began to seem like an antique before it was off the drawing board. It was this thought that preoccupied Ken now.

"It's a new age."

"What?" Yamada put his needles down.

"We're being left behind. Everyone else is developing new aircraft. That's what's been getting me down."

"Look, there's something else I wanted to discuss with you." Yamada's large hand pressed down on the slender bamboo knitting needles, and he glanced around. There were just the two of them in the junior officers' room. "I'm a doctor. A doctor's job is to cure people's illnesses. Working here, I'm involved in treating all the new ailments that come with your line of work. But you know, it's like being ordered to come up with medical solutions for technical backwardness. For example, how to enable men to withstand inadequate oxygen, inadequate air pressure, and G sickness. To train men to cope with high altitude on their own—that's a lot easier than coming up with new airplanes with pressurized cockpits, and it doesn't add any weight to the plane. But it seems to me they've got it backwards. They should first come up with a pressurized cabin in which a man can operate safely, and if that involves extra weight, then develop a more powerful engine to cope with that weight. That's the logical way to do it. But that's not how the people in Air Command see it."

"It costs more, that's why."

"Right. Look at how we're trying to deal with the G-force problem. The Americans came up with an anti-G suit for pilots, while we've made the whole thing the pilot's own responsibility. Made him wear extra loincloths, made him press parts of himself to keep the blood from flowing down from his head. We tell them it's impossible for the pilot; they say we're lacking in samurai spirit."

"Doesn't make any sense," Ken said, nodding. "The generals, oh they understand that the aircraft are products of advanced technology, but they can't grasp that the more advanced the technology becomes the more it ignores basic human physiology. They've never piloted planes themselves. They have no idea what it feels like to experience one-fifth normal air pressure and a temperature of –50° at 10,000 meters, or what the so-called pinball effect does to the body when you're diving and get hit by 3G or 4G. Their only concern is how fast the plane will fly, how much maneuverability it has, how high it can get. They think they can win as long as the plane performs. They don't think about the pilot's physiological condition."

"That's it, exactly. The generals make all their plans, and we're stuck having to wipe their asses for them."

There were footsteps in the hallway, and Ken and Yamada immediately stopped talking. They heard loud voices, lots of them, the loudest being Kurokawa's. The door to the senior officers' room opened, and the group went inside. It was quiet again.

"That itself doesn't bother me," Ken continued. "The generals aren't perfect, and they need help from us, their subordinates. What I can't bear is this spiritual stuff they always fall back on. They're dealing with airplanes, with science and technology, but when it gets down to the nitty gritty they'll start talking about 'Japanese fighting spirit.'"

"Yes. That's the problem. That's what I meant."

"Fighting spirit . . ." A bad memory cropped up in Ken's mind.

It had been the beginning of May. The mock dogfight between the Hayate and the Mustang had just taken place. A conference was held in the Colonel's office, with the generals from Air Command and the staff of the Inspection Department present.

Colonel Imamura had said: "Today's combat exercise involved veteran pilots. Why don't we try it again, but this time with two rookies with no combat experience? Major Wakana, what do you think?"

"An interesting idea," he had answered, nodding in agreement.

Wakana and Iwama decided Ken should take the Mustang and Lieutenant Sugi the Hayate. So the second round was set.

As a test pilot, Ken had become quite familiar with the Mustang, but of course he had never been in actual combat. And Sugi, too, though he had been undergoing rigorous training for the last two months under Major Kurokawa, had no fighting experience either. The two young men were graduates of the same class in flying school and thoroughly competent technically. All in all, they seemed a reasonable choice for the second mock dogfight. But then General Okuma of Air Command had vetoed the selection of Ken as the pilot of the Mustang. The captured plane was too valuable, he claimed, to allow an inexperienced young officer to fly it. They couldn't afford an accident. Major Wakana argued that Ken had been in charge of testing the captured plane, he knew it better than anyone else, and he had superb flying skills to boot.

But General Okuma wouldn't listen. "I'm absolutely opposed to Kurushima flying that plane," he said.

"But there's nobody else qualified to do it," Wakana replied, equally insistent.

"Let Major Kurokawa pilot it again."

"But then it won't be a dogfight between rookies." This came from Colonel Imamura. "Frankly, sir, why are you opposed to Kurushima?"

"All right," Okuma said. "Just between ourselves, I find it hard to stomach the fact that that man has Yankee blood in his veins. You may not like me saying this, but the idea of letting someone with American blood fly an American plane makes me feel damned uncomfortable. Now wait, Major Iwama, I recognize that Lieutenant Kurushima, your subordinate, is a fine officer. I don't deny that at all. But just consider it for a minute: here we are with this precious trophy, the one and only Mustang we've managed to capture. Now if, just *if*, there was an accident, it would look a bit funny, wouldn't it? So let's get a *pure*-blooded officer to fly it."

Owing to General Okuma's opposition, the second mock dogfight was put off indefinitely. And the next day, Ken found that he'd suddenly been dropped from the team inspecting the Mustang, too.

It was Major Wakana who told him what had happened, adding a word of consolation: "General Okuma's an old graduate of the Army Academy. He basically doesn't trust people like you or me who went

to civilian schools. In fact, he probably hates the whole idea of technicians occupying senior positions at all. So don't take it personally."

It was true that graduates of the Army Academy occupied all the
key positions, even in their department. Unlike people from civilian
schools, or NCOs like Mitsuda, or the young pilots from the Junior Air
Academy, the Army Academy men considered themselves an elite,
and were given special treatment. Back at the Kumagaya flying
school, Hanazono, who had been at the Academy, had often come
down hard on Haniyu and Kurushima for their lack of military discipline. The three of them later became friends, but there were still
moments when Hanazono seemed intent on keeping a distance
between himself and the other two. And when the other Army Academy graduates, Major Iwama and Major Kurokawa, went out drinking,
they would invite Hanazono along but not Ken. When Colonel Imamura held his occasional banquets Hanazono would be invited, but
Major Wakana and the other technical officers wouldn't. That wasn't
all. It seemed that Hanazono was in the habit of giving his fellow
Academy graduates little reports on Ken and the others. Why else
would Major Kurokawa, soon after that night in Shinjuku, have said to
Ken with a dirty grin: "You boys having yourselves a good time now,
are you?"

"Why the sudden silence?" asked Yamada. "What were you saying
about 'fighting spirit'?"

"It's quite a big problem, actually." Ken stood up, took the diagram
of the B-29 off the wall, and pinned it to a drawing board. As he
began tracing the outline of the plane, he said, as if joking, "I wonder
how much *Japanese* fighting spirit I've got."

"What're you talking about? You're full of it."

"Then what about Yankee fighting spirit?"

"What the hell's that?" Yamada dropped his knitting needles on the
floor.

"Well, my mother, she's a Yankee."

"I don't know about that, I can't see inside you."

"Then how can you be sure I have the Yamato spirit?"

"I . . ." Yamada was at a loss for words. His huge body seemed to shrink a little.

"Don't worry about it. Anyway, General Okuma's right, I *do* have the Yankee spirit in me. For example, if the Yankees can build this B-29, I can build a perfect model of it." He started drawing the contours of the plane again.

Suddenly Momotaro began barking. The door opened and Sugi, wearing his flying suit, came in.

"Hey, Sugi!"

"So you were both here." He picked up Momotaro. "You're getting big."

"What's up, Sugi?" Ken asked.

"We got our marching orders."

"Wow," Ken and Yamada both said together. "Where are you going?" "When?"

"As soon as the rains let up, we're heading for China. The Imperial Army's first Hayate squadron."

"China!" Ken seemed surprised. "I thought the big battle was going to be in the Philippines. Isn't that why you guys have been doing all that training for combat over the jungle?"

"We thought so too. But they told us the U.S. Air Force has been reinforced on the China front, so we've got to go and take care of that first."

"After the rainy season ends. That would be the second half of July. That's only a month from now," said Yamada.

"I guess so. A summer campaign."

"Well, anyway, congratulations. The very first campaign with the brand-new Hayate!" Ken picked up a model of the Mustang in his left hand and a model of the Hayate in his right and swung the two planes around in a fierce air duel. It ended, of course, with the Mustang falling to the floor.

"Kurushima, you're still a kid!" One by one, Sugi picked up the model planes on Ken's desk. "They're really perfect, aren't they? Hey, as a going-away present for me, why don't you make me a model of an enemy plane? I can use it for training at the front. How about a

Curtiss P-40 or a P-47 Thunderbolt? Or maybe a P-38 Lightning?"

"I can't do that. I'm not a toymaker, I'm a soldier."

"Then give me this Mustang."

"Well, okay, if you insist, it's yours."

"Thank you. I'll take good care of it. By the way, Yamada, since I've given you the good news, how about some Pilot's Good Health for me? Why don't we all have some in fact?"

"You're really getting greedy. Still, I guess I can give you some. Sure, and if you run out, I can make some more."

"It's just medicinal alcohol mixed with something weird," said Ken.

"I know. But a good vintage from the Yamada Distillery can be pretty special."

The three of them set out under large oiled umbrellas with the words "Inspection Department" inscribed on them, and walked through the rain to Yamada's room in the Aviation Medicine Institute.

5

Only the main runway was open; the rest of the airfield was occupied with plane after plane, each with its engine running. The roar was tremendous, echoing from the mountains to the east where the sun had just risen, into the blue sky beyond. Forty Hayates and ten 97 heavy bombers, plus the gliders each bomber trailed, cast long shadows, and each plane was being checked over by a maintenance crew.

A send-off ceremony was in progress, with *sake* bottles and cups laid out on tables. At the center of a large group stood Colonel Imamura, Major Iwama, Major Wakana, Major Kurokawa, and the technician Aoyagi, with the junior officers on each side. Sugi and Hanazono were in their flying suits; Ken, Yamada, and Haniyu in full uniform. They had to raise their voices over the roar of the airplanes.

Ken, lifting his *sake* cup, said to his two friends, "Take care of yourselves. May 'the luck of the warrior' be with you."

"Thank you," said Sugi, raising his cup in return. "It's a strange feeling—all five of us here from the same class at flying school, and now two of us going away. We're depending on you others. Make us some good planes to fight with."

Yamada stuck out his fat fist. "A hand has to have five fingers or it's not good for anything. You two guys have to survive. Survive, and return here, and we'll make new planes together."

"I don't plan on surviving," said Hanazono, his eyes gleaming. "I'm ready to die."

"Don't overdo it, now," said Yamada. "That's a noble way to feel, but the longer 'the luck of the warrior' lasts the better it is for everybody."

"You know the situation in China as well as I do. They're counter-attacking, and they have a huge material advantage. Forty Hayates aren't going to change anything. We're all going to die. The real question is what happens then. You guys have to come up with better planes, and continue the struggle."

"Yes, yes, of course." Yamada offered him some more *sake*. "Let's drink."

"I can't fly when I'm drunk," said Hanazono, downing what remained in his cup in a single gulp.

"A little more won't hurt you," Yamada said, refilling his cup anyway.

"Haniyu," Hanazono called out. "Haniyu, I'm drunk. Since I'm drunk, I can tell you. I want to apologize. I want you to forgive me, before I go off to die."

"What're you talking about?" Haniyu gave him a sad, boyish smile.

"When we were in training together I was always down on you, said you hadn't enough 'fighting spirit' and stuff like that. I was really hard on you. I'm ashamed to remember it. I apologize."

"What do you mean? I'm the one who should be thanking you. I was a bit neurotic back then, and you helped me get over it."

One by one, the engines fell silent; the tests were over and the maintenance crews swarmed to the tables. Their tunics were covered with oil. Colonel Imamura beckoned the head of the maintenance team to his side.

"Thank you for all your good work. The 22nd Squadron is now all present. I would like to give a toast to Squadron Leader Iwama and all the men of your division, wishing you the best of warrior's luck and every success on the battlefield."

Each of the fliers called the men attached to his plane over and filled their cups. Most of those on Hanazono's and Sugi's planes were still teenagers, and some of them embarrassedly refused the drink, others took one gulp and frowned as it went down.

Ken waited for a chance to say goodbye to Iwama, but the Major was surrounded by bigwigs from Air Command, among them General Okuma. Ken didn't feel like butting in. He tried nodding at him, but failed to get his attention. Ken was joined by Yamada and Haniyu and together they were about to call out to the Major when they were interrupted by Aoyagi, the technician.

"There've been some changes in the design of the Ki-94. We were going to put propellers fore and aft to increase speed, but that would make ejecting difficult. We've succeeded in making an experimental pressurized cabin. All that's left is the supercharger, and that's turning out to be the biggest problem. I'd like to take a look at Lieutenant Haniyu's design for it."

"Oh, that? I was just trying out an idea, there's no specific plan . . ."

"No, no, it's damned good," Aoyagi said, turning to Ken. "I even asked Major Wakana if he could let him come out to Nakajima Aircraft to work with us. He told us the Lieutenant's too busy here now, but maybe sometime in the future. Anyway, come and see the plane, it'll be ready soon. We should have a prototype by this fall."

"I look forward to it."

"Just as with the Hayate, we want to get everything ready to move quickly into production as soon as the experimental model is approved."

"I'd love to be the test pilot for it."

Major Iwama broke in at this point. "Hey, Kurushima! And Yamada and Haniyu!" he said cheerfully. Lifting a bottle labeled "From the Imperial Palace," he poured each of them a cup. The three young men immediately stiffened, and received the *sake* with proper formality.

"Your very good health, sir," they said.

"Thank you. You did a lot for our squadron. You know, I'm just a pilot, I don't know anything about all that technical stuff. But you technical officers really helped us."

"Squadron Leader, sir." Ken wasn't sure what he wanted to say, but he blurted out, "Why were Sugi and Hanazono chosen for the squadron and not me?"

The Major, a head shorter than Ken, looked up at him. "Is that what's bothering you? To tell you the truth, I don't know. It was an order from above."

"I wanted to accompany you into battle, sir."

"But you've got important work to do here at home. The Inspection Department needs talented technical people like you."

"I understand, sir, but any soldier worth his salt would want to fight in the plane he's worked to develop."

The smile vanished from Iwama's face. He glanced at both Ken and Aoyagi. In place of his normally placid expression, there was a hard look on his face. "It's not easy to say this in front of Mr. Aoyagi, who invented the Hayate, but the fact is that your plane is already out of date. The Hayate might, at a pinch, be a match for the Mustang, but against the B-29 it's useless. Wouldn't you agree?"

"Yes," said Aoyagi.

"We'll give it everything we can, but still . . . The real question is, what happens next? Aoyagi, you've got to come up with another plane —a high-altitude fighter capable of taking on the B-29. That's the top priority for all you young fellows. It's because I know that you'll follow up on this that I can now go off to fight reassured. You understand?" His tone had suddenly softened.

"Yes, sir, we understand." Ken's head felt hot, the heat rising from inside him. He realized that Iwama was setting out in the full expectation of his own death.

"All right, let's go." Iwama surveyed his squadron of fliers and abruptly raised his hand. "Listen everybody! We're leaving in ten minutes!" He said goodbye again to the VIPs present and walked to the lead plane.

"Hey, wait!" Major Kurokawa came running out of the barracks, his large body lurching as he headed in Iwama's direction. "Your sword, you forgot your sword!"

"Damn it, you're right." The Squadron Leader scratched his head in embarrassment and, with a laugh, took the sword and boarded his plane.

The head of the maintenance crews waved a white flag. The two men standing by each plane shouted "One, two, three," and began to turn the propellers. The engines, already warmed up, sucked in the air and burst into life. The Squadron Leader waved his hand left and right. Chocks were removed and, with Iwama in front, the planes filed onto the runway. The air filled with the roar of thousands of horsepower, then one plane after another flew off, gleaming in the sunlight. The men on the ground waved their hands in farewell.

As the fighters rose into the sky, the crews boarded the 97 bombers. Following them, the transport planes took off. Three of the bombers trailed gliders filled with 800 kilos of equipment. The gliders hit the ground once as they left the runway, but managed to lift off. Applause rose from the ground.

"They're gone," said Yamada.

"Now the hard part starts," said Ken. Yamada and Haniyu couldn't tell if this referred to the crews who had just left or to them.

V

THE ECHOES

1

There was a stir around him, and it woke him up. On the station platform Ken saw a swarm of people in mourning clothes. They were all either old people or middle-aged women, and their black clothes were faded and wrinkled. Each time a passenger stepped down from the train with a white box hung from his neck, they all bowed. On the box was written "The Heroic Spirit of [rank and name]," and inside it was a dead man's ashes. Mingling with the mourners was a group of schoolchildren with their names sewn on the shirts of their uniforms.

Haniyu also awoke. Yamada was still asleep, his snoring as loud as ever.

Ken and his two companions had only been told last night they could take today—Sunday—off, so their visit to Karuizawa had been decided in a hurry. They had been up since four that morning, and had taken the first train from Ueno Station. Ken had tried to phone ahead several times, but he hadn't been able to get through. Their trip would only be a day visit, since Ken and Haniyu were due to leave base on Tuesday to transfer a couple of new Hayates, fresh from the factory, to Hankou in China.

The third-class carriage adjoining theirs was jammed with passengers, but even in their second-class carriage people were standing in the aisles. Around them, mixed in with the civil defense clothes, women's baggy working trousers, and soldiers' uniforms, there were also white cotton blazers and colorful dresses, as if the train were just making its leisurely way to a resort.

The door opened and a group of foreigners came in. The military policeman in charge of them looked around, but there were no empty seats. The foreigners seemed to have come with almost no luggage; most of them were in their everyday wear, each carrying a single suitcase, and they looked exhausted. One of them, an elderly lady, addressed Ken in a language he didn't know. Ken shook his head.

"I'll bet it's German. Yamada can speak German," said Haniyu, trying to wake him up. Ken stopped him, and spoke to the old woman in English.

"Are you German?"

"No," the woman laughed, switching to English. It was the English of a non-native, every word carefully enunciated. "I am Spanish. What nationality are you?"

"I'm Japanese."

"Oh." The old woman stared at him in open surprise. His fellow countrymen were never this straightforward about it; when they were curious about him they would look at him on the sly, while pretending not to. The Spanish woman wasn't like that. Ken actually preferred it.

"I'm of mixed blood . . . Where do you live in Japan?"

"Yokohama. We have been there for twenty years. We have an import business—wine and corks. Suddenly we get an order to move to Karuizawa. We were very surprised. We are nationals of a neutral country, and there is no reason for us to relocate. So we protested, but they ordered us out anyway, saying there was some kind of secret defense installation in our neighborhood."

The woman turned and gestured at an elderly man, evidently her husband, and a girl of fourteen or fifteen with a boy around ten, no doubt their grandchildren.

"You've been through a lot. Why don't you sit down?" Ken stood up to offer her his seat. Haniyu stood up with him. Yamada rose, bewildered, the sleep still in his eyes. The old woman sat down, along with her granddaughter. The man in a cotton blazer in the other seat ignored them, his eyes on the forests and mountains streaming past the window. The foreign pair squeezed the little boy between them.

The military policeman, a corporal, came over. "You're not allowed to split up from your group. Get back with the others," he told them.

In broken Japanese, the Spanish lady assured him: "We will not run away. We will not run away from this train."

"No! I told you to stand over there!" He seemed to be trying to impress the three officers in front of him.

"Come on, man," Ken said to him calmly. "These people are tired."

The MP looked up at his face suspiciously. "And who are . . . ?"

"All right now," said Yamada, his thick shoulders pushing him aside. "You're meant to be kind to old people and children."

The man couldn't argue too hard with an officer, so made up for it by shouting at the other foreigners: "Hey! Didn't I tell you you're not allowed to talk!"

They immediately fell silent. The policeman glanced at Ken and Yamada. There was resentment in his eyes. "I have to look after the whole bunch myself. If there's an accident or something it'll be my responsibility."

When the Spanish pair stood up to return to their group, Ken put his hand into the pocket of his uniform and switched on his portable radio. Ignoring the startled policeman, he gave the Spaniards a wink and told them to sit down again as a clear, metallic voice on the radio reported: "As previously announced by GHQ, our brave forces on the island of Saipan chose self-annihilation over surrender on July 16th. Mobile units of the enemy's forces attempted a landing on Guam on the twenty-first, followed by Tinian on the twenty-third. Our troops are presently locked in battle with these enemy units. The enemy's goal appears to be to use these islands in the Marianas to launch air raids on Tokyo, and the Eastern Division has ordered a redoubling of air defense alertness on the home front. Each household is to maintain emergency food rations, drinking water, firefighting implements and water, and is furthermore advised . . ."

The train started up a steep incline. They passed through one tunnel after another, and each time they emerged the foliage shone bright green as sunlight filtered through the trees.

"This past June, due to the calm and diligent air-defense efforts of the public, damage was kept to an absolute minimum during the bombing of Kyushu by enemy bombers . . ."

Eventually, the train pulled into Karuizawa Station. In the square outside were rows of aproned women from the Women's Patriotic League, along with city dwellers who had come with their belongings in rucksacks to barter with the locals for food. But, as usual in this resort, it was the foreigners among the crowd who caught one's attention. The group that included the Spanish family was being led by the Military Police to the Peony Inn, the old hotel that stood in front of the station. There was a new wooden sign on the inn which read "Karuizawa Military Police Substation." Outside it, they seemed to be giving out rations: a group of Germans, with swastikas sewn on their shirts, stood there in line, herded by policemen.

"It's as if we've come to a foreign country," said Haniyu.

"It feels that way, doesn't it? This is one of the relocation areas for foreigners," Ken explained. Right after the war began an order had come from the Interior Ministry severely restricting the movement of foreign residents; special permission from the governor and the police was needed every time a foreigner wanted to travel outside his prefecture. Enemy aliens, the Americans and the British, were under the strictest surveillance, while their military people had been interned as prisoners of war. Any place near a defense installation was of course off-limits, and certain cities and prefectures banned foreign residents entirely. Recently three areas—Hakone, Karuizawa, and the part around Lake Yamanaka—had been designated compulsory residence districts for foreigners, and forced relocation had begun. Karuizawa, which had always had a large contingent of foreign residents, now had the nationals of some forty countries living there. Add to this a stream of Japanese who owned villas in the locality and had come to escape the city bombings, and the result was an explosive growth in population.

There were no horses to be seen in the stables. The gardens of many villas had been dug up and turned into vegetable patches, with beans, onions, potatoes, and eggplants struggling up in the volcanic soil.

"There seems to be a food shortage here too," said Yamada.

"Yeah, the place has really changed." Ken looked around in amazement. "I didn't get up here last summer. It's been two whole years."

"Two very long years," Yamada chimed in. "Two years scurrying about at the mercy of the Hayate."

The Kurushimas' old whitewashed Western-style house came into view. "There it is," said Ken, pointing at the villa. Haniyu and Yamada hurriedly tugged at the sleeves of their uniforms and adjusted the belts in which they carried their swords.

Ken pulled open the lattice door at the front entrance, but there was no sign of anyone around. He showed his two friends out to the garden. Here too the flowers and trees had been uprooted and replaced with tomato and taro plants, a rustic scene out of harmony with the elegant veranda and windows of the villa. There was the sound of a bowstring being released. Beyond the vegetable patch, on the archery range, stood Saburo Kurushima in a kimono, with a bow in his hands. When he noticed Ken and the others, he put down the arrow he was about to notch.

"Papa, we were suddenly given leave. This is Lieutenant Yamada and Lieutenant Haniyu, of the Inspection Department."

"It's a great honor to meet you, sir." They both saluted.

"I'm Ken's father. I've heard a lot about you."

"We're honored, sir." They were as stiff as boards.

"Nice of you to come all the way out here. Make yourselves at home. Ken, your mother took Anna and Eri to church. Yoshiko's here. As for me, I've just finished two sets."

He headed for the house, and they followed him. His hair was still abundant but noticeably whiter. He had also lost quite a bit of weight, and his shoulders seemed thinner than before. He bent forward as he walked, which made him look like an old man.

As they mounted the veranda Yoshiko came out to greet them. She gave Ken a smile so large it seemed to envelop him. "Master Ken!"

Ken introduced his two friends, then said: "I'm going to church to see my mother and sisters. What are you two going to do?"

"Don't know," said Yamada, exchanging glances with Haniyu.

Saburo motioned to them: "Well, young men, why don't you both take a seat?" and they sat down stiffly in the wicker chairs.

Eri was counting the wrinkles on Father Hendersen's face. *Are there really twenty-three between his eyes and his lips? No, twenty-four. Why has he got so many of them?* The pastor, to cover his embarrassment at the way Eri was staring, smiled at her, and she smiled back, an angelic little smile from the cute little girl whose head Father Hendersen was so fond of patting. The pastor went on reading the Bible in English. He read slowly and deliberately, so that the policeman in the last row could understand—not, of course, that that was likely. He had to read that way or the policeman would get suspicious, for he was listening for one word: "peace." To the policeman's ears that word meant anti-war propaganda and, as had happened once before, if it ever cropped up he was liable to round up the entire congregation and haul them off for questioning. Hendersen read the Bible slowly, avoiding that single word "peace."

Why does he have to do it so slowly, when there are White Russians, Italians, Swiss in the congregation, people who don't know all that much English anyway? As Eri stared at the broad shoulders of the Russian in front of her, she started to measure them. Someone poked her in the side. It was Maggie. "Don't stare like that. Pay attention to the reading." Maggie was glaring at her. Eri bent her head slightly and listened.

> Love your enemies, bless them that curse you, do good to them that hate you, and pray for them which despitefully use you, and persecute you;
>
> That ye may be the children of your Father which is in heaven; for he maketh his sun to rise on the evil and on the good, and sendeth rain on the just and on the unjust.
>
> For if ye love them which love you, what reward have ye . . .

Someone opened the church door and came in. Who in the world could be so rude as to enter just as the service was finishing, Eri wondered, and stealthily turned around. To her astonishment, she saw her brother standing there in military uniform—right there in this den of pacifists. And her astonishment immediately turned to joy. She hadn't seen him since the family had moved up here to escape the bombings. Eri gave Margaret a nudge. Maggie gave her another disapproving look. Then Eri pointed to the back of the church. It was fun to watch Maggie's face slowly turn red.

Father Hendersen noticed Ken, too, and an expression of surprise crossed his face—he wasn't much good at hiding his feelings—which made several people in the pews turn their heads. Ken walked down the aisle, his boots echoing loudly. Eri gave Margaret a little shove to make room, and beckoned Ken into the narrow space between them. Ken sat down. A hymn began, and Ken sang out, his rich, smooth baritone voice engulfing them.

The congregation emerged from the little wooden church into a soft, cool breeze and the sound of birds in the surrounding woods. After Ken gave Alice a hug, Eri rushed into his arms.

"Ken! I can't believe you're here. It's been so long."

"Eri, you look well."

"Ken, Ken, how long are you here for? You'll stay for quite a while, won't you?"

"Only for a day, I'm afraid. I've got to get back tonight."

"Only one day? What a gyp!" Eri was furious. What was wrong with the Army anyway?

Ken gave Anna a hug and kissed Margaret on both cheeks, and then the whole group, with Ken and his mother in the middle, moved off down the slope. Alice took her son by the arm, her conversation bubbling out. When she realized that her huge hat kept her from seeing his face properly she swept it off and handed it to Anna. Eri tried to smooth her mother's hair. Most of the shops in town had their shutters down, but people were out, the Tokyoites among them obvious from their dress, with several men in knickerbockers.

A young man in hunting cap and dark glasses came over. "Hey, Ken! It's been a long time." It was Ryoichi Koyama, son of the owner of the Peony Inn.

"Ryo-chan! I didn't recognize you. How's business?"

Ryoichi nervously looked around, then answered, "It's a complete disaster. Just as we were getting in gear for the summer season, all of a sudden the Military Police took us over."

"Why don't you come over to our place today?"

"Okay, I'll be around as soon as I can. But you won't see me on horseback. They requisitioned our entire stable. The tennis court's reserved for 'friendly' aliens—we Japanese can't use it any more. They say the pool's still open. I've got to go now—got some errands to do."

Ryoichi hurried off, dragging his bad right leg along.

A group of Germans came their way. The Germans liked to walk in groups, but these weren't walking so much as marching, under the direction of a middle-aged woman with a swastika proudly displayed on her blouse, who signaled to them with her right hand as if conducting a small orchestra. Unsmiling, ignoring anyone who wasn't German, they moved briskly past in neat formation. Compared to them the other foreigners seemed listless, their clothes old and worn, the luster gone from their skin, their hands dry and chapped. Bells began to clang. Eri saw some German boys coming, riding bicycles with the Nazi flag flying on them, their thin legs sticking out of leather shorts. *Deutschland über alles* they came racing along, and when a little old lady, French perhaps or Swiss, told them to watch out, the boys shook their fists at her, loudly ringing their bells.

Alice laughed as she talked to Ken, a loud, hearty laugh. How long it had been since Eri had heard her mother laugh like that.

Eri began thinking about how they were going to spend the day with Ken, as it was still eleven in the morning and they had the whole day ahead of them. *Tennis is out. There's the swimming pool, but the water hasn't been changed in months and it's too dirty to swim in. There's horseback riding* (she had started taking lessons so that someday she could ride with Ken), *but all the stables have been emptied by the Army. So there's nothing to do. The war has ruined everything. Everything! How about going on a picnic? Hiking? Now that's patriotic. Left! Right! Left! Right! Mount Hanare isn't high enough, Mount Asama is too high. We'll have to find a mountain in between, somewhere with nice scenery and not too far away . . .*

On the veranda, Saburo was well settled in his wicker armchair, calmly smoking a pipe, but the two young officers were still buttoned up in their full uniforms. *Papa's always like that,* thought Anna; *he means to be a good host, but he just doesn't have the sense to tell them to take their jackets off and make themselves at home, offer them something to drink or a cigarette. And the poor fellows have got their heads lowered, listening to a lecture from His Excellency . . .*

Both of them stood up to be introduced to Anna and her mother. Ken had often spoken about them. The tall, fat one was Lieutenant Yamada, a doctor who loved animals, and the slim young man with pale skin, so much smaller than Ken but of average build for a Japanese, was Lieutenant Haniyu, son of the commander of the Japanese forces in China and, according to Ken, a good violinist. Haniyu's face was different from the photographs of the general Anna had seen in the newspapers; he was classically good-looking—his mother's genes, presumably. As for Yamada, he didn't have any of the citified refinement one normally associated with military doctors, who tended to come from the upper crust. He was also older than she had imagined, perhaps even thirty. She felt slightly disappointed. He was so fat it seemed as if the buttons were going to fly off his uniform and, to make matters worse, there were ugly sweat stains under his armpits and down his back.

Alice clapped her hands. "Welcome, all of you. I'm going to feed you. I'm going to give you a real feast. So make yourselves at home. And take off those uniforms. Ken, don't you have something casual for them to wear?"

"Yes, I do. Okay, you guys, let's go upstairs and change."

Each of them had different luggage. Ken had an Italian leather trunk the family had used in Europe, Haniyu his violin case and a valise, and Yamada a large cloth pouch that was so full the zipper wouldn't close—rather like the body of its owner.

When the guests went up to the second floor, Eri began skipping about like a kindergarten child. "Hey, hey, what're we going to do with Ken and his friends? I think we should go hiking. The weather's great, and if we climb Mount Sekison we'll get a wonderful view from the top. Why don't we make some boxed lunches and go? What's the matter, Anna, you don't think it's a good idea? Maybe you're right, hiking *would* be a bit childish for those big men."

"No, I'm not against it . . ." Anna was thinking what a baby her sister was. *Boxed lunches? Why, we don't even have any rice. Ever since summer the town has been bursting with new arrivals, and the ration situation has gotten so bad that last week all they had to hand out were some dried-out sweet potatoes. And just when I was thinking that I'd have to go and barter for some food from the locals, here's Eri talking about boxed lunches for a hike. The girl is living in a dream world. But then . . . what about Mama?* "A real feast," *she promised them. Using what?*

Anna went into the kitchen, with her mother and Eri in tow. All they found, though, when Yoshiko had a look in the rice tub, the vegetable bins, and the icebox were some wheat flakes, flour, potatoes, onions, and a few loose vegetables.

"It's worse than I thought." Eri looked crushed.

But it was their mother who was the most crestfallen. Wringing her hands, she cried, "This is terrible! My son's come home and I can't even feed him. I don't have a thing to give his friends."

Eri hugged her and tried to calm her down.

"All right," said Anna in a quiet voice. "I'm going out to sell something for food. If I go to Saku or Ueda, I'm sure I'll find something."

Eri was worried. "But Anna, we don't have anything left to trade with."

With the rush of city folk heading out there to barter for food, the farmers in the vicinity had become highhanded. They wouldn't accept cash, only things—useful things. Up until last year the locals had been dazzled with foreign things, and happily took English tea plates, French embroidery, and Parisian jewelry boxes. But then it dawned on them that such articles weren't much use to them in their everyday lives, and they began asking for something more Japanese—lengths of cloth and kimonos, futons and lacquerware. The Kurushimas, whose possessions were almost all foreign-made—things they'd picked up during their long years abroad—abruptly ran out of items to barter with. At that point Anna's possessions had come in handy. Arizumi, her former husband, had been a fancier of traditional Japanese things, and had had several kimonos made for her. One by one the kimonos had fed the Kurushima household. But recently even these had run out.

"My family can probably help," Yoshiko said. Yoshiko's people lived in a hot-spring village near Ueda; her mother Toku still tilled her fields there.

"Oh, no, we can't ask you every time," Anna protested. They had already been helped out of several tight squeezes by her.

"No, it's perfectly all right. My mother's on her own, and she's got more than she can eat. And it's Master Ken, after all, who came all the way here to see us."

Anna thanked her, but insisted that they first make an effort themselves and only go to Toku as a last resort.

"Sorry for interrupting, but we happen to have brought some rations with us." Yamada, who had slipped into the kitchen so abruptly he startled Eri, dumped his cloth pouch on the kitchen table with a thud. He was dressed in workman's trousers and short sleeves. "Here's enough rice for several big bowls." He took out four envelopes of rice wrapped in his Army socks, and a heavy-looking carton. "These are pilots' rations. This one's chocolate, this is vitamins, and here's some anti-cold supplements—plus some Pilots' Good Health . . ."

"What a lot of stuff!" Eri was all eyes. "But what's the last one—a health drink?"

"It's just plain liquor, actually. Here, take it all." He shoved the carton in the women's direction.

"Why, thank you very much," said Anna, bowing deeply.

Yamada bowed back, his face red. "If you're going out bartering, let me go with you. I could carry things for you."

"Oh no, we wouldn't want to trouble you." She felt a bit uncomfortable, realizing that he might have picked up their conversation a few moments ago.

"I'm sorry, I couldn't help overhearing." Suppressing his embarrassment, he forced the words out. "But I'm an expert at scrounging. Before I went in the Army, in Tokyo, I used to do it all the time. And today I'm in charge of our group, so I feel it's only my duty . . ."

Eri burst out laughing. "I think, Mr. Yamada, that you really *want* to go out bartering."

"You're right, I do." He gave a forced smile, and wiped at the sweat on his face.

"Well then, I would appreciate it," said Anna with a smile. She felt it would in fact be easier if someone else were with her. In the past, she had always gone out with Eri or with Ryoichi, and never alone. "It's Eri's idea that afterwards we all go hiking up a mountain."

"I'm no good at that sort of thing. You can see how heavy I am," he said, shaking his head.

"Eri, I'm going to make some rice balls with the rice Mr. Yamada brought." She tapped her sister on the shoulder. "You go and discuss the hike with the others."

"Oh, but you've got to come too or it won't be any fun."

"I'm not very good at walking up mountains either. I'd prefer to haggle with the locals for food—it's easier."

"I'll go talk to the others, then." Eri bounded out of the kitchen, unable to contain her excitement.

Yamada glanced around the kitchen. "Can I help with anything? I'm actually a pretty good cook."

"Oh no! We can't have a man in the kitchen!" Anna glared at him. Yamada walked out, a bit crestfallen.

"Why don't you let me come along?" said Yoshiko.

"No, there's no need. It's something I want to do myself." There was confidence in her voice. It was also a fact that Anna was better at bargaining with the locals than Yoshiko. Yoshiko was all too aware of her own roots in this region; it was impossible for her to swallow her pride and go through the humiliation that hard bargaining entailed, whereas Anna, giving up her own pieces of clothing one by one, would press on until satisfied.

Eri came back. "They all agreed to go! But they're sorry you won't be coming."

"Oh Anna, why don't you go?" said her mother. "I can do the bargaining."

"No, Mama, you can't," Anna laughed. As a Japanese citizen Alice was free to go where she pleased, but her appearance made people automatically assume she was a foreigner, and the family was worried she might get stopped and interrogated at one of the checkpoints the police had set up around Karuizawa. Her imperfect Japanese would only make her seem more suspicious. Also, the give-and-take of bargaining was simply beyond her language ability.

Yoshiko washed the rice, put the pot on the stove, and lit the fire. Anna and her mother peeled some onions. Just then, a man appeared at the kitchen window. His face was deeply tanned, and he stared in sharply at them. Yoshiko opened the door when he knocked on it.

"Wanna buy some meat?"

"What kind of meat?" Yoshiko said suspiciously.

"Beef." The man pulled out a slab of meat from his cart, which was covered with a straw mat.

She peered at it. "It does look like beef." Drawing back, she whispered to Anna, "Black market."

In English Anna told her mother, "This man's selling black market meat." She then inspected the meat carefully, prodding and sniffing it. "Mmm, it's quite fresh. This being a special day, I'm sure we'll be forgiven for buying something on the black market." She switched back to Japanese. "How much do you want for it?"

"I ain't selling for money. I want *things*."

Alice stepped forward. "What kind of things?"

There was a gleam in the man's eyes. "You people're pretty rich, aren't you? I want some gold."

"We don't have any. We gave all our gold to the war effort."

"That's gold, ain't it?' The man pointed at the little crucifix hanging at her neck. It was an heirloom.

Alice shook her head angrily. "No! You certainly can't have that."

"I ain't selling except for gold. It's a nice cut of meat." The man wrapped it in newspaper again and hid it beneath the straw mat. Then, with a wicked look in his eyes that said, *You'll change your mind when you get hungry enough,* he slowly wheeled his cart away. After a while, they saw him suddenly yank the handles up and break into a run.

"What happened?" asked Anna.

Yoshiko went out to look.

"It's strange. There's nobody around."

"He must have thought he'd seen a policeman. He seemed in quite a hurry."

Just then, they heard Yoshiko scream. She rushed back into the kitchen and pointed outside. "Oh my God!—there's something horrible lying out there."

"Don't scare me, Yoshiko. What is it?"

Anna and her mother ventured outside, led by the maid. At the foot of a huge larch tree lay a hideous-looking thing. It was a bull's severed head; its blackish blue eyes were open wide, and its horns gleamed like metal. On the grass was a stream of blood.

"How disgusting," said Anna, looking away.

"That man! He just dumped this on us." Yoshiko's voice was filled with outrage. "We should tell the police."

Alice touched the bull's horns and pressed its eyeballs. "Good and fresh," she said in English. "They're not squishy at all. We're in luck. Yoshiko, don't we have a big pot just the right size for this?"

"Mama, just what have you got in mind?" Anna sounded astonished.

"I'm going to make a delicious meal out of it. Just leave it to me. But you must promise not to tell the others. They might find it a bit off-putting."

"But . . ."

"It's all right, Anna. *Tête de boeuf* is a specialty of mine."

Yoshiko, with a dubious look on her face, brought out the giant pot and helped Alice lift the head by the horns and, with a cheer, dump the whole thing into the pot and shut the lid. The three women had quite a job lugging it into the kitchen; they had to turn the pot on its side and roll it in. Just as they got inside, Eri appeared.

"You go into the living room," her mother ordered. "We're busy making the boxed lunches."

"What's that?"

"Pot roast. Now don't worry, dear, the lunches will be ready in time."

As she shooed Eri out Alice slapped the pot and gave the other two a wink.

2

A long line had formed by the bus stop in front of the station. They were right at the back of the line and there was little chance of getting on, but they decided to wait anyway.

As they waited in their hiking outfits, Eri and the others stood out among the crowd of women in baggy farmer's trousers and men in laborers' rubber-soled shoes. There was a lot of staring. And, sure enough, two military policemen wandered over, clumping along in their boots. It was Margaret they first approached. The look in their eyes gave Eri the chills.

"Where're you going?"

"We're going for a hike in the mountains," Margaret answered in fluent Japanese.

"A hike!" It was the last answer he expected to hear. In a softer tone of voice he asked, "Which mountain?"

"Mount Sekison."

"Let's see your travel permit."

Ryoichi stepped forward. "She's Swiss. People from a neutral country are allowed to travel freely within the prefecture without a permit."

"Hmm." The policeman looked stumped. He was a private. "Show me some identification," he told Margaret.

"Yes, sir." She pulled out her passport. Ryoichi had reminded her to bring it along when they'd set out, and she had slipped it into the pocket of her rucksack.

The other policeman, a sergeant, stared hard at Ken. "That one, too, let's see some identification."

"That one . . . Oh, you mean me? Yes, sir." Ken, with a great show of deference, handed him his military papers.

The man stiffened, as if he'd received an electric shock, but managed to salute and say, "Please excuse my mistake, sir!" and returned Ken's papers. "Is this Swiss person with you, sir?"

"Yes, she is." Ken smiled at him. "We're doing some 'physical training for victory.'"

The bus came. It was a charcoal-driven vehicle with a huge pot fixed to the back which belched white smoke. The line began moving, people jostling each other, and in no time at all the bus was full. As expected, they couldn't get on without a struggle. When Eri finally got onto the step, she found herself being pushed firmly inside by Haniyu. Haniyu's body was crushed against her; she could feel his body heat. Eri closed her eyes, enjoying the sensation.

The bus followed its usual route, heading west. Ten minutes later they made a stop. Some passengers got off, and at last the door shut, with Ken, who had been riding with half his body hanging out, finally managing to get inside. They started climbing a slope. The bus churned up a cloud of dust at the rear.

At Oiwake they got off and began walking. When they reached the mountain trail, which led through a larch wood, a cool breeze touched their sweaty faces.

"Those MPs are a damned nuisance," Ken said to Ryoichi.

"Karuizawa is crawling with them. I don't remember seeing those two, though. They must be new arrivals."

"You sure seem to know your law—that bit about neutral nationals."

"No, I'm just an amateur, but our place is full of cops, so it helps to know where you stand."

The path sloped gently uphill. When the larch wood ended they found themselves facing a forest that backed against the foothills. A wind rose, sending white waves across a field of pampas grass that lay in between. Beyond the red leaves of the birch trees they could see Mount Asama, smiling like a bonze, a plume of smoke above it. Haniyu stopped walking and stood there. Eri stopped too.

"Isn't it pretty?" Haniyu stroked a frond of pampas grass. It was still young, slightly wet, with shades of vermilion at its stem. "And soft."

"Look how far it stretches," said Eri, gazing out into the distance, where the white grass seemed to foam at the edge of the trees.

"They remind me of ghosts, these white fluffy things. When people die their souls must float around like that."

"What?" Eri looked curiously at his prominent brow and nose. His talk seemed a bit "off" for such a young man.

A nightingale called, so close they felt they could hear it breathing; but they couldn't see it. From somewhere another nightingale called in response. Ken and Margaret were in the lead, with Ryoichi walking a few paces behind them. From a distance Ken's long legs seemed to tangle with Ryoichi's. Haniyu and Eri started walking again, side by side.

"Your brother's a superb pilot. Most of the men in the Inspection Department are veterans, and some have shot down a lot of enemy planes. He's as good as any of them. He's a born pilot."

"And you . . . are you a born pilot too?"

"No, I'm useless. I just don't have any gift for it. I just don't have, you know, any vertical sense. An airplane moves the length and breadth of a cubic world. But my sense of motion is limited to the ground, it's a surface sense."

"But . . ." Eri didn't know what to say. She couldn't begin to imagine what a cubic world was.

A swarm of dragonflies came, flying against the wind and filling the blue sky with their wings. Haniyu held his hand up to the swarm.

"We have a trainer plane called the Red Dragonfly. Three years ago I did my training in one of them. It seems like yesterday. I've been together with your brother ever since flying school."

"I've often heard him talk about that time."

"What did he say?" Haniyu looked a little worried.

"He talked about when you were in the hospital for something, and him flying past your window in a Red Dragonfly. I was surprised they were allowed to do that."

"They weren't. It was you brother's idea of a prank."

The two of them caught up with the others.

"We're going to go through the forest now," said Ryoichi. "Stay together, so nobody gets lost. Ken, you take the lead."

"Okay!" Ken stood in front and looked back at Eri. "Eri, don't start saying you're tired and hungry. You keep falling behind."

"That's not the reason," said Ryoichi with a wink. "It's the attraction of Mr. Haniyu that keeps making her fall behind."

"Ryo-chan, you . . . !" Eri pinched him on the shoulder. She meant it as a joke, but it made him yelp. "Oh, I'm sorry, are you all right?"

"I'm *not* all right. I'm wounded. People who play the piano should know how strong their fingers are."

As soon as they entered the forest the path became steep. There were large and small volcanic rocks strewn about, and it was hard to walk. The sound of the cicadas poured down on them, they were out of breath and, darn it, just as Ken predicted, Eri found herself racked with hunger. Margaret, her thin legs clad in dark blue pantaloons, was following strongly behind Ken. Even Ryoichi with his lame leg ambled up the slope, sometimes kicking rocks out of the way. *Darned if I'm going to let them get ahead*, Eri swore to herself, and she clambered gamely up the path.

Haniyu began to sing. He had a rich tenor voice.

> Come, my friends,
> all of us together,
> let's spend the day
> walking in the hills.
>
> The weather's warm,
> the sky is clear,
> the view unrolls
> over radiant fields.

Ken joined in. Ryoichi took the lower notes; he had a surprisingly attractive bass voice. Margaret didn't know the words but she soon picked up the tune and hummed along.

> The sun is high
> in the autumn sky,
> so let's set out—
> a perfect day.

The pampas grass
beckons hither,
and woodland birds
are calling to us.

"What song is that? It's lovely."

"It's an old schoolchildren's song, 'Walking in the Hills.' "

Haniyu's voice rang out with other tunes. Eri was impressed, deciding he must have had proper training; he also seemed to know folk songs from almost every region in the country.

"Did you learn singing somewhere?"

"Yes, a little. My violin teacher also gave me some voice lessons."

Haniyu got tired after a while, and Ryoichi took over. Mostly he sang American folk songs, beginning with Stephen Foster. Ken, Eri, and Margaret loved it and joined in. Both Kurushimas were crazy about thirties jazz and country music. Here they were belting out one "enemy" song after another right in the middle of a war—they'd be in big trouble if anyone heard them—but Eri knew it would be all right as long as they had Ken and Haniyu, Army officers, with them, so she sang at the top of her voice. But then she noticed that Haniyu wasn't joining in.

"Don't you like this music?" she asked him.

"I'm not used to it. I was raised in a house where my father sang military marches and my mother sang traditional ballads. But I like it fine. Nothing wrong with American music."

Eri was glad that, at a time when both adults and children went around shouting "Anglo-American swine!" this young man could see them as human beings. In the Kurushima family nobody called them "swine," just as nobody ever said "Jap." Alice had been depressed to see the word "Jap" all over the newspapers Saburo had brought back from the United States with him. She would never allow such language in her house.

"Listen!" Ken told the others, and they all fell silent. Beneath the light whistling of the wind there came the sound of a waterfall. Everyone suddenly sprang to life, and in a few bounds climbed up to the ridge from which they could see the falls.

"Look, the water's red!"

"It's called the 'Waterfall of Blood.'" Drops of reddish spray rose in the dappled light shining through the treetops. It had been a year since Eri had visited the place. Before, she used to come out here several times a year. It was as if the summer didn't properly end for her until she had seen this waterfall.

"There's a way to get right down beside it," said Margaret. "Why don't we go?"

They descended the cliff until they reached the valley stream, and then marched in a line up the narrow trail. The path was slippery and Ryoichi, who was walking behind Margaret, lost his footing. As he fell backward he almost made Eri fall too, but Ken held him up and Haniyu supported Eri. Haniyu smiled. He didn't seem to want to let go, and Eri let herself remain helpless for a few lingering seconds.

Somehow they managed to reach the cave facing the waterfall, with three stone Buddhas in it. It was large enough for ten people to sit inside. The waterfall, which was now so close they could almost reach out and touch it, had an eerie sort of beauty. Just as its name suggested, it seemed as if blood were pouring from a wound in the mountain.

"It really is red. I wonder why," Haniyu said.

"The source is way upstream. The water's clear there, but almost immediately turns red. Probably iron in the water," Ryoichi explained.

A breeze blew through the forest trees, and the crisp leaves came tumbling down. The ground was covered with bright red and yellow leaves.

"Oh yes, now I remember!" said Ryoichi. "Last spring someone spotted a bear over there."

"Where, where? Near here?" asked Eri, frightened.

"Straight ahead. They found a bear living with its cubs inside a hollow. In the end some soldiers came and shot them."

"They didn't have to do that. A bear and its cubs aren't criminals."

"No, but they're hungry these days, and there's a chance they'll attack people."

"But what a pity. Killing them because of a *chance*."

"It can't be helped. And people are doing it to other people, aren't they?"

"You think there are any more of them lurking around?" Eri gazed at the dense foliage on the opposite bank of the stream. There stretched a darkness, thick with trees, out of which a bear might easily emerge. The wind groaned in the treetops, and the cries of the birds seemed to be warning them of danger.

"It's perfectly safe," said Haniyu, aware of Eri's alarm. "We're enough to make any bear run away."

"I'm hungry. Let's have some lunch," said Ken. Eating inside the cave would be too gloomy, so they decided to open the wooden lunchboxes by the log bridge upstream from the falls. The rice balls and grilled corn were delicious on their empty stomachs. A steady breeze brushed their cheeks, and Eri found herself stretching out and looking straight up at the sky and the clouds.

"That must feel good," said Margaret, who followed suit.

Eri stole a glance at the men, who were laughing and joking a little way off, and realized there was something different about her own feelings this time. *Usually when Ken comes home after a long absence I stick around him all day*, she thought, *but this time I've stayed with Mr. Haniyu. Almost as if I were ignoring Ken on purpose. No, that's not it. It's because Ken's with Margaret I'm leaving them alone, that's right*—or so she told herself. But her eyes kept drifting toward Haniyu's handsome profile. She was aware of Ryoichi glancing sideways at her with a teasing look in his eyes, and nearly made a nasty face at him.

Eri turned to Margaret and looked into her green eyes.

"Do you like Ken?" she asked her quietly.

"Of course."

"Well, do you . . . love him?"

"Of course I do," Margaret replied, with no hesitation at all.

"Really? I'm so glad."

"Eri," she whispered, "you mustn't tell him."

"Okay."

"You swear?"

"Yes, it's a secret."

Margaret turned away and fell silent. Eri, wondering why, stole a glance at her. She was astonished to see her crying.

"Hey, what's the matter?" She couldn't think why but she felt like crying herself.

"I'm so happy you insisted on inviting me along today."

"Oh, is that it—because you're happy?" Eri felt reassured. But the sadness in Margaret's voice made her eyes blur with tears.

"I'm from a neutral country, so I'm fairly free. But the police, and especially the MPs, as you know, aren't too keen on Japanese people associating with foreigners. Today my mother didn't want me to come along with you. She was afraid I might cause you all trouble."

"What are you talking about! It's no trouble at all. There's no reason why it should be."

"It's not that simple, Eri." A tiny wrinkle appeared on Margaret's nose, as if she were about to sneeze. "My mother was originally British, and the British are enemies."

"Well, *my* mother was originally American."

"That's right, and that's why she's under surveillance."

"I know." There had been many little incidents. Time and again her mother had found some strange man following her when she went out. Letters came to the house which appeared to have been opened, the return address on the back slightly askew. A policeman masquerading as a postman had questioned Yoshiko about what went on in their home.

"And something else." Margaret had assumed a rather adult tone of voice. "There's a rumor going around that there are hidden weapons somewhere around here, and the authorities are afraid of foreign spies."

"That's ridiculous. If such things really existed even Japanese people wouldn't be allowed near them. At the very least there'd be No Entry signs."

Ryoichi said they ought to be moving on, and the group got to their feet. The path ahead was even narrower and steeper. There didn't seem to be any hikers these days, for the trail lay under thick stalks of striped bamboo. Ryoichi took the lead, stripping the bamboo away as he climbed. Margaret, who had been going strongly until then, started to show signs of fatigue, and Ken deliberately slackened his pace so as not to get too far ahead. Ryoichi, Eri, and Haniyu pushed on without them. After a while they sat down on an outcrop to wait for the other two.

"They're really slow."

"Maggie's gotten so thin. I'll bet she doesn't get enough to eat. She looks undernourished."

"Her family's been through a lot," Eri sighed, as she thought of her friend's circumstances. After the war began the Anglican church had been shut down, and Father Hendersen and his family had moved into a small cabin by Kumoba Pond. By summer, however, with the forced relocation of foreigners, the demand for church services had grown, and the pastor was allowed to open the old church for Sunday services. But the Military Police and the Thought Police, always on the lookout for "pacifist activities," interfered constantly, and the services were conducted under the strictest surveillance. With all the stress the pastor's wife Audrey, who had a heart condition, had taken to her bed. Margaret had been busy nursing her.

"I'll go look for them," said Haniyu, heading back on the path they'd been following.

A short while later Margaret appeared, supported by the two young men. There was sweat gleaming on her pale face.

"Maggie, you look exhausted. We'd better turn back."

"I also suggested we go back," said Ken, "but she absolutely refuses, and insists on climbing the rest of the way." There was concern and vexation in his voice.

"Well, we *are* almost at the top," said Ryoichi.

"I'm all right. There's nothing wrong. I can make it." Margaret climbed on in front.

"She's pushing herself," said Haniyu. "You can see she's totally exhausted, but she's determined to go on. She's overdoing it. I can tell because I do the same thing myself."

"You do?" Eri gave him a doubtful look. He was in the prime of life, a young man who looked good in his uniform, and just as good in an open-collared shirt and tennis cap.

"I've been pushing myself my whole life . . ."

After negotiating the path that zigzagged up a sudden incline, they at last came out onto a flat place covered with creeping pines. The summit was a rounded knoll about another fifty meters further up. Margaret, stumbling, climbed this last bit, with a dogged Eri close behind. When they reached the summit they all sat down and gazed around them.

Over the brownish mountainside moved shadows of clouds large and small, bending as though over creases in cloth, with every detail, each crag and scrubby pine, prominent. The whole thing was like a luminous and intricate illustration. Into the passing clouds rose white volcanic smoke, maintaining an unchanging shape as if insisting on its being a permanent part of the mountain landscape.

Margaret stood up and very slowly turned around.

"What're you doing, Maggie?" asked Ken.

"When you turn like this you can hear the different sounds of the wind. As if the mountain's speaking to you."

"No kidding," said Eri, who got up and tried it. The wind passed over her ears, whistling high and low depending on the direction, as though playing a tune.

"This is a famous spot for echoes," said Ryoichi. "Somebody try shouting."

Ken called out, "OO-EE!" Once, then twice, an echo returned.

Then Haniyu tried. His high tenor voice came back even higher, like the voice of a woman.

Margaret shouted at the top of her lungs. Her clear soprano voice turned into bright echoes like children's laughter.

"What if we all try shouting together?" suggested Eri. Their shouts dissolved in the air before returning as the cries of a dozen people.

Margaret's hair was blowing in the wind, her face full of color again. Eri jumped up and planted a loud kiss on her friend's cheek. *This stupid war*, she thought. *Haniyu and Ryoichi are pure Japanese;*

Maggie comes from a neutral country, with half of her blood an enemy alien's. Papa is pure Japanese, but Mama's Japaneseness is messed up by her having been born in an enemy country. And Ken, Anna, and I are Japanese with enemy alien blood in us. The women have it better, we can get by without having to kill anyone. But Ken, what a weird situation he's in: half Japanese, half American, obliged to kill Americans (his other half). What a stupid war, caused by incredibly stupid people—Americans and Japanese! Everything around us—even our echoes—seems to be saying that.

"Come on, let's do it again," Eri insisted. They all shouted once again, and clarinet echoes came back to them. The sky, the mountains, the clouds, and the wind all cooperated in producing echo after echo.

"I'll be all right, we can go now," said Anna to Yamada as she got up from the shrine veranda. But when she grasped the handlebars of her bicycle they still felt heavy, and right away she started pouring sweat again. Even though her throat was parched the sweat came, robbing her body of all its liquid. Her ears ached with the sound of the cicadas, like metal rasps being rubbed together.

"You must be exhausted. Why don't we rest here a bit longer?" Yamada said to her gently, even though he had already stood up to go.

"But we're running out of time." The sun was getting low in the sky, and she was worried. They had to find something to eat soon if they were going to get it home in time to prepare it for dinner.

They had already been turned down twice. Since she was trying to trade a formal visiting kimono she had her eye on farmhouses where there might be a young wife in the family. At the first house a young woman had appeared who had shown an interest in the kimono. Anna thought the deal was set, but that lasted only a few minutes— until the mother-in-law came out and put a stop to it. At the second house an old woman told them they had nothing to sell, no rice, no vegetables, and shooed them away like dogs. They came to the dark, dense woods surrounding a shrine, and decided to drink some water and rest a little, but the water in the fountain for pilgrims was covered with mosquito larvae. So they just sat down on the veranda of the main shrine building for a short break.

There was a road that led from behind the shrine into the fields. Along it stood several straw-thatched farmhouses. Oppressed by the glare of the sun, Anna pedaled hard on her bicycle, feeling sorry for and concerned about Yamada, who had followed along like a loyal servant, oblivious to the heat. It was particularly embarrassing when she had to pull out her kimono in front of him.

They came to a fairly spacious-looking farmhouse, with its main wing extending sideways with several large rooms in it. In the earthen-floored kitchen they found the women of the house stuffing sweet potatoes into straw bags. The young wife, who was about the same age as Anna, was directing the work of the other women and girls, who were either her younger sisters or her daughters. Anna set her heart on getting some of those sweet potatoes.

The woman's face tensed as she spotted the two intruders. When they spoke to her she stood in the doorway, as if to hide what was going on in the kitchen. They suggested an exchange. She shook her head.

"No. We don't have anything to sell. These potatoes are for the Army, they're taking them all."

"Would you consider trading some rice or some beans for this?" Anna lifted the package, wrapped in cloth, from the rack of her bicycle and placed it with great care on the farmhouse veranda. From the wrapping emerged a magnificent silk garment, with beautiful designs on its sleeves.

"Nope. We don't need stuff like that." The woman scarcely glanced at the kimono; only her hand moved slowly over the garment, checking its worth.

"Ten cups of rice, six cups of beans, and a few vegetables. How about it? You couldn't buy it anywhere for that price."

"Naw, that's too expensive," the woman answered.

"But it's pure silk, and it's as good as new."

"I don't want it. We don't need any luxury stuff like that." A glimmer of interest in the woman's face seemed to go out and, ignoring them, she went back into the kitchen. Anna called to her again, but she didn't seem to hear. Dejectedly, after wrapping up the kimono again, Anna pushed her bicycle out through the farmhouse gate.

With a good deal of hesitation, Yamada ventured a proposal. "You told me not to say anything, so I haven't. But why don't you, just once, let me try to negotiate? Next time you don't say anything and let me do it."

"Well, all right, but it's just not our lucky day. I imagine we'll end up having to ask old Toku for food again."

"Yes, but let me at least try. Just once." Yamada's round shoulders were hunched a bit diffidently.

They reached the riverbank. Boys in loincloths were swimming from a little island in the middle of the river. Mount Asama, unlike the view from Karuizawa, stood sidewise, broad and languid, with clouds swirling about its middle. The wind was pleasant on their sweaty skin.

There was a farmhouse facing the river. One entered through the middle of a storage room. Above the entranceway, and to the left and right, were piled sacks of charcoal and firewood. On the left in the front courtyard was a cowshed, and on the right was the main house. Yamada tiptoed into the courtyard and surveyed the family quarters.

"It's an elderly couple. Let me try out my plan." He took a piece of charcoal from one of the sacks and blackened his palms with it, then his cheeks and forehead.

"What are you doing?" said Anna.

"Sorry, but would you mind smearing some of this on your face, too? You can wash it off later. Now listen. We're going to turn ourselves into a miserable young couple whose house was destroyed in the air raid on Yahata, who lost their child and everything they owned in the bombing and managed to escape to the countryside. Don't worry, I'll do all the talking. You just have to nod and say 'Oh yes' and 'That's right.'"

"But how could we possibly . . . ?"

"Don't worry. Just leave it all to me."

Anna was nervous as she rubbed the charcoal on. She was a wretched actress.

Yamada plastered mud over his pants and shirt and deliberately wrinkled his clothes. Then, leaving his bicycle by the road, he walked in, swinging his big behind, with Anna following. He slid open the glass door of the family quarters and, in a pitiful voice, called out, "Is anybody there?" His manner was so convincing that Anna almost burst out laughing. From inside the house a rather refined-looking old woman appeared.

"Ah, excuse me," Yamada panted. He staggered and grabbed one of the pillars. "We're sorry to bother you, but our house was wiped out in the air raid on Yahata, and we escaped up here. We've got some money. We were wondering if you could maybe sell us some food . . . D'you have a glass of water?"

The old woman gaped at them and hurried inside, reemerging with a kettle of water and two glasses.

"This is my wife." Yamada gestured at Anna with his chin. "You'd better drink some water . . . You see, she's expecting . . . hey, you'd better sit down and get some rest."

Anna, mustering a skill that surprised even herself, pretended to be on the verge of collapse. She sat down on the veranda and drank as if she hadn't seen water for days—which wasn't difficult since she was genuinely thirsty.

"So your house was destroyed in the air raid, was it?" the old woman said. "I heard it was terrible over there."

"Yes, ma'am," said Yamada, his shoulders slumping with dejection. "It was horrible. These gigantic bombers—they call them B-29s— came with their engines roaring and dropped firebombs on us. You ever heard of firebombs? They're different from regular bombs. When a firebomb hits it explodes and spreads flames all around, and in a few minutes all the houses are just ash."

"Really!" the old woman said, nodding. From inside the house her elderly husband now appeared. The two of them sat on the veranda, and were all ears as Yamada told his story.

"The firebomb is a steel cylinder—it's got six sides, like this," he continued, gesturing with his hands and body, and gulping water. "They come in double clusters of eighteen of 'em. And when they drop one of those big bundles, why, you should see it, they scatter all over the place, like a fountain of red flames. It's like fireworks, they're real pretty in the sky, but, wow—when they hit the ground, they cause a hell of fire. Just one of those cylinders, when it hit our house, it burst right into flames."

"Were a lot of people killed?"

"Yes. Women and children. It was indiscriminate bombing, there were blackened bodies all over the place."

"Oh? Women and children too?" The old man's mouth was twisted in anger.

"Our side put up a good fight. We downed some of their planes. I even saw some men who'd parachuted from one of those bombers taken prisoner."

"Monsters! They'll kill even women and children!" The old man's moustache was trembling. "They ought to be cut to pieces."

"Yes, right . . . well, what happened was that me and my poor wife here, bombed out of our house, we had nowhere to go. My wife is expecting. I didn't know what to do. I remembered visiting here in Shinshu when I was a student, so I thought we should try coming up here again . . . We were hoping maybe you could sell us some food. We can pay for it." He took his wallet out and flashed some bills at them.

The old woman brought out some bean cakes and potatoes. Then she added some more beans and some sweet potatoes, until there was so much they could barely carry it all, and the old couple let them have it for twenty yen. The rucksacks almost split as they stuffed the food in. Finally, after thanking them with loud and heartfelt thanks, they were on their way.

Outside, they shoved the rucksacks on the racks of their bicycles, then pedaled furiously until they reached the highway, soaked with sweat.

"I was so worried. I was sure they'd see through it . . . ," said Anna, putting her hand on her chest in a gesture of relief, now that the farmhouse was out of sight.

"We did it, though, didn't we?" Yamada laughed as he wiped his face.

"But it still bothers me a little. You know, as if we tricked them."

"Everything I told them, about the air raid and about the prisoners, is true. I heard it from your brother, who went to inspect a B-29 that had been shot down over Kyushu. And he also copied the way people down there speak, so I even managed a bit of an accent. Also, what we paid for the food was just about the market price."

"Okay, well, I suppose it's all right then . . . I don't know how to thank you."

"That's all right. The real work is going to be getting all this stuff back to Karuizawa, isn't it?"

"Yes, just lead the way, sir!" she answered, like a good soldier.

The highway forked at the river and soon started climbing steeply. The same road they had easily descended earlier by bicycle was a struggle now, made even harder by all the baggage they had. After trying several ways of balancing their cargo, they realized it would be easier just to carry the rucksacks on their backs. Yamada insisted on carrying Anna's too; he wouldn't take no for an answer. He tied her bag onto his and set off up the road—a tower of strength, with a tower of stuff on his back.

What a funny man, Anna thought. *It wasn't long ago that he was complaining he was much too fat to go mountain climbing, and here he is, climbing hills, and still going strong.*

"I hope you'll forgive me for pretending you were my wife like that."

"Oh, don't worry . . ."

"But to say you were pregnant. That *was* a bit much! Your brother'll kill me."

Anna didn't reply, only smiled, feeling slightly uncomfortable.

3

It was around four o'clock when Eri got home with the others. She took a bath and had just finished changing when she heard a voice at the front door. Her hair was too untidy for her to go herself. From somewhere her mother shouted, "Eri! Go see who it is. Yoshiko and I are busy in the kitchen."

"Yes, Mama." Eri reluctantly bundled up her hair, tied a scarf around it, and went to the front door.

There was a policeman standing there.

He was a balding, middle-aged man, breathing heavily and covered with sweat. The sweat dripped down into his eyes, and when Eri appeared, he frantically searched his pockets for a handkerchief but couldn't find one.

". . . Is this the home of Mr. Kurushima, Mr. Kurushima the Ambassador . . . the home of His Excellency the . . ."

"Yes it is."

The man bowed. "I'm sorry to, to trouble you, but . . . there's big trouble . . ."

"What? What is it?"

"If you'd be so kind as to come with me, right away . . . there's big trouble, and I don't understand a word they're saying."

"I'm sorry but could you tell me who you want to come with you and where you want them to go?"

The man gave a low bow. After finally pulling a wrinkled handkerchief out of his pants pocket and wiping his forehead and neck, he took a deep breath—and made another bow to Ken, who had come out to see what was happening, and then Yoshiko, who was close behind. "Sorry, I should have explained earlier. My name is Yoneyama, I'm a patrolman from the Karuizawa Police Station. A crowd of foreigners is trying to storm the police station. They're speaking a bunch of foreign languages, German, English, who knows what else, and we've no idea what they're saying."

The patrolman smiled in relief and wiped his face again. By now his handkerchief was drenched. He rolled it up in both hands to wring it out.

"And?" Eri asked impatiently.

Eri seemed to unnerve him. "Yes, ma'am, well, we thought that in the family of His Excellency Ambassador Kurushima, there should be someone who understands English. Get one of them to come over here, no, ask one of them if they'd be so kind as to . . . the chief told me himself to . . ."

Eri looked back at the others for advice.

In the course of the conversation, her father had poked his head out of his room. "In other words you want someone to interpret for you," he said.

When he recognized the Ambassador the patrolman stood stiff as a stick. "Ah, yes, an interpreter. Yes, sir, that's it."

"Eri, you go and help them."

"Me?" Eri puffed out her cheeks in a big pout. "I was just going to have some fun with Haniyu and Ken. Besides, policemen scare me, and I've never interpreted for anybody in my life."

But her father had already disappeared inside.

"All right, I'll go," Eri said to the worried-looking policeman. "Give me a few minutes. Please take a seat."

She quickly fixed her hair and changed into a pair of plain farmer's trousers. The patrolman had come by bicycle, but the Kurushimas' two bikes had been taken by Anna and Yamada, so Eri had to sit on the rack of his bicycle. He rode off unsteadily. Before long, he'd wobbled into the undergrowth at the side of the road. Eri managed to jump off in time, but the patrolman needed help extracting himself from the bushes.

"You ride," he said, picking off the burrs, "I'll run along behind you."

When they arrived at the police station they found a crowd of foreigners shouting angrily at the occupants. Alongside an old man in worn clothes waving his fist was a fat woman shoving her chest at them in a gesture of outrage. From the swastikas on their sleeves and blouses Eri recognized them as Germans.

Patrolman Yoneyama pointed Eri out to his helmeted colleagues who were guarding the front door, and showed her inside. In the station were five representatives of the German group, who stood glaring at the Chief of Police. Yoneyama introduced Eri to his boss.

The latter rose to his feet and gave her a salute. He was shorter than Eri, with a crew cut and narrow eyes. She couldn't tell how old he was; he might have been forty or a bit younger. When he saw that Eri was just a girl he seemed disappointed and withdrew the name card he was about to proffer, then thought about it again and handed it to her. In large characters it said, "Ryumei Takizawa, Chief of Police, Karuizawa District."

"These people here are representatives of one of the foreign residence areas. There seems to be some sort of misunderstanding. But we're just no good at foreign languages, so Captain Maruki"—he pointed at a lanky, thirty-year-old policeman—"he graduated from college, and he's supposed to know some English, but when he tried talking to them it got a bit too complicated . . . You speak English, don't you?"

"Yes," Eri nodded, "a little."

Maruki explained to her briefly that, as usual, the foreigners were complaining about their rations.

Eri addressed the German representatives. "Do any of you speak English? I can interpret for you."

A bearded old man with thin legs sticking out of a pair of shorts stepped forward. "I do. What country are you from?"

"I'm Japanese."

"Oh really?" The man looked her up and down, then nodded as if finally convinced, and began speaking in a very correct King's English. "The problem is that the foreigners' rations are not being distributed fairly. The day before yesterday, Friday, wheat flour was distributed. It was supposed to come to a kilo per person, but when we got home and measured it it was only seven hundred grams. When we made inquiries about the other residence areas, we discovered that *they* had been given a full kilo per person. So we came here to protest to the police, but their answer was that they'd measured the rations themselves and each of us had been given a full kilogram. However, we know for a fact that we were indeed given short rations. We continued to protest, but have yet to be given an appropriate response. Then yesterday we received information that the police have been siphoning off our rations. We organized an investigatory committee who followed the police from the station, and we found, to our astonishment, that the sacks of flour were being taken to the chief's home! In other words, the Chief of Police has been stealing the foreigners' rations!"

"I see," said Eri, uncertain whether she should translate this into Japanese. The look of expectation in the chief's eyes made it even harder for her.

"What time was the flour taken to his house?" she asked.

The old man, after a brief discussion with the other Germans, answered precisely, "Yesterday, Saturday afternoon, from 2:15 to 2:20."

"Can you prove that those sacks of flour were part of the rations intended for the foreigners?"

The old man again consulted with the others, but this time there was no clear answer. A woman in a Nazi uniform addressed Eri. She had bony cheeks and a harsh-looking face. She spoke in German-accented English.

"The sacks of flour carried to the chief's house were identical to the sacks of flour distributed to us."

Eri gave a wry smile. "That doesn't prove that the sacks at the chief's house were rations intended for you."

"Wheat flour is not distributed to the Japanese. It is meant for the foreigners. We have a right to be guaranteed our food supplies. Time and again we have suspected the chief of diverting our rations. We Germans are not being given enough to eat. We are starving, and it is entirely the fault of the police."

"I think you're wrong," said Eri. "We Japanese people don't have enough to eat either. The whole country is short of food. You're not hungrier than anybody else."

"Even if the Japanese starve, we Germans should not starve. It is a matter of race."

"I don't care what race you are—it's the same for all of us."

"That is incorrect. We are *not* the same as you."

The old man in front cut the woman off. "What we are demanding is . . ."

"I understand. You want equal distribution of the rations, one kilo per person, right?"

"Exactly."

The Police Chief, who had been observing Eri's exchange with the Germans with growing discomfort, wanted to know what they were talking about.

"It's complicated."

"Please translate everything they said."

"Okay. Some of them had different opinions, and it took a bit of an effort to get a conclusion out of them. Anyway, the problem is that in the rations the day before yesterday the residents in their area only got seven hundred grams each, when they're entitled to a kilo. They want to be given the rest of their fair share."

"That's all?"

'They claim that the police pocketed the rest of their share."

"That's not true. What proof do they . . . ?"

"This woman says that if they're not given their fair share she'll make a legal complaint. Can't you just give each of them another three hundred grams?"

"But . . ."

"They say that some of them saw sacks of flour being carried from the police station to your house."

"Is that what this is all about?" The chief was agape. "That stuff belongs to me. I've had it stored at the station for a long time. It's not rationed food."

"I told them the same thing—that just seeing some sacks at your house doesn't prove that you stole them."

"Of course it doesn't."

"The main thing is, as long as they're given their full share they'll withdraw their protest."

"All right, tell them the following. I can't do anything now because the present allotment's already finished, but from the next round on, the rations will go to their district first, and the next time they'll get an extra three hundred grams each."

Eri translated, and the Germans held a consultation. The Nazi woman delivered their conclusion in English: "Have him put what he said in writing and sign it."

The chief nodded. Eri drew up a document, read it to them and, on getting the representatives' agreement, got it signed. The Germans, satisfied, withdrew from the police station, and the crowd outside quietly dispersed.

"We're very grateful to you, Miss Kurushima," the Police Chief said with a somewhat exaggerated bow. "You did a great job. They were here since this morning, and they wouldn't calm down. Dragged me out of my house on a Sunday. We hadn't a clue how to handle them, and then you come along and take care of the problem in less than ten minutes."

"My English was useless," said Captain Maruki.

"Let me make you a proposal," said the chief. "You know the foreign population hereabouts is increasing daily, and we're having to negotiate with them all the time—who gets to live where, who gets the rations given out by the food supply office, how the ration tickets and then the actual rations are distributed. Captain Maruki here, he's just overwhelmed by all the English this involves. I wonder, Miss Kurushima, if you could come and work for us as an interpreter on a part-time basis?"

"Oh, I don't know if I'm good enough . . . I'll have to discuss it with my father."

"Yes, please do that. Then I'll go and visit you to make a formal request."

Eri left and began walking home, but patrolman Yoneyama came running after her.

"This is the chief's bicycle. He wants you to use it to go home with."

"Oh, but then I'd have to ride it back to return it."

"No, it's one he isn't using."

"But I couldn't . . ."

"I tell you what. I'll ride along with you on another bike. And then I'll bring both bikes back myself."

"That's crazy. You can't manage two bikes at the same time. No, I'll walk home."

"No, I couldn't let you do that. Here, you ride and I'll run along behind you. I can certainly use the exercise."

So Eri went home the way she had come, pedaling, with the middle-aged patrolman puffing behind her.

4

Ryoichi had taken Haniyu out to show him the surrounding district, and Ken was in the living room, cooling down after their exertions. In a corner of the room his mother was polishing the silverware. Ken tiptoed up behind her. Alice immediately sensed his presence and held up a silver plate like a mirror to catch his reflection. Ken smiled at her smiling face at the bottom of the plate.

"Mama, you've become a bit thin."

"I haven't become thin. I've become *slim*, like a pretty girl."

"Food's getting hard to come by these days, isn't it?"

"Well, yes, there's no meat anywhere, and we don't qualify for foreigners' rations. We can't eat the way we did in Tokyo."

"That's right, it's been a whole year since you got out of Tokyo and moved up here."

"I heard you went to see the Nagata-cho house this spring. Yoshiko told me."

"Yes, after I'd been drinking in Shinjuku with the guys from the Inspection Department, I stopped by. You wouldn't recognize it, it's like an empty shell. All the furniture is gone, along with all the pictures on the walls."

"But we only brought some of our things up here. Everything bulky we left there, and Papa's books are all still in the house."

Ken glanced at the photographs on the mantelpiece. At their home in Tokyo the pictures had been carefully arranged in order—his parents' wedding, each child's birth, travel, other posts. Here they were crammed into a small space, all jumbled up together. One photograph in the back had fallen down, and Ken righted it. It was a picture of Lauren. With a pleasure akin to rediscovery he gazed at her, her chest and waist. Sweet memories of that night in Chicago returned. At the same time he thought of what had just happened with Margaret. When the group returned to the house after their hike up Mount Sekison, his mother had asked Margaret and Ryoichi to stay for dinner, but Margaret had declined, saying she had to look after her bedridden mother. Ken said he would accompany her as far as the pond near her house. On the way Margaret had suddenly turned down a small path. Ken followed but she moved quickly ahead. At the end of the path was a cemetery, and she ran in. Ken followed and caught up with her, and there they embraced. The tops of the surrounding trees bent in the wind. Maggie stayed with her eyes closed. Her thin face was beautiful, and he felt wonder and joy at what he'd just done and at the same time regret, with her being so young. *When I let her go she said, "No!" and clung to me. "Ken, it took a long time, didn't it? A long time before we got to this." "But . . . ," I wanted to say, "you're so young, and I'm not sure I could make you happy," but I stopped myself. I have no future. When the enemy attacks get worse I probably won't survive. Only if the war ends and I'm still alive will I be able to make her happy. But I didn't say anything, and Margaret waited and waited for me to speak. Finally I just said, "Please understand. Right now I can't promise you anything," and Maggie just nodded, the shadows of the branches crossing her face. She looked sad, close to tears. I walked her to the front door of her house. "Take care of yourself, Ken." "I will." "When are you coming next time?" "Don't know." "Anyway, please take care." Without turning around, she shut the door behind her.*

Ken put Lauren's picture back and said to his mother, "These days we're on twenty-four hours alert, and it's next to impossible to get a day's leave."

Alice put down the silver plate and slowly turned until she was face to face with him. "Ken, there's something different about you."

"What do you mean?"

"You look as if something's troubling you."

"Really?" Ken remembered the unpleasant exchange with General

Okuma. But to discuss it with his mother would only make her worry. "Well, it's probably because I'm working on a new fighter plane. It's reached the end of the first stage of development."

"Oh, is that it?" There were wrinkles beneath her eyes, and she still looked preoccupied.

"What's the matter, Mama?"

"Well," Alice began, as if it took some resolve to get the words out, "the other day I heard somebody talking about a boy, half-American like you, who was drafted into the Army. They made life hell for him, apparently. I was just worried that something similar might have happened to you."

"Oh, don't worry, I'm okay." Ken hugged his mother and patted her lightly on the back. "Don't forget, I was raised here by myself, ever since I was a kid. Also, I'm physically strong, and a little bit of harassment never bothered me. Mama, it's unlike you to be worried about this sort of thing."

"I suppose you're right." The smile returned to her face. "I'm sorry. Here I am seeing you after all this time and I have to bring up something unpleasant like that. I don't know what's happened to me. Maybe it's age. I've started worrying about little things."

"You're not old at all." As Ken comforted her, he looked beyond the veranda at the garden outside. His father was crouching there, weeding the potato patch. He was bent over, an old man now. Ken felt a wave of sadness at the thought that his parents were coming toward the end of their lives.

"Ken, there's one favor I want to ask you."

"Anything, Madam Ambassador." He swept off his cap and gave her a courtly bow.

"Oh, it's no big deal, I'd just like to see you in a kimono. It's been so long."

"A kimono? No problem at all. Actually I sort of wanted to change anyway."

They both went up to his room on the second floor. Alice took out a man's formal kimono from the paulownia chest, and laid out the inner and outer layers on the bed.

"No, Mama, that's a winter kimono. It's the middle of summer. I need a light yukata."

"Oh, is this the wrong one? I wanted to see you in *this*."

Ken smiled at his mother's mistake and took a yukata out of the drawer. Yoshiko or Anna must have put the clothes in order, for the summer things were arranged neatly together, all ironed and starched. His mother helped him tie the waistband, but she tied it too high above the waist, and the effect was strange.

"It's all right, Mama, I'll do it myself."

As Ken was winding the stiff sash smartly around his waist, his father, also in yukata, slipped into the room.

"Alice, I'm going for a walk. Ken, will you join me?"

Ken looked back at her.

"Yes, go," she said. "It's been a long time since you've gone for a walk with your father."

The darkening road, lined with huge fir trees, was deserted except for an occasional child passing on his bicycle.

"How are things in Tokyo?"

"This July they began moving schoolchildren out to the country-side. The relocation's been speeded up after the air raids on Yahata and Nagasaki. This morning the train was jam-packed with people escaping from the city."

"Saipan's fallen, and Guam and Tinian are about to go, too. It's a grave situation. There's a possibility even Tokyo might be bombed."

"No, not just a possibility. It's a matter of time. The Americans will be building bases for their B-29s in the Marianas. That would put Tokyo within range. It's only 2,500 kilometers from the Marianas to Tokyo, and the B-29s have a range of 7,000."

"Is the B-29 so powerful?"

"Yes, it is. I inspected one that had been shot down over Kyushu. It's a real monster. It can go 700 kilometers per hour at 10,000 meters. None of our planes can touch it."

"I see . . ."

The flower bed in the center of the intersection had been turned into a stand of corn. The cicadas fell silent, and for a moment all was still. The shadows of the two men stretched down the empty road behind them.

"We're desperately trying to come up with a high-altitude fighter that can take them on."

"Will you develop it in time?"

"To tell you the truth, it's almost impossible. The designs have gone forward, but we don't have the materials, especially the duralumin. With all the skilled workers away fighting and with the lack of fuel, production in the factories has fallen off badly."

"America always had an industrial base in its huge automobile industry."

"Papa, when you left for the negotiations you told me to 'do my duty.' I understand now how you felt at the time. Doing one's duty even with something impossible."

"I'm thinking of making one more effort for peace," he said, his shadow swaying behind him. "We've got to end this war sometime. And the sooner the better. Once they land in Japan it'll be too late. I know that saying this, let alone acting on it, would probably get me branded as a traitor, but I've *got* to do it. Do you understand?"

Ken smiled. "The son fights to win the war and the father fights to end it."

"Exactly." Saburo smiled too.

"It's strange," said Ken. They had reached a place called Six-Road Intersection. A bit further on was Kumoba Pond, and on the edge of the pond was Margaret's house. "It's strange," he repeated. "Yet talking like this seems so normal . . . Deep down I think winning the war is an empty thing. The side that murders more wins, that's all. Victory will mean nothing but the satisfaction of having slaughtered millions of people. And yet a person fights for his country, he kills people, and that act of murder is the 'duty' he has to fulfill. Try even whispering that in the Army, though, and you'd cause a riot. 'Pacifist!' 'Traitor!' they'd say. A death worth dying, a death for the sake of other people—I'm not afraid of that. It might sound like I'm bragging, but I really do feel that way. But I'm not sure dying for war is a worthy 'duty.' Maybe it's because of my American blood, because I can't be truly Japanese, that I have these doubts. There's a high-ranking officer, incidentally, who treats me like that, as if I were only half human. But even if I was completely Japanese, I still don't think I could accept dying for war as a worthy death."

"Do you regret having become a soldier?"

"No," Ken said firmly. "I have no regrets about being a soldier, or about being Japanese. That's not what I'm trying to say."

His father remained silent.

"Nor am I trying to discredit the men who lose their lives in war. I'm just questioning the cause they die for. The fact is that the rulers of this world can come up with any number of 'duties.' In the Army, the whim of any superior officer can turn into 'an order from His Majesty the Emperor.' One 'duty' can be manufactured after another, and each of those 'duties' can rob a young man of his life. And I'm sure the same thing happens in the U.S. Army. That's how armies work."

Ken and his father had reached the pond. Several young foreigners were still swimming in the chilly water. On the far side was the little red-roofed cottage where Father Hendersen and his family lived.

Ken, almost as if he couldn't stop himself, continued talking. "We all swear loyalty to our country, and an army is a part of that country. As long as armies exist, people will be obliged to fight wars. But what if all the armies disappeared from the world? Then we'd be free from having to murder other people, from being murdered ourselves, from being shut up in the tombs of unknown soldiers. Do you think that's just a fantasy?"

"No, Ken, it's not a fantasy," his father said gently. The two of them were sitting on a log bench by the water's edge. A few foreign girls with wet hair passed them on their way home, and then there was no one, just the still reflection of the clouds and Mount Asama on the surface of the weedy green water. "What you have in mind is the diplomat's ideal: that all the countries of the world should gather at an international conference and sign a treaty to abolish their armies and destroy their arsenals. And when that day comes, no young people will ever be praised again for killing young people of other countries.

And they'll no longer feel obliged to consider their own death an honor. Yes, that's it, that's the diplomat's ideal."

"If it were a question of dying for an ideal like that, I would gladly give my life. But . . ."

The word "But" seemed to vibrate in the air around them. Ken was gripped by the forlorn thought that perhaps his so-called ideal was indeed a fantasy, nothing but a cowardly dream to excuse his own fear of death. He threw a pebble into the pool and watched the ripples expand, scattering the images reflected there—mountains, clouds, and forest trees.

"It's not a fantasy," his father said slowly, as if waiting for the water to settle. "As I just said now, the only way to save lives is through peace negotiations. Ken, three years ago I did my best to keep the war from starting, but my efforts weren't enough. When I returned to Japan the following year, Prime Minister Tojo said to me, 'Now I'd like you to begin thinking about how we might wind this war up, if we have to.' I was astonished that a man in his position could say something so simpleminded, so irresponsible—as if a world war could just be switched off. Starting a war is easy, but peace is too complex for them. Actually . . ."

Someone was approaching. Saburo immediately fell silent. It turned out to be an elderly couple, probably from Tokyo, the old man in hemp shorts and a pith helmet and sporting a goatee, and the old woman in an elegant long dress that trailed over the ground. A closer look showed that the man's shorts were covered with dirty marks and that the lady's dress was in tatters. Both had hollow eyes and seemed to be short of breath. The old woman stuck her hand out at Ken. Ken didn't understand the gesture, but his father took a ten sen coin out of his pocket and handed it to her. The couple bowed and walked away, still breathing hard.

"Actually," Saburo continued, in a deliberately casual-sounding tone of voice, "an early peace would be the best thing for this country. We were completely unprepared for a long, drawn-out war. Tojo thought he could achieve a quick victory. Not just the Army thought that way, but the Navy too. Look at Admiral Yamamoto—he gave us a brilliant lightning strike on Hawaii, but nothing to sustain it afterwards. It's those one-shot politicians and soldiers, always playing to the gallery, who've taken the country down the wrong path. Before we end up surrendering, which would be an awful fate, we have to conclude a peace treaty with the best conditions we can get. The other day I had a talk with Prince Konoe—he's living up here—and Yoshizawa, the ex-Ambassador to London, about suing for peace. For example, asking the Soviet Union to intervene. I'd even go to the Soviet Union—that is, if the powers-that-be still want me around—or anywhere. I'd do anything to put an end to the hostilities. What do you think, Ken?"

"If there's a way to make peace, yes, that would be best. But do you really think the Americans would be interested? From what I've seen they're hot for revenge. Look at Attu and Saipan, look at the air raids on Kyushu where they seem to think nothing of bombing ordinary civilians."

"It's the 'logic' of revenge. Because two thousand Americans were killed at Pearl Harbor, millions of Japanese have to be killed."

"All that matters to them now is victory."

"Yes, but for them, too, an early peace would surely still be preferable, would reduce their losses. Listen, Ken, I'm not just thinking about what I can do for Japan, I'm thinking about your mother's country, too."

Ken grinned. "Do it, Papa, do it."

"Ken . . ." His voice faltered. "Until peace is achieved I, I want you to stay alive. For your mother's sake."

As they moved away from the pond the darkness thickened around them, isolating the single small light in the Hendersens' house at the edge of the forest. Ken thought of Margaret and suddenly felt embarrassed at his own pomposity, deliberating the fate of nations—the world, the war, the development of the new fighter—when all that really mattered was Margaret. Walking behind his father on the way home, he pictured her white face in the darkness.

Anna loved that time of day when, though the damp night air was already clinging to the trunks and branches of the surrounding trees, the summer sunlight still lay on the adjoining field.

She could hear the sound of a piano. Eri was in the parlor playing the second movement of Mozart's Sonata in B Major. She could also hear her father's and Ken's voices on the veranda.

In the kitchen Alice and Yoshiko were hard at it, pouring cooking oil, draining boiling water. Anna remembered her mother's excitement when they came back with all that food—potatoes and beans and bean cakes. "You just watch me!" she'd said. What was really surprising was that she had already taken that bull's head, cleanly skinned it, removed the meat and the tongue, and even gotten at the brain inside. The meat would become a stew, the tongue a steak, the brain cutlets—nothing was going to waste. Even the bone could be turned into an ornament. It was amazing. All her life she had had cooks at her disposal. When had she learned to cook herself? Even Yoshiko was impressed. Maybe the secret was in those notebooks she wrote everything down in. There were dozens of large notebooks, numbered on the back, which she kept in the locked cabinet next to the mirror stand. Normally she was oblivious to little details, either ignored them or managed to forget them, but sometimes she displayed an astonishingly detailed recall of things. Maybe she had some old family recipe for bull's head recorded there!

Yamada joined her, his crew-cut head still wet from the shower. He evidently didn't have anything new to change into, for he was in his khaki shirt and workman's trousers.

"Thanks for all your help this afternoon."

"Don't mention it," he said in a country accent.

Anna stifled a laugh, but then remembered his refugee act at the farmhouse, and the laugh burst out.

"We're a couple of real pros, aren't we?" said Yamada, laughing too.

Eri finished her piece. Haniyu took up his violin and began a duet with her, the Kreutzer Sonata.

"Well, well," said Saburo, entering the parlor with Ken. Alice also poked her head out of the kitchen, wiping her hands on a cloth.

Haniyu was like Yamada and Ken in the way that once he was out of uniform the soldier in him completely disappeared. The difference was that he wished he never had to put the uniform on again; one felt it was almost painful for him to slip back into it. Not only that, but the sky blue shirt and white trousers he'd brought with him looked perfect on him. Eri couldn't take her eyes off him, and whenever he looked in her direction she almost fluttered in response. Anna was only too aware of how infatuated her sister was.

Eri had probably pleaded with him to play his violin, and he seemed uncomfortable in the opening notes, but gradually relaxed as they found a common rhythm. The first movement ended, and after a slight pause, they attacked the next part. There was a warm round of applause when it was over.

"Bravo! Bravo!" The loud voice, jarring in that room, was Ryoichi's. When had *he* slipped in, Anna wondered. "You ought to give up the Army and make your living as a violinist. It's people like me who ought to be soldiers. Untalented. Disposable."

"Hey," said Ken in a scolding tone. "There happen to be three officers in the room. You'd better watch what you say."

"Yeah, Ken-chan? You don't exactly fit the Japanese soldier image yourself. Damn it, if it weren't for my bum leg I'd make a finer soldier than you. Courage, obedience, ideals—I've got them all!"

"Yes, but you lack the other qualities mentioned in the Imperial Rescript for Soldiers, courtesy and simplicity. Three out of five isn't good enough . . . Anyway, it's your turn to play something. Come on."

"I can't do anything classical."

"Oh, jazz is okay."

"If I played any of that the Military Police would be on your doorstep."

"Didn't you tell us they're all over your place already? Come on, play us a tune."

Ryoichi, with his sly smile on his face, took Eri's place at the piano and glided into Gershwin's "Summertime." Haniyu and Yamada watched with eyes wide as Ken and his younger sister immediately started dancing.

"I don't know this sort of music at all," Haniyu said to his fat friend. "If a musician doesn't know it, how the hell am I supposed to?"

"Pretty unique, the Kurushimas, aren't they?"

"They sure are."

Ryoichi played three pieces in a row. Since Yoshiko had begun setting the table, Eri and Anna got up to help, lighting some anti-mosquito coils under the table and bringing in the chairs.

Alice asked her husband to choose a wine from the cellar. Saburo nodded, and went out with a wine basket. The wines he had collected over the years had been decreasing bottle by bottle; since the beginning of the war, there had been no new bottles to replace them. Now there were only a few left, and he wouldn't touch them except on very special occasions.

After a few minutes he reappeared with a bottle lying in the basket. He carried it in slowly, careful not to disturb the sediment at the bottom. Anna remembered how Tanaka, before he was killed in the war, also used to bring the wine to the table on its side, not letting the sediment move, and how proud he was when he poured it all out cleanly. But her father, being clumsy, knocked his elbow on the door of the parlor and shook the bottle up. Not only that, when the time came to uncork the wine he absentmindedly stood the bottle up, again defeating the whole purpose of carrying it slowly up the stairs.

Alice rang the bronze gong, the signal for dinner. The gong had been used for the same purpose at their house in Nagata-cho.

It was the custom in the Kurushima house for Saburo and Alice to sit at opposite ends of the long dining table. On Saburo's right sat Haniyu, Ryoichi, and Eri, and on his left were Ken, Yamada, and Anna. Anna couldn't help grinning when she noticed the obvious disappointment on Eri's face when she was seated away from Haniyu.

Yoshiko appeared in a "Flemish-style" embroidered dress. It was a dress only worn at formal dinners for important company, and it had been a long time since Anna had seen her in it. However, unlike the old days when their cook Tanaka and the other maid Asa had been with them, Yoshiko now had to prepare and serve the food herself, which kept her busy, one moment disappearing into the kitchen, the next going from guest to guest pouring the wine. In due course, she pushed the cart in with the pot of stew on it. As she removed the lid, steam rose and filled the room with a delicious smell.

"Madam Kurushima's special dish," she announced, fanning the pot with the lid.

"Wow!" said Ken, stretching half out of his seat for a look. "Incredible. It's been years since we had a feast like this."

Alice threw out her chest and smiled. Yoshiko ladled the stew onto everyone's plates.

"It's delicious," said Yamada.

There was a strange look on Eri's face. "It's real beef! There must have been a special ration."

Anna tried to eat, but the image of the bloody bull's head ruined her appetite. Peering carefully at the lump of meat, she noticed two holes in it, and bristles at the edge of the holes.

Eri quickly sensed something odd about Anna's behavior. "What's the matter, Anna? Aren't you hungry?"

"It's all right, Eri, I'm just a little tired." She poked at the meat with her knife.

"The bargaining must have been hard work," said Haniyu. "Those rucksacks certainly looked heavy."

"Mr. Yamada carried mine for me. He really saved the day. And how was your hike?"

"We had a wonderful time," Haniyu answered. "Hiking's obviously a luxury these days. We didn't see a single person the whole time."

"We reached the top of Mount Sekison," said Ken. "We could hear the echoes really clearly."

"Yes," said Ryoichi. "It's always been a good place for echoes, but today it was spectacular. Maybe because the air's dense toward the end of summer. By the way, when I got home I got called in by the Chief of the Military Police."

"Why?" asked Ken.

" 'Called in' isn't quite right." The muscle at the corners of his eyes began to twitch, which always happened when he was tense. "Since 'home' is now a Military Police station, I bumped straight into him, and he took me into one of the rooms and started interrogating me. The problem, as I'd suspected, was Margaret. Ken, don't glare at me like that. The chief kept digging and digging. He wanted to know just what we were doing climbing that mountain with an Englishwoman."

"Margaret's not English, she's Swiss."

"*I* didn't say it. He did."

"If you'd just explained that she's Swiss . . ."

"I did. But he said that as long as she's got English blood in her, that makes her English."

"The moron! Then what about me? Does that mean I'm American?"

"No, in your case it's all right, because you've Japanese blood in you. In other words, there's no logic to it. For them the only thing that matters is the fact that Margaret is pure Caucasian. Caucasians are foreigners, and foreigners are enemies. Even our allies, as long as they're white, *smell* like enemies to those people."

Ken thought about it for a moment and then said, "But how did they know we climbed the mountain?"

"Oh, they know. They're monitoring everybody full time. Probably when we got off the bus at Oiwake they had a spy nearby. They're very nervous about the movements of foreign residents."

"But Margaret's still a child."

"She is not," Eri protested. "She's the same age as me."

"Well, pardon me!" Ken placed both hands on the table and bowed down till his nose touched the table.

"How awful, though." Eri shivered. "They even interrogate you about Maggie taking a hike. So, what did you tell them?"

"Of course I told them it was just a hike."

Anna explained the gist of the conversation to her mother. Alice surveyed her guests and said, in English, in a loud voice: "The other day, I was talking with Father Hendersen in front of his house, and on my way back two men who seemed to have been waiting for me stopped me. They wanted to know what the pastor and I had been talking about. I immediately realized they were Military Police. It was their bright-colored shirts and berets that gave them away, they've got it into their heads that if they wear anything loud or colorful they can pass as Karuizawa residents. So I told them off. How dare you go swanning around in those flashy clothes when my son is in the Army Air Corps, working night and day to defend the nation! Shame on you, I said, you ought to be in the Army! And they ran away!"

Laughter erupted around the table. Anna interpreted for those who hadn't understood.

"But Mama," Eri interrupted, "what language did you tell them off in?"

"Why, Japanese, of course."

"You could say all that in Japanese?"

"I said: '*Anata-tachi, nani wo asonde iru ka? Baka! Uchi no musuko wa rikugun ni gohoko shite iru yo.*'"

"Well, *that* should have gotten through to them!" Eri clapped her hands in delight. "But is anything going to happen to Maggie?" she asked uneasily.

Ryoichi was silent for a moment. The constant twitching in his face made it hard to see what he really felt. "Don't tell anyone that I told you this, because if it gets out I'll be in big trouble, I really mean it. But I happened to find out that the Military Police are secretly checking people's mail. This is something that the Tokko have been doing too—it's part of the rivalry between them."

"What's the Tokko?"

"The so-called Thought Police."

"Are they scary?"

"Yeah, they're scary. They've got special powers. They can pick up anyone they suspect of 'unpatriotic attitudes.' The new civilian Chief of Police here is said to be one of them."

"The chief? But he doesn't seem scary at all."

Saburo, who had been listening to this, asked, "Eri, what happened with you and the police today?"

"The Germans had been making a fuss. They claimed that the chief had been stealing their rations. But they couldn't prove it, so they settled for an increase in their rations at the next handout. Oh yes, and the chief said he wanted me to interpret for them in the future too, he said he'd be coming over to ask your permission. But if they're

Thought Police I don't want to do it. Papa, what should I do?"

"Well, at least by enabling them and the foreigners to understand each other you'd be helping other people. You don't have enough to keep you busy anyway."

Eri shrank from her father's gaze. Ever since the family left Tokyo she had stopped going to school. The girls' school at Komoro was too far away for her to commute there. Saburo had suggested that she study at home but, unlike her sister, she didn't like books, so she ended up with nothing to do all day, and her fecklessness had occasionally gotten on her father's nerves.

"It's a good idea," said Ryoichi. "To get in with the Thought Police could be very useful for your family. And I can tell you honestly that . . ." Even the indiscreet Ryoichi couldn't continue what he wanted to say in front of Alice.

"I don't like the idea of special treatment," Eri said.

"It's not just for your family, it could be useful for other people too. For Maggie, for example."

"Why Maggie?" Again a shadow of unease crossed her face. She had heard things from Anna. Anna had been told that the Thought Police had marked out Father Hendersen, ex-Ambassador Yoshizawa, and a few others for special surveillance as "pacifists." Their father's name had also been mentioned, apparently.

As if to distract them from this line of conversation, Yoshiko wheeled in the next course. Eri took a bite and exclaimed in delight, "Wow! Broiled tongue, I can't believe it. And soft cutlets. This is incredible!" Even Anna, at the sight of her favorite salad—a mixture of cabbage, tomatoes, and cucumbers—finally recovered her appetite. "What happened, Anna? You're not tired any more?" Eri asked.

"I'll bet there's a mist tonight," said Yamada.

Anna opened the blackout curtain and looked out. A milky-white mist lay heavy over the ground beyond the veranda. "How did you know?" she asked.

"I was born in mountain country. I can usually tell when there's enough dampness in the air for a mist to rise."

"Ryoichi, can you get home in this mist?"

"No problem. Around here I can make my way blind."

"Ryoichi, Lord of Karuizawa," said Ken. "But Karuizawa's changed a lot, hasn't it? Today when we were by the pond we met a couple of people we thought looked rather grand, but they turned out to be beggars."

Ryoichi nodded. "There's been a huge increase in beggars and thieves. The White Russian refugees who came here from Manchuria are penniless. The Germans from Batavia are always short of food; they caught some of them stealing from the farmers' fields. And the Japanese are suffering too. When the population explodes like this there isn't enough to go around."

"Oh, I told the Germans off about that at the police station," said Eri. "I said they're not the only ones having a hard time."

"A lot of foreigners don't seem to understand that the Japanese have a different diet, and they're quick to complain. When there's no bread distributed they immediately assume that they're being excluded from the rationing. When the authorities try to make up for the lack of bread with sweet potatoes they get furious. But the Germans and Italians are Axis nationals, and at least they *can* complain. Americans, Canadians, the enemy aliens can't say a thing."

"By the way, Ken, how's your flying—getting better?" his father asked abruptly. Anna had hoped the conversation would stay away from airplanes.

"Kurushima," said Yamada in Ken's place, "is at the very top, one of the two best pilots in the entire department. I myself am one of the worst."

"He's a born pilot," Haniyu agreed. "Not only can he fly but he shoots well too. He's good enough for actual combat."

Ken waved his hand. "No, no, I'm not that good. They're overdoing the praise."

"I'd love to watch you all flying," said Eri.

"All right, next time the three of us will fly here," said Yamada. "We'll skim right by the peak of that mountain you all climbed today, then head over to that farmhouse in Komoro. Yes, we'll zoom over where you hiked and where we went bartering, and then we'll swoop in and do a loop, a loop right over your house . . ."

"The day after tomorrow we're flying to China," Haniyu said. He was a little drunk. Ken quickly gave him a sign, and he fell silent.

"What's that, Ken? You're flying all the way to China?" his mother started to ask.

"No, no, Haniyu and I go to China," Yamada replied in quite good English. "Your son stays in Japan."

"Oh." She seemed relieved. "Well, since we're finished with the main course, I would like to inform you that there's a Bavarois for dessert. Unfortunately I can't, because there isn't any."

"Mama," said Anna, "what about the pilots' food Mr. Yamada brought? Why don't we serve that?"

"Good idea." Alice had Yoshiko bring in the cardboard box from the kitchen.

"Oh, look!" Eri picked up each piece and showed it to everyone as Yamada explained.

Anna removed a piece of chocolate from its silver wrapping and placed it in her mouth. It was sweet, a sweetness she'd completely forgotten. "I haven't had anything sweet like this in ages," she said, giving Yamada a smile.

After the meal, Haniyu began to play the violin. This time it was a light piece. Eri had never seen the score, and she stumbled at first when trying to accompany him, but finally got the hang of it.

Ken got up to dance with his mother. Yamada approached Anna and said in an apologetic voice, "I don't actually know how to dance."

"Oh, nor do I."

"You mean there's someone in this house who doesn't dance?"

"There certainly is. I can't handle any difficult steps, and my father can't dance at all."

"I'm relieved to hear it."

"It's gotten chilly. You must be cold."

"Not at all." Yamada folded his thick arms and scratched them. "I actually prefer the cold."

Anna had just put on a sweater when Ryoichi came up and whispered, "Now there's a fine couple." Anna, thinking he was teasing her and Yamada, began to protest but then realized his eyes were on Haniyu and Eri. She felt relieved, but at the same time, to her surprise, a little disappointed.

Ken was dancing with his mother on the sliver of lawn near the veranda. In the wan light escaping from the blackout curtains, the mist looked as if a great flock of sheep was passing through the larch wood.

"Ken, what are you thinking?"

"That I wish all that mist was sherbet."

"If it were winter I'd make you some right away."

"You dance just as well as ever—still full of energy."

"Oh, I'm still young. Still in my twenties, dear."

"Ha ha . . . Do you go over to Maggie's place a lot?"

"Oh yes, almost every day."

"How's her mother?"

"Oh, her heart problems aren't actually that serious. But she's the worrying type. She's obsessed about her husband getting killed. And no wonder. As soon as the war started all their Japanese friends turned their backs on them. No one comes to see them any more. You were there this morning, you saw how almost his entire congregation is made up of foreigners now. I thought at least I should go occasionally, to give them some comfort . . ."

"When we were hiking today I got worried about Maggie. She doesn't seem happy."

"How can she be? For foreigners now, this country isn't a comfortable place to be."

"What about you, Mama?"

"Me? I'm Japanese. I'm perfectly comfortable here, thank you."

"But . . ."

"What are you thinking? I happen to be the mother of a man who is a magnificent Japanese officer. I don't give a hoot what the cops or the Military Police think."

"Good. But Mama, you're strong—Maggie's weak. Use some of your strength to help her, could you?"

"Of course I will . . . Ken, do you have to leave tonight? Couldn't you at least stay overnight?"

"I can't. There's an assignment I can't get out of tomorrow. I've got to catch the last train back today."

"That assignment doesn't involve any danger, does it?"

"No."

"You're not going to China, are you?"

"No, Mama. Why are you so suspicious?"

"Just a mother worrying. Just wanting you to stay alive."

"I will always stay alive."

"Yes, always, always."

Alice pressed her face to her son's chest. Ken hugged her.

Ken had meant to make his way through the mist to visit Margaret, but now decided not to. To see her again would only bring pain. Instead he resolved to stay with his mother right up to the last moment, and he went on stroking her soft, warm back.

VI

THE DEVIL'S TRILL

1

Flying in formation was easy when one was in the second or third plane. Major Kurokawa, who was in the lead plane, had more than fifteen hundred hours of flying time under his belt and had made innumerable round trips between China and Japan. Everything would be all right as long as Ken just followed him.

Ken looked over at Haniyu, who was parallel to him, on his left. Unaware that he was being watched, Haniyu stared straight ahead. Ken waved, but he didn't notice. *All right then*, Ken thought, *I'll waggle my wings at you*. But if he overdid it, Mitsuda, in the bomber behind, might get suspicious. Ken finally gave his wings a little flip. But Haniyu still didn't notice.

Altitude 2,000 meters. Below, his view of the sea was completely clear except for occasional small clouds that floated like half-constructed forts. Over the Chugoku Mountains to his right and the Shikoku Mountains to his left, however, lay a heavy covering of cumulus clouds—gigantic columns that looked heavy and solid, not floating in the sky but anchored to the earth. The islands, large and small, of the Inland Sea didn't seem like islands so much as the fragments of continents that had sunk in the ocean. In front of him the tops of mountains poking above the clouds were strung out like road markers. He couldn't be bothered to check his position now against the map. *Just trust the leader, and follow him*. It was nice not having to think.

Ken looked back at the plane behind him. He could see Mitsuda, with his thick eyebrows, in the cockpit and, lined up behind him, the six crew members. A twin-engined heavy bomber was a big plane. With a full load of aircraft parts on board, it looked like a huge bird winging its heavy way through the air. Ken raised his hand and waved. Mitsuda responded. He seemed to be pointing down.

The lead plane waggled its wings and began descending. Ken opened the throttle. Haniyu, oblivious, stayed at the same altitude, then finally noticed and began following the others down, but too fast, so that he pulled out in front. Altitude 1,500, 1,000, 500. The pressure on Ken's eardrums was painful. He swallowed hard, and it got better. The lead plane flipped its wings again, a signal to look down.

What was that below? It looked like a long, narrow island.

No, it was a battleship. Over the radio came Mitsuda's voice: "That's the *Yamato*." The famous *Yamato*. It was enormous.

How many guns did it have? The big guns on the main turret, the countless high-angle guns—it was bristling with them. It didn't hide its function, it proclaimed it: a killing machine. In that respect it was different from most airplanes, which kept their guns hidden in order to maintain speed. Ken had loved model airplanes as a boy, but he'd never taken any interest in model battleships; he just couldn't bring himself to like all those guns sticking out all over them. Tiny figures were visible on deck, dwarfed by the massive conning tower and the huge funnels. Wrapped in layer upon layer of heavy steel plates, this was a fortress, built without regard for gravity. The buoyancy of water was so much greater than the buoyancy of air.

But that steel fortress was helpless in the face of an aerial attack. Look at Pearl Harbor. Look what happened to the *Repulse* and the *Prince of Wales*. You could build three hundred planes for less than the *Yamato*, and bombs and torpedoes would easily do it in. He should have been feeling pride and awe at the sight of this "unsinkable" battleship, the largest in the world, the pride of the Imperial Navy, but he was surprised to find himself imagining for a moment that he was an American pilot about to attack it. He could just hear General Okuma going on about his "enemy blood." But anyone who knew the power of airplanes would see that complex and bombastic hunk of steel as hopelessly out of date.

The guns shone. The deck gleamed. The flags were red. It really did look almost like an island. Ken couldn't get rid of the fantasy of attacking it. At the same time, he couldn't shake off the fear that it was aiming its guns at him, ready to spew fire at him.

He flew on past it. Below him now were the naval docks at Kure, cruisers and destroyers at their berths. With a curse, he realized he'd lost sight of the lead plane. He opened the throttle, searching the sky around him, then saw the 97 bomber and the two Hayates and chased after them at full speed.

Over the radio came Major Kurokawa's voice: "Where were you?"

"I'm sorry, sir. I wasn't paying attention." He concentrated on staying in formation.

They flew away from the coast, out over the sea again. Past the Straits of Shimonoseki and then over Kyushu. Soon, ahead of them, was the airfield at Gannosu. The plane was fully loaded with ammunition, and if he wasn't careful with his flaps he'd hit the runway too hard and break his wheels. Following the lead plane in, making constant small speed adjustments, he managed a three-point landing. Here they would refuel and then take off for Shanghai.

It was a civilian airfield which the military had temporarily requisitioned. The men who came running out of the hangars had apparently never seen a Hayate, and they crowded around. Leaving the maintenance work to the crewmen who emerged from the bomber, Ken and the other pilots went inside.

Major Kurokawa spread open a map. "Here's the flight plan. It's now 11:22. We'll take off at 1300 hours. Our first objective will be Chejudo Island off the Korean peninsula, our second, Shanghai. A total of 1,000 kilometers, flight time two and a half hours. First, Chejudo Island. That's easy, just set your compasses due west and fly straight. Then reset 30° south for Shanghai. In this case our landmark will be the yellow water at the mouth of the Yangtze, fanning out into the sea. If you aim for the spokes of the fan you'll reach Shanghai. Got it?"

"Yes, sir," Ken and Haniyu replied crisply. Mitsuda gave the slightest of nods, as if to say it was all so simple he already understood.

"Now, then." Kurokawa removed three long-barreled pistols from a bag at his side. "I'm going to give each of you one of these. You know how to use them?"

"Yes, sir," Ken answered. "We had firing practice at flying school."

"Okay. Now you each get ten bullets. Seven you use on the enemy and three you keep. Why do you keep three bullets? Mitsuda, you're not saying anything. I imagine you know."

Ken and Haniyu exchanged glances. Neither knew the answer.

"One bullet is for your fuel tank, so you go up in flames. The other two are for you to kill yourself with. You shoot yourself in the fore-head. If you're still not dead you shoot yourself again. Got that?"

"Yes, sir," answered Haniyu in a hoarse voice. Ken's legs were shaking. He tried to repress the tremor, but it only got worse.

"We'll be heading over enemy territory. There are enemy sub-marines out at sea, just waiting for some little fish to catch, and enemy planes all around China. If you're forced to land it'll be in enemy territory, and that's where you'll need the gun. Okay, let's have some food!"

The Major removed the lid from his rice bowl and stuffed the con-tents into his mouth. Mitsuda poured tea. Ken and Haniyu also began eating.

"If we encounter an enemy plane, do we have permisssion to engage it?" asked Ken.

"No, you idiot!" Kurokawa sounded angry, but there was a glimmer of a smile in his eyes. "Our mission is to transfer the new planes to China, not to fight. If you spot an enemy plane you just turn and escape."

"With the extra fuel tank you can't fight."

"Right," said Kurokawa. "Don't forget, the extra fuel tank is also cargo. You're forbidden to jettison it."

Kurokawa sprinkled his rice with pickled plums, dried meat, and boiled vegetables, and wolfed down the mixture, along with a cup of tea. His shoulders were hunched up aggressively, and he sprayed bits of rice around as he spoke.

"How're the planes doing?"

"My propeller is a bit off," said Ken, adding that he had asked the crew to take a good look at it.

"Mine's got oil pressure problems. The planes they're turning out these days look like rush jobs to me. Damn it, it's hot!" Kurokawa wiped the sweat off his forehead. The building faced the sea, with its windows open, and there was a good breeze coming in, but the glare from the runway, the tin roofs, and aluminum sidings still made it feel like a furnace. "I've got bad memories of this place." He finished his rice and stood up. Sticking his head out the window, he gazed at the sea and the red and white signal flags flapping in the wind. "It was three years ago. A squadron of Tsubasas was taking off for Taiwan, when the second plane veered off the runway and crashed into the crowd of people seeing them off. A propeller can really cut. It just sliced through that crowd. There was blood, bits of bodies, flying everywhere. Sorry to bring this up during a meal."

They left on schedule. The three planes entered the runway together. The extra fuel tanks were full and the planes even heavier than usual. They lumbered along for what seemed like ages, but the wheels wouldn't leave the ground. Just before the runway ended and the sea began, they managed to get off the ground. Ken was about to execute a turn when the foot he had on the pedal suddenly slipped on something wet. It was oil. Where was it leaking from? There was no way he could fly a thousand kilometers in this state.

"First Lieutenant Kurushima here. Sir, I've got an oil leak. I'm turning back to have it checked."

"All right, you fly alone. We're going ahead."

"Yes, sir."

He made a turn over the sea and landed again at the airfield.

"What's wrong?" It was an older man who came up, one of the civilian maintenance crew.

"I've got an oil leak."

"I don't know much about fighter planes."

"I'll look at it with you. Give me a hand anyway."

Ken borrowed a pair of overalls and got to work in the small cockpit, his hands soon becoming smeared with oil, the sweat pouring out. Maintenance, he realized, was hard physical labor. It took a great effort just to unscrew a single bolt from its narrow groove. The maintenance man unscrewed bolt after bolt and removed the covering. After two hours of work they finally found the problem: there was a leak in the undercarriage oil pressure pump, which had seeped through. Two other maintenance men pitched in, and by the time they got the leak fixed it was a little before four o'clock. If he took off now it would be dusk when he reached Shanghai. He had absolutely no confidence about flying over unknown territory at night. No, even in the daytime he had never flown over the sea for two and a half hours alone. Okay, so he would escort a civilian flight to Shanghai, letting it show him the way. He went to the office and asked if there was anything scheduled for Shanghai that day.

"Today's flight left this morning."

"What about tomorrow?"

"The next flight is a week away."

He had no choice. He would fly alone.

He managed to take off at 1600 hours. He flew due west. As far out as the Goto Islands he could work out his position on the map. Altitude 3,000 meters. Then he was flying over water. Man-eating sharks and submarines lurking down there somewhere—everywhere. He had his life vest on, but what good would that do? Yet he found himself fidgeting, checking the straps of his parachute. *What's the matter, Ken, you getting scared? No, I'm not scared. Just weighing up my chances.*

Thirty minutes passed, then an hour. The needle on the fuel gauge began to twitch. There should have been some sign of an island by now, but all the way out to the horizon there was nothing but the sea. He thought he saw a small island but it turned out to be the shadow of a cloud. *I'm marooned in blue space*, he thought, *blue above me and blue below.* The foot pedal was slippery. Maybe they hadn't gotten all the oil out. Suddenly he lost speed. He opened the throttle, but there was no response. The engine was at full power but he couldn't get speed. Without lift, a plane crashes. An air pocket? *No, the propeller must be malfunctioning again; the pitch is too shallow.* At this rate the engine would overheat. He'd had the crewmen check it over and over again, to make sure the electrical connections were all right . . .

He started falling. He dropped a good 700 meters, and he could see the crests of the waves. He injected more methanol to cool the engine, and again pressed the switch that adjusted the propeller's pitch. This time it worked. He zoomed straight ahead. Then, right below him—could it really be?—yes, an island. It was Chejudo. Shore. Land. He was saved. He could get the propeller fixed here. At the foot of a mountain he spotted a small landing strip. It was too small, and there didn't seem to be any service hangars, just a hut that looked like a storage shed. It would be impossible to take off from such a short runway. *Go on, go all the way to Shanghai. Somehow the plane will hold out.*

O Lord, Ken began to pray in English, *I'm depending on you. I place my life in your hands.*

Over the sea again. (He was still thinking in English.) *I don't have enough fuel to turn back, I've got to go forward.* A strong wind was blowing from the northwest, around fifteen meters a second. *I've got to revise my compass navigation.* He made a quick mental calculation—the ratio between the wind speed and his air speed. *Just keep flying in this direction. Don't get blown off your flight path.* The sky above him was blocked out by gray cumulus clouds. The plane was getting blown about. If he could climb to 7,000 meters he'd be above the clouds, in calm air, but then he wouldn't be able to find land. He remembered the visual flight he'd made at flying school. Back then a sudden break in the clouds had saved him, and he'd had the solid ground of Japan below him. That wasn't the case now. Now it was waves . . . huge waves. Ditching it in water this rough was out of the question. He would just continue flying in what he reckoned was the right direction. *O Lord, I stand before you alone. Are you watching over me?*

It was only the day before that he'd been dancing with his mother in the mist. His mother's body had been warm, and smelled nice. The mist had flowed around them—it had been like a dream. Lauren had smelled nice, too, when he'd danced with her. And then the fragrance of Margaret's body in the damp air of the cemetery came back to him, stronger than any of the others. Suddenly Ken was gripped by desire. Surrounded by sea and sky, his mind shrank to nothing. Only desire, the desire that burned through his body now, was proof that he was alive.

The thick cloud cover broke and he could see, here and there, patches of blue sky. Rays of sunlight reached the surface of the water, and the waves sparkled like schools of fish, their silver scales glistening. The engine and the propeller hummed in perfect sync and the plane carried him safely forward. His life depended on a machine constructed of innumerable parts. He moved entirely in accordance with its designer's own sweet will.

Two and a half hours had passed. Time for land to start appearing. There was no change in the color of the sea, no sign of any yellow water fanning out. *Am I lost?* His chest became constricted, gripping him like an iron strap. *Don't panic.* He made another calculation, the wind speed in relation to his air speed. He was right on course. *Just a little more, another ten minutes.* But the sea showed no change at all. *Hey, what's that?* A shape like a black ship, submerged beneath the sea. *A submarine? It must be. Friend or foe?* He couldn't tell. It slipped further and further away. *Should I go back and check on it? No, that would take me off course, and I can't afford the extra fuel.*

The sun sank toward the horizon, enthroned in red, with thousands of red torches waving in the sea. Then, abruptly, it was gone, swallowed up in the waves. The firmament went dark and the sea grew murky, as if a cloud of ink had oozed up from the bottom. He had thirty minutes' worth of daylight left. The warning light began to flash on the fuel gauge. The wing tank was nearly empty; only the fuselage tank was left. Time crept relentlessly forward; stars began to glitter. He turned on the radio. There was only static. He couldn't hear a thing. Compared to the Mustang, the Hayate had poor radio reception. It was only good for communicating with other planes in formation or with the airfield when taking off and landing. Suddenly he remembered his American portable radio and switched it on. There was a broadcast in Chinese. So he must be near the mainland. Somehow he would make it. He was seized with happiness, and gazed out at the dim night sky. A red flame trailed from the exhaust. Among the stars sprinkled over the vast sky was one bright, steady light. *Is it a star, or a city? It can't be a city. They said Shanghai was under strict blackout orders.*

He decided to head for that star, feeling that just making the decision would help calm him down. He had only thirty minutes of fuel left. Ten minutes passed. The Chinese broadcast grew louder. He was nearing land. Was he imagining it or was the color of the water down there really changing? He couldn't actually see the color, but he sensed a change. Fifteen minutes to go. Islands. He checked his map. There was no mistake. The Zhoushan Islands. He headed up the Yangtze River, a straight band of white. He felt as if he were driving up a highway. And where it split into the Huangpu and the Suzhou, there would be Shanghai. Even at night the white river would be his salvation. He flew straight at a small cluster of stars; the stars became square, then turned into the lights shining in buildings. Large buildings lining the riverbank. It was Shanghai. The buildings of the foreign concessions.

Suddenly he found himself caught in a searchlight beam. They must have seen the rising sun insignia on his wings, for they didn't shoot. Friendly territory. Black buildings on the riverbank, black ships docked here and there in the Huangpu. A bridge. Still caught by the searchlight, Ken began descending. He turned on his red and blue wing lights and proudly made his way down, skimming over the Garden Bridge he knew from photographs, to the airfield which lay to the north. The city slipped behind him, and he came to what looked like a flat plain. His flying was so accurate it surprised even him. Suddenly there were red runway lights. Permission to land. Without the slightest hesitation he went down, and safely touched the ground.

"We were worried. Did you get lost?" Major Kurokawa was there to greet him.

"Yes, sir, I did."

"It's amazing you got here. How did you home in on us? It's enemy territory all around here."

"I listened to a radio broadcast."

"With that radio? Hey, isn't that American?"

"My father brought it back as a souvenir."

"Courtesy of the Ambassador, eh?" Kurokawa turned the radio dial roughly with his thick fingers. Chinese came over the speaker. "That's not a Shanghai station, it's an enemy broadcast from somewhere nearby. They're bad-mouthing us."

"Kurushima!" Haniyu had come running over, arriving out of breath. "It's a good thing you were late. An hour earlier and you would have flown right into an enemy air raid. Several B-25s attacked, escorted by P-40s and P-51s. Major Kurokawa, in a Hayate, shot down one of the P-51s."

"Well, get yourself some food and rest. Tomorrow, after checking enemy movements, we'll be going to Hankou."

The airfield was wrapped in darkness, and there were so many stars they looked as if they would spill out of the sky. The wind was cool and refreshing, like an autumn breeze, but there were masses of flies and mosquitoes. Next to the service hangar was a room with bunks in it stacked like silkworm trays. Mitsuda and the maintenance crew were already sleeping there. Ken wolfed down the cold rice balls Haniyu gave him, and then dived into an empty bunk. Despite the mosquitoes buzzing around him, he was almost instantly asleep.

When he woke up the next morning all the others were already gone. Ken jumped out of the bunk and went out in the morning sun to look around. He was shocked by what he saw. Steel girders sagged in the hangars, and there were holes in the roofs. Everywhere were the skeletal remains of airplanes that lay on their sides, and there was a burned-out enemy plane that had been shot down. Though surrounded by a peaceful-looking countryside, where the yellowing ears of kaoliang fluttered as far as one could see, this place was a battlefield. A patrol plane, finishing its rounds, returned to the airfield. A truck packed with ammunition departed. The barrels of antiaircraft guns and machines guns gleamed tensely in the sun.

He ran to the edge of the field, where Major Kurokawa and the others had gathered beside the Hayates and the bomber, their shadows stretching across the runway. Fortunately the three planes were undamaged. The crewmen were at work, wiping oil from the exhaust ports and inspecting the engines.

"Okay," said Kurokawa, "after breakfast we take off. Let's get out of here—and get some revenge."

It was afternoon when they reached Hankou. Among the airmen who came out to meet them Ken spotted Sugi and immediately went up to him.

"How're you doing, Sugi?"

"Oh, same as usual. Hey! I can't believe you guys got here." His face was thin and lined. He looked old. "Been having diarrhea. It's a damn nuisance. But I managed to shoot down some Bs."

Ken looked around. "I don't see Major Iwama."

"Actually . . ." Sugi started to say something, but then began walking. "It's so hot out here. Let's go to my room." Ken followed him, along with Haniyu and Mitsuda.

The airmen's quarters were a makeshift barracks much like their old quarters at Nakatsu. The dust-smeared window was half broken, and the door was gone.

"It lets the breeze in. The damned Bs blew the door away."

A young NCO named Okano served them tea. The fresh Chinese tea soaked into their parched throats. Then Sugi dropped the news.

"The Squadron Leader is dead."

It came as a shock to all three of them.

"This place is hell," he continued. "Their air power is overwhelming. There are so damned many of them. You shoot them down and they just keep coming like flies. And recently there's this great big fly called the B-29. The B-29 is . . ."

"I've seen it," Ken interrupted. "I examined one that had been downed over Kyushu."

"Then you know. Even the Hayate is no match for it." Sugi smiled, and the wrinkles spread all over his face. "The Hayate's a damned good plane. It can down a P-40 or a P-38 without much trouble. With the P-47 and the P-51 I'd put it about even. Even I managed to . . ."

"How many have you bagged?" Haniyu had been waiting to ask the question.

"Oh, not that many." Sugi, embarrassed, turned to the young Corporal serving tea. "Okano here's our ace, he's had twelve kills, including three Mustangs."

"The Lieutenant has downed seven planes," said Okano.

"That's damned good," said Ken. "I wouldn't mind seeing some real combat myself. I'm tired of testing planes."

"What happened to Major Iwama?" Haniyu asked impatiently.

There was a pained look on Sugi's face. "It was just a week ago. All of a sudden at dinnertime we got this order from the Squadron Leader. Eight men were to fly to Shinkyo, in Manchuria, then mount an attack on a secret enemy air base from there. Departure would be at 1900 hours. So eight men capable of night flying for 700 kilometers, with me, Hanazono, and Okano here among them, were picked. The Squadron Leader seemed in a really bad mood. He kept muttering about 'those assholes at headquarters'—this from a guy who never criticized his superiors. I found out later that there'd been a stream of conflicting orders all day. Go left, go right, no, stop, come back, go out and attack—generals moving us around like chess pawns. They play one piece, then change their mind and withdraw it, and meanwhile we're going through hell to suit them. The Squadron Leader, he just couldn't take it any more, it seemed."

Corporal Okano sighed. "I remember there was something wrong about the way he led us up and away. Usually he was real smooth, but that time he zoomed up like some rookie pilot. It was so steep I thought he was going to stall. A night flight normally means a slow cruising speed, right? But we went flat out, arriving at Shinkyo before we knew it."

"Anyway, things got worse there," Sugi carried on. "The local maintenance crew only managed to attach the extra fuel tanks we needed to three planes—in the rush of leaving we'd forgotten to bring the buckling gear. So it was only the Squadron Leader, me, and Hanazono who took off on our attack, without getting any sleep, either. Plus this kid here, Okano, who said he'd come along even without the extra tank. Okano—you finish the story."

"Yes, sir." The Corporal, who couldn't have been more than eighteen or nineteen years old, got up, his cheeks red with embarrassment, looking as if he were making a formal report to a superior. "We took off around midnight, but visibility was zero. I soon realized that only the Squadron Leader and I were flying in formation."

"You've got to explain how that happened. First of all, after taking off I noticed my extra tank was leaking and I turned back. And Hanazono, when he tried to take off in the dark, ran off the runway, got caught in the fence, and flipped over. He was quite seriously injured. He's in the Army Hospital in Shanghai now with a bad concussion and a broken right leg."

Ken and Haniyu groaned. Mitsuda, smoking a cigarette, remained silent.

"Yes, sir. Well, the Squadron Leader and I flew west for sixty minutes, following the course of the river, then, just as the sun was coming up, we reached the enemy airfield and divebombed it. There were thirty P-40s down there. As they were starting up their engines we swept them with our machine guns, then turned and let them have it again, two or three more times. There was a lot of smoke and flames. They turned their antiaircraft guns on us, but, hell, they couldn't touch us. Just then we saw an enemy plane trying to take off, so the Squadron Leader dove on him. But he didn't fire. Just as I was thinking maybe his gun was jammed, he crashed into it. He killed himself—burst into bits. A real hero's death . . ."

The Corporal broke down, sobbing.

Sugi patted the boy on the shoulder. "It's okay," he said, and told him to sit down. "This kid tried to fly back, telling himself it was his duty to report how Iwama died. Mind you, he didn't have an extra fuel tank, so when he finally reached friendly territory he was out of fuel, and did a belly landing on the bank of the Yellow River. Then he walked back to base."

The group watched helplessly as Okano went on crying. The ashes from Mitsuda's cigarette dropped onto his knees.

A wounded soldier tottered by on crutches. Perhaps he was just learning how to use them, for the tip of one stick slipped on the linoleum floor, and he would have tumbled over if a nurse hadn't caught and held him. The wounded soldier was missing a leg.

All the large wards to left and right were packed. There weren't enough beds, and the wounded lay on mats in the corridors too. Ken was reminded of a warehouse. A soldier with no arms was being fed by one of his buddies. The buddy only had one arm. A man whose eyes and mouth were visible through the bandage that swathed his head was clumsily trying to manipulate his chopsticks, staining the bandage with *miso* soup. And there was a man who, no doubt because of the heat, had stripped to his shorts and was angrily swatting with a fan at the flies that swarmed over the open wound on his skinny back. A penetrating smell of carbolic acid and ammonia mixed with the smells of sweat and feces and food. Ken felt slightly nauseous.

"I remember when I went to visit you in the hospital," he said to Haniyu.

"Oh, but . . ." Haniyu looked around and sighed. "That was at home. This is different. It's almost like . . ."

"What?"

"Like an asylum for the crippled and the lame. There isn't a single man here who's going to go home whole."

Ken nodded and looked away from the patients. He was worried about Hanazono. What did "seriously injured" mean?

When they reached the officers' ward on the second floor, there was a white cloth over the doorway and they couldn't see inside. It seemed like an ordinary hospital room. They asked for Lieutenant Hanazono at the nurses' station. A military doctor in shorts and a white coat appeared and led them to the end of the corridor.

Looking away from them, he said: "This patient is normally not allowed any visitors. But the Commander in Chief, General Haniyu, made a special request, so we're letting you in. Which one of you is Lieutenant Haniyu?"

Haniyu saluted. The doctor looked him over.

'Did you do your training together?"

"Yes, we did."

"I see. Then I can tell you the facts."

"How bad is it?"

"The broken leg is no big problem. We can remove the cast in about five weeks. The problem is the concussion. There was serious hemorrhaging, and he's suffered a loss of memory. He's conscious, but he's lost some of his mental capacities. Please keep your visit under five minutes, and keep the conversation simple."

"I understand," said Haniyu. "The loss of mental capacities—will he recover?"

"We don't know yet. We probably can't expect a complete recovery."

The doctor led them inside. Over the doorway was a sign saying "Psychological and Neurological Section." The room had a small window with bars on it. There Hanazono lay with his head wrapped in bandages. The air was damp and stifling, with a lingering smell of human waste.

"Hanazono, it's us. It's Kurushima. Can you hear me?"

There was no answer. That face which once shone with authority had a fixed, dull expression, and sweat was all that shone there now. When Haniyu spoke to him, his eyeballs moved slightly. Then suddenly he groaned, "Woah!" like an animal, and twisted his body. He tried to rise, but couldn't. They realized that his four limbs were tied to the bed. Once again he gave that animal groan, and his coverlet slipped off, revealing the diaper he had on. The doctor quickly put it back.

"He can't even take care of himself down there."

"Hey, Hanazono!" Ken called out to him again, but nothing happened. Below his greasy forehead the eyes were dead. He lay unmoving, like a dead insect. Ken signaled to Haniyu, and they left the room.

"Does he ever say anything?" Haniyu asked.

"Yes, one word," the doctor replied. "*Kaachan*."

"*Kaachan* . . ." Haniyu and Ken looked at each other. The word meant "Mommy."

A few minutes later they were walking along the Suzhou River in the direction of the Garden Bridge. Two nights before, Ken had been looking down on that steel bridge from the air. He had had the illusion of another city underneath it, and now realized why, for the river was crawling with junks and sampans. On the riverbanks were innumerable stalls selling Chinese dates, green plums, noodles, and ginkgo nuts. There were people everywhere: women in high-collared clothes, old men with goatees, barefoot boys.

Yes, this was a foreign land. It seemed impossible that he had reached it in a little over two hours. Ken moved to avoid a passing rickshaw, and watched the dark gleam of the driver's shins as he loped away. In the seat was a plump matron, no doubt on her way home from a shopping expedition; the footrest was crammed with vegetables, caged chickens, and boxes of candy. The man hauling the rickshaw was elderly and malnourished.

Jostled by the crowd, they crossed the bridge and, after paying a thirty-sen entrance fee, went into a park. They were now in part of the International Concession. This was another world from the bustling streets across the river. There were ancient plane trees in neat rows, and few pedestrians about. There was a grassy hill and a pavilion in front of a fountain where one could stop to rest. From here the stately buildings that lined the Huangpu riverfront were visible. Haniyu pulled out his map and identified some banks, the British Embassy, and the Chamber of Commerce.

"It's like being in a different country," said Ken.

"In other words it's a colony. Located in Chinese territory, but with no freedom for the Chinese. They say there used to be a sign in this park that read 'No dogs or Chinese allowed.' That regulation wasn't abolished until after the First World War. Which isn't so long ago."

"It was run by the English and the Americans, right?"

"Yes. England, the United States, and us. The city council consisted of five Englishmen, two Americans, and two Japanese. Now it's three Chinese, three Japanese, and two from other countries."

"So the rest were driven out."

"Right. But in their place they've got Japan expanding its power. I heard from my father that, deep down, they hate us, and that there are anti-Japanese movements everywhere, like underground water. There've been cases of our people being attacked. You're not supposed to move around by yourself in the city."

"Are *we* taking a risk?"

"Maybe." Haniyu looked about him, as if checking for enemies, and touched his sword and pistol. "Let's go somewhere a bit livelier. Why don't we have some Chinese food?" He began to walk quickly away. In a short while they were on Nanking Road.

The thoroughfare had countless signs jutting from each side, and a constant surge of noise bouncing off the walls and windows. Steam from wonton noodles drifted over them, along with the smell of fried ginkgo nuts. When Haniyu caught sight of a restaurant his father had mentioned, he said "Let's eat here." A waiter in traditional dress greeted them politely and ushered them into an inner room. The place appeared to be an Army watering hole as there were Japanese officers everywhere, and, sure enough, they noticed Major Kurokawa and Warrant Officer Mitsuda at one of the tables. There were four plates of food on the table, along with a brown bottle of mao-tai. The two men were already quite drunk.

"Hey, sit down!" said Kurokawa. "We're all taking that early flight back to Japan tomorrow, so we might as well stay up all night . . . Haniyu, did you get to see your father?"

"Yes, sir. But only for five minutes. He seemed busy—some new strategic plan or other."

"But at least you got to see him. That's good. People should see their parents while they can."

"I heard about the new plan," said Mitsuda, sticking his face out, proud to be privy to the latest information. "Enemy air power has made sea transport difficult, so we're going to open a land route between north and south China, and bring supplies in from Indochina."

"That's one possibility . . . ," said Haniyu vaguely. Privately he took a dim view of babbling about military secrets like this.

"We saw Hanazono," Ken said to Kurokawa. "He's lost his memory. It seems unlikely he'll ever completely get better."

"Poor guy." There was a pained look in his eyes.

Ken filled Kurokawa's glass and then everybody else's. "Let's drink a toast in memory of Major Iwama, and another to the fighting spirit of the Hayate squadrons."

Kurokawa nodded. "The fighting's going to get harder and harder from here on. So let's live it up while we can—we won't be able to eat and drink like this at home. Okay, then, a toast!"

The four men clinked glasses and drank down the mao-tai in a single gulp.

The Major began to sing; it was a song about the Red Hawk squadron he'd been attached to at the beginning of the war. Ken and the other two soon joined in, their loud foreign voices showing no concern for their surroundings. The waiter attending them probably despised them for it, and none of the people outside on the street— the little girls, the priests, the skinny barefoot coolies, the students, the resistance fighters—none of them had the slightest interest in what these men might be feeling as they sang. Ken in fact felt a sense of emptiness, and the feeling made him sing even louder, and that in turn made the emptiness even worse. In his mind there flashed an image of the vacant expression on Hanazono's face.

2

"Please remove your clothes." At Yamada's request, Ken—now back on home ground—took off his jacket, shirt, and trousers and stood there in his loincloth. He seemed to have faithfully observed the late Major Iwama's rule that "an airman should always keep his loincloth clean, so as to be presentable when he dies."

The medical orderly gave a little cry of astonishment. Yamada understood his reaction: he himself, when he'd first seen Ken naked, had been astonished at his hairiness. It was the complete opposite of the smooth hairlessness of most Japanese.

Yamada tied a rubber tube around Ken's chest and fastened it with adhesive tape. He placed the electrodes of an automatic thermometer under his armpits. And on his arms he tied an automatic pulsimeter. Then he fitted Ken in a thermal suit, with the electricity on, being careful not to loosen the rubber tubing or the electrodes.

"Great. It's a perfect fit." Yamada touched the sleeves. "Yours is extra large, we had it specially tailored for you."

He tied anti-G devices on Ken's stomach and legs.

"What's this tube you got around me?"

"I invented it myself. When you inflate it, it constricts your stomach and below, so that when G hits you the blood doesn't drop to your feet."

"It's really tight. I feel a bit faint."

"Ah, a sign that the device is working." Yamada let some of the air out.

He had him put on a helmet with an oxygen mask attached. As he was adjusting it so it wouldn't leak, Major Wakana peered in, along with the technician Aoyagi and Haniyu.

"How's it going?"

"We're just about ready."

"He looks like a diver," said Haniyu.

Ken went out first, followed by the doctor and the medical orderly, carefully carrying the automatic instruments. The group walked slowly to the airfield.

There, waiting for them with its engines already started, was a Hayate with its paint stripped off for ultra high-altitude flight, its bare duralumin gleaming.

"How's the supercharger this time?" the Major asked Aoyagi in his abrupt way.

"It worked well in the ground experiments, but we won't know for sure until we test it in actual flight."

"That's obvious." There was a deep furrow in his forehead. "What are the chances?"

"I'd put it at fifty-fifty, sir." The technician's scrawny neck looked thinner than ever. "We tried to copy the P-51, but the stuff we're getting from the factories these days is worse than ever, and we can't get an even mix of fuel and air."

Wakana turned to Yamada. "Lieutenant, how much do these anti-G things and the thermal suit weigh?"

"About ten kilos, sir."

"That's a lot. Hey, is that stuff going in too?"

"Yes, sir, those are automatic devices to monitor the pilot's blood pressure, pulse, breathing, and body temperature." He knew what Major Wakana was thinking: in order to attain high altitudes this Hayate had had everything not strictly essential removed from it—the bulletproof shield, the radio, the machine guns, the lights, the emergency medical kit. But he had two more things to add: one a cage with a rabbit in it fitted with an oxygen mask; the other a steel pressure chamber, akin to a cash box, which held another rabbit. "Altogether these weigh another thirty-five kilograms."

"You mean you're putting an extra forty-five kilos in there?" Wakana waved his fist to show his dissatisfaction.

"It can't be helped. The heavy stuff, the pressure chamber, is the most important part of the experiment."

Ken entered the cockpit. Yamada stuck his head in and fixed up the various measuring devices. Ken began to sweat.

Effortlessly he climbed up and up. At 5,000 meters, the clouds and the mountains were all below him. It was cold, and hard to breathe. He switched on the thermal suit and started the flow of oxygen. The plane was performing above its normal standard, having been lightened. Wisps of autumnal cloud floated by. Already 6,000 meters. Tokyo Bay and the Izu Peninsula spread out beneath the tips of his wings. 7,000. The rudder was getting stiff. He was losing some speed. Even at full throttle the air-speed indicator twitched downward. 8,000 meters. He had never been up here before. A slight headache. Quickly losing speed, he leveled out and got some thrust back. He climbed higher: 9,000, then 9,500. Pulling on the control stick gave him another two, three thousand meters, but damn it, the air just wouldn't support his wings. Below him were the streets of Tokyo, the commuter trains of the Chuo and Yamate Lines, and Shinjuku. He was being pushed to the east. When a plane reaches 10,000 meters it encounters a fierce westerly wind, and especially around the beginning of autumn the seasonal winds add their effect, with speeds getting up to sixty or seventy meters per second. He was supposed to be going 250 kph, but it felt as if he'd stopped—right over the Shinjuku entertainment district. Slowly, slowly he gained more altitude. 10,500, then 11,000. He felt as if he could go even higher. Breathing was difficult; he was almost out of oxygen. But the supercharger was working well. Good job, Aoyagi. Could it be a mistake?—no, there it was, 12,000, and he could still go higher. Pegasus the flying horse, working its wings, making its way skyward. It was quiet here, not a sound. *A room in Chicago. I remember the roses on the wallpaper. The second floor of the Consulate. A girl calling my name. Me saying "Lauren?"* Pegasus still flapping its wings. But, hey! 11,000? Yes, no mistaking it, he'd lost height, must be an air pocket. *In the darkness beneath the desk, a girl laughing. "Lauren, where are you?" I hear my name being called, but it isn't Lauren's voice, it's my mother's. Mama* (he was thinking in English now), *there's some strange bird coming at me. What kind of bird? A silver bird. It's huge, and it's coming right at me . . .*

Approaching from below him on the right, Ken saw an enormous object gleaming in the sun. His mind cleared and he focused hard on it. Four engines on its wide wings, a tuna-like nose pushing ahead of it. It was nothing less than a B-29. He had recently made a model of one, so he knew its every detail. Its guns fixed fore and aft, left and right, had no dead angles. Ken, rather than sensing danger, felt excited by the beauty of it. What a lovely piece of work it was, every bit of it designed for long-distance, ultra high-altitude flights. The bomber didn't seem to notice the tiny Japanese plane with its back to the sun; it maintained its leisurely flight path, four white streamers trailing from its propellers. How confident it was, invading hostile air-space without a single fighter escort. Ken waited for it, using the westerly wind and hiding in the sun. It was 1,000 meters below him. *Dive, and crash into it! Do it! Now!* He made a large turn to the right and swooped down behind it . . . But, damn it, he'd come down too far. He'd miscalculated the distance, forgetting how big the target was, with its wingspan of 43 meters—twice the size of a Japanese bomber. The upper half of his field of vision was now blocked by a sheet of silver. He could clearly see the face of the American gunner. The man swiveled his weapon at him and fired, but missed. The huge plane then flew off behind him. Ken realized what a big mistake he'd made. Why had he been chasing the thing in the first place? He hadn't been thinking. He headed down. 650 kph. He was out of oxygen. *Before I faint, just keep falling!* Smoke was coming from his arms. The wires were burning him. He couldn't find the switch. The switch! . . .

Yamada was in a Hayabusa. All around him Japanese planes were racing each other upward. But the B-29 was moving further and further away, the swarm of fighter planes way behind it as it drifted away into the blue, sending out streams of white from its engines . . .

Yamada had watched Ken take off in the experimental plane, then gone to the officers' mess to get something to eat, when the siren had suddenly gone off. At first he thought it was the signal that always announced the start of work at the nearby aircraft factory, but, no, it was an air raid siren. Soon a message from the Eastern Division came over the loudspeaker: a single enemy plane had entered Japanese airspace over the Boso Peninsula and was heading for the capital. The capital! There hadn't been a raid on Tokyo since the B-25s had attacked in 1942. Then an order for a sortie was announced. Recently, in preparation for the coming air raids, an emergency fighter squadron had been formed, with Major Kurokawa as its leader. Haniyu, Ken, and Mitsuda were members of it. Yamada was head of an emergency medical team.

They'd all looked up at the sky. The silver four-engined plane was flying from west to east. "It's flying low, real low," somebody said, misled by the size of it. In fact it seemed so low that they imagined its occupants were bound to see the generators and ammunition dumps at the base. It looked as if they might catch up with it if they gave chase. Shouting "Start 'em up!" to the ground staff, they each ran to their planes. The planes were a motley collection: Hayates, Hiens, Hayabusas, and even an ancient 97. Yamada himself wasn't called out, but when he saw the others dashing off, he was caught up in the frenzy, not so much because he wanted to fight but so as to see for himself close up just what this rumored B-29 looked like. Still wearing his white medical coat, he had jumped into a Hayabusa that the ground crew had just started up. "Lieutenant, sir, where's your helmet?" "I don't need it. Get out of the way!" "The oxygen set isn't . . ." "Just let me get airborne!" He roared down the runway in pursuit.

Once in the air, Yamada quickly realized how futile this was. To make matters worse, horizontal vision in the upper sky was unexpectedly bad. He just hadn't been thinking, he'd simply rushed off. Beyond the black harvested rice fields the blue Tama River pointed the way back to base. Since the runway was crowded he passed over it once and circled. On his second pass he noticed a Hayate with its rear trailing down, descending as if it were about to stall. It was Kurushima's plane, and there was something very wrong. There was another plane in front of Kurushima, but he was ignoring the red flag signaling him to wait and was heading straight for the runway. His rear wheel struck the ground hard, and he brought down the front wheels with such force that they almost broke. It was only just short of a crash.

When his feet touched the ground, Ken felt the earth rolling and pitching beneath him, and he stumbled. He planted both feet firmly on the ground, but he couldn't keep his balance. A member of the maintenance crew held him up. He took a deep breath, filling his lungs with soothing air, but he couldn't get rid of the awful rasping in his ears or the throbbing headache, which made him feel as if his headband might burst open. The voices of the ground staff sounded distant, as if heard over a wall. No, not just their voices—people's faces, hangars, everything looked different.

"Is this the Inspection Department?" he asked.

"Yes, sir." A shadow of astonishment crossed the man's face. "Are you all right, Lieutenant?"

"Yes."

"There's blood coming from your forehead, sir. Shall I take you to the emergency room?"

"Please. I've got a bad headache."

He lay down on the examination table and a medical orderly attended to him. It was an old corporal who had been a barber in a provincial town before joining the Army, and who even now occasionally gave haircuts in his spare time. He swabbed the wound with surgical cotton. "It won't hurt, sir, it won't hurt," he kept repeating, as if talking to a child. "You've got a bad cut there. We're going to have to stitch it up."

"Where's Yamada?" asked Major Wakana as he entered the room. Ken tried to get up and salute but was told not to. The Major seemed in a rage.

"Dr. Yamada joined the sortie, sir," the orderly answered. "We've got to stitch this up. We can't leave a scar on this handsome face."

"Why the hell would Yamada want to tag along? Has everyone lost their heads around here!"

"You don't have to stitch the wound," said Ken, getting up from the table. "I've been banged up like this before when I played rugby. Just put a bandage on it. Major, I've got something to report. At an altitude of 12,000, no, 11,000 meters I encountered, and gave chase to, a B-29."

"You did?" Wakana's face suddenly brightened. "Which was it?"

"I beg your pardon?"

"Was it 12,000 or 11,000?"

"I think it was 11,000."

"Don't you remember exactly?"

Ken couldn't answer.

"We have to know the exact altitude of the B-29. It's important data, so make sure you remember when you make your formal report. By the way, how high did you get?"

The headache was excruciating, and he couldn't think straight. "A little over 12,000 meters."

"A little over? What was your exact altitude?"

"I can only remember getting up to 12,000."

"You encountered the B-29 right after that?"

"Yes, sir."

"And that made you forget?"

"Not exactly, sir . . ."

"Everyone's lost their wits around here! What the hell is the matter with all of you? Kurushima, what is your main duty nowadays?"

"High-altitude flight testing."

"Your job is collecting data—performance and physiological data—on high-altitude flight. Correct?"

"Yes, sir."

"Then carry out your duty! Of course the B-29 is important, but that was an unexpected incident. The important thing is the experiment itself."

"Yes, sir."

Yamada came running in. He checked Ken's thermal suit. "Damn it, you've ripped the wiring and rubber tubing!"

Ken had forgotten. He was used to removing his oxygen mask and the parachute harness, but had left the wires plugged in, and they were now broken.

Yamada roughly pulled the bandage off Ken's forehead and examined him. "This is bad. The bleeding hasn't stopped. Lie down. You idiot, you haven't even let the air out of the anti-G suit. No wonder the bleeding won't stop. Orderly! Is the needle and thread sterilized?"

"Yes, sir, it's ready." The old soldier put it on a tray.

As Yamada finished putting in four stitches, Major Wakana said, "Why did you abandon your emergency medical post and take off like that?"

"I guess I let myself get carried away," Yamada answered as he cut the thick surgical thread.

"You neglected your duty."

"I didn't neglect it. I just wanted to see the B-29 closer up. It's a hell of a plane."

"Your duty, Lieutenant, is medical and physiological research. Your duty was to wait for Kurushima's return, to remove the technical apparatus and make precise records of the data."

"Well, I'm sorry. There's nothing wrong with the data, we've got it all. As expected, my little inventions worked rather well."

"And what about the research animals?"

"The rabbits? The poor things died from lack of oxygen."

"What do you mean?"

"I mean they were able to survive a long high-altitude flight until they no longer had the necessary amount of oxygen to stay alive."

"All right, collect all the data, and afterwards both of you come to my room."

After Wakana left, Yamada wrapped a bandage around Ken's head. Sticking out his long tongue, he said, "What's wrong with that guy? Something's eating him."

"Probably one of the Academy officers. 'You technical people are getting flabby!'—that sort of thing . . . My headache is still really bad."

"Take some oxygen and you'll soon feel better." Yamada told the orderly to prepare a tank. "Apparently you went for six and a half minutes at 12,000 meters with your oxygen off. What an amazing guy!

Any ordinary human being would have suffocated."

Yamada began removing the thermal suit. There was a sharp pain in Ken's right arm, and he groaned. Overheated wiring on his forearms from his wrists up had left serious burns.

"This is bad. When it got too hot you should have switched it off."

"I couldn't find the switch. The headache did something to my brain."

After being treated for the burns, he took some pure oxygen. His headache improved immediately, and he finally felt human again.

As Ken was filling out the experiment records in the research lab, an NCO working for the department chief came in with an order for him to show up immediately in the chief's office. The senior representatives of various commands had arrived and wanted to hear in detail about his encounter with the B-29.

"All those bigwigs at one sitting! Who came from Air Command?"

"I don't know, sir."

"What does he look like?"

"He's got a moustache."

"It's Okuma. What a pain."

"Kurushima, I have a suggestion," said Yamada. "Take your models of the B-29 and the Hayate. Those brass hats are a bunch of half-wits. A verbal explanation won't mean anything to them."

"Good idea." On his way there, Ken stopped in at the officers' room and picked up the two brightly painted model airplanes.

The atmosphere in the chief's office was stiff, with medals and epaulets conspicuous. After announcing his name and rank, Ken was introduced to the others present: Lieutenant Colonel Asai from Imperial Headquarters, Lieutenant Colonel Shimamoto from the Defense Command, and General Okuma from Air Command. Major Wakana, the top technical officer, stood at the chief's side, and their high-ranking visitors sat on the sofa facing Ken. Ken expected an interrogation, but when they saw the models of the B-29 and the Hayate, the staff officers cried out in admiration. "Well done!" one of them said. "I wish *we* had something like this at headquarters." "You'll just have to wait your turn," the chief told him with a laugh. "We're inundated with requests for them from other squadrons." Ken then smoothly reported on the recent incident, speaking confidently about altitudes and conditions in the upper atmosphere. With the B-29 in his left hand and the Hayate in his right, he explained how after reaching 12,000 meters —as recorded on the automatic data recording device—he had made a wide turn and approached the enemy plane from behind.

"All right. I get the basic idea. I have a question," said Lieutenant Colonel Asai after listening to him. "What's this high wind you referred to?"

Major Wakana jumped in to explain. "It's a westerly wind encountered at 10,000 meters above sea level. When seasonal monsoon winds combine with it, it can get up to sixty or seventy meters per second, which is 200 to 250 kilometers per hour. There was a record of the phenomenon in the data book of the B-29 that was shot down over Yahata. They called it the 'jet stream.'"

"Fascinating!" said Lieutenant Colonel Shimamoto. "We could use this 'jet stream' to send over bombs to America."

"Bombs?" The smooth-faced Asai turned to him, his mouth agape.

"Yes. Put bombs on balloons and send them into the 'jet stream.' At that speed, you could reach a target a great distance away. In fact we've already got our technical research people looking into the possibility of bombs attached to balloons made of special paper."

"What good is that going to do?"

"A lot, actually. First of all, you don't need any fuel. And the 'jet stream' happens to cover the entire North American continent. We could deliver bombs over the East Coast, bombs over the southern states. We could even drop them in the Gulf of Mexico."

"Let's get back to the point," General Okuma demanded, medals quivering.

"Hang on." Shimamoto still had a smile on his face. "This 'jet stream' *is* the point. Because of it, Lieutenant Kurushima was able to achieve stable flight at 12,000 meters, and the enemy was able to gain the necessary speed to escape."

"So what?"

"It has an important bearing on the air defense of the capital, for one thing. This incursion by a single plane was no doubt carried out from a base in the Marianas. It entered our airspace over the Boso Peninsula and turned west over the northern suburbs, and then escaped. Probably its object was to photograph Tokyo. But there's a real possibility that next time they'll set out further west, by Mount Fuji, turn eastward and take advantage of the 'jet stream.' If we can get our squadrons up there at high altitude, stable and waiting with their backs to the sun, why, we can swoop down from behind and attack them. What's more, just like Lieutenant Kurushima here, we'll have a speed advantage if we can dive on them."

"I like the sound of it." Asai rattled his sword.

"Sir, I have something to say." It was Ken. "The problem is a shortage of planes that can reach 12,000 meters. This time we were only able to get to that altitude by removing all the heavy equipment—the guns, the communications equipment, the bulletproof shield, everything."

"Why, of course you remove everything." Shimamoto nodded for emphasis.

"You do?"

"With all the equipment removed, you wait up there and when the B-29s come you crash into them. It can't fail."

"That's it—Kamikazes." Asai jabbed at the floor with his sword. "In the Philippines we've already had magnificent results with Kamikazes attacking enemy ships. If we're not willing to use suicide planes, we'd be failing in our duty to protect the Emperor."

Ken had a creepy feeling as he surveyed these two: Shimamoto, with the smile never fading from his face, as if he'd been born with it fixed on his doughy features; and Asai, with his soft white hands folded over his sword.

"Well, Lieutenant Kurushima, do you have any thoughts on the matter?" asked Shimamoto.

"Yes, sir, I do. At 12,000 meters the air is extremely thin, making it very difficult to maintain a stable horizontal position. In my experience just touching the control stick sends you down 500 or 1,000 meters. Also, at ultra high altitude when you execute a turn you can easily lose a couple of thousand meters. In other words, sir, chasing an enemy plane is one hell of a problem."

"A little extra training could take care of that." This was Asai's contribution.

Imamura, the department chief, who had been silent until then, adjusted his glasses and asked, "How was the supercharger?"

"Aoyagi's improved version worked quite well this time." Ken gave the chief a hard look. "But I gather it's not being mass-produced yet."

"That's a major problem. The engines. They just don't operate well at really high altitudes."

"There's one other thing," said Ken. "The physiological problem. At 12,000 meters the temperature is –55° centigrade and the air pressure is one-sixth of that on the ground. Oxygen is reduced to four percent. Hanging around in such conditions would induce severe physical pain."

"Nothing that extra training couldn't cure," Asai insisted.

"But with our present oxygen equipment, staying at that altitude for any length of time just isn't possible. And if we added more oxygen, the extra weight would cut back on performance."

"Piloting problems, physical pain, technical difficulties—those are all *details*. We don't have *time* to quibble over details. The fate of the nation is at stake."

Ken wouldn't quit. "I believe the correct solution is to put all our efforts into producing an ultra high-altitude fighter. The Ki-94 presently under development at Nakajima Aircraft is being designed with a pressurized cockpit and an improved supercharger to achieve better results at high altitude. If we could just get it produced . . ."

"Produced? *When?*" Asai's voice was high-pitched. "The Americans are building huge bases in the Marianas, and they'll be bombing Tokyo any day now. Can you get those planes out in time?"

"I don't know, sir. But if we put our backs into it . . ."

"Putting our backs into something we don't even know will work? You call that a solution? Is that what makes you technical officers tick?"

Ken's face was burning hot. "Kamikaze tactics involve the loss of men and planes. It would be better to complete an advanced fighter . . ."

"You coward!" General Okuma cut through the argument. "Trying to save your own skin, are you?"

"What do you mean, sir?"

"You said you got so close to that B-29 you could have touched it. Then why didn't you crash into it?"

Ken didn't answer.

"Are you aware of the term 'destroy the first wave'? Shoot down all the planes in the first enemy attack—that's Air Command's basic strategy. Isn't that right, Asai? Lieutenant Kurushima's actions today amount to a dereliction of that fundamental duty."

Ken kept silent, his eyes fixed on the General.

Ken's chief shook his head. "No, the purpose of his flight was to gather data on high altitude performance."

"But, my dear Imamura, downing that plane was surely more important than any data you could have gathered. There's no question that the object of today's enemy incursion was to photograph Tokyo. Lieutenant Kurushima, did you have some *reason* for letting an enemy plane you were perfectly capable of downing escape? Or was it your mother's blood that stayed your hand?"

Ken still remained silent. *Here we go again*, he thought—*enemy blood, tainted blood*. He looked away and stared at the stains on the ceiling.

"Oh, come now," said Lieutenant Colonel Shimamoto. "It's thanks to the Lieutenant that we discovered a way to bring the B-29s down. On behalf of the Defense Command, I propose that we put all our efforts into developing suicide planes. I want the cooperation of you people in the Inspection Department. Major Wakana, I'll be counting on you."

"Yes, sir." There were deep creases in Wakana's forehead.

Several days later, Ken and Yamada paid a visit to the low-pressure, low-temperature experimental chamber at Nakajima Aircraft's factory in Mitaka. At the request of technician Aoyagi, they were to test the pressurized cockpit of the Ki-94 then under development.

Ken, in his electric thermal suit, opened the thick steel door and slipped into the cocoon-shaped cockpit, identical to that of the actual plane when completed. The steel door slid smoothly shut, locking him in.

Aoyagi's voice came over the intercom. "All right, close the canopy."

Ken did as he was told. It wasn't a simple thing like the canopy on the Hayate, but with double rubber insulation.

"Commence pressure reduction."

An electric motor started up with a low throb. The needle on the altimeter slid up to 1,000, then to 2,000.

"Please turn on the pressure switch."

A small electric motor behind him went on.

"Is the cabin pressure rising?"

"No, there's no change on the gauge."

"Something's wrong. How do you feel?"

"Fine. Try reducing the air pressure a bit more."

At 3,000 meters the temperature inside went down. White mist began to swirl in the chamber. Crystals formed on the canopy. In actual flight they would be blown away by the wind, but here they clung to the glass. At 5,000 meters the oxygen started to flow; the pressure, however, remained unchanged. He tried to use the intercom to contact Yamada and Aoki, but he couldn't speak. The low air pressure, he realized, made it impossible to use his voice. Gradually his consciousness dimmed, but the thermal suit was working all too well, making him feel hot. At 10,000 meters all around him turned dark. He had the feeling he was about to see something—a feeling he'd experienced in the air when that B-29 had hoved in sight. Yes, it was the darkness in a corner of a room, in the Chicago house where he'd been playing with Lauren; he should be hearing her name at this point, and her soft white shoulders would appear. There was a sharp pain in his ears; he tried swallowing, but the pain wouldn't go away. It felt as if his eardrums were about to burst.

"My ears hurt." He'd finally got his voice back.

"Try holding your nose and swallowing real hard," Yamada suggested. Ken remembered doing that before. Three times, and it worked; the pain was gone. He was back down to 2,000 meters now. The temperature went up, and he began to sweat. He switched off the thermal suit, but still his whole body felt on fire.

"I'm hot."

"It looks like we can't get enough pressure," said Yamada. "You're suffering from pressure loss symptoms."

The steel door opened, and people came running over. Ken pushed against the canopy, but the insulation had frozen up and it wouldn't give. With help from the outside he finally got it open.

Yamada looked worried as he took Ken's pulse. "You were unconscious for three whole minutes. If we'd taken the pressure down to the 12,000 meter level you would have been in danger, so we immediately called off the experiment."

They investigated what had gone wrong. Aoyagi discovered that the valve on the ventilation shaft in the pressure chamber had frozen over, blocked by the moisture from Ken's breath. It was a truly elementary problem, but certainly not the first time (there had been a similar hitch with the Hayate's governor) that a complex piece of machinery had been fouled up by something very simple.

"You're lucky to be alive," said Yamada. "But you always manage to get through. If it had been me I wouldn't have survived."

Ken was limping. "The joints in my knees hurt."

"That's a low pressure symptom. You need some oxygen." Yamada put an oxygen mask on him. Several minutes later the pain in his knees eased.

Aoyagi was watching him with a worried expression on his face.

Ken, in an encouraging tone, said, "Just quickly fix it and get a test plane ready as soon as possible. We have to hurry."

"We already have one, with the pressurized cockpit built in. But there are still lots of little things to be ironed out."

"I want to be the first to test it."

"It's still too dangerous."

"Anyway, let me take a look at it."

In one corner of the factory grounds stood a hangar guarded by MPs. There was a wooden plaque on it with the words "No Unauthorized Entry" inked in black. Inside the building was a Ki-94, the plane Ken had seen in blueprints—even built a model of—but here was the real thing with its wings spread, as if ready to take off.

"It's magnificent. I'm ready to fly it."

"Impossible . . ." Aoyagi shook his head weakly, but then proceeded to give a detailed and confident description of its makeup: the materials used, the weaponry, the canopy, the anti-moisture glass. As he spoke, he occasionally coughed.

"Are you all right?" Yamada asked him.

"I haven't been getting much sleep these days," the skinny technician replied, "and I can't seem to get over a cold."

Ken made a proposal. A formal, public test of the plane would mean the factory taking responsibility as the producers, but if they tested it while it was still under development they could keep it secret. He offered to try it out like that. Aoyagi promised to discuss it with his superiors.

On the train back Yamada said quietly, "You saw those red marks on Aoyagi's cheeks? That's a sure sign. He's a serious case of tuberculosis."

When they got back to the Inspection Department, Haniyu showed them a mimeographed circular that had just come in relating to the defense of Tokyo.

1. We anticipate high altitude raids on the capital by enemy B-29s, flying singly and in groups above 10,000 meters.
2. The Air Corps is organizing special attack forces to deal with these raids.
3. Each squadron is to organize a special unit of four planes, whose aim is to carry out collisions with enemy aircraft at ultra high altitude and destroy them.
4. The planes in these special units will be divested of armor,

communications equipment, and all other heavy equipment, with the single goal of improving high altitude performance.

5. Members of the special attack forces will in principle consist of non-married volunteers. Further details will be supplied by the general staff.

"Now that's a clear set of orders," muttered Yamada.

"A little too clear if you ask me. I've got a bad feeling about this." Ken scowled. It was sinister the way they were going to apply his experience in the Hayate to making suicide planes more effective. He remembered his argument with the senior officers, Okuma's angry voice shouting "You coward!"

"Are we going to have one of these special units here?" asked Haniyu. There was a worried note in his voice.

"We're not directly under division command, so we're not required to," said Ken.

"But if we're going to be inspecting Kamikaze planes, there's no way we can avoid having to organize our own squad."

"What do you mean, inspecting Kamikaze planes?"

"They made Major Wakana chief inspector. They've already placed orders for suicide planes from Nakajima Aircraft, along with Mitsubishi and Kawasaki."

"Even Nakajima!" Ken pounded the table with his fist.

A week later the maiden flight of the Ki-94 was carried out at the aircraft company's Tachikawa airfield. The test pilot was Ken. It was a top-secret affair, attended only by officials from the company.

Ken had a smooth ascent. However, when he got above 5,000 meters he began losing power; the supercharger wasn't working and the turbines were unsteady. Even at full throttle he couldn't get any more out of it. But the pressurized cockpit functioned perfectly even at 10,000 meters. It was much easier than when he had struggled to control the Hayate with his oxygen mask and thermal suit on. Then suddenly, at 11,000 meters, the windshield burst. In an instant all the air blew out. Ken felt a sharp pain in his eardrums. He placed the oxygen mask over his nose, but his body seemed to swell like a balloon. He felt his skin crawling, all down his back. *Dive! Dive!* The blast of air through the broken windshield tore his goggles away. He was flying blind now. But he was used to abrupt descents. At 3,000 meters he pulled back on the control stick. *Come on, flatten out.* He could just see the airfield even without his goggles. *Stay calm and bring it in.* He managed to land in one piece.

"Are you hurt, sir?" Aoyagi was out of breath. "Why didn't you bail out?"

"Bail out? It never crossed my mind. All I thought about was getting this crate back on the ground."

Yamada noticed blood pouring from a vein in Ken's neck where a shard of glass must have cut him. Fortunately it had missed the artery, and a little first-aid took care of the wound. Technicians were checking the ruined windshield.

Ken saw Aoyagi standing alone away from the others, and went over to him. But before he could start discussing his flight Aoyagi interrupted, his lips trembling: "We just received an order from headquarters. We're to cease production of the Ki-94 immediately. It came along with another order—that the factory is to put all of its resources into producing Kamikaze planes."

3

The first plan for remodeling fighters into suicide planes was drawn up at the Air Corps' Technical Research Institute. But the institute's work then shifted to designing unmanned, radio-controlled planes, and the Inspection Department was ordered to take over the research and training for manned Kamikaze flights. It was decided that, within the Inspection Department, the bomber section would concentrate on anti-ship suicide missions, while the fighter section would undertake the remodeling of planes for use against both ships and B-29s. Major Wakana's group was chosen to work on the B-29 side of the operation.

"It's an order," Wakana told them. Even Ken, who had proposed that the experiments on the Ki-94 be restarted after he came back from Nakajima Aircraft, realized, from the tone of the Major's voice, that he had better keep his objections to himself.

One morning shortly afterwards they were shown a film in the officers' room. It had been produced by their counterparts in the Navy. Off a beach somewhere floated life-size mockups of American Liberty and Victory ships, and they watched wingless aircraft crash into them, with bits of propellers scattering in all directions and engines bursting through the sides of the ships, followed by thunderous roars deep inside them as the bombs placed in the fuselages ripped through the steel plating and exploded. This was all taken with high-speed film, which showed every stage of it in great detail.

"They must have spent a fortune on all that research," said Mitsuda.

Ken, too, was impressed by the work that must have gone into it, comparing it with the knee-jerk response of their own top brass to the threat of bombing raids. In order to get the fuselages, stripped of their wings, to crash at the same speed as real planes, they had added rockets, applying to this problem the same ingenuity they'd used to catapult planes into flight from ships. The recent successes against enemy battleships in the Sulu Sea in the Philippines hadn't been suddenly improvised. Even so, Ken found it hard to understand the mentality of scientists singlemindedly bent on making something whose sole purpose was to kill other people.

When Wakana asked him for his reactions to it, Ken thought for a second, then said "Maybe the anti-ship planes need an internal explosive device, but against B-29s, carrying a large bomb that high obviously isn't possible. It seems to me we should be studying whether a simple collision would be enough to bring them down. It's tricky, because the weight of a plane stripped of its heavy equipment might not be enough for an effective collision."

"I agree. We should be looking at the weak points of the B-29."

"Not only that, we should be thinking about a system that would allow pilots to eject immediately before or at the time of the collision."

Wakana nodded. "That's the way our research should go." He seemed in a very good mood, completely different from when he'd laid into Ken for arguing in favor of continued research on the Ki-94.

"I'm against it," Haniyu said quite abruptly.

"Oh? Tell us why." Wakana turned to him, surprised. Haniyu rarely ventured an opinion.

"If ejecting is an option, well, people are weak, and saving themselves would be their first priority, which defeats the whole purpose of it. Collision has to mean a sure hit and a sure death." This phrase— "a sure hit, a sure death"—was one the newspapers used in connection with the Kamikaze missions.

"Hmm." Wakana thought it over. He seemed unsure of himself. "What do you think?" he asked, looking for some further comment from Ken.

"I think making ejection impossible would in fact lower the hit rate. It's human instinct to avoid dying in the first place."

Haniyu was obviously agitated, and red in the face. "The fate of the nation depends on the outcome of this phase of the war. A soldier has to be prepared to lay down his life at a time like this."

When had he changed? His overexcitement seemed almost irrational. Ken spoke gently, hoping to calm him down.

"It's because the future of the nation is at stake that I want to save as many soldiers' lives as possible. It's easy to make suicide planes, but it's not so easy to make new pilots. You can mass-produce Kamikaze planes, but they won't work if there's no one left to fly them."

"I don't know what to think . . ." Wakana looked at the two of them.

Haniyu was silent, so Ken spoke again. "We've worked all this time to develop fighters. The aim of the fighter plane is to down the enemy without being downed yourself. The proper course now is for the enemy to be attacked and brought down by remote-controlled planes. The present emphasis on suicide planes basically comes down to wasting precious human lives as substitutes for a homing mechanism, simply because the mechanism wasn't developed in time. Even now, though, we should be giving priority to saving pilots' lives in combat."

The naval officer who had brought the film they'd been watching was a stocky-looking figure, a Captain. "What the hell's going on here?!" he bellowed suddenly. "All this *gaijin* bastard can talk about is 'precious lives.' His life is that important to him, is it? Then he's no different from those damned Americans. The Navy wouldn't put up with this kind of talk for a second. Look at the suicide submarines at Pearl Harbor, look at the Kamikazes. We die the samurai way—a dozen enemies for just one of us. And this bastard doesn't even *look* Japanese. Well, I can forgive that, but I warn you, the only way for us to defeat an enemy with a huge material advantage is for each of us, each loyal subject of the Emperor, to give his life *willingly* for the Empire. Parachutes for suicide pilots? The idea makes me SICK!"

The officer picked up his projector case and film and, kicking the door open, left the room. A moment later, they heard his motorcycle roar away.

"Well," Wakana nodded weakly, "there are various sides to the question. Here's what I'd like us to do. Let's come up with a plane in which, right at the moment of collision, the canopy opens, allowing the pilot to escape. But let's make it difficult to open before actual impact. That's the compromise I propose. What do you think?"

Haniyu nodded slightly. The red was gone from his face; it was pale now, almost white. Ken kept his mouth shut and reluctantly nodded his approval.

Their planes had been built to withstand air friction and high speeds; nobody had thought about collisions. Even though they had a detailed understanding of the B-29's structure, they still had no idea what part would suffer what kind of damage when crashed into. The same was true of the Hiens and Hayates (the other planes couldn't achieve the necessary altitude) that were to be remodeled into special attack planes. There were huge guns on the B-29, two 12.7-mm. machine guns on both the upper and lower decks fore and aft, along with a 20-mm. automatic cannon and another two 12.7-mm. machine guns at the rear. Their experience with the B-29 in Kyushu had shown them that these eleven guns, all firing at once, threw out a fine net of bullets, with no dead angles at all.

After long debate they came to the conclusion that they wouldn't understand anything until someone actually tried a real collision. Their only hope lay in the fact that the bomber hadn't been designed with the necessary power or guns to specifically fend off a suicide attack by Japanese planes.

Ken went to visit the Nakajima factory in Mitaka. In one corner of the factory floor, which was covered with tools and equipment for remodeling the Hayates, stood the Ki-94, like a piece of junk waiting to be removed.

"Too bad, isn't it?" Ken said to Aoyagi. "A little more effort and we could have completed it."

"It's nobody's fault," the other man replied with a shrug of his thin shoulders. "But we didn't work all those years to make something like this." He indicated one of the stripped-down Hayates, and sighed, the sigh turning into a cough. Did he have a fever? His eyes were red, the sockets hollow-looking; even his blink was weak.

Ken sat in the pilot's seat and closed the canopy. Compared to a real fighter, everything about the remodeled plane felt tawdry. On the tin instrument panel were the minimum four gauges necessary for flight: altitude, speed, revs, and direction. And that was it. The seat was made of plywood, and the control stick had no button for firing the guns. Instead there were electrical outlets for the oxygen set and the thermal suit. Ken imagined flying at a B-29 in this toy of an airplane, and the thought made him immensely depressed. No, even if he managed to destroy the bomber and died a hero, he still wouldn't want to die in a jalopy like this. Was he a coward for thinking such thoughts? Did Haniyu really mean it when he'd said that? He hadn't spoken to him since then. He would see him in the officers' room and nod, but hadn't exchanged a word with him. It was as if they were avoiding each other. But what was truly incomprehensible was Wakana's attitude. How strange that the man could shift his mental gears, without the slightest hesitation, from developing an advanced fighter plane to gutting aircraft for suicide missions. *No*, he thought, *I'm no better than the rest of them. Look at me, someone who once told his father he wanted to build something that would last . . .*

Aoyagi knocked on the canopy. Ken tried to open it, but it wouldn't budge. Then he noticed the double-turn knob that Wakana had invented—you couldn't operate it without letting go of the control stick—and finally got it open.

"There's something I have to tell you." Aoyagi led Ken behind the Ki-94. "Yesterday I had an X-ray, and they discovered shadows on both my lungs. I'm going to be hospitalized. I'd like to thank you for all you've done for me."

"That's terrible."

"The disease is at an advanced stage. I probably won't be around much longer. I hope you'll see the rest of our mission through." Suppressing a cough, he gave Ken a deep bow.

"Take care of yourself." Ken shook his hand. It felt hot to his touch.

As Aoyagi walked away he was hit by a blast of wind, and his shoulders shook like a paper fan.

It was the end of November when the special attack units of the 11th Air Division, responsible for the defense of the capital, were given an official name by Prince Higashikuni: "Masters of the Sky." According to division orders, Sky Masters were to be chosen for suicide missions from each fighter group, with oldest sons and married men exempted. In principle the suicide pilots were all volunteers; in reality those who met the criteria of being single and second, third, or fourth born were mainly to be found among the recent graduates of the Junior Air Academy. And their youthful passion led to a phenomenon observed in all the squadrons: that those who failed to volunteer were immediately branded as cowards. Also, when the squadron leaders shouted "Kamikaze volunteers, raise your hands!" it was hard for any youngster, however reluctant, to resist the peer pressure. Ken, whose job was to hand over the remodeled planes to the Sky Masters who came from each squadron to pick them up, was increasingly depressed by reports of what had been happening.

One morning, in one of the Inspection Department's maintenance hangars, he got to know one of these young volunteers. It was just as the special mark of the Masters of the Sky was being painted on the plane, bright red lines extending to the rudder. A boy in an airman's uniform saluted Ken. It was a vigorous salute.

"Sir, are you Lieutenant Kurushima?" the young voice asked.

"Yes, I am."

"I'm PFC Honda of the 47th Fighter Squadron. I've come to take delivery of my special attack plane."

Ken gazed in surprise at his boyish face. The youngster, embarrassed, looked down at the ground.

"How old are you?"

"Seventeen, sir."

"Seventeen? Were you at Kumagaya?"

"Yes, sir, the fifteenth class."

"When I was there—it must be already three years ago—I did my flight training with the eleventh class."

"Oh, did you, sir? Then you're way ahead of me."

Now Ken was the one to be embarrassed by the look on the boy's face.

"Not by that much. You must have joined your squadron recently."

"Yes, sir, on August 1st."

"Three months ago? Have you ever flown a Hayate?"

"Yes. I'm more used to the Shoki, but since I volunteered for this unit I've been training every day in a Hayate."

"I see." Ken nodded, and led the boy over to where the remodeled planes stood in a row outside the hangar. Three more young airmen from the same squadron were waiting there. Saluting, they walked over.

"Here are your planes. They're basically the same as the regular Hayate, but the control stick is lighter. Okay, climb in and try out the equipment."

The four of them briskly boarded the planes. The rudders and flaps moved this way and that.

"All right, deplane!" When he shouted the order all four boys immediately climbed out and lined up at attention.

"How does the equipment feel?"

"Very good, sir," Honda answered.

The four pilots all had suntanned, boyish faces. They looked like brothers.

"Did you all volunteer?"

"Yes, sir. In our squadron everyone volunteered, and the four of us were chosen."

"Honda, are your parents alive?"

"No, sir. Only my mother. My father died when I was eight. But it's all right, as I'm the youngest of three children."

"Did you tell your mother you were volunteering?"

"Yes, sir. I wrote her a letter yesterday. I asked our Squadron Leader to send it on completion of my mission."

"I see. And your mother . . ."

"She'll be very proud of me. When she saw me off from my village—it's in Fukushima prefecture, sir—she told me to be happy to give my life for my country."

"Next week you'll be joining pilots from other squadrons for special training. All right, you can return to barracks now."

The four teenagers saluted and left. As Ken was walking off, thinking it was time to get some lunch, Honda came running after him.

"Lieutenant Kurushima, sir!" The boy gave a formal salute. "I have a question to ask."

"What?"

"Sir, what kind of person is your mother?"

"Why do you ask?"

"I was wondering, sir, because you look like a foreigner."

"My mother is a Japanese citizen, but she was originally American. I'm of mixed blood."

"Is that right, sir?" There was excitement in his eyes.

"What do you think about that?"

"I think it's wonderful, sir. America is a great country, even though it's the enemy. It's big. And it makes great airplanes."

"Hey, I'm Japanese, you know!"

"Yes, sir, but when we win the war you'll go to America, won't you?"

"Would you like to go there?"

"Of course, sir, I'd love to. But only after we win the war."

After we win the war . . . Ken walked off with large strides, averting his eyes from the smiling face of this boy who was about to die but was talking cheerfully about the future. The short-legged private tried to keep up with him, but finally gave up and walked away.

When Ken reached the officers' mess, Yamada came straight over. His mouth was full, and bits of rice sprayed out behind his hand.

"Sugi! Sugi's dead!" he blurted out.

"What!" The bowl of soup Ken was holding spilled on the floor.

"It happened ten days ago. He was on a sortie in southern China, and was attacked by a combined Chinese-American force."

When the 22nd Squadron was ordered back to Japan at the beginning of November, Sugi had been given another tour of duty with the 25th Squadron and had remained in China. Twenty of the Hayates had been handed over to the other squadron. Sugi was assigned the job of training their pilots in the new planes.

"Even Sugi." Ken stuffed some red sorghum rice into his mouth, but it was tasteless and he spat it out. "Have you told everybody?" He pointed with his chin at Haniyu, who was in a corner, eating alone.

"It was Haniyu who told me. He was crying."

"Crying . . ." Ken half rose to go over to him, but Yamada stopped him.

"Don't. He wants to be left alone."

Ken stood up. He just couldn't remain seated. Anger, sorrow, frustration filled him, running in a black stream through him.

"Hang on, where're you going?" Yamada called after him as he strode away.

"I don't know. For a walk."

"Let me come with you."

"I want to be alone."

"Me too."

"Don't follow me."

"You're going where I was about to go."

The two of them reached the Aviation Medicine Institute and went up to Yamada's room on the second floor. Ken went straight to a cupboard and took out the air gun he'd lent him.

"Shoot some birds?"

"Maybe."

They left together. It was a fine day but there were heavy clouds moving in the sky, sometimes blocking the sun. Using the rear gate they set out into the adjacent mulberry fields. The bare branches of the trees looked like black thorns. The woods too were black. There was frost remaining on the path beneath the trees, and when they tramped along it the soil stuck to their shoes. They could hear the chilly sound of the nearby stream, but no birdsong.

"Sugi, you fool, why did you have to die?" Ken loosed off a shot at the empty sky. From somewhere came a hollow echo.

"Iwama, Hanazono, and now . . . ," said Yamada. Hanazono had been shipped back to Japan, but he was still comatose, confined to a ward in the Army Hospital in Kofudai. They said he would never recover.

"And Aoyagi's been hospitalized." Ken told him about Aoyagi's lungs.

"So he did have it. There was TB written on his face. Did you know that he'd been getting by just on rations?"

"No."

"All he had to eat was stuff like potatoes and beans. He wouldn't touch the special rations they gave out at the aircraft factory. So he was undernourished. One of his superiors spoke to me about it. I warned him myself, but he wouldn't listen. He's a strange, stubborn fellow."

"Trying to make do with rations these days is like committing suicide."

"Maybe that's what he wanted. He once told me that he was tired of building fighter planes, sick of making what he called 'murder machines.'"

"Murder machines?" Ken felt as if some secret weakness deep inside himself had suddenly been exposed. "Well, that's all they are."

A crow flew into the dark foliage of a cryptomeria tree. Ken's arm automatically reacted. He aimed, but didn't pull the trigger. He was sure he could have bagged it easily, but he just didn't feel like killing it. Instead he went down to the bank of the stream and fired into the water. When the ripples died away and he could see his own face, he fired again.

"Are there fish down there?"

"I'm imagining there are." He kept firing.

"Hey, tomorrow's Saturday, why don't we go out and get drunk? We can invite Haniyu. And Mitsuda maybe, too."

"Good idea. I tell you what, why don't we have a party at my family's house in Tokyo? They've all moved out to the country and the house is empty."

"Excellent. I've never been there. Sounds interesting."

4

The shop window was bare but for a single flying cap. When they went inside, however, the walls were lined with flying suits, long mufflers, and other pilot's gear, and the glass cases were crammed with goggles, badges, and key chains. They were impressed; it was all they had expected, and more. Mitsuda called out a couple of times, and in due course the bald old owner appeared, stifling a yawn, from behind the heavy double curtain, apparently fashioned from parachute cloth.

"Oh. Warrant Officer Mitsuda. And some people with you."

Mitsuda, wearing a civil defense uniform, introduced his three friends, who were all in blazers. When he realized they were officers too, the old man was more than usually polite: "Members of the armed services have always been valued customers in my little shop. Warrant Officer Mitsuda, for one, has been coming here ever since the war with China began." As he said this he stared for a second at Ken's foreign face, then looked away, only to take sidelong glances at the violin case Haniyu was carrying.

"Today we're having a dinner for a friend who was killed in action, and we'd like some commemorative item, something the same for all of us."

"Let me see, sir." The old man thought for a moment, then showed them some wallets decorated with pictures of the Hayabusa and the Hayate, and then some appointment books with the Air Corps insignia on them, but none of them was to everyone's liking. Somebody suggested a scarf, which would be useful at high altitude. The old man said he happened to have four nice woolen mufflers left. He brought them out from inside. They liked them; there was a comic-book effect to them, with yellow stars on a green background, and a rising sun in the middle. He told them the wife of one of his relatives had woven them herself, using the "choicest" wool (he kept using this word). They paid the full price of five yen, and Yamada also bought an emergency medical kit small enough to fit in the trouser pocket of an airman's uniform.

They put on the scarves and went out into the street. There was a damp wind, and leaden clouds hung darkly in the sky. It looked as if they were in for some rain. They quickened their pace. Civilians in air defense garb and padded hoods, carrying water and first aid kits, had become a common sight on the city streets, so the four of them stood out, and people turned their heads as they passed. In blazers and fedoras, with Ken swinging his duffel bag crammed with food, Mitsuda his rucksack full of vegetables, and Haniyu his violin, they might have been a group of itinerant musicians. Yamada seemed proud that he alone looked like an ordinary pedestrian. But even he attracted stares, a big fat man lugging a straw bag filled with bottles of liquor.

As they climbed the hill that led from the Ogawamachi intersection toward Ochanomizu, they were surrounded by people using their Saturday afternoon for air defense drills. As usual, a middle-aged official of the Police Defense Association was barking orders at the housewives lined up for a bucket relay. In front of each house was a container full of water and a fire extinguisher made of cloth tied to a bamboo pole. All such preparations were made on the assumption that air raids were imminent, and yet the local inhabitants seemed relaxed about it, compared with the Inspection Department, which was predicting massive bombings to come. The women laughed as the water from the buckets spilled on their faces, and children splashed in the puddles.

They took the urban loop line and changed to the subway. When they emerged at Toranomon there was nobody about on the street. This seemed strange, until a defense volunteer stopped them and told them to take shelter as an air raid alert had gone out. Ken turned on his portable radio. The broadcast spoke of "a single enemy plane moving north toward the capital from the Izu Peninsula," so they went back to the subway and waited underground. It turned out that the plane was on a reconnaissance mission and backed off because of the rain clouds covering the city. "The enemy aircraft is heading south, without dropping any bombs." Shortly afterwards they heard the siren announcing the all clear. People streamed into the streets; automobiles and streetcars started moving.

Yamada, who had graduated from medical school in the provincial town of Matsumoto, was unfamiliar with Tokyo's streets. The area around Akasaka and Nagata-cho was completely new to him. He was all eyes as he passed mansion after mansion, each with a garden like a wooded park, and he lingered by the exotic buildings of the Mexican Embassy.

"Here we are!" Ken called back to him. Where Ken stood were high stone walls lined with azaleas, and a magnificent granite gateway. Deep inside the walls was a white building similar to the Kurushimas' villa in Karuizawa. The house was not some halfhearted imitation but a genuine Western-style mansion, complete in all its details.

As Ken opened the gate with his key and led his friends to the front door, Yamada's heart began to pound. So this, he thought, was where Anna grew up. These trees, these stones had all been touched by Anna's gaze. After returning from Karuizawa that summer, he had written a thank-you note to her parents and, along with it, a letter to Anna. It had been close to a love letter, the first time in his life he had tried to express his real feelings in writing. There had been no answer.

As Yamada stared around the grounds, Mitsuda said, "My, my, quite a palace our Lieutenant lives in."

"It sure is," Yamada agreed. "I thought I knew everything about him after being at flying school together. It turns out I didn't know much at all."

Ken called out from inside: "There's no one home, so come on in." He pushed aside the newspapers that had piled up in the hallway. "I thought my father was using the house on his occasional trips to Tokyo, but it looks like nobody's been here for weeks."

As they walked down the corridor in their slippers, the dust rose around them. In the rooms, bare of furniture, spiders had spun their webs. The window glass was smeared with dirt. At the sound of rain pattering on the roof, Ken said cheerfully, "We got here just in time. The gods are with us!" He seemed to have suddenly sprung to life. Haniyu and Yamada went on a quick tour of the parlor, where the sofas and cabinets were still in place, and the terrace and garden, then joined Mitsuda and Ken who were cleaning the dining room and kitchen. They managed to get the place reasonably tidy. But when it came to cooking, Ken and Haniyu, the pampered city boys, were useless. A nap was in order for one, violin practice for the other. Mitsuda and Yamada took over the kitchen.

The actual food for their dinner was a gift from Mitsuda, the scion of a fisherman's family on the Chiba coast. He had just been given a batch of seafood from his home village, so he set about making some sashimi and sushi, cutting the tuna, mackerel, yellowtail, shad, and squid into professional-looking slices. Somehow he had laid his hands on some white rice and seaweed, and he had even brought along some meat, vegetables, and vegetable oil, which Yamada proceeded to turn into a stew. It had been Yamada's job to supply the booze, and he had several bottles of Pilots' Good Health which his job had enabled him to rustle up, plus two bottles of real *sake*, obtained in exchange for some of his moonshine.

At some point Ken, who had been out in the rain, contributed some birds he'd shot.

"You brought your air gun along?" Yamada asked.

"No," Ken explained, "there was an old gun on the second floor, from my school days, and it still worked." He told them that over the wall, in the forest on the estate of Prince Konoe, there were lots of birds at this time of year.

The rain fell thick and dark and cold. They lit a fire in the coal stove, laid out the food dish by dish, and, with Mitsuda's jacket over the chandelier as a makeshift blackout curtain, began their banquet. Mitsuda, wearing a sushi chef's *happi* coat and headband, served the others, then started eating and drinking himself. They all scooped the stew from the soup bowl, wolfed down the birds, each fried whole, and in the course of this half-Japanese, half-Western, half-elegant, half-primitive meal, proceeded to get quite drunk. The remains of the fish, fowl, meat, and pilots' rations clung to the expensive (was it French or English?) dinnerware.

"Hey, Kurushima, have some more!" Mitsuda proffered a piece of sushi on the palm of his hand. "What's the matter? I made it with my own hands!"

"You eat *my* food!" Ken answered, stuffing a fried bird into Mitsuda's mouth. "Eat!"

"I can't. I'm scared of birds. I'm a flier—they fly too—they're the one thing I can't eat."

"You're hopeless. Imagine it's an enemy bird. Eat it!"

In the struggle that ensued between the two men Ken was of course bigger, but Mitsuda, who had been out on the fishing boats since he was a boy, was no weakling. As Mitsuda was cramming the slab of sushi into Ken's mouth, Ken knocked against the table, sending several dishes crashing to the floor.

"Stop it, you two, no fighting!" Haniyu shouted angrily. "You're officers, aren't you? Mitsuda, let's have a little dignity!"

Mitsuda rounded on him. "Dignity? What the hell do you mean? Dignity's for the officer corps—not the likes of me. For the sons of generals, not fishermen. For ten long years, since 1934, I've been working for the Army, and I'm still just a warrant officer. Oh, I've seen action, plenty. North China, Manchuria, Malaya, Burma. Do you know how many kills I've had? Exactly thirty-seven. I've been blooded, boy, so don't talk to me about 'dignity.'"

"That's not what I meant," said Haniyu, his voice now calm again. "You're our top pilot and I respect you for it. It's just that . . . well, we shouldn't be fighting *here*."

"Fighting? We weren't fighting." Mitsuda seemed to have run out of steam. He sat down with a thud, like a spent rocket.

"Come on, let's drink." Yamada picked up a bottle of *sake*, but it was empty. They had drunk all the Good Health too. "Listen, you guys, we're out of fuel. The Japanese Empire has run out of gas."

419

"Out of gas?" said Mitsuda. "Then use pine oil. That's what we do back home. Only problem is, will the Hayate fly on pine oil? Will it reach those B-29s?"

"Hey, Ken," cried Haniyu. "Don't you have any liquor stashed away somewhere in this house?"

"Wait here a minute," he said, and staggered off.

He was drunk, but he was alert enough not to let any light seep outside. He climbed the stairs without turning any lights on, and managed to reach his room in the dark. Pulling the blackout curtain over the window, he switched on the bedroom light. His books and papers and pens were covered with dust. A younger version of himself dressed in a rugby uniform stared back at him on the wall, looking like an entirely different person. In these few years the war had utterly transformed him; still in his mid-twenties, he felt like an old man, with no future to look forward to. Once, in this room, he had dreamed of doing things. Now the future held nothing at all, a blank, like the rainy darkness outside the window. Ken tore down the photo of himself and threw it in the wastebasket. He walked on down the corridor, passing the storeroom, then his mother's room. He turned the doorknob but it wouldn't open. Alice had the habit of keeping her own bedroom door locked. He entered the room that had once been Anna's and was now Eri's. The sound of the rain suddenly seemed close by. Was the window open? No, the glass was broken. He turned the switch, but the light didn't come on. He felt his way along the wall. There was nothing in the room, it was completely empty . . . except for one small, yes, a doll, a doll on the shelf. An American doll. It had been Anna's favorite when she was a little girl. Its head was gone.

By the time he reached his father's study his eyes had adjusted to the dark, and he could dimly see inside. He peered at the window. Despite the rain there seemed to be wisps of light in the sky, which must have been the moon shining above the clouds. The room, the desk, the bookshelves, and the sofa were exactly the same as before, proof that his father used this room on his occasional trips back to

Tokyo. He pulled the blackout curtain over the window and turned the light switch. The lamp on the desk, cleverly wrapped in black cloth, came on.

On a small shelf beneath the bookshelves were bottles of Western liquor: brandy, whiskey, gin. Some hadn't even been opened. *Thank you, Papa.* Ken removed a bottle of Courvoisier XO and a glass, sat down on the sofa, and began to drink.

On the bookshelves were rows of books about diplomacy. Half were in English; most were large, thick tomes. He wondered why his father, for whom these books were so precious, hadn't taken them up to Karuizawa for safekeeping. With glass in hand he wandered from bookcase to bookcase. Pretending he was his father, he sat down at the desk. Then he noticed, right in front of him, an album. It lay there as if his father had been looking at it one day and then forgot it.

It was a photo album. There were neat captions in white. "February 4th, 1910. Vice Consul in Hankou." Ken had just been there. *Papa was born in 1885, so he was twenty-four at the time, just about my age now. We look quite like each other.* "August 15th, 1912. Honolulu." "April 16th, 1913. New York." "June 26th, 1914. Appointed Consul in Chicago." Then Alice Little appeared. His mother as a young woman. *Very much like Anna now, with traces of Eri as well—no, Lauren. That smile, those soft shoulders. The spitting image of Lauren. Then Uncle Norman. And Norman's father, James Little, my grandfather.* "July 3rd, 1914. The annual meeting of the Chicago America-Japan Society." The two young people stood with their arms around each other's shoulders. "October 3rd, 1914. Wedding at the Little house in New York." The young couple; the door to the New York townhouse above a wrought-iron stairway. Americans sat interspersed with Japanese, most of whom were diplomats. "November 18th, 1916. Anna is born." *Some hospital somewhere. Mama in the hospital bed, holding the baby. Aha! The next one is me.* "January 8th, 1919. Ken is born." *I've never seen this picture before. It wasn't among the photographs on the mantelpiece in the parlor.* The album evidently consisted of the pictures that meant most to Saburo personally, pictures he had arranged and pasted with some care. Ken skipped through the album and got to the end. "November 3rd, 1941. Foundation Day. Fine weather." It was the portrait of father and son taken at the photographer's studio in Akasaka, just before Saburo left for the United States. *I was in flying school, had just made lieutenant. My new uniform didn't quite fit, there were wrinkles all over it. Papa's hair was still black. Three years ago. A time when war between Japan and America still seemed avoidable.*

Ken heard footsteps. He closed the album, got up, and took the glass of brandy in his hand.

"Where were you? Everyone's been waiting," said Yamada.

Ken, with a wry smile, handed him a glass. "Drink up, there's plenty more where this came from."

Yamada downed the brown liquid in a single gulp. "What is this? This is pure alcohol!" His throat was on fire.

"It's brandy."

"I've never had anything as fancy as this before."

"You're supposed to drink it slowly. You *imbibe* it."

Yamada gradually got used to the taste. The liquid, after sucking the moisture from his throat, was now burning in his belly. "This stuff dries you out."

"What do you mean?"

"Alcohol has a dehydrating effect on the body."

"Well, maybe it does. But drink up anyway."

"Is this your father's study?" Yamada looked around the room, taking in the black wooden desk, the bookcases overflowing with books, the gold lettering on their spines, and the large wooden bed with bas-relief designs. "The whole house is completely Western!" he said in amazement. Yamada, who had been brought up in the mountains of Shinshu, had known only a life of tatami mats and earthen floors, followed in the Army by a life of wooden bunks and straw futons. When he sat on the bed he was astonished to find his bottom sinking deep into the mattress. Enjoying the softness of it, he raised the glass of brandy, careful not to spill its contents. He quickly found himself experiencing a high-class, Western inebriation.

"I've got to tell you something," he blurted out. "I wrote a letter to Anna."

Ken put his glass down and looked at him intently. Ken's large eyeballs were dilated from the alcohol. There were hints of blue in his pupils.

"It was a love letter. But I didn't get an answer."

"Really . . ."

"Did you . . . did you hear Anna say anything about it?"

"No, nothing."

There were times when it was impossible to tell from the expression on Ken's face what he was thinking. It was like the faces of some American actors in the movies. Even when he was sad he didn't cry like the Japanese; when he was in trouble he never seemed to panic. Repressing his feelings, he remained expressionless.

"I see. Well, that's all right. I've already given up. I suppose it was hopeless from the start—the third son of a farmer in a mountain village and the daughter of an ambassador."

"Anna," said Ken with a faint smile, "can't write Japanese."

"I don't believe it! She speaks it beautifully."

"No, it's true. She never spent much time in Japanese schools, so she hardly knows any *kanji* characters. And writing a letter in English would only make the authorities suspicious."

"Really . . ." A small sun began to rise in Yamada's breast. "Kurushima, there's a favor I'd like to ask you. It means a great deal to me. Could you please ask Anna how she feels about me? If the answer is nothing much, I'd like to know for sure. I like her. I love her."

"Certainly." Ken's voice was gentle and clear. "The next time I see her I'll ask her. I promise. But of course that's assuming that I do see her, that I live that long."

"Thank you." Yamada bowed his head and stared at the slim, elegant crystal glass with its intricate decorations that he was holding in his fat, inelegant hand.

Clumsy footsteps were heard. Mitsuda and Haniyu came banging in. Mitsuda grabbed the bottle of brandy and shouted, "Look at this! First-class cognac! This is good stuff. I had some of this once at the house of some Dutch people in the East Indies." He then downed it straight from the bottle, shouting between gulps, "I'm out of fuel . . . and, like the Air Corps, I'm a bit battered but, what the hell, cheers! *Banzai!*"

Yamada snatched it from his hands and, giving both of them a glass, filled them up.

"Okay. First, a toast to the Air Corps of the great Imperial Army! *Kampai!*"

The toast was then repeated. "To the Ki-94, plane that never was!" "To Major Iwama!" "To Lieutenant Sugi!" "To our fighting ace, Warrant Officer Mitsuda!"

Suddenly Haniyu stood at attention. "It is my honor to propose a toast . . . ," he began. Ken and Yamada struggled upright. But when Haniyu went on, ". . . to our Commander in Chief, His Majesty the Emperor," Mitsuda waved his hands and said, "Stop! Don't ruin the atmosphere!" and refused to join in.

Haniyu, glaring at him, continued, "And let's give a toast to the Masters of the Sky. Actually, you should be toasting me. Because I just volunteered. So drink to me!"

Mitsuda turned to him. "Haniyu, your joke isn't very funny."

"I'm not joking. I volunteered for the Kamikaze squad."

"You honestly did? . . ." His voice was heavy with emotion. "I salute you. *I* couldn't do it. I'm sorry. I'm truly sorry."

"Hey," said Ken. There was a certain strain in his voice, as if it were he himself he was trying to encourage. "To the valiant Lieutenant Haniyu, our Master of the Sky."

Yamada quickly filled everyone's glasses with brandy, and the four of them drank it down. Ken's and Haniyu's glasses touched with such force that both broke, while Mitsuda smashed his on the floor. Yamada, not quite knowing why, felt he should follow Mitsuda's example, and he too hurled his glass down, but it bounced on the carpet without breaking and rolled away.

Haniyu picked up his violin and began to play. It was Tartini's "The Devil's Trill," which he had often played at the Aviation Medicine Institute. As always when he played, he closed his eyes and lost himself in the music. He didn't look like an Army officer at all, let alone a Kamikaze pilot whose mission was to crash into a B-29. Mitsuda bent his head close and listened intently. Ken turned the light off, pulled back the blackout curtain, and opened the window all the way. The fresh night air streamed in, wiping the smell of alcohol and nicotine away, and the waves of music mingled with the sound of rain covering the earth.

Six days later, the B-29s came. Not one by one, and not on reconnaissance. Seventy of them came at once, in an enormous air raid. The bombing of Tokyo had begun.

5

"Aren't you cold?" Patrolman Yoneyama stirred the embers in the stove with his stick.

"No," Eri answered, as she went through the translation she'd just made of the ration schedule for foreigners. There had been the name of one fish she hadn't been able to translate. There wasn't enough meat to go around, so the authorities had substituted fish, but she just couldn't think of the English name for it. *Umi unagi,* literally "sea eel." Reluctantly she spelled it out in Roman letters, and decided to ask her father later.

"Lousy firewood," said Yoneyama, pushing a bundle of it inside. "Look at this. It's like a bunch of chopsticks. There's no way we'll get any heat this way. You'd better come closer."

"Ah, thank you." Eri moved from her seat at the desk and stretched out her hands at the stove.

The policeman stacked alternate layers of firewood and coal, skillfully coaxing the flames out. He looked pleased at the sound of hot smoke rising in the stovepipe. "We've got a nice fire going now," he said. He kept pushing his hair back from his grimy face with hands that were smeared with coal dust.

"For a simple man like me, why, everything here is different. Take this firewood—I've never seen such miserable stuff. Back at my previous post, it was always brushwood. And the people here, they won't pick up a piece of coal with their hands, they've got to use tongs. So fussy. These people must bathe in milk, I thought. And then yesterday, when I went out to the Mampei Hotel on some business for the chief, there was this fine young lady staying there who sent a taxi back just because it was five minutes late. These days there aren't that many taxis at the station, and the hotel must have gone to some trouble calling one, but that didn't mean a thing to her. Oh, I'm sorry—here I am saying bad things about fine young ladies when I've got one right in front of me."

"I'm no 'fine young lady.'"

"Sorry, anyway." The patrolman poked with his fingers at the sweet potatoes he'd placed on top of the stove. "That's funny," he muttered. "They aren't getting soft. I guess frozen potatoes won't cook on this."

It was past three in the afternoon, and the feeling inside the police station was that the day's business was just about done: men were closing the lids on the inkstands and wiping their fountain pens with newspaper; some were putting stacks of documents back on the shelves, others sipping cold, coarse tea.

The door to the interrogation room swung open and Captain Maruki, the lanky head of the Internal Security section, came out. With his strange gait, he looked as if he were floating over the floor. When he spotted Eri the look in his eyes softened. Eri gave him a slight bow. The atmosphere in the room had changed; there was now tension in the air. According to Yoneyama, Maruki was a member of the Thought Police. He had told her that the chief was one, too, along with a couple of the patrolmen. But none of them wore special uniforms, and when Eri pressed him on the matter Yoneyama admitted that he wasn't absolutely sure; he'd just heard rumors, that's all. But there *was* something different about Captain Maruki. Once, when a young man from a relocated family had been arrested for "anti-war attitudes," it had been Maruki and the chief who had taken charge of the investigation. If it was the Tokko who took care of "thought crimes," then Maruki must be Tokko. And he seemed to scare the regular personnel stiff.

He was kind to Eri, though—a little too kind, and it gave her the creeps. His English was good enough for ordinary dealings with the foreigners, but when things got complicated he asked her to interpret. His manner with her suggested something more than just a working relationship. That's what gave her the creeps.

Behind the Captain was a White Russian boy, with a patrolman at his side. He had been caught stealing potatoes from the barn of a farmer's house. He didn't speak English, only French. Eri had gone to a French-speaking school when her family had lived in Belgium for three years, and she was able to interpret. Her English ability alone had impressed the chief and Maruki; they were bowled over when they heard her French. The praise came thick and fast: "Amazing . . . But what else would you expect of an ambassador's daughter."

The boy was obviously malnourished. His skin was sallow, and his sunken cheeks were so white they looked powdered. Eri had translated the details of his miserable home life, and that seemed to have persuaded the Captain to release the boy after giving him a severe reprimand. His father was missing, his mother was bedridden with consumption, and the boy (who was fourteen) had been hired as a field hand at a local farm, but lost his job when winter came. Both he and his mother were starving, and he had stolen out of desperation. The Captain, given clear proof that the foreigners' rations weren't enough to survive on, began muttering about the laziness of the prefectural officials concerned, and finally decided to let him off.

"Are the potatoes cooked yet?" Eri asked.

"They're still hard, but they should be edible."

Eri wrapped the baked potatoes in newspaper and went out to give them to the boy, who was lingering in front of the station, evidently at a loss about what to do. The boy thanked her in good French, giving her a faint smile. She turned quickly away and ran back in.

"You gave that kid the whole lot?" A disappointed look crossed Yoneyama's face as the loss of the food sank in.

"It's freezing outside."

"Yes, the roads have frozen over."

"It's hard when it's so cold. This winter has been unusually bad."

The face of the Russian boy really had looked as if it had been dipped in flour, and his discolored lips, which seemed almost transparent, were trembling with cold.

"That air raid yesterday seems to have been terrible. Tokyo Station burned to the ground." The patrolman poured some hot water from the kettle into a teapot.

"Let me do it," Eri said.

"No, no, you always pour it. Here." He handed her a teacup.

A detective who had been up to Tokyo had returned that day at noon and told everyone about the air raid. Tokyo Station had gone up in flames, and the people who had taken shelter under the railroad bridge at nearby Yurakucho had all burned to death. The bombs had done great damage to the Ginza entertainment district, and people bombed out of their houses were wandering about like ghosts. Several dozen B-29s had dropped incendiary bombs, which seemed to be much more devastating than ordinary ones.

Eri grew worried about her father and sister, who had been staying at the house in Nagata-cho the past two days. Previously the enemy planes had only targeted armament factories, but since the start of this year they had begun indiscriminate bombing of civilian districts as well. Saburo had decided that he had better rescue his library and bring the books to Karuizawa. He and Anna had made several trips to Tokyo. When Eri conveyed her concern to the chief, he called police headquarters in Tokyo, who told him the Nagata-cho district hadn't been targeted yet, which was some relief.

"At least they're not going to attack Karuizawa," said Yoneyama. "It's full of Americans."

Just as the patrolman began to sip his tea, the door to the police station burst open. An elderly, white-haired foreigner in handcuffs was pushed inside by two detectives on his left and right. The foreigner, in black clothes, was Father Hendersen.

Patrolman Yoneyama looked at his watch. "At this time of day?"

Captain Maruki had evidently been waiting for this. He immediately stood up and pointed to the interrogation room. Soon after he disappeared inside, the chief and his deputy followed him in. There was a general stir among the rest of them, the episode suggesting they had a major criminal in their charge.

"What is it? Is it someone you know?"

"Yes. He's our pastor. He's not the sort of person to do anything bad."

"Oh." Yoneyama seemed at a loss for words. "He's a priest?"

"I'll go see what's happening," Eri said, and stood up. But a glance from the patrolman told her to stop.

"You'd better not. That's the Thought Police."

Eri counted five people who had gone into the interrogation room. She poured tea into five cups and placed them on a tray. She knocked, and pushed the door open.

Father Hendersen, his handcuffs and his coat removed, had bent his tall frame uncomfortably into a small chair. The Chief of Police, Takizawa, who was interrogating him, gave her an angry look.

"What is it?" Captain Maruki demanded in a sharp voice.

"I brought some tea."

"Put it over there," he said in a softer tone of voice.

When Eri left, the chief followed her out and asked her quietly if she knew him.

"Yes, he's our pastor."

"Can he speak Japanese?"

For a second she was astonished, then realized what was going on: the pastor was hiding the fact that he was fluent in the language.

"He can hardly speak it at all. He's memorized a few phrases from the Bible, but he doesn't know the meanings of individual words."

"Then please interpret for us."

"Yes, sir."

The pastor gave no sign of recognition as Eri stood between the chief and Captain Maruki. With Eri translating, the questioning began.

"Did you distribute a document containing anti-war propaganda?"

"I distributed a pamphlet quoting the Lord's gospel."

"Did the Lord's gospel have anti-war sentiments in it?"

"The Lord forbids the killing of people."

"Does war constitute the killing of people?"

"It depends on the purpose of the war."

"Is the Greater East Asian War a war in which people are being killed?"

"The nature of the present war is not for me to analyze. However, I do believe that people are being meaninglessly slaughtered in this war."

"And who's doing this meaningless slaughtering? The Japanese side or the Anglo-American side?"

"Both sides."

"You acknowledge that England and America are enemies of Japan?"

"For one who believes in God, there are no enemies but the enemies of God."

"Let's get this clear. Are England and the United States not enemies of Japan?"

"I am a citizen of a neutral country, so I look at things impartially. I do not consider Japan to be an enemy of the United States or Britain."

"In other words you're saying that America and England aren't enemies of Japan?"

"For a citizen of a neutral state, the matter is impossible to judge."

The chief seemed stumped for a moment. He looked at Maruki. Then he pulled a sheet of mimeographed paper out of a drawer. It had been typed in English.

"Have you ever seen this?"

"Yes I have. I wrote it."

"Would you agree that it's a work of pacifist propaganda?"

"It's a prayer for peace."

"In other words, an anti-war act giving assistance to the enemy."

"I cannot say whether it can be interpreted in that way. Peace is more than just the absence of war; it is a state of spiritual serenity."

Eri did her best to translate all this correctly, but the word "peace" had vastly different meanings for the pastor and the Police Chief. As the chief kept repeating the same questions, and the pastor kept responding from a Christian perspective, the gap between them only grew wider.

Then an envelope was brought out. In it was a letter the pastor had sent to the diplomat of a third country (the name seemed vaguely Russian) who had been relocated to Hakone. The letter contained the latest details concerning the foreigners' situation in Karuizawa. It constituted, the chief said, an act of espionage.

"I didn't write that letter."

"We found it on your desk."

"I don't know anything about it."

"You don't?" The chief gave a scornful laugh. "But the typing is from your typewriter."

"I don't know anything about it."

Now, suddenly, there was a frightening look in the chief's eyes. He ordered Eri out of the room. When Yoneyama asked her what was happening she said, "There seems to be some misunderstanding." The pastor had answered all the chief's questions without flinching, and yet Eri had the feeling he was hiding something, and it worried her. The interrogation room, its thick wooden door shut, was quiet now. She hung around in case they needed her again, but even at five o'clock, as the staff was getting ready to leave, there was no sound from inside. She watched the others getting their coats, not knowing whether she should stay or go.

"It's time to go home, Miss Kurushima." Yoneyama lived quite close to the Kurushimas' villa, and it was his daily task to escort her home.

"But . . ."

"There's nothing you can do. There must be some reason, something we don't know about."

"But I just . . ."

"Miss Kurushima." He sounded a little more insistent. There were a few men staying on for night duty. Among them were two rumored to be members of the Thought Police.

"You go ahead. I'm worried about the pastor."

"You'd better leave," he whispered, "otherwise . . ."

Just then they heard a sound from the interrogation room. High, then low, it was like the muffled whine of a dog. She stood there rooted to the spot, stiff as a statue.

She recognized it: it was the sound of someone being tortured.

She had never actually seen it happening, so she didn't know exactly what they did. But, along with the handcuffs and ropes, she had seen some strange metal instruments in that room, and she had watched as people were dragged out of there. In the case of foreigners, they let up during the intervals when she interpreted; the men doing it—usually the chief and Captain Maruki—didn't want her to see. So she had made it a habit to deliberately serve some tea as the torturing was beginning. The moment she knocked they would stop and awkwardly try to hide what they were doing.

Without the slightest hesitation, Eri now poured some tea into the cups, walked up to the door, and knocked. She tried to push it open, but it was locked. It had never been locked before. And, for the first time, groans continued after she knocked. A well-built sergeant—rumored to be Tokko—came rushing over and pushed her away. "You can't go in there today. That prisoner is a spy," he said. "You'd better go home, miss."

With the word "spy" still echoing in her head, Eri went outside with Yoneyama. It was already getting dark, and since bicycle lights were forbidden they had to hurry. Eri pedaled her bike, clutching the handlebars as she sped along the icy, potholed road. After saying goodbye to the patrolman in front of her house, she turned suddenly and called him back.

"There's something wrong. There *must* be some kind of misunderstanding."

Yoneyama told her in a low voice to keep quiet about it. "There are things we just don't know about."

"He simply couldn't be a spy," she said urgently.

Yoneyama didn't answer. In a moment he was gone, swallowed up in the darkness.

Alice, who had grown markedly thinner in recent weeks, had taken the clothes down from the screen where she had hung them to dry, and Yoshiko was checking the pot of food she had placed on the stove. In order to save fuel, and so as not to worry about carrying out the blackout regulations in each room, the family had moved into the parlor. They did all their cooking, eating, and sleeping in the one big room. Cots had been brought in, with curtains hung between them, and the vicinity of the stove had been turned into a little kitchen, with pots and pans, dishes and condiments stacked around it. There were traces of the "Flemish" style Alice had been so proud of in the lace draped over the sofa, but the smoke from all the cooking had made it almost unrecognizable.

Yoshiko greeted Eri with a bow. "Welcome back. Dinner's just about ready."

"There's a telegram from Papa." Her mother handed her a slip of paper. It read, "HOUSE UNDAMAGED RETURNING TOMORROW SABURO."

"What a relief about the house," said Yoshiko, as she put the lid on the pot and checked the fire. "They say the air raid in Tokyo was something awful."

"Tokyo Station and the Ginza were destroyed. We've got to get the rest of our things up here as soon as possible."

Their dinner consisted of wheat dumplings and boiled cabbage flavored with soy sauce. It had been the same food for a week now; there had been no rations for half a month. The three of them said grace and took up their spoons, but as Eri tried to eat, her stomach ached at the thought of what they were doing to Father Hendersen.

"Anything new at the police station?" her mother asked.

"No." Eri put on a smile. "Every day's the same."

"Isn't it hard work?"

"No, it's okay. I'm used to it now."

A couple of dumplings and three mouthfuls of cabbage, and the meal was over. Her family's meager fare made Eri feel bad about the three baked potatoes she'd given to the Russian boy. It was wrong to think that way, but she couldn't help it. And then she found herself imagining how the pastor must have looked as he was being tortured. She could almost smell the blood and the sweat. But she couldn't tell her mother about it; Alice would immediately barge into the police station and demand his release. For an American-born woman to defend Father Hendersen, whose wife was English, would only end up hardening their attitude.

"Something's bothering you, isn't it?" Alice said to her daughter. "Go ahead, tell me what it is." Anna had often teased Eri that "the contents of your heart are printed on your face," and even Eri knew she wasn't very good at hiding her feelings.

"No, nothing," she said unconvincingly. It would have helped if she could have thought of something cheerful to talk about, but there were no cheerful subjects any more. Ken was in the fighter squadron defending Tokyo, her father and sister were in the city while air raids were going on, Maggie's mother was sick, and now the pastor was under arrest. Ambassador Yoshizawa was under police surveillance for being sympathetic to the Allies, there wasn't enough food, it was cold, everybody was run down, people were dying in droves . . .

Eri lifted the lid of the piano. The summer day when she had played that duet with Lieutenant Haniyu—that had been her last pleasant memory. Mozart's Piano Concerto, K. 570. She flipped open the music book and began playing the score in front of her. Gradually everything painful, everything sad, seemed to melt away and, spreading from her fingertips, a softer world returned, the world she'd known as a little girl going to Professor Duval's house in Brussels for piano lessons. Then she started playing some Chopin preludes, one after another, in no particular order. She had memorized them all. Whichever piece she played she felt buoyed up, like wandering into a wood in early summer. She banged them out, enjoying herself now . . . until abruptly the joy disappeared when she looked across the dim room at her mother's drawn face.

"Mama, you've gotten so thin."

"Really? My weight hasn't changed at all since summer. I've still got lots of energy."

"Have I gotten thinner too?"

"You haven't changed at all, you've always been thin. And you play just as well as ever."

An idea came into Eri's head, and it immediately popped out. "Mama, can I telephone Ken?"

"Ken?" She was surprised. "Well, you can if you want to. But you know he's living in the barracks now. I don't know if it's a good idea to have a girl calling him there."

"Anyway let me try."

The hallway was cold, and her socks crackled as she walked. Taking the receiver off the hook, she tried to call Ken's barracks, but there was no answer. So she called the house at Nagata-cho. The moment Anna answered, her eyes filled with tears.

"Eri! I tried to call from here, but I couldn't get through. The house is all right. Did you get Papa's telegram?"

"Yes. Thank God the house is okay . . . Is Papa there?"

"He's out at the moment. I'll have him call you when he gets back. What is it?"

It wasn't something she could talk about on the phone. If the police heard the word "spy," there would be enormous trouble. The police often had information that could only have come from wiretapping. (Why, then, she wondered, had she telephoned in the first place?)

"It's nothing. Everything's okay."

"Eri, you sound strange. Has something happened?"

"No."

She hung up and went to the washroom, where she dabbed at her eyes with water that was kept continuously running to keep it from freezing over. Her mother was sewing and Yoshiko darning some socks when she came back.

"Ken wasn't in. I'm going to sleep. Good night."

She heard the sound of ice cracking somewhere outside. Someone treading heavily, creeping up to the house. A detective, a military policeman. Boots, like those worn by the sergeant—the Tokko agent —who had told her, "You'd better go home now, miss." Eri began shaking, making the bedsprings creak. Listening intently, she could hear firewood crackling and splitting in the stove, her mother's regular breathing, the tick-tock of the grandfather clock.

Mama, what should I do? Tell me. What would Papa say? In the darkness, Eri was trembling, helpless and trembling. The cold penetrated to her core. *I'm cold, so cold. Ken's away, he's busy. Would they understand? Nobody understands me. I'm all alone.* The tears began to flow. She heard the muffled whining of a dog. She heard the pastor's groans. She couldn't stand it any more and leapt out of bed and threw herself at her mother's knees.

"What is it, girl?"

"What should I do, Mama? Tell me!"

Her mother's soft hand touched her hair. "It's all right. It's about Father Hendersen, isn't it?"

"How did you know?"

Holding Eri's face in her hands, Alice made her look straight into her eyes. "Someone who saw the pastor being taken away came and told me. You must have seen him at the police station."

"Mama, I'm worried. The police can do terrible things to people. And what about Maggie and Aunt Audrey?"

"Eri, listen to me carefully." She had her sit next to her. "I'm going to go to the Hendersens' house and check on things. I tried to go during the day, but a detective was standing guard and I couldn't get close. It should be safe now, no policeman's going to stand around all night and freeze. You wait here. I'll let you know what I find out."

"I want to go too. It's too dangerous for you to walk alone on the road at night."

Yoshiko also offered to accompany her.

"No, if there are too many of us we'll stand out. I'll go by myself."

"No, Mama! I want to go too."

In no time at all her stubborn daughter had slipped into her clothes and was ready to go. Alice shrugged. She wanted to bring the Hendersens some food. From their own meager stock she picked out some canned salmon, potatoes, and pieces of pumpkin, dividing the goods between two rucksacks which she had Eri carry, while she herself lugged a large bag stuffed with firewood. When they got out to the road, there was a bright moon in the icy sky, and countless stars.

If they were careful they might make it without a flashlight. However, when they got to where the road was lined with fir trees, the darkness became impenetrable; they couldn't see a foot in front of them. Eri drew close to her mother and peered around. There wasn't a soul about, only the whistle of the wind in the treetops. She shone the flashlight on their path.

"Eri, we've got to hurry."

"I know. Oh, watch out for that rock."

They deliberately went through the cemetery, and came out by the pond. On the other side they could see the light of the Hendersens' house.

"Mama, watch you don't fall in."

"It's all right, it's frozen solid. We could probably walk across."

Eri thought she heard somebody and turned the flashlight off. The sound of the wind in the emptiness around them mingled with the barking of a dog. The stars glinted like innumerable souls frozen in the sky, and Eri, for the first time in her life, felt true fear. There was no one to protect them, no sign of any god in that vast, cruel sky.

"Mama, I'm scared."

"It's okay, girl. I'm here. I'm with you."

Alice rang the cowbell at the front door and whistled three times. The door immediately opened. Margaret, in her nightgown, beckoned them in.

"It must have been hard getting here on a night like this."

"Don't worry about us. We heard they took your father away."

"They did. It's horrible!"

Audrey waved at them from the sofa where she lay. When Alice took her hand she began to cry. "Don't get excited, dear, it's bad for your heart." But Audrey sobbed uncontrollably. It was Margaret who, still calm, told them what had happened.

That afternoon two detectives had barged in and started ransacking the house. But they didn't find anything, taking only the Sunday announcement sheet from the church, the typewriter, and the mimeograph machine with them, along with the pastor himself. He was under suspicion for "divulging state secrets." Policemen had stood in front of the house until evening, so nobody had gone out. Their rations had just run out, and they hadn't eaten any dinner. Her husband's arrest had sent Audrey into hysteria. Margaret said she was still behaving oddly.

"Oddly, in what way?" Alice asked.

Margaret wiped her mother's eyes. "Mother, it's Aunt Alice, Mrs. Kurushima."

"Oh, how kind of you to come. Welcome! Maggie, serve them some of that pound cake we just bought."

"We don't have any pound cake."

"Really? Did we eat the whole thing? Well, then, give them some hot chocolate."

"Mother, it's Mrs. Kurushima."

"Linda, how good to see you."

"Dear, it's Alice . . ." Alice gently stroked her friend's hand.

"Linda. It's been years. Five? No, ten years." She broke down again.

"Mother!" Margaret shook her. "Wake up! It's Mrs. Kurushima."

"I know her. It's Linda Preston, my cousin."

"You see, she's been like this," said Margaret. "What's wrong with her? What should I do?"

Alice beckoned her from her mother's side to a corner of the room and whispered, "We'll have a doctor examine her tomorrow. I'm sure she'll be all right. The shock of having your father disappear like that has affected her mind. Let her get some sleep."

They helped Audrey move to her bed in the adjoining room where, to their surprise, she lay down quite calmly. They placed a blanket over her. It was icy cold. From the moment she entered the house Eri had noticed that the fire in the large Swiss stove was out. She put some of the firewood her mother had brought with her into it, and lit it with some newspaper.

"Maggie, I'll have Yoshiko bring over some more firewood tomorrow. Tonight you make do with this." Alice placed a frying pan on the stove and proceeded to fry some thinly sliced potatoes.

Eri told Margaret, "I saw your father at the police station. Don't worry, he looks all right."

"Really? How long do you think they're going to keep him?"

"I don't know. But I'm sure his arrest was a mistake. How can they call a church announcement a piece of pacifist propaganda?"

"I hope you're right." For the first time that night a faint smile appeared on her pale face.

"Your mother'll get better once your father comes back."

"But what if . . . what if he doesn't come back?"

"That's not going to happen. It's all a mistake."

"Dinner's ready!" Alice called, stirring the frying pan. A delicious smell rose from the dish of potatoes fried with salmon and ketchup. "Take this to Audrey. Maggie, you have some too."

It was after eleven when Alice and Eri left the Hendersen house. In the deep night outside, it seemed as if the whole world had frozen over.

6

The next day Father Hendersen still hadn't been released. The questioning went on and on, the chief and Captain Maruki taking turns. Several times Eri, using tea as an excuse, went in to see what was going on. The pastor's eyes were red and swollen. He was bent over and there were blue marks on his hands and wrists, evidently from having been tied up. As the hours went by the chief's mood got worse. Three members of Father Hendersen's congregation were brought in and interrogated in a separate room, but soon afterwards were released.

In the afternoon, Eri was astonished to see her father appear, wearing an overcoat with a leopard-skin collar over a black silk suit, his top hat in his hand. At one glance the police took him for a VIP, and he was ushered into the anteroom with the deepest of bows.

"How is the pastor doing?" he asked his daughter.

"He looks very weak. They kept him up all last night interrogating him."

"I see . . . Your mother told me about it, and I came over here at once."

The chief came out and, at a sign from her father, Eri left the room. A policeman was called in to take notes. Saburo was evidently giving a statement about the case. Thirty minutes later he emerged. The chief saw him to the door, saying as he bowed him off, "Miss Kurushima, we don't have any more work for you today, so you can go home with your father."

Eri walked alongside him, pushing her bike.

"What happened?"

"Well . . ." He seemed to be lost in thought. He wasn't a talkative person, but when he did speak he always said clearly what was on his mind. Eri waited.

They turned off the main road onto a path that led through the fields. Eventually her father said, "Eri, I'm afraid it looks as if Father Hendersen is in a lot of trouble."

She held her breath, and gazed at the serious face beneath the top hat.

"They have proof. Notebooks, letters. Even a wireless transmitter they discovered on the roof of the church. They got the names of his Japanese accomplices, and arrested them."

"So he is a spy."

"The evidence points that way. They're going to transfer him to a prison in Tokyo."

"I just can't believe it."

"I don't want to believe it either. But they have proof, and lots of it. And he tried to conceal it. For example, he lied about not speaking any Japanese, when in fact he wrote notes and letters in excellent Japanese."

"Then . . ." Eri remembered how she had "interpreted" for him the previous day. She broke into a cold sweat. "What happens to a spy?"

"The firing squad." There was pain in his voice. "You mustn't breathe a word of this to your mother or to Maggie. It'll only worry them more."

"Just having him arrested made Aunt Audrey lose her mind. Poor Maggie!"

The little stream was frozen over, the water gurgling faintly beneath the ice. The murky sky seemed so close it would crush the earth. Eri made a vow to herself. *I'll visit Maggie tonight. I'll take her food and firewood. I don't care if the Thought Police are watching. I'll do it for Maggie. I'll do it every day.*

VII

THE FROZEN POND

1

The seagulls rode on soft cushions of wind. They seemed to have stopped there in the middle of the sky, their wings lazily stroking the air, their eyes fixed on the horizon where the ocean boiled with the heat of the setting sun. From a tiny point in the distance they stretched, innumerable, across the sky, flying in a perfect line, away to another tiny point on the other side. The almost endless line of birds swayed up and down on the transparent, silky wind.

There was a bang, and the line broke, the gulls scattering across the sky, and one of them fell, smeared with blood, to the sea. There was another bang, and another one fell, and another, until the sea was stained with the blood of the fallen gulls . . .

Ken awoke, and looked at the other fighter pilots asleep on the floor and on the tables around him. In the leaden light of the morning sky, they lay like corpses lined up in a common tomb. The bugler sounded reveille, and miraculously the pilots rose from the dead; they stirred, rubbed their eyes, and got to their feet. Those who had been sleeping in their flying suits put on their boots, ready to move out at any moment.

An announcement came over the loudspeaker: "This morning at six o'clock an enemy task force was spotted just out from Kujukuri Beach. It appears to be the same formation observed previously proceeding north from Iwo Jima."

"So they're coming, huh?" a voice said, and another added, "It sure sounds like it," and another chimed in, "We'd better hurry up and eat."

Without bothering to wash their faces, the men ran to the mess hall, gobbled down balls of cold rice, and proceeded to the pilots' room on the second floor. The large, five-sided room had windows all around it which afforded a sweeping view of the airfield and the sky above. Beyond the row of desks and chairs where the pilots waited for their assignments was a slightly raised area containing the command room and the radio room.

The loudspeaker broadcast both civilian radio and military reports from Air Defense Headquarters, mostly of impending American attacks. The B-29s had first appeared in the skies over Japan last November. Their initial targets had been the aircraft factories—Nakajima Aircraft outside Tokyo and Mitsubishi Aircraft in Nagoya—but with the new year they had begun firebombings of civilian targets as well. The damage was getting serious. The Army had thrown together fighter squadrons using every man who had ever piloted a plane. They were in a constant state of alert now. In the intervals between the American bombings the pilots were kept to a busy schedule testing new aircraft, examining downed enemy planes, training for flight at the high altitudes where the B-29s roamed, and training for the Sky Masters squadron.

As they assembled in the pilots' room a warning came over the loudspeaker. Ten minutes later they heard the announcement of an imminent attack. "The Eastern Division reports several formations of enemy light aircraft entering Japanese airspace from over Kashima and heading toward the northern Kanto plain." There followed two official announcements from Air Defense Headquarters. "The light aircraft invading over Kashima have been identified as Grumman F-6-Fs. Approximately 60 planes, heading due west at 5,000 meters. There is a possibility they may split up and attack various airfields across the Kanto plain." And then "Additional Grumman F-6-Fs have been sighted entering Japanese airspace over the Boso Peninsula and over Izu. The total number of enemy aircraft is estimated at more than 200. All fighter squadrons immediately prepare for combat!"

The pilots all stood up at once. The booming voice of Wing Commander Kurokawa rang out. "Hold it! And listen up. As you can see, we have a covering of stratocumulus clouds at between 1,000 and 1,500 meters. The enemy is going to come down through those clouds. Which is good for us, because we're at a disadvantage at ultra high altitudes. This is our chance to show the Yankees what we've got. As you boys well know, the Grumman F-6-F has three 12.7-mm. cannons on each wing, for a total of six, and it can do about 600 kph at 5,000 meters. Whereas our Hayate has 20-mm. cannons and does 620 kph at the same altitude. Which means we can catch them. Warrant Officer Mitsuda, you have anything else to add?"

"Yes, sir." Mitsuda rose from his chair. "In my experience, the Yankees always fly in pairs. While one plane is attacking, the other's backing it up from above or behind. So you have to look out for the second plane even while you're fighting the first. And remember that trick they have when one of them suddenly climbs and the other drops, and they're both spraying the air with six guns—you're dead if you get caught between them. So if you see them coming at you, make sure you dive away *to the side.*"

"Okay," said Kurokawa. "Scramble!" The pilots saluted and dashed out of the room. Ken remained standing at attention in front of the Wing Commander.

"Lieutenant Kurushima, sir. The plane I was working on the day before yesterday has been handed over to the 18th Squadron. Sir, I haven't been assigned another plane."

"Then you stand by until you *are* assigned one." The floor seemed to sag under the weight of Kurokawa's thick legs as he walked to the stairs. Then he stopped. "All right, you can transfer a captured P-51 to the Army airfield at Ueda. We got the plane from the Navy, and we haven't finished examining it yet. Headquarters want all captured enemy aircraft moved up to Ueda for safekeeping, but we haven't had time to do anything about it. So you can fly it up there now."

"But, sir, then I won't be able to join in."

Kurokawa flipped around. "Lieutenant, moving a captured aircraft is just as important. You're the only one around here who knows how to operate those Mustangs." (He pronounced it "Ma-su-tan-gu.") "Just make sure you fly with your rising sun insignia showing, so our people don't mistake you for the enemy."

"Yes, sir."

"Oh, and Kurushima, take the train straight back. A lot of the trains aren't running these days, but you get yourself on any train you can find. Understand?"

"Yes, sir. I'll be back as soon as I can."

The pilots were racing across the tarmac. Today the planes remodeled for action against B-29s were parked off to one side of the runway, and the Hayates and Shokis equipped for battle against enemy fighters were being started up. One after another they took to the skies.

Ken caught sight of Haniyu running to his plane and quickly set after him. "Hey!" he called out.

Haniyu stopped in his tracks, his shoulders heaving. "You going out on the attack too?"

"No. I'm flying a captured Mustang up to Ueda."

"Oh . . ."

"Haniyu, be careful."

"Don't worry. There're no B-29s today. It's not my turn yet." Haniyu had finished his Kamikaze training.

"Well, there might be some later today."

"I'll go for them when they come."

"Yes, well, just be careful when your turn does come."

"Okay, okay." Haniyu smiled, then dashed off in the Army running style, both hands on his hips.

The Mustang was parked, like an uninvited guest, at the farthest edge of the runway. The soldier guarding it, who knew Ken, told him the plane had a full load of fuel and ammunition.

Yamada came running over. He was covered with sweat.

"Hey!" said Ken. "Are you flying too?"

"No, I'll be taking care of the casualties in the emergency room. I heard you were going up to Ueda, so I came to say goodbye."

"You didn't have to do that. I'm not even fighting today, I'm just transferring a plane."

"Are you going to stop in Karuizawa on your way back?" The Ueda airfield wasn't far from where Ken's family now lived.

"I won't have time. I have to come straight back by train."

"Oh . . ." He seemed disappointed. "Well, see you," he said, waving his hand.

Ken sat in the cockpit of the Mustang, watching the crestfallen Yamada walk away. He had probably wanted Ken to ask Anna if she would marry him. But how on earth was he supposed to help him with this in the middle of a raging war? He himself hadn't seen anyone in his family for months. No one saw their families any more.

After the planes in the fighter squadron had all left, Ken finally took off. Almost immediately he spotted a formation of seven Grummans approaching just below the clouds, shifting up and down like a shoal of little fish. It was a strange maneuver; they were probably trying to avoid antiaircraft fire. Abruptly the American fighters went into a dive and began strafing the airfield. Ken considered joining in the fight, but then noticed a Japanese plane diving to attack them, and remembered his orders were to get the Mustang safely to Ueda. Avoiding the opposition, he flew off toward the mountains, heading north. He stayed just below the clouds; that way he could disappear if he met any enemy planes. He maintained an altitude of about 1,500 meters and a speed of 400 kph. After a while he spotted the runway of the Kumagaya flying school directly below him. Red Dragonflies were lined up, and little figures were darting toward them. Suddenly a flash of light burst right in front of him. It was antiaircraft fire. They were firing at him from the ground. Startled, he burrowed into the clouds. Flying blind now, he switched on his radio. With disturbing clarity he could hear a conversation in English.

"Big Henry here. Come in, George."

"George here."

"Paul?"

"Yes, sir."

"Bob?"

There was no answer.

"Bob. Where's Bob?"

"Paul here. Sir, Bob was taking on the gang a few minutes ago at AD 10421."

"You see those green and black points right below us?" Evidently he was referring to things on his radar.

"Yes, I see them."

"Those are hangars. Let's take 'em out."

"George here. My radar shows a point at 9M."

"Is it the gang?"

"I don't know, sir. It's only one plane, a small one. Looks like a fighter."

"Okay, George, reconfirm."

"Okay."

Ken cautiously banked to the west, making for the mountains. He could get off their radar if he flew between the hills. Seconds after he banked the clouds thinned away, and he saw the potbellied outline of a single Grumman in the distance. He couldn't make out the stars on the American plane. They probably couldn't see the markings on his plane either.

"George here. It's strange, sir, but it looks like one of our P-51s."

"A P-51? But there aren't any in the attack today. Watch out, it might be a Jap Tony. Firing order for ground target cancelled. Attack formation!"

"No, sir, it *is* a P-51. It's not a Tony."

"Call it up."

"P-51, identify yourself."

Ken had to respond. He turned the switch on his radio to transmission. As long as they thought he was one of them, he might as well have a little fun.

"F-6-F, identify yourself."

"What the . . . P-51, state your unit!"

"This is Captain Little, Ken Little. How's it going, George?"

"All right, Captain. But what're you doing over here, sir?"

"Reconnaissance. But it's so damned cloudy my visibility's close to zero. Hey, George, you're from Texas, aren't you? Let me guess. I'll bet you're from Dallas."

"Close, sir. Houston."

"I'm from Chicago myself. This your first time over Japan, George?"

"Yes, Captain. But it's kind of a letdown, there isn't much resistance. We did a little strafing down in Tokyo this morning. Zoomed right in. You shoulda seen 'em running around to get away. A whole schoolyard full of little Japs."

"And you shot them up?"

"Yes, sir. You shoulda seen it. They were tumbling all over the place."

"Big Henry here." The voice was quite distant. "Did you get confirmation?"

"George here. Not yet, sir. But it sounds like an American. A Captain."

"Watch out, George, it might be a trap . . ." There was a wave of static, and the voices faded away.

Ken dropped below cloud level. To his left was Mount Myogi, its peak enveloped in clouds. To his right was—my God!—a Grumman, maybe 30 meters away. There was no mistaking that star on the fuselage. He found himself staring right at the pilot, a young man with acne on his face.

"It's the gang!" the man shouted in horror.

"Hey, George? Take it easy!"

The Grumman started a sudden climb, trying to escape into the clouds. Ken was right behind him, in a perfect position to shoot. His finger automatically reached for the trigger. Then he thought, *I don't have to do it, those aren't my orders.* He decided to lose him.

Suddenly he was attacked from behind. The Grumman he'd just allowed to get away had turned and was coming down at him, spitting fire. Ken took two hits in his left wing. He cut his speed, dived sharply to the left, and let the Grumman get in front of him. Then he carefully aimed his 20-mm. cannons and fired. There were three bursts of sound, and the Grumman sucked in a cluster of flashing tracer bullets, flapped its tail upward like a choking fish, and went into a tailspin.

It was Ken's first kill. Amazed at how easy it had been, he watched the black spot spin through the air until it burst into a reddish black plume of smoke in the forest below. Ken felt a shudder in his fuselage. Two more Grummans were attacking him from the clouds.

Should he try shaking them off by flying close to the ground—he knew this country well—or should he climb high and outrace them? He quickly decided on the former course.

Directly below him a highway twisted through the mountains. He was flying so low he could almost touch the hairpin curves of the road as it snaked through the snow-covered pass. Ken followed the road up, staying at an altitude of 50 meters. The Grummans, perhaps afraid of antiaircraft fire, were at 500 meters as they trailed him. They were so close to the mountainside they would probably crash if they tried to nose down to get him in their sights. All they could do was follow him. When Ken got through the mountain pass he reduced his speed and flew over the villa area of Karuizawa. He was almost skimming the ground. He spotted the roof and garden of his own family's house. That was probably his mother in the garden. Then he spotted a red roof at the foot of Mount Hanare. Maggie's place. What was she doing right now?

The Grummans were still trailing him, looking for a chance to close in. They weren't using their radios, not wanting to be overheard. Right in front of him rose Mount Asama. The top half of the volcano was swathed in clouds. Ken headed up, going flat out for cover. The Grummans, outrun, took several shots at him but missed. He climbed halfway up the mountain, then banked to the left in cloud, rolled over, and returned to his original position. By this time the Grummans had lost him. Ken attacked as they wandered along below the cloud line. He hit the first plane easily, watching it go down in flames.

"Paul, where are you?"

There was no answer.

There was only one of them left now. It must be Henry, their leader. Ken rolled away and swept over the plateau, leaving the Grumman far behind. He made for Mount Asama again and, like a magician doing a disappearing act, vanished in the clouds. This time when he came out he headed straight for the Chikuma River, where the Ueda airfield was. Fortunately there were no other planes landing or taking off. Just as he touched down and hit the brakes, a Grumman zoomed in right over his head—not Henry, but another guy. Ken opened his canopy and tumbled to the ground. Another American fighter roared in and opened fire. Ken's Mustang began to shake, then burst apart, spewing black smoke. There were three Grummans attacking—no, four. Ignoring Ken as he dashed across the runway, they concentrated all their fire on the captured Mustang, pouring round after round into it. The Mustang exploded. Showers of oil and metal rained onto the shelter at the edge of the runway. Then they strafed the rest of the airfield. The meager antiaircraft fire was useless against them, the Grummans free to roam at will. Columns of fire shot from the hangars, and the older fighters on the runway were soon enveloped in flames. Ken's mission had ended in disaster.

The railroad station in Ueda was mobbed. There was a sign pasted on the wall: "BECAUSE OF AIR RAIDS ALL SERVICE ON THE SHIN-ETSU LINE FOR TOKYO HAS BEEN SUSPENDED INDEFINITELY."

Ken pushed his way through the crowd to the wicket, where a white-haired ticket collector stood. People were grabbing the old man by the arm, demanding when the train would be leaving, and patiently he was answering their questions. But when he saw Ken approaching he fell silent and stared at him. Ken realized how strange he must look. The uniform he had packed in the P-51 for his return to Tokyo had been reduced to ashes. Over his flying suit he wore an overcoat he'd borrowed at Ueda, and a helmet someone had given him. The cap was smeared with oil, and the overcoat too small, the sleeves so short it looked as if it was a dwarf's. He had already been challenged twice because of his strange attire. The first time was when he tried to leave the airfield, and the MP at the gate had suspected him of being an American pilot who, after bailing out of one of the Grummans, had stolen a Japanese uniform and was attempting to escape. Then as he passed the police box in front of the railroad station the policeman had run out, demanding to see his ID. And now the ticket collector was staring at him open-eyed.

"I'm with the Air Corps," said Ken. There was a glimmer of relief in the old man's eyes as soon as he heard him speak Japanese. Ken continued, "Can I get to Tokyo if I change to the Chuo Line?"

"I don't know for sure, but I heard there aren't any trains running on the Chuo Line either."

"What a mess! What's the situation on the Shin-Etsu Line?"

"Well, the phones are down, so I don't know the latest news, but I did hear that the trains have been running part of the way, from Karuizawa to Tokyo. So you might have some luck if you walk to Karuizawa and try to get on there."

As he pushed his way back through the crowd, Ken thought about his situation. It was now ten-thirty. If he walked the twenty miles from here to Karuizawa through the snow, it would probably take him until dusk. He remembered the old BMW motorcycle he'd left with Toku, his family's old maid, at her house in the hot-spring village of Bessho. It would save a lot of time—if the motorcycle still worked.

"Are the trains running to Bessho?"

"Yes, they are, the track up to Bessho hasn't been bombed."

He checked the timetable. The next train left in seventeen minutes. The "train" consisted of a single car on a little one-way track. It was empty, and Ken could sit where he liked. The train set off at a leisurely pace, crossed the Chikuma River, and headed toward the wall of snow-covered mountains on the horizon. The bells at each little railroad crossing rang sharply as they chugged across the plain of withered rice paddies. Whenever they rounded a curve all the swaying hand straps slapped against the luggage rack at once. Ken recalled how, when he was very small, and Toku took him for a ride on this train, he would wait with great anticipation for this to occur. Sometimes, when the train was going too slowly, or was too crowded, the hand straps failed to slap against the luggage rack. He remembered how disappointed he had been.

2

The road from the station was all uphill. It was lined on both sides with old inns. There was a ravine along one side of the road, with a loud, gurgling brook at the bottom. When Ken peered down he could see large patches of snow remaining in the shaded parts. After the last inn there was a block of souvenir shops, but every door was shuttered. The entire town seemed dead. Past the hot-spring district he came to a village where farmhouses with thatched roofs clung to the steep, terraced slopes. Women squatting in open sheds, exposed to the wind, were plaiting straw into ropes. Children in bulky cotton padded jackets were playing in the yards. Old men bent over in half as they bowed to him. All the young men were gone. And yet how different it looked from war-ravaged Tokyo, where people cowered in their air-raid hoods, how peaceful each house seemed, how nostalgic it all was. The sense of nostalgia became even stronger when Ken saw Toku's house. Slipping between the barn and the cowshed, he made his way into the inner courtyard.

The old woman, who had been picking strings of dried persimmons from the eaves of the farmhouse, gave a cry of astonishment and joy. "Why, Master Ken! What are you doing here?" She seemed startled by his appearance as well. "Did you get wounded somewhere? There's blood on your face . . ."

"Oh, it's nothing. I might have grazed it when I jumped into the air raid shelter. I flew up to Ueda from Tokyo, and ran into an enemy attack. I've got to get back to Tokyo as soon as possible, but the trains are only running from Karuizawa. So I thought maybe I'd take my old motorcycle."

"I see," said Toku, with a worried look. "I don't know if it still works."

"Let's have a look."

Holding the basket of dried persimmons carefully in her arms, Toku looked Ken over from head to toe with the gentlest of eyes. "What a strapping young man you've become! Since you've come all this way you really should take a hot-spring bath, have some dinner, and spend the night here."

"I can't, I'm afraid. I'm still on duty, and I've got to hurry back."

Toku led Ken to the tall stucco storehouse at one side of the court-yard. It was like a museum: all the things he had once used were preserved there like artifacts. When he removed the white dust cloth from one of the wicker trunks and looked inside, he found his tennis racket, his ice skates, his skis and riding boots. The old woman had even kept the blades of his skates clean all these years; there wasn't a bit of rust on them. In another trunk he found, neatly arrayed, his childhood toys: building blocks, a rocking horse, a little catapult, a water pistol, and a top. And there, sitting in the corner, was his BMW. When he took off the canvas covering, the intrepid machine looked as if it had just been polished.

"Hey!" he shouted in admiration, grabbing the handles.

"Whenever I come in here it all reminds me of the years I spent with you, Master Ken. So I end up coming here a lot."

"This machine just might run." Ken removed the cowling and peered inside. If only the batteries were still good. He found an old battery charger. It worked. The needle on the fuel gauge began to flicker. There was enough gasoline to make it to Karuizawa.

"This'll get me to Karuizawa three hours before the train."

"Oh, I *am* glad." Toku's face crinkled with delight. "Then you can go for a bath and have something to eat, after all."

Ken nodded. Toku helped him change into a bathing robe and black *tabi* socks. These were Ken's own clothes, smelling of camphor but preserved without a single wrinkle. Then, with his towel and soap under his arm, he set out in wooden clogs. At the bottom of the hill was a small inn where Toku said they would let him use the bath if he mentioned she had sent him. He was about to go in when, abruptly, he changed his mind: he remembered the grand old inn he'd passed on his way through town. It stood beside a tall, white-walled storehouse, and the entrance was magnificent. Ken used to go there to play with a friend who was the owner's son. The inn was built in pure Japanese style, with detached suites connected by rambling wooden corridors, and sulfuric water piped directly into the bath in each suite. It was just the kind of traditional architecture that Ken loved. He decided that if he was going to take a hot-spring bath, he might as well enjoy a little luxury.

He stood in the entrance hall and called out. He recognized the white-haired man who came out as his friend's father. The old man was wearing a stiffly starched civil defense uniform.

"I'd like to use one of your baths if I might," Ken said, bowing. It was the custom for large Japanese inns like this to open their baths to travelers for a small fee.

"What?" said the proprietor, his eyes suspiciously comparing Ken's face and his kimono. "We don't do that here."

"But I thought they were open to travelers during the day."

"We only let registered guests use them."

"What is it?" From far down the corridor a soldier emerged. He was wearing a white doctor's gown. "What do you want?" The man was walking with a cane fashioned out of a pine tree branch. His left leg was wooden. When he was told about Ken's request, he peered down at him in a hostile way. "This inn's been requisitioned as an Army hospital. Locals aren't allowed in here."

"I'm not a local."

"No? Then what are you? You're a foreigner, aren't you? A *gaijin*. That's even worse. *Gaijin* are forbidden here."

"What's going on?" A Sergeant came out in uniform. He was wearing a medic's armband. "A *gaijin!*" he shouted in a husky voice. "What are you doing here? This area's off limits for you people."

Ken turned on his heels and walked away.

"I'm Japanese," he said, kicking at the gravel with his wooden clogs. He was sick of having to account for his appearance. The

Sergeant's expression and tone of voice reminded him of the NCO who had tormented him back in boot camp. But he was also sick of having to pull rank on bullies like him.

Ken ended up heading for the inn Toku had told him about. He recognized the little establishment with the faded wooden sign saying "Hot-Spring Bath." Toku had often brought him here to bathe during the summer vacations. A maid came out in baggy peasant trousers and immediately ushered him inside. The dining room was filled with elementary school students, sitting straight up on their heels in the formal style, their schoolbooks resting on their laps, as a teacher stood in front of a blackboard lecturing. "Children evacuated from Tokyo," the maid informed him.

Ken remembered the wooden corridor that led to the bath: you went down a flight of stairs and then out to a place right on the river-bank. He hurried ahead of the maid.

There was a look of surprise on the maid's face. "Haven't I seen you before, sir?"

"Yes, when I was a little boy . . ." And he told her about Toku.

"Ah, the family that Toku-san used to work for . . . Then you must be the Kurushimas' son."

"Yes."

"My, that's a long time ago. But I remember you very well. Your mother is the American lady. Don't you remember me? We used to live next door to Toku. I'm Mamoru's mother."

"Mamoru. Of course! How is he?"

"He was killed in action. In the Philippines. Last year. October."

"I'm sorry . . ."

"Well, here's the bath!" She sounded as if she was trying to cheer herself up. "I'm afraid it's a little dirty because all the children have been using it. But I hope you enjoy it."

Ken was alone in the quiet changing room. Removing his clothes, he walked down to the bath. The air was chilly.

The sulfur water splashed from a little cascade near the river and flowed into three pools made of green stone, where the water became cooler the lower one went. Ken began with the lukewarm pool at the bottom. As his cold skin warmed slightly, he moved up to the top bath, letting his body slowly submerge in the scalding water. The surface of the water was hard at first, as if rejecting this alien thing, then seemed to relax its tension and make him welcome. He lay on his back and stretched out. His stomach and legs floated up on the surface. Like a child he flicked at the water with the tips of his fingers. The steam rose in a single cloud, danced and whirled through the air, and escaped through the window high above the bath. Yes, thought Ken, everything's just the way it used to be—the spurt of water, the wooden enclosure, the dance of the sulfuric steam; it was all the same as when Toku brought him here as a boy. He remembered how the maid would come into the bath with him.

In 1927, when Ken was eight years old, his father was transferred from Chicago to Athens, where he was Consul General. On the way to assume his new post he brought his family to Japan for a visit. When the family departed for Greece, Ken was left in Toku's care, living with her in a rented house in Tokyo while he attended elementary school, and spending his summer vacations up here in Toku's village. Things continued like that for five years, until 1932, when his father returned to become Director of the Trade Bureau in the Foreign Ministry. Ken moved with his family into the new house they built in Nagata-cho, on the bluff above the Sanno Hotel. That year Toku's daughter Yoshiko joined them as a maid.

In 1936, his father was appointed Special Envoy to Belgium. Ken was left in Japan again. Toku came down from her village to Tokyo, and the two of them lived together for a second time until 1940, when he graduated from the Yokohama High School of Engineering. Ken had been in the old woman's care for altogether nine years.

Time . . . Time whirled like a cloud of steam, divided in several directions, and drifted away. But memories of those days with Toku lingered like some of the bright wisps near the ceiling above him.

War . . . War wasn't some abstract, invisible evil, it was the new fighter planes rolling out of the factories, it was the blood of soldiers. He saw it in the eyes of Kamikaze pilots as they took off to meet their death, he heard it in the roar of B-29s. Firebombings, Grummans strafing the ground . . . the war assaulted him, corroded his everyday life. As he sat in the hot sulfuric water, he could feel the blood pulsing through the veins in his skull. He recalled how the Kamikaze pilots always took a final bath, as a rite of purification, the night before their missions, and suddenly he thought, *Today I too finally killed some-body. Two Americans, George and Paul, who crashed before they could open their parachutes. For all I know the bullets I fired actually hit them. I've got blood on my hands. Hands that pushed the firing button, hands that took the lives of two young men.* Ken rubbed his hands together in the bathwater. He felt as if he could rub and rub but never get the sticky blood off.

He jumped out and started washing himself outside the tub. The soap Toku had given him was brand-new, American. His father must have bought it in the States on his way back from Berlin after resign-ing the ambassadorship. Japanese soap these days was extremely coarse. When you dipped it in water it smelled bad, like whale oil. But this soap smelled like perfume; the scent of civilization, the fra-grance of his mother's native country. Ken rubbed a thick lather from it, and looked in the mirror. The person he saw there wasn't Japan-ese; he saw someone as white as the man he'd murdered today. *No wonder people see me as a gaijin, an outsider, an American.*

But then he thought, *I don't give a damn about my body, in my heart I know I'm Japanese. I think in Japanese, I went to a Japanese school, I'm a soldier in the Japanese Army. And yet, unlike other Japanese soldiers, I just can't bring myself to simply see Americans as "the enemy" and kill them without batting an eyelid. In the Army killing a man is a virtue. To shoot down, to sink, to overwhelm, to wipe out—how they boast of acts of murder! No one considers it a record of homicide. The enemy simply isn't human. But for me, he is. Just as my mother is human and I am human, Americans are human. They just don't fit the definition of "enemy."*

Yet how many Americans must think of "the Japs" as less than human. The way George machine-gunned those schoolchildren at their morning assembly—obviously for him they didn't rate as human beings.

What a horrifying, stupid war this is!

He was freezing. He couldn't stop shaking. He stood there pouring bucket after bucket of hot water over himself. Then he dived back into the pool—just as he had as a boy—and swam underwater. His skull felt compressed in the thick, hot water. First he swam from one side to the other, and then he made his way to the little cascade and swam among the rocks and pebbles strewn below it, twisting his body, feeling as if he'd turned into a fish. The sensations returned of that time, long ago, when he used to go swimming in the Chikuma River.

Suddenly he had the feeling someone was watching him. He poked his head above the surface. He must have been imagining things, for there was nothing but the sulfuric steam, the sound of the cascade, and the glitter of the water. Why couldn't he remain a child forever? Why couldn't he just run away from the war? Why not? Why not? . . . He remembered the look of grief on Margaret's face the last time he left her to return to the Army. And he thought, *I'm somebody who can make her happy, but there isn't a single promise I can make to her now. How can a man who may die at any moment make promises to a woman? And so Margaret is left with her grief. And I with mine.*

As he toweled off and slipped back into his kimono, he heard the thin, high-pitched voices of children laughing. One of the sliding doors was yanked open, and half a dozen little boys jostled with each other for a peek.

"It's true!"

"I told you it's a *gaijin!*"

"He's really tall!"

When Ken gave them a smile, they all screamed and ran away. A moment later they regrouped and cautiously poked their heads around the door again.

"What school are you boys at?" he asked them.

"The Hongo Motomachi Elementary School, sir," one of the smaller ones answered, and another boy gasped, "He speaks Japanese!"

"Ah, so you're from Tokyo," said Ken. "I'm from there too." He went out into the corridor, with the boys following.

The smallest of them looked up at him. "Are you Japanese?" he asked.

"I sure am."

"Darn it, I thought he was a *real* foreigner!" The boys nodded to each other; they seemed to have finally agreed on Ken's nationality.

It must have been recess time, for the dining room and the garden were filled with noisy children running about. Some of them noticed Ken and stared at him with open curiosity, but most were engrossed in their games. With bad complexions and bony bodies, they were obviously city boys.

Ken was flushed from the hot bath, and he found the cold wind refreshing as he walked through the deserted streets of the village. When he got back to Toku's house the old woman was waiting for him. She seemed delighted as she ushered him to a seat beside the sunken hearth. The firewood was burning vigorously in the hearth, and it was warm there. His dinner was laid out on a large black lacquer tray; slices of carp washed in cold water, fresh mountain greens, steamed vegetables, and pickles filled the fancy red lacquer bowls that had once been used by the resort guests.

"Hey!" said Ken, admiring the spread.

"It's country food, nothing special."

"No it isn't, it's a feast." In fact, considering the times, it *was* extravagant, the sort of meal prepared only on special occasions.

Over the hearth dangled a *jizai-kagi*, a rope suspended from the ceiling with a hook on the end, to which was fastened a large iron kettle.

"Go ahead and start," said Toku, as she lifted a hot bottle of *sake* from the kettle and filled Ken's cup. Ken downed it in a single gulp. He had gotten through the entire day on a single ball of rice, and the hot *sake* hit his empty stomach with a jolt.

"Make yourself comfortable," the old woman said. Ken had been sitting in formal Japanese style. He relaxed, crossed his legs, stirred the sesame oil in the red lacquer bowl, and started in.

"Delicious!"

Toku proudly watched him eat; he could have been her own son. There was also a certain sadness in her eyes, as if she knew this would be their last meal together.

He raced his motorcycle up the slope. The weather had cleared, and the huge white shape of Mount Asama stood like a giant laughing at the sky. The sun had come out just as he drove away from the banks of the Chikuma River, which glittered with ice. Watching his long shadow flicker across the withered rice fields gave him a rough idea of his speed. The cold wind sliced his ears and made his eyes ache with cold. But Ken's heart was on fire: he had resolved to visit his home in Karuizawa, no matter what. Even if only for a few minutes, he wanted to see his family—Mama, Papa, his sisters—and he had to convey Yamada's feelings to Anna, and ask about hers. Then he thought of Margaret. In fact, wasn't it Margaret he really wanted to see? It had started the moment he spotted the red roof of her house as he flew over Karuizawa that morning. But equally strong was a feeling of hesitation. For one thing it didn't seem right to go to meet your lover while you were on military duty. And then he thought how painful it would be to have to leave her once again. The slope grew steeper, and he was beginning to slide about on gravel and volcanic ash. The road was very rough and uneven here. What worried him more was his gasoline; the fuel gauge was flickering near zero.

An Army truck came roaring past him, leaving the bicycles and carts behind in a cloud of dust. Ken's BMW could go faster than the truck, but he didn't want to risk a flat tire, and he certainly didn't want to call attention to himself, so he went easy on the throttle. Toku had washed his flying cap and overcoat—he had no idea how the old woman had managed to get them dry in time—and she had let out the sleeves and hem of the overcoat, so he now looked roughly presentable.

The air was bitterly cold when he got up to Oiwake, and the pond by the roadside was completely frozen over. The bare trees were veiled with gleaming strands of ice. He could see right through the forest to the different colored roofs of the villas.

Not far from Karuizawa Station, his engine suddenly stalled. He stamped on the kick pedal again and again, but the damned thing wouldn't start. He was out of gas. He had used up more fuel than he anticipated. He got off and started pushing. Now even the elementary students on their bicycles left him behind.

He was surprised to find the station quite still and quiet. All the employees had withdrawn inside. There was a sign on the wall that said, "BECAUSE OF BOMBINGS IN UEDA AND NAGO, SERVICE NORTH HAS BEEN SUSPENDED. A TRAIN IS EXPECTED TO DEPART FOR TOKYO LATER TODAY BUT THE SCHEDULE REMAINS UNCERTAIN."

Ken called one of the station employees to the ticket window. This too was an old man, who told him, "Word is the train's going to be very late getting here. Come back at five." It was now 3:42. He had an hour and a half.

"Hey, soldier!" The old man called him back. "You got a ticket? You can't get on without one. Only people commuting to the munitions factory can use it. We don't sell tickets to anyone else."

"Let me talk to the stationmaster. I have to get back to Tokyo on military business."

"I am the stationmaster." Ah, yes. Ken noticed the gold bars on the old man's cap. "Even soldiers can't buy tickets without special written permission. If I just sold you one I'd get in trouble."

Obviously protest was futile. Ken would just have to go home and think up some way to deal with this.

3

The two military policemen tapped at the cowling and peered into the apple box tied to the back of Ken's motorcycle. Although they saluted when they realized he was an Army officer, they continued to eye him suspiciously. The older of the two, a Sergeant, spoke first.

"Where're you coming from?"

"From Ueda."

"Where're you going?"

"To Tokyo."

"What's in here?" The Sergeant pointed at the apple box.

"Some vegetables and rice." Toku had packed them for him when he left her village.

The Sergeant moved away a little and had a few words with his colleague. Ken tried to put himself in their place: just what would *he* make of a foreigner wearing a Japanese Army greatcoat and flying suit, with a load of rice and vegetables on his German motorcycle? He decided he had better explain himself.

"I'm a First Lieutenant in the Air Corps. This morning I flew to the airfield in Ueda. I'm on my way back to Tokyo now."

"Your name?" asked the Sergeant, with the blank expression that was typical of the Military Police.

"Kurushima."

There was a flicker of recognition on his face. His chinstrap slipped off, revealing a line of untanned skin.

"Kurushima? The same as the Ambassador?"

"Yes. I'm his son."

Ken thought that would take care of any remaining doubts. But instead the expression on the Sergeant's face became even more severe.

"You'll have to come with us to headquarters."

"I can't, I'm in a hurry." But the Sergeant moved beside him and, with the other man pushing the motorcycle, escorted him in a fixed direction.

The corridors of the Peony Inn, the old hostelry in front of the station which belonged to the family of Ken's friend Ryoichi, were swarming with policemen. On a door in the lobby, just inside the main entrance, was a sign that said "Commander's Office." Ken was kept waiting a few minutes before the commander called him in.

Inside the office was a large charcoal stove. The commander was an Army Captain, around thirty years old, with a knife scar on his left cheek. He was sitting up so straight it looked as if his body were in a cast.

"Well now, Lieutenant Kurushima, please take a seat. Do you smoke?" He held out a package of Golden Pheasant cigarettes.

Ken helped himself to one immediately. As the commander lit it for him, Ken noticed his fingernails were blue with ink.

"May I see your military ID?"

"I didn't bring it with me. There was a sudden enemy attack this morning, and I had to take off under emergency conditions."

"Are you carrying *any* identification?"

He thought of having Ryoichi come in and identify him. But then the whole idea of having to identify himself at all began to offend him—what other Japanese officer would be put through all this? So he didn't answer.

"Lieutenant." The commander blew out a puff of smoke. With an unexpectedly mild look on his face, he told Ken, nodding at each of his own phrases, "This is Karuizawa. As you are well aware, it's a compulsory residence area for foreigners. Just the other day there was a young man from Canada—an enemy nation, as you know—who actually escaped disguised, believe it or not, as a Japanese soldier."

"I understand your concern. But my family happens to live here. Right behind the livery stable on the New Karuizawa Road."

The commander examined the map on the wall. He had the Sergeant bring him some documents, which he began to look through.

"What's your father's first name?"

"Saburo."

"And your mother's?"

"Alice."

"*Arisu*? Well now, that's a strange name. Is your mother a foreigner?"

"She's a Japanese citizen now, but she was born in America."

"So you, Lieutenant, would be of mixed blood, a 'half'? . . . The fact is," he said with a prissy little laugh, "we know all about you. It's all in these documents. We just wanted to make sure who you were. By the way, why were you sent to Ueda?"

"I was transferring an airplane there."

"I see. Yes, that explains the flying suit. Now then, Lieutenant, exactly what kind of airplane was it?"

"A military aircraft. I'm not allowed to tell you anything more."

"What time did you arrive at the Ueda airfield?"

"Around ten o'clock this morning, right in the middle of an enemy attack. Sir, you've now identified me, and I'd like to be on my way. My orders are to return to Tokyo as soon as possible."

"Just a minute. You said you arrived at Ueda at ten. It's now four o'clock. What were you doing in the six hours in between?"

"I was visiting an acquaintance in Ueda."

"Ah, I see, that's where you got the motorcycle and the food. That explains it. Tell me, who is this 'acquaintance' of yours?"

"That's personal. You have no right to ask." Ken resolved not to reveal Toku's name to the police. He would do anything to avoid getting the old woman in trouble.

"Because of my position I'm afraid I *have* to ask." The man's cheeks flushed red in the light of the stove, and his scar gleamed like a strip of bacon.

"I refuse. I am an officer in the Imperial Army. I demand that you let me go."

"A *technical* officer," said the commander, with a hint of derision. "And because you're a technical officer, you're privy to a lot of military secrets. Therefore, as a military policeman, I have no choice but to ask you that question. You do understand, don't you?"

"This is incredible!"

"Lieutenant, if we wish to we can easily investigate all your activities. But," he said, "we want to hear it from you yourself." Suddenly he softened his tone of voice. "We know all about your mission. You transferred a captured Mustang from the Eastern Kanto Division to the Ueda airfield. Correct? But we want to know exactly what you were doing in the six hours after you accomplished your mission. Where were you? Traveling by motorcycle for six hours, you could have gone quite far, couldn't you? Say, as far as Lake Nojiri? As far as the homes of the neutral aliens by Lake Nojiri?"

"Just what are you accusing me of?" asked Ken, half in anger and half in disgust.

"I'm not the one who suspects you," replied the commander, with a significant glance at the Sergeant and his partner. "It's the Army high command."

"I don't know what you're talking about."

"Come now, Lieutenant," he said with a condescending smile, "you must have some idea."

"No, I really don't."

"You, sir, are under suspicion. The Army is keeping an eye on you. And our orders are to report all of your movements over the last six hours. So tell us, what were you doing?"

"I refuse. I've done absolutely nothing to put me under suspicion."

"You refuse to cooperate?"

"Yes. I do."

"Well then we have no choice but to make a thorough investigation ourselves. It won't be very difficult. We have the license plate of your motorcycle, and we can find out where that apple box came from. Until we clear this up you'll have to remain here."

"This is outrageous!" Ken blew up at them. "I'm a member of the fighter squadron defending the Imperial capital. How dare you keep me up here when Tokyo is being subjected to daily bombardment! That's aiding and abetting the enemy. And you call yourself an Imperial officer?"

The man winced at Ken's outburst, an uneasy smile on his lips. "Now, Lieutenant, don't get excited."

"How can I not get excited! Give me that phone. I'm going to talk to my commanding officer."

"The lines to Tokyo are all down at the moment."

"Well, you can investigate me all you want. I'm going."

The MPs made no attempt to stop him as he stormed out of the room. Slamming the door behind him, he walked right into Ryoichi Koyama, who seemed to have been eavesdropping.

"Oh, sorry!" said Ryoichi. "I heard they'd brought in an officer who looked like a foreigner, and I came to see if it was you. Are they finished with you?"

"I'll have nothing more to do with these people."

"Really got to you, didn't they?" Ryoichi peered into the commander's office. He glanced at the policemen in the hallway, then, deciding it was safe to do so, followed Ken out.

At first Ken pushed his motorcycle along slowly, so that his crippled friend could keep up with him, but his anger got the better of him and he ended up walking with large, impatient strides. Ryoichi struggled to keep up, bobbing up and down like a diver plunging then coming up for air.

"You know, Ken, those MPs have been really putting the screws on lately. Any *gaijin* who gives them the slightest cause for suspicion gets dragged off. With your foreign face, I wouldn't go walking around Karuizawa alone. Everyone's getting hysterical about spies. Even in Tokyo they picked up the Anglican Bishop. And our pastor here was arrested by the Thought Police last year. I heard he died in prison—they tortured him."

"What? You don't mean Father Hendersen?" The whole day had brought nothing but strange and depressing news.

"You didn't know?" Ryoichi seemed as astonished as Ken.

"How the hell could I?" said Ken sharply. "My family couldn't exactly discuss it in their letters, could they?"

"Of course not," said Ryoichi in a calmer tone of voice. "I heard that Tokyo's being bombed to smithereens, but there isn't a word about it in the papers. Yet somehow the foreigners in Karuizawa always manage to find out what's really happening. I just heard there was a huge air raid on Tokyo today—three hundred carrier-based planes and a hundred B-29s. The neutrals up here knew all about it, down to the last detail. There must be spies around somewhere, but how're the police going to find them out of several thousand *gaijin*? The result is that the competition's gotten real hot between the MPs and the Thought Police, and they're arresting everyone in sight. By the way, Ken, what *are* you doing up here?"

"I had a mission in Ueda."

"A mission, huh? You flying back to Tokyo?"

"No, it's not possible."

"Oh. Okay, Ken, I've got to go now. Sorry to have to say this, but people get suspicious if they see one talking with a *gaijin*. See you around, Ken. Take care of yourself." And he bobbed off down the road, dragging his bad leg.

Ken turned off the main road onto the path between the rice paddies, back behind the livery stable. The stable was empty, and the courtyard was littered with broken bottles and rotting carriage wheels. Beyond lay a frozen stream, silent and gray. The only bright thing in the landscape was the tips of the icicles hanging from the snow-covered roofs as they glinted in the light of the waning sun.

He heard chickens cackling in the garden, and went around to look. The garden had been turned into a vegetable patch. There on the edge of it he saw his mother, walking behind a rooster with a large basket in her hand.

Ken flung his motorcycle to the ground and ran to her.

"Mama!"

Alice dropped the basket.

"Ken! What on earth are you doing here?"

He hugged her, noticing that she seemed to be a whole size smaller. "I don't have much time, I'm afraid. I've got to go back on the five o'clock train. I just wanted to see you before I left."

"Well, at least you can come inside for a while. We've got some coffee. We might even have some sweets."

"Where's Papa?"

"He's been in Tokyo the last three days. He took Anna with him."

"Tokyo? The firebombings are getting worse and worse."

"That's why they went—to get all his books and diplomatic papers out before it's too late."

"And where's Eri?"

"Oh, you didn't know? Last summer the police pressed her into service. She's been working as an interpreter."

"So you're all alone here."

"I've got Yoshiko with me . . . she must be off doing the laundry now. Ken, you've gotten so thin! They must keep you busy in the Army. What did they send you up here for this time?"

"I had to fly a plane up to the airfield at Ueda. But it was destroyed in a raid."

"I can't believe they're bombing all the way up here in the mountains. Today I saw an American plane for the first time. Ken, were you in danger? You've got cuts on your face."

"It's nothing, just some scratches. The other pilots have been dying almost daily. All of them younger than me. Compared to them, I've got it easy."

Alice looked intently at her son, drawing him into her large green eyes.

"Ken, don't die."

"Don't be silly, Mama." He held her tightly in his arms. "Didn't you always say it's not up to us whether we live or die, that it's the will of God?"

"Yes. But Ken, you mustn't die."

He kissed her on the forehead and stroked her soft shoulders.

Yoshiko was standing on the veranda, watching them. Ken waved to her.

"Wait a minute," his mother said. "I've got to put the rooster back in the coop." She took up the basket and started picking some shiny green buds on the ground. "Look—new shoots, even in this freezing weather. The rooster eats them. I thought if the rooster can eat them, so can we. So I let the thing find the shoots of grass and I pick them."

"That sounds typical of you."

Yoshiko had joined them. She was even more emaciated than Alice. The deep wrinkles on her face made her look a full ten years older. Her red cheeks were wet with tears. "You look well, Master Ken . . . I can't believe you're really here."

"I stopped by your mother's village. She gave me a real feast. But I'm only here for a quick visit—I'm taking the five o'clock train."

"You've got a whole hour. Why don't you come inside?"

He hardly recognized the parlor. Most of it was occupied by two large beds where the women slept, with laundry hanging to dry around them. A tiny fire was kept burning in the stove, giving off only a little heat. Ken wanted to call his base, but they told him the phone had been out of order for three months. No repairman would come. Yoshiko removed the kettle from the stove and poured him a cup of hot green tea. As he sipped the fragrant tea, Ken remembered something he'd had at the back of his mind.

"I don't have a ticket for the train. I suppose I could sneak on board if I had to."

"You don't have a ticket?" his mother cried. "Then they absolutely won't let you on. When Papa and Anna went to Tokyo, we had to go through the Foreign Ministry to get them tickets a whole month in advance."

"What if we asked Miss Eri to help?" Yoshiko suggested.

"You mean ask the Chief of Police?" Alice grimaced.

"Well, this is an emergency, and it's fair enough, surely." Yoshiko turned to Ken, as if looking to him for support. "After all, Miss Eri wanted to quit but the chief insisted she stay on, saying she was indispensable to them as an interpreter. So he does owe us something. Last year when they arrested Father Hendersen your father begged the chief to let him go, but they wouldn't hear of it. Those people are two-faced, they are—all nice and polite when they need something from you, but when you ask *them* for a favor, forget it! They owe us

472

at least a railroad ticket, and by God I'm going to get it from them!" And she dashed out of the room before either of them could say a word.

"I heard Father Hendersen died last year."

"Yes." Ken's mother gave a deep, despondent sigh. "He was murdered, by the Chief of Police. They claimed he died of an illness, but I don't believe a word of it. The chief's a member of the Thought Police—and a brute. Poor Audrey collapsed with shock. Maggie's been taking care of her. Sometimes I go over to help. I usually take some food. They don't get enough to eat on the foreigners' rations."

"Oh, Maggie."

"Yes, the poor child."

"If I had time I'd like to go and see them."

"She'd be overjoyed if you did. I'm pretty sure the girl's in love with you."

"I wouldn't bank on it . . ."

Ken was wondering just how much his mother knew about their relationship, when she said, "Eri told me. It seems Maggie told her everything."

"Oh, it's all just a big game for Eri. She's been dropping hints about it for years."

"Well, you're certainly right about *that.*" Alice smiled.

"By the way, Toku gave me something for you." Ken went to get the apple box on the back of his motorcycle. The box was packed with rice, sweet potatoes, and dried trout.

"We owe that old woman a lot. If it weren't for her, we would have starved to death." She made the sign of the cross. "Let's share some of this with Maggie and her mother. Why don't we cook some sweet potatoes now?"

"I'll do it." Ken carried the box into the kitchen and washed the potatoes in the sink. On a sudden impulse he opened the icebox to see what else they might have. It was empty. The bread shelf, the rice bin, the vegetable containers were all empty. Ken felt like weeping as he carried the washed potatoes into the parlor and put them on the stove. He suspected his mother hadn't eaten anything since morning.

She had probably spent the whole day walking around looking for shoots of grass.

"Mama." He knew how much his mother hated being pitied, and how she disliked imposing on people, but if she left Karuizawa and moved in with their old maid at least she would get enough to eat. "Mama," he repeated, and found himself staring into her eyes. She was eagerly waiting to hear what he had to say.

"What is it?" She gave him a smile that had the warmth of an old-fashioned lamp.

Ken smiled back. "Before I go there's something I want to ask you."

"Go ahead."

"Why did you leave me alone in Japan when I was a little boy?"

"Because . . ." The smile faded and a shadow crossed her face. "Your father is a diplomat, and a diplomat's family drifts from nation to nation, like a ship without an anchor. The children on board the ship get to see all the countries of the world, but before long they forget the harbor from which they first set sail. And yet they *do* have a harbor, every person has a harbor somewhere, the place they once set out from. A port of origin. Papa and I thought it was especially important for you because you were a boy. And so we left you in Japan. As your mother it was terribly difficult for me to . . . but I . . ."

"I see. So you decided this should be my port of origin . . ."

"Ken, I was born in America. America's a place where people have gathered from all over the world. And there are some people who, once they've settled there, never give the slightest thought to the harbor they originally set out from to get there. But to my mind people like that are cut off from the very root of their existence. I'm sorry for them. Only when you know your origins can you lay anchor in that new harbor, America."

"And what about you, Mama?"

"My parents set sail from Scotland and laid anchor in America. I set sail from America and laid anchor here in Japan. I've spent my life wandering from country to country, but I always knew that the ship I sailed in had an anchor, and a port to return to."

"You mean . . ."

"Yes. I'm Japanese. A Japanese who was once an American. Whose parents were once Scottish. And to me that's the most natural thing in the world."

"So you boarded the same ship as Papa, and sailed under his flag."

"Exactly. And I've never regretted it, not for a single moment. I'm proud of what I've done. Despite everything, Japan is a wonderful country."

Ken tossed a larch twig on the fire and gazed intently at the bursting sparks.

"Ken." His mother took his face in her hands and looked straight into his eyes. "I want you to fight bravely for this country. But I want you to stay alive. Because if you die now you will only have died for Japan. But if you live you'll live for both Japan and America. This war can't go on for much longer, and when peace comes you'll be a bridge between the two countries. I want you to stay alive till then."

Ken remained silent as his mother buried her face against his chest. The wood burned briskly in the stove. There was the sound of footsteps approaching.

"What a disgusting man!" Yoshiko announced. "When Miss Eri asked him for help, he said it was 'theoretically possible' to issue a ticket for Ken, but that he'd have to interview him first. 'I'll be in serious trouble with my superiors,' he said, 'if I give permission for it without first making a thorough and *responsible* investigation.' All he talked about was his 'principles' and his 'responsibility.' He forgot all about his obligation to Miss Eri. A real man would have just shut up and written out the permission."

"Thanks, anyway," said Ken. "At least he agreed to see me. I'll go talk to him."

"Oh look, they're almost burned!" Yoshiko grabbed the blackened potatoes from the stove and tossed them on a dish.

Alice poured them some coffee she'd bought on the black market. They then cut the sweet potatoes into round slices, added some salt, and started eating. After a few minutes Ken looked at his watch and stood up to go. The two women wanted to come to the police station with him, but he told them not to. He gave his mother a hug and shook hands with Yoshiko.

"Ken!" Alice flung herself at him again. "Don't die."

"I'm not going to die," he said firmly.

"God bless you."

"I'll be back again sometime. *Sayonara.*" He bowed to them and walked away with long strides. When he got to the stable he turned around. His mother and Yoshiko were still there watching him, frantically waving their hands.

The door of the police station flew open and Eri dashed out. With her short hair and pantaloons, she looked like a boy.

"Ken!"

"Eri!"

Normally they would have embraced and kissed, but they were conscious of the people around them and merely stood there looking at each other.

"You look okay."

"You look pretty good yourself."

Eri showed him into the chief's office. Sitting there behind a huge desk was a surprisingly unimposing, thin, middle-aged little man. His small head, cropped short in the military style, gleamed as though it had just been polished.

"Allow me to apologize for the inconvenience we've caused you." The chief stood up and gave Ken a salute, then indicated a small wooden chair. "I'm required to ask you a few questions, otherwise there'd be all sorts of trouble. Your sister here" (he glanced at Eri) "has been indispensable to us. As you know, we're here to assist the foreigners—and you know how difficult foreigners can be, with all their strange customs. Every time a new bunch of *gaijin* arrives from Tokyo we have to find them somewhere to live. We work with the local government to make sure they get sufficient food rations. You might say we're a combination real estate agency and grocery store for them, and when they don't speak Japanese we're absolutely helpless. Well, your sister's English is the real thing, and we're completely dependent on her, especially when those damned Germans—most of the foreigners are either White Russians or Germans and, let me tell you, the Germans are the worst!—with their arrogance and the way they treat us Orientals, they completely ignore our orders. Well, Miss Kurushima comes and talks a storm at them, and that shuts 'em up right away. Yes, sir, I don't know what we'd do without her. Er, Miss Kurushima, could you wait outside for a couple of minutes? I'd like to talk with your brother alone. Just one or two minutes."

As soon as Eri left the office the chief lowered his voice.

"I understand you'll be returning to your squadron in Tokyo."

"That's right. I'd like to get on the five o'clock train."

"Your ticket has been approved. You can pick it up at the station-master's office."

"Thank you very much."

"No problem. By the way, Lieutenant . . ." His eyes nervously roamed the door and the windows. "We understand you just saw your mother."

"Yes, I did."

"Did you talk to her about anything in particular?"

Here we go again. Ken steeled himself.

"No . . . I hadn't seen her for some time, and we talked about family matters."

"You didn't talk about the late pastor, did you? Father Hendersen?"

"No, we didn't. Why do you ask?"

"No particular reason. I just . . . Your father's away now, isn't he? Can you tell me where His Excellency went?"

"I understand he went to Tokyo to remove his books and diplomatic documents from our house. He's afraid they might be destroyed in the bombing. But why should you be interested?"

"I'm afraid I can't tell you why. But there's a very good reason." He paused. "Would you like to know the reason, Lieutenant?"

"Not particularly." Ken shook his head. "It's none of my business how you go about your job."

"Actually, Lieutenant"—he was obviously put out—"in this case it is your business. It concerns your parents. One might say your parents are in some danger."

"What kind of danger?"

"You see," he said, with a triumphant grin on his face, "you are interested, aren't you?"

"How can I *not* be concerned when you tell me my parents are in danger?"

"Well then, I'll let you in our secret. But first you must tell me something. A trade, Lieutenant. This afternoon you were questioned by the Military Police. I want to know what they asked you."

"It has nothing to do with you. They asked me about a military matter."

"A military matter! I thought so!"

"And that's why it has nothing to do with you."

"Oh, but it has a great deal to do with us. And with the danger your parents are in."

"Are you telling me the danger has something to do with me?"

"Exactly," the chief said happily, stretching his little arms and grabbing the edge of his enormous desk.

"The Military Police asked me how I got from the Ueda airfield to Karuizawa."

"And did you tell them?" The chief's eyes gleamed with curiosity.

"Yes, I did." Ken spoke deliberately, in a clear voice. "I told them that since the trains weren't running I walked. That's all I said. They released me right away."

"All right. Now I'll tell you our secret. Since you're an Imperial officer I feel I can trust you with this information. The authorities suspect your parents of being pacifists. Pacifists working to undermine the war effort. The fact is, your father has been seen in the company of the pro-English former Ambassador, Yoshizawa, and the moderate former Prime Minister, Prince Konoe. Your mother has also been a frequent visitor to the house of a suspected spy, Mrs. Hendersen. *That* is the evidence."

"But it's ridiculous."

"Yes, I agree. But I'm worried about your family, because these days ridiculous rumors, when repeated often enough, tend to turn into the truth. Since Miss Eri is a girl, she wouldn't understand how seriously the authorities take your family's behavior. So I'd like you to warn her. I think she would listen to her older brother."

"You want me to warn Eri?"

"Yes. Warn her to stay away from the Hendersens' house."

"I understand," Ken answered automatically.

"Excellent, Lieutenant! This has been a most useful meeting." The chief gave him a military salute and handed him the authorization for his ticket. "I won't need any money for this. Miss Eri asked that the fare be deducted from her pay. Goodbye, Lieutenant. We're counting on you."

"That was a long two minutes," said Eri as they left the police station. "What was it about?"

"Just chitchat. The guy's a real chatterbox."

"His chatter's a ruse. He throws out a smoke screen of words to trick you into telling him what he really wants to know. Are you sure you didn't tell him anything?"

"Oh, I was careful. He seemed very interested in Papa."

"He asks me about him all the time. So I tell him all sorts of silly little things. How Papa cuts his nose hairs in the morning, how he uses an American Gillette when he shaves, how he stumbled on a rock in the garden. And that fool puts it all down in his little notebook."

"What happened to Father Hendersen?"

"The chief killed him with his own hands, that's what I think. I saw him when they brought him out after his interrogation. He was as white as a ghost, and he could hardly stand. I wanted to quit when I saw what they'd done, but I decided to stay on for Mama and Papa's sake. As long as I'm working there, even that man can't lay a finger on them. Ken, look at the time! You're going to miss your train."

It was three minutes to five. They broke into a run. When they reached the station they found a notice saying that the train scheduled to leave for Tokyo at five had been delayed. The passengers sat with their heads wrapped in air-raid hoods and the collars of their over-coats turned up against the cold wind blowing into the open waiting room. They looked like bits of baggage. Ken went up to the ticket window to get some information, but there was no sign of anyone on duty.

"What're you going to do?" asked Eri.

"I'll just have to wait."

"It's freezing in here. You'll catch a cold." Eri untied Ken's woolen scarf and wrapped it around his face. "This is a good muffler. It looks handmade. Ken, I'm sorry, but I've got to go. The Germans are waiting for their food rations."

"Thanks for everything, Eri. You really saved the day. I didn't have much time, but I'm glad I got a chance to see you and Mama."

"When will you be back?"

"With the war like this, who knows."

"How are your friends, Yamada and Haniyu?"

"Oh, they're okay. But Haniyu's in a special attack squadron."

"What's that?"

"The Kamikazes. They crash their planes into American B-29s."

"Oh, my God!" Eri gasped. For a moment she was a little girl again. "Don't they die when they crash?"

"Not necessarily. They're allowed to bail out just before impact."

"Thank heavens!" Eri gave a deep sigh. "I'm sorry, Ken, but I've really got to go. Come visit us again as soon as you can. And take care of yourself. Please take care of yourself."

Eri opened her arms, but since everyone in the waiting room was staring at them, they couldn't actually embrace. She walked away with a look of regret. Two or three times she turned back. He noticed how bony her backside was, and realized it was emaciation that made her look like a boy.

The stationmaster loudly cleared his throat and addressed the crowd: "This is an emergency announcement. The train delayed by an enemy air raid has been further delayed. It is now due to arrive at approximately seven o'clock. The departure time for its return to

Tokyo will be announced after it arrives. However, we cannot guarantee that it will leave at seven . . ."

A few muttered complaints were heard, and a few of the passengers rose from the benches and headed for home, but most of them remained seated, their heads hung in resignation. They were used to waiting.

Ken immediately went outside. Two whole hours! It was like a gift from heaven. There was time to see Margaret.

He wanted to take the shortest route, so he hurried along the narrow paths that zigzagged across the rice fields. The dirt paths were crusted with a layer of hard snow, and it felt like walking on paved city streets. In a few minutes the sky above him was blanketed with leaden clouds. When he reached the area where the villas were, the damp, heavy air clung to him like a slick of waste oil. Here the summer guests used to stroll and enjoy the cool, refreshing breeze; now it was completely deserted.

A wall of black lacquer was how the sheer slope of Mount Hanare appeared to him, and the cold was even sharper than before. The forest here, filled with evergreen trees, was especially dismal in winter. The gathering darkness seemed to press the houses flat against the earth. The red roof of the Hendersens' house was covered with a thick layer of larch needles, and the gutters in the eaves were rotting away. The white birch door pillars tilted to one side; the door itself teetered on its hinges. He looked at the chimney. There wasn't the slightest sign of heat. Nor could he see any light behind the curtains.

Somewhere behind him he heard the sound of twigs breaking and turned around, seeing a shadow moving behind the lone withered tree in the garden next door. Was he being followed? Or was there always a lookout posted here? Ken crouched beneath the fence and watched the tree for a few minutes. During that time he couldn't hear a single sound from inside. The house might as well have been deserted.

No, there was nobody in the garden next door; he must have been imagining things.

He rang the doorbell three times, and finally after the third time he heard some movement inside. He could sense someone peering out from behind the curtains, and then the door slowly opened.

"Oh my God, Ken!"

"Maggie!"

"Come in! What are you doing here? I just can't believe it!"

As soon as she shut the door behind her and refastened the chain, Margaret flung herself at him. He grabbed her by the waist, and they hungrily kissed each other's lips.

"It's you, Ken. It's really you, isn't it? Let me see your face."

"It's so dark in here, how can you see anything? Is the light broken?"

"Let's go inside. We keep the doorway dark on purpose. The police are always watching."

They went into the parlor, which looked out over the pond.

"So it *was* a policeman out there."

"Did you see somebody?"

"I had a feeling there was a man in the garden next door."

"Oh him? That's a detective. He's always there. But Ken, if he saw you you're in trouble."

"Don't worry about me. After all, I'm not doing anything wrong. But I *was* worried about you. I heard your father died. I'm very, very sorry."

"Thank you."

"How's your mother?"

"She's in the next room. She's sleeping now, so we have to be quiet."

They looked at each other. Margaret's eyes were so different from his mother's. For a moment they made him think of pools of cold blue water. Her small face felt smooth when he touched her. When she smiled there were deep creases beneath her eyes, and her face was framed by long, flaxen hair. She was beautiful. The sudden rush of desire he felt made him flustered, and he started talking to conceal his discomfort.

"I must look ridiculous," he said, unbuttoning his overcoat to reveal the flying suit he was wearing underneath. "I had to fly a plane up to Ueda today."

"You look fine." There was exhilaration in her voice. "I've never seen you in your pilot gear before. It makes you look heroic. I'd love to see you actually flying."

"As a matter of fact I flew right over your house this morning. Just before ten. You didn't hear any planes go by?"

"Yes, I did hear something. But we have to stay hidden in here, and I couldn't go out to look. Of course these days even if you do look out there's nothing you want to see." She hung her head.

Ken didn't know what to say. He looked at her again. Her whole face seemed pale and slightly swollen. Ken noticed the frayed, washed-out blouse she was wearing beneath her sweater. He felt a pang when he realized it was a summer blouse.

"You'd better stay longer this time," she said, her large, round eyes teasing him with a smile. She seemed to have banished all the misery and loneliness from her face in order to give him this smile. "I'll make you some dinner. I know, I'll make you a pie with the flour your mother gave us."

"I'm sorry, Maggie, but I won't have time to eat. My orders are to return to the squadron as soon as I can. I've got to get back to Karuizawa Station by seven . . ."

"You mean we've only got two hours?" She looked as if she might burst into tears. "It's been so long since I saw you. Forget about the train. You can stay here tonight."

"It just isn't possible. I've got my orders."

"Your orders? You mean your war, your murdering war." Margaret was shaking. She glared at his military overcoat. "Well go, then, go back to your horrible war!"

"Maggie!" He took her by her thin shoulders. "It can't be helped. I'm a soldier."

"Yes. And I'm the enemy, aren't I?" She was crying. He had never seen her cry before.

"No, you're Maggie. My beautiful girl."

"Am I?" Her eyelashes brushed against his face.

"Yes, really." Ken held her tight, as if to squeeze all the sadness from her body.

"Maggie!" an old woman's voice called out from the next room. Margaret reluctantly pulled herself away from him. He tried to hold her back but her eyes told him "Don't." Then with slow footsteps, as if delaying an unpleasant task until the last possible moment, she went into the next room. A few minutes later she returned with her mother in her arms. Audrey was wearing her nightgown. Ken helped Margaret lay her down on the sofa. Audrey's blond hair, streaked with red, was tied back in a bun. But her cheeks were hollow, her eyes sunk deep in their sockets. It was painful to look at her.

"How nice of you to come, young man. You look so well. What a handsome sailor you've become!"

"He's in the Army, Mother."

"Oh yes, the Army. I know that, Maggie. Oh, it's so cold in here. Why don't you light the stove?"

Ken looked around the room. There wasn't a single piece of firewood anywhere.

"Here, Mother, put this on." Margaret draped a blanket over her legs.

"Now, tell me all about the Royal Navy. What kind of ship are you on?"

Margaret winked at Ken, so he decided to humor her.

"It's a big ship. In fact, it's an aircraft carrier."

"Oh . . . but they sink, don't they? Battleships sink, don't they? How awful. The Japs are sinking all our ships!" With a scream, the mad old woman kicked off her blanket and tried to stand up, then tottered to the floor.

Margaret moved quickly to her side. "Come on, now, let's go back to sleep. It's time for your medicine."

"No, Maggie. Can't you see we have a visitor? This nice sailor's come to see us—the least we can do is heat the stove. It's so cold. So cold! We're all going to die, it's so cold!"

Ken tried to help lift her up off the floor. He slipped his hands under her arms.

"How dare you! How dare you touch a lady!" she suddenly screamed.

"Come on, Mrs. Hendersen," he said gently, pointing to her room.

"Don't you call me Mrs. Hendersen! What impudence! Get out, leave my house at once!"

"Mother." Margaret was equally gentle with her. "It's Ken. Ken Kurushima."

"I've never seen this man in my life. It's disgraceful, a sailor in the Royal Navy, and look at him! Look at his shaved head. Why, he looks just like a Jap! How dare you call me Mrs. Hendersen!"

"I think I should leave," he said to Margaret in Japanese. "I'll come again."

"Wait! Don't go. Just wait here until I give her her medicine."

It was a firm order, and the very act of giving it seemed to give her thin arms strength, as she swept her mother off the floor and carried her back to the adjoining room. The screams continued for a few minutes, and then the house was quiet again. Margaret came out of the bedroom wearing an overcoat.

"She's gone to sleep. That medicine always works. I'm sorry if she gave you a shock. She's never recovered from Father's death . . . Ken, why don't we go outside? I want Mother to sleep and I could use a little fresh air."

The two of them went out to the edge of the pond.

The pond was frozen over. Ken put one foot on the ice. The ice creaked, but it held him. Boldly he tried the other foot. A long crack opened ahead of him.

"Ken, it's dangerous!"

He stepped back onto the shore and crouched down beside her. He dug a little hole in the ice and peered through it. He could see algae swaying on the blue and black bottom of the pond. Dim reflections of the clouds swirling past above them were tangled with the languid green weeds.

Ken picked up a pebble and threw it. It skimmed the frozen surface of the pond with a dry, melodious echo.

"It's as if the pond is singing." Margaret followed suit and threw another pebble across the pond. Hers gave a rhythmic sound, *karan koron karan koron*, and landed even further away.

Then Ken picked up an even larger stone and threw it with all his might. It skimmed the ice with a heavy, sonorous ring, hit the little island in the middle, and ricocheted away.

"Sounds like you, making a speech."

Ken looked at her. Her face was full of life again. "Remember when you used to skate at the rink up in Kutsukake? You were really good at it." He remembered the first time he ever saw Margaret skating. One winter in Karuizawa, at the outdoor rink in the garden of the Kutsukake Inn, he noticed a Western woman leading her daughter over the ice. He had been intrigued by the sight of the little girl with flaxen hair—she must have been eight or nine—whirling round and round the rink. "You were good at everything you did. Skating, swimming, riding, tennis . . ."

"No, Ken, *you* were the athlete."

"Let's play tennis again sometime."

"Yes. We could play now if you want to."

It was getting darker and darker. The black mountain seemed to swallow up the surrounding dusk and swell into the sky like some giant beast. It was already after six. Ken couldn't tell for sure, but he had a feeling someone was watching them, someone's eyes were fixed on them in the shadow of the house.

"We don't have much time. Let's go for a walk."

They strolled around the pond and came to a dam that marked the beginning of a little river. They followed the river for a while. Only the pools by the bank were frozen over; down the middle ran a ribbon of clear water which retained the dim light of dusk, gurgling against the ice clinging to the roots of the dead trees at its edge. Ken pulled out one of the roots and held it up. It was festooned with icicles like curling fingers.

"It's so pretty," said Margaret, stroking the ice.

He let the thing drop into the river and, taking her by the hand, embraced her, kissed her.

"Ken, I'm so happy . . . ," she said, letting her whole body fall against him.

"Margaret, I love you." The air was so cold it felt like black ice, but warmth rose from Margaret's soft body to penetrate deep inside him.

Somewhere in the distance a man was still watching them. *Go ahead and look. Look all you want. No matter how much you bastards stare at us, forbid us, make fun of us, I still love Maggie.*

"Ken, I love you."

Walking shoulder to shoulder, they set off back to Margaret's house. They found her mother sleeping peacefully, and they continued their lovemaking on the sofa.

4

It was the next morning when Lieutenant Ken Kurushima finally returned to his base. An hour after his train left Karuizawa it had to stop for what seemed an eternity while the tracks destroyed in an air raid were repaired. It was midnight when they started moving again, only to be delayed by a snowstorm, and it wasn't until after seven the next morning that the train finally pulled into Ueno Station in Tokyo. All the city trains were running behind schedule because of the snowstorm. Ken had to change trains several times. These ran for several miles, stopped for an air raid warning, then started up again. He finally reached Tachikawa, in the northern suburbs, after ten, and boarded a bus for the airfield, arriving back exhausted and hungry.

The airfield had been devastated. A good half of the hangars were destroyed, their iron frames twisted and exposed. Purple flames were still licking the sky from the bunkers where fuel had been stored. He felt a twinge of pain each time he passed a wrecked airplane. Hayabusa and Shoki fighters, and even his own proud creation, the Hayate, smoldered on the ground, battered beyond recognition. He couldn't believe it. *What a shame, what a goddamned shame!* Headquarters had been blasted away, with just its foundation stones remaining. Only the pilots' room and the medical institute were still standing among the ruins.

He stood without moving where the bus driver let him off, right in the middle of it all. He was too stunned to go anywhere. Looking down, he saw Momotaro playing at his feet, and he followed the dog indoors.

The animals' hutches were all burned to a crisp. Peering into a mound of tangled wire, he found that the rabbits and white mice had fused together into ashy lumps. The whole building looked ready to collapse: the wooden paneling had been blown away, the floor was a jumble of broken test tubes and spilled chemicals. There was nowhere to walk. But Momotaro led him through the debris, and he managed to climb up to the second floor. There, among the shattered window-panes, the desks and chairs that had all slid into a pile at the lower end of the floor, sat Yamada.

Ken called out. Yamada languidly lifted his head. His eyes didn't seem to be focusing.

"Is that you, Kurushima? They finally came. The bastards finally came."

"Are you all right?"

"Everything's gone. The animal lab, the anti-G suit—all my work has been blown away." He lifted the helmet he was holding on his lap and showed it to Ken. It was an experimental pressurized helmet he had just designed. It had a large bullet hole through the middle, and the apparatus at the back had been torn to shreds.

"You can make another one."

"No, I can't. The factory where I got the material for it has been destroyed."

"Where is everybody?"

"Everybody? . . . Oh yes, everybody. They're all in the pilots' room. That's where they moved headquarters."

Snow was drifting through the broken windows. Ken found it hard to believe it could get this cold.

"I'm going to report back. Why don't you come with me? You'll freeze to death here."

"I want to check the damage a bit more." As Ken walked away, Yamada called out to him: "Haniyu's missing. He went out on a sortie against the B-29s this morning, and he didn't come back. Also, Wing Commander Kurokawa was seriously wounded and is in the hospital. His right leg was shattered—it's amazing he kept on flying like that. He was bleeding badly when he landed, but I managed to tie up the artery. They'll probably have to amputate. Lots of dead and wounded around here. Yes sir, thrills aplenty."

"So Haniyu . . ." Ken remembered his smile just before he took off yesterday, the way he ran with his hands on his hips. He remembered the young man feverishly playing "The Devil's Trill" on his violin, and Eri's face as she watched him singing. Bits and pieces from all those days together came back to him, all jumbled up . . .

Only a few minutes after Ken had finished reporting, they received news of a B-29 shot down over the Kanda area of downtown Tokyo. It was reported that parts of the American aircraft were still intact. Major Wakana was appointed to lead an investigative detail composed of Ken, Yamada, Mitsuda, and several technical people who were bomber specialists. Two trucks set out through the driving snow, heading for the center of the city.

As they drove through the suburban towns of Tachikawa and Mitaka, Ken noticed streets here and there where bombs had fallen, but nothing prepared him for the devastation he saw as they approached the middle of Tokyo. Row after row of wooden houses had been incinerated. Sheets of zinc roofing, hunks of porcelain, and twisted water pipes lay scattered on the ground. In what had been the greatest city in all Japan, you could now see clearly all the way to the horizon, the whole area now just one vast stretch of rubble, with the survivors sifting through it like stray animals foraging for something to eat. As Ken sat there beside Major Wakana he strained to take it in, but his eyes were so heavy he couldn't stay awake.

He woke up to the sound of an air raid siren. The streetcars had halted, and passengers were scurrying into nearby shelters. Ken could see the moat and the great stone walls of the Imperial Palace. They felt the earth shudder as a burst of high-pitched antiaircraft fire went up.

"Major, shouldn't we be taking shelter somewhere?" said the driver.

The metallic throb of bomber engines could be heard approaching low over the city.

"No," Wakana answered in a shrill voice. "They're still some way off. Drive on!"

Sharp streaks of light rained down on far-off streets, and as each hit the earth there was a flare of red. A heavy snowfall had muffled the city in white, and only the places where the bombs hit loomed large and bright, like photographic enlargements.

"It looks like they hit Nihonbashi," said the driver.

They were approaching Yasukuni Shrine, the shrine of the war dead. The grove surrounding it was blanketed with snow. Somehow these hallowed grounds had managed to escape with their sanctity intact, but when Ken's little convoy passed the shrine and reached the top of the slope, they saw that the lowlands of the Old City ahead of them were all ablaze. In the distance, innumerable fires large and small ringed Ueno Station and the bridge at Nihonbashi. Directly below them the streets of Kanda were dotted with points of flame. It was as if some giant hand had sprinkled red and black ink over a field of white powder. The wind shifted from minute to minute, sending thick clouds of smoke mixed with snow across the road. The soldiers choked on the burned-smelling air.

Books burn well, and Kanda was full of bookshops. As one of the stores burst into flames they saw reams of paper flutter up into the air. Fires were spreading from shop to shop, from house to house, from street to street. Two entire fire brigades had been called out, but they were wasting their time. A few people could be seen hurling snowballs at the flames, laughing hysterically.

"What're we going to do, sir?" asked the driver.

"Can we get down this slope?" Wakana asked.

"Yes, I think so. We've got chains on."

"Then go. Our orders are to recover what's left of that B-29."

As soon as they started down, the truck began to slide. A crowd of people escaping the fires had spilled onto the road, and it was only by honking wildly that the driver made his way safely through. The road ahead, though, was now blocked by a jumble of fallen telephone wires. They had to make a detour. The snow fell relentlessly. At the side of the road they passed women placing their sleeping babies on singed blankets, old men tightening the ropes around the belongings they'd piled onto wooden carts, officials of the neighborhood associations barking instructions into their megaphones.

Yamada had been silent so far. "It's barbaric," he muttered. "They're just civilians."

"There it is!" cried Wakana. Leaning against a telephone pole was a huge silver wing with the star of the U.S. Air Force on it. A section of the road had been roped off, and debris from the fallen B-29 was arranged in the middle of the street like an exhibition of war loot. Hundreds of people lined the sidewalks watching. A gang of old Army Reservists came up pulling a cart piled high with fragments of the B-29's wings and cowling. Proudly they began lowering their trophies to the ground.

"God, it's huge," said Yamada, gazing up at the wing.

Even Ken, who had seen one of them before, found himself marveling again at the sight of it.

Spread on the ground before them were the bombardier's seat, the radar set, machine guns, the radio, a single boot, a helmet, and an oxygen mask, all of them scorched and damaged. An old man with white hair, evidently the local civil defense chief, explained where each item was "captured." With a look of great pride he told them how bits of the giant airplane had been scattered over twenty blocks, from Jimbocho all the way to Suruga Hill, and how he was quite sure they would find a lot more of it. It was almost as if he had shot the thing down himself.

"What's this?" Ken picked up a small, thick book.

"Probably a Bible," said Yamada. "The Yankees always carry one."

Ken read the black lettering on the brown cover: *Flight and Operational Manual, Boeing B-29, 1943.* "This looks important. They found one in the wreck in Kyushu, but most of it was too badly burned to read. It should tell us everything about it."

Wakana grabbed the manual from Ken and stared at its inscrutable text. "You're right, it *is* important. I want you to get to work translating this as of tonight." The Major bustled around the neat assortment of fragments. "The engines," he shouted suddenly. "Where the hell are the engines? Without them this is just a pile of junk."

Taking offense at this but unable to complain, the civil defense chief turned away and started shouting at onlookers, telling them to keep back. The crowd of primary school children, office workers in civil defense suits, and old women in tattered kimonos seemed far more interested in the display than in the block of buildings going up in flames on the other side of the road. One young man kicked a piece of the wing, shouting, "Goddamn it, this feels good!"

"Out of the way! Out of the way!" a voice called, and a squad of civil defense workers led by a policeman came pulling a cart on which lay a bundle wrapped in a straw mat. As they lowered the bundle, the straw mat fell away, revealing the corpse of a young American pilot. The crowd surged forward.

The left half of the face had been blown off, but the right half showed handsome, regular features. The young man's unopened parachute was still strapped to his back. Ken ordered the civil defense chief to search him for any personal effects. Squatting by the body, he started going through his pockets and found a pistol, a knife, a water canteen, an aluminum lunchbox, and a bundle of maps tied together. The lunch was half eaten. Burned scraps of beef were stuck to the box.

"They get more to eat than we do!" someone shouted.

When they opened the pilot's bulletproof vest and undid the top of his flying suit, they found a round identification tag hanging from his neck: KENNETH HAMILTON STUART B. 1923. He was twenty-one years old. *Ken, you and I have the same name.* In his pocket they found a photograph.

"Let me see that," Ken said, taking it from the civil defense chief. It was a baptism picture. The boy's mother had written "God bless you" on it. There was a small imprint at the bottom of the picture which said: "San Jose, Calif." So this Ken was a boy from California. Mentally Ken made the sign of the cross. He was ashamed of himself for not doing it openly in front of the crowd. He thought of George and Paul: *the two American pilots I killed were also young men like him.* He could feel, pressing on him like a heavy weight, the grief of their mothers when they were notified of their sons' deaths.

Yamada tapped him on the shoulder. "The Major's calling us. They found one of the engines."

Under the direction of Warrant Officer Mitsuda, the whole collection was loaded onto the trucks. By now the fire had devoured all the buildings on the other side of the road. White smoke smoldered among the charred remains.

They drove past the street where, last November, Ken, Yamada, Mitsuda, and Haniyu had bought identical scarves with rising sun designs on them as emblems of their friendship. All the shops had burned down. The black ground was dappled with snow.

"I wonder what happened to the old man who ran it," said Yamada.

Ahead of them were a few blocks that had escaped intact—a district of publishing companies and printing shops—and they could see the silhouettes of people working in the windows. Their guide, an old Army Reservist, pointed to the house where the B-29's engine had been found. He told them the massive piece of machinery—eighteen air-cooled cylinders—had fallen through the roof and the second floor, landing right in the middle of the living room on the ground floor. There it still lay, on its propeller.

The house was empty. Apparently its occupants had moved to the countryside, as had most Tokyoites who had someone in the countryside to take them in.

The living room was thick with the smell of gasoline. The slightest spark could blow the whole place up. Major Wakana ordered the police to evacuate the surrounding houses and keep the onlookers at a safe distance.

As Ken was searching the bottom of the engine for the supercharger, he noticed another engine half-buried in the earth beneath the floorboards. He called everyone over to look, but they couldn't see very well in the dim light. Ken wanted to use a flashlight, but they couldn't risk a short-circuit in the gasoline-filled room. So first they had the technicians stop the fuel from leaking, then they opened the doors and windows to air the room, and only then did Ken crawl under the floorboards with a flashlight. What he found was an engine from a Hayate fighter. There was no mistaking it. The B-29 had been brought down by a Kamikaze. Ken noticed a piece of cloth entangled in the air condenser. He gasped. It was Haniyu's muffler. It had the same design as the other ones they'd bought. Ken yanked at it and tore it out of the engine. The shredded cloth was smeared with blood and clumps of hair.

5

Feeling as if the morning sun was dazzling him, Ken opened his eyes, but found himself in a dim, gray room. There were signs of dawn outside: the stars had faded in the pale blue sky, and the hills loomed black and distinct against it. The snow had finally let up. Ken couldn't stop shaking—apparently his fever hadn't yet subsided. Yesterday, after his detail had hoisted the engines from the B-29 and the Hayate onto the truck and returned to the air base, he had started getting chills and a terrible headache. When Yamada examined him, he had a fever of 103°. He was told he had a bad cold, but there was a chance it might turn into pneumonia, and he was ordered to stay in bed. Yamada put him on one of the examining tables in the emergency room, laid four blankets over him, and placed ice packs filled with snow on his forehead. He also gave him various shots. This should have sent him quickly to sleep, but instead the freezing sensation in his head kept him awake. Too much had happened in the past two days—no, the past few months—with one overwhelming incident coming after another. Now each in turn appeared to him like a dream, then faded away . . . though nothing faded entirely, bits lingering in his fevered mind.

"Anna wasn't there," he told Yamada, breathing painfully. "She was in Tokyo with my father."

"Oh . . ." Yamada sighed. "Ken, I think I'm in love with her. But I've told myself it's wrong to fall in love. I may die any day now, like Haniyu."

"Yes, like Haniyu," he repeated mechanically. His own thoughts were of Margaret. Suddenly he decided to tell Yamada about it.

"When I was up in Karuizawa I let myself fall in love with a woman, too. In fact I'd been in love with her for quite a while, but like you I told myself it was wrong to take it any further at a time like this. Well, yesterday I changed my mind. I decided I'm going to marry her, and I took it further."

"You did? Just like that? That takes guts."

"It wasn't guts, it was the opposite. No, it was neither. It just happened naturally, that's all. She's someone you know."

"I can guess who she is. But what about the consequences?"

"The consequences? Well, I've thought about it. We may die tomorrow. But then maybe we won't. There's a good chance we won't survive, but to let that dominate our lives—a man's *and* a woman's lives—when we don't know for sure, is just presuming . . . Guts doesn't really come into it."

"I see . . ."

"And if you really love Anna, for God's sake tell her, tell her now. If you survive you won't regret it, and if you die at least you won't carry the secret to your grave."

"You've changed, you never used to talk like this. It makes me feel uncomfortable."

Ken gave a loud, cheerful laugh, and was soon asleep.

Now, some nine hours later, he realized that what he thought was the morning sun was really a dream image of Margaret.

He tried to stand up. He seemed to be floating lightly—not a bad feeling at all. Quietly, so as not to wake the comfortably snoring Yamada, he slipped on his sweater and overcoat, and put on his flying cap. He pushed the door open, and the cold air felt refreshing on his hot cheeks. As he walked along, checking the firmness of the snow-covered ground with each step, his breath trailed from his mouth like a white streamer.

The main runway was lined from one end to the other with little black spots; they were people clearing the snow. As he came nearer he could see, alongside the soldiers, local women who had been drafted to work there. It was hard labor. First they swept the snow into piles and shoveled it into large straw baskets. Then they hung the baskets on bamboo poles. Two of them shouldered each pole, with the basket of snow dangling in the middle, and carried it to the edge of the runway. They had probably been working like this since midnight, when the snow let up. About two-thirds of the runway had already been cleared, revealing the red earth underneath. The soldiers and women worked silently in the freezing cold. Mechanics were attending to the planes in the hangars and on the approach paths. Under the glare of spotlights, they fastened screws and hammered the bent duraluminum back into shape, all the while blowing on numb fingers.

To the east, beyond the runway, he could see the Tachikawa aircraft factory. Yesterday's fire was finally under control. Across the plain stretched a peaceful snowscape. The horizon was first a thin band of red, then streaks of gold spread above the red, and a bright orange sun pushed its way into the sky. Sparks of gold fell across the snow-covered plain like a thousand star shell flares. The airplanes and the wind tee began to cast long shadows.

As the sun rose it gave off a little warmth. Above the purple range of the Chichibu Mountains stood a distinct red Fuji. Since being stationed here Ken had grown used to the sight of this mountain, but he had never had the leisure to appreciate it in its full glory. Suddenly he thought, *Please, let nothing happen today.* After its ferocious attacks of the past two days, surely even the U.S. Air Force, with all its firepower and fighting spirit, would want to take a breather.

The chilly blue sky held a promise of spring, and the sweet smell of the plum blossom in front of the control tower was a clear sign that winter was coming to an end. *Soon the snow'll melt away, the cherry trees will burst into flower, and when spring's in full swing, Margaret and I will marry. I don't care if she is a foreigner, I'm going to marry her. And if this war ever ends, we're going to travel to her country, to Switzerland . . .* For a moment, he felt a pang of remorse as he remembered Lauren. *I was going to meet you when peace comes. If only peace would come . . .* Peace. He could no longer even imagine the world that word referred to. All the duties binding him (not obligations but duties, the word his father used)—the development of a new fighter plane, his research on ways of countering attacks at high altitude, the actual fighting he had done—all these tasks he had undertaken so that his own country, the port he had laid anchor in, might win the war. But now there wasn't a chance in hell that Japan would win. Ken could see with his own eyes that the gap in air power was just too overwhelming. Right after Pearl Harbor they had been able to maintain a certain edge. The Zeros and the Hayabusas were better planes than any of the fighters the British and the Americans put up against them, and their own pilots gave as good as they got. But when the Yankees started building P-51 Mustangs and Grumman F-6-Fs, and then the massive B-29s, the Japanese planes hadn't a chance. And now the bombings were taking their toll on the aircraft factories. They weren't turning out finished products with the skill they once did. They were running out of spare parts, they were getting sloppy on the assembly line. And once the planes left the runway they were being flown on watered-down fuel by inexperienced pilots. For the first time, a new thought had forced its way not just into his mind but into the minds of those around him: that Japan was headed for certain defeat, and that until that day came, it was their duty—their "impossible duty"—to fight on.

Yamada came over, his plump shadow trailing behind him like a clown.

"You're up early. How's the fever?"

"I feel a bit hot, but I must be a lot better, because this cold air actually feels refreshing."

"Glad to hear it. But you'd better be careful, the flu this year has been as persistent as the B-29s. Ha ha!" Yamada took a deep breath. "Nice weather we got today. It'll probably get a little warmer. Hey, let's go eat. I heard they repaired the mess hall."

Engines were being started up. The propellers began whirring on two planes, then five. Some of the aircraft began taxiing onto the auxiliary runway, since people were still at work clearing the main one. The sun had climbed high above the horizon, and the snow on the roofs of the hangars gleamed silver-white.

The officers' mess had been destroyed, and a temporary dining area, with wooden tables and benches, had been set up inside a tent. As Yamada and Ken were eating breakfast, Major Wakana came over and sat down across from them. Wakana hadn't shaved, and white bristles were prominent on his pointed chin.

"We got the B-29 engine to work," he told them. "We spent all last night checking it out. The cylinders, the supercharger, and the running gear were all in perfect condition. Unfortunately, some of the wiring and an exhaust port were damaged, but we can probably fix them."

They had never seen the Major in such a good mood. It was rare enough for him to even sit at the Lieutenants' table. He chattered on and on about the engine.

"We're going to fiddle about with it in the workshop this morning. Kurushima, I'd like you to give us a hand. That damned wiring is a problem. A real pity. If only our pilot had crashed at a steeper angle."

Ken bristled at the insinuation that Haniyu had bungled his mission, that he hadn't killed himself quite "correctly." But he remembered that he was under suspicion, and had to be careful with his superiors, so he bore his indignation in silence.

In a casual way, suggesting the thought had just struck him, he asked, "By the way, sir, have Haniyu's remains been found yet?"

"No. However, judging from the damage to the engine, we figure he must have crashed a bit below the center; the B-29's propeller probably cut his cockpit to shreds, so his body must have been chopped up into little bits."

Ken and Yamada looked at each other. It sounded as if he was talking about meat. Ken remembered the way one of his superior officers had described an accident at the air show: when one of the planes ran off the runway and plowed into the crowd of spectators, there had been "a burst of red spray."

"But, sir, even the 'bits' haven't been found. I have a request. I'd like to be assigned to the search party."

"There's not going to be a search party." Wakana was becoming irritated again. "Judging from the scientific evidence, it's obvious that the pilot is dead and his remains can't be found."

"I don't mean to contradict you, sir, but scientific deductions always include the possibility of error."

"I'm well aware of that, Lieutenant. But a more urgent task is to test that bomber engine."

"No, sir. If Haniyu's body has been scattered about, then recovery of those remains will become more difficult the longer we wait. That, surely, is the more urgent task."

Wakana slammed his bowl of *miso* soup on the table. "Get your priorities straight! We're being pounded by that plane, so discovering its weak points is *crucial*! You, Lieutenant, will spend the day getting that B-29 engine running. That's an order."

"Yes, sir." There was to be no further discussion. An order from a major to a lieutenant was tantamount to a command from the Emperor, even if the Imperial Will itself was flexible—determined by the whims of that superior.

When Wakana left, Ken and Yamada glanced at each other. They couldn't say a thing about him in front of the other men, but each knew exactly what the other was thinking.

Dressed in a mechanic's overalls and lying flat on his back, Ken peered up into the narrow space between the engine's cylinders and began unfastening, one by one, the electric cables there. The tips of his oil-smeared fingers were bleeding, cut by the split copper wiring; his back and buttocks were numb from lying on the freezing ground. At this rate, his cold was bound to get worse.

Just then, an air raid warning came over the loudspeaker. Taking advantage of the weather, three squadrons of light aircraft had been spotted over the Boso Peninsula heading for Tokyo, with another eighty heavy bombers—it could only mean B-29s—coming from further west. All available planes were to take off immediately. Several of the bomber specialists had been helping to clean the B-29's cylinders, but they all left. Major Wakana was called over to headquarters. Only a few mechanics and Ken remained behind.

As they finished repairing the broken cables, they heard the roar of airplanes approaching and the tattoo of rapid gunfire. "Take cover!"

someone shouted, and the mechanics all jumped to their feet and ran for the shelter outside. Ken recognized the sound of Grumman F-6-Fs, firing 12.7-mm. cannons. Bullets came whizzing through the roof of the hangar and bounced off the building's metal frame. Ken stayed where he was; rather than try to make it to the shelter, he'd be safer here under the engine. But the next burst of gunfire, after riddling five planes being refitted for Kamikaze missions, hit the fuel tank of the B-29 engine. A few seconds after Ken rolled away the thing burst into flames. Ken heard two, then three explosions behind him as he ran out of the hangar and jumped into the open shelter. There was the sound of antiaircraft fire. He looked up and saw six Grummans coming in, two at a time, in a dive-bombing formation. A dozen Hayates and Shokis were in flames on the runway, along with several hangars. After a final sweep around the airfield the enemy planes fled away toward the horizon, and a few seconds later disappeared. It had been a lightning attack.

"Are you all okay?" Ken shouted. One by one the mechanics emerged from the shelter. Luckily nobody had been injured. The B-29 engine they'd been working on since the previous evening, however, had been reduced to a blackened lump of metal.

Then came the distinctive throb of B-29s. Eight of the giant planes, their silver fuselages looking dangerously beautiful in the blue sky, were coming in from the west. Ken couldn't see any vapor trails, though. They were surprisingly low, at around 6,000 meters, presumably in order to get cover from carrier-based fighters. Ken narrowed his eyes and, sure enough, spotted an escort of several Grummans above them. The whole leisurely procession was passing to the east. As he searched the western sky, he saw another squadron of American planes following behind, just silver sparkles in the sky around Mount Fuji.

Ken turned to one of the maintenance crew. "Hey, do you have any Hayates ready for flying?"

"Yes, there are five reserve planes for the fighter squadron. They weren't hit in the raid just now."

"Good, start one up for me. I'll be taking it up."

The man looked at him dubiously.

"What're you waiting for, soldier? I'm a member of the fighter squadron."

Yamada found him putting on his flying suit in the changing room.

"What are you doing? You've still got the flu. You can't go up in your condition."

"It's all right. Those guys are only at 6,000 meters. It's no big deal."

"Don't be a fool. Even at that altitude your air pressure's cut in half."

"It's *all right*."

Yamada looked incredulous. All the pilots knew the dangers of flying with influenza. It made the Eustachian tubes swell, blocking the passage of air between the middle ear and the nasal cavity. The intense pressure of trapped air could rupture the eardrum. Pilots were absolutely forbidden to go up if they had the slightest symptoms of flu. Yamada kept shaking his head, but Ken refused to listen.

"You're being reckless, Kurushima . . . Incidentally, they found Haniyu's body. He landed on the banks of the Kanda River. He was half buried in the ground, but he was in one piece. Haniyu was reckless too. He hadn't bothered to strap his parachute on."

"So they found him? At least they can give him a decent funeral now."

"Mind *you* don't forget your parachute."

"Don't worry." Ken tied the parachute straps around his waist.

"Be careful." He touched Ken's forehead. "You've still got a fever."

"I'm not a Kamikaze. If I attack I'll do it with my guns."

"Of course! Look, for God's sake, don't do anything crazy. Come back alive."

"Oh, I'll be back." Ken smiled at him. "You know, I don't think Haniyu came in from the front at all. I think he came down on them from behind, aiming for the cockpit. I looked at that B-29 engine myself, and that's the only conclusion I could reach."

"Then why didn't you tell Major Wakana?"

"There's no point. You can't disagree with him. He's the great expert on engines."

Yamada followed Ken out to the plane and watched him climb on board.

"Shouldn't you tell headquarters you're going out solo?"

"The squadron's been given an order to attack. I'm a member of the squadron."

"But there's been no order for solo attacks."

"Well, Lieutenant Yamada, why don't you just go and report me? I'm going up alone, orders or not. Look, the whole damn sky is plastered with enemy planes. How can I stay down here and not do anything? And another thing, Yamada. I am truly sick of following orders."

"I know how you feel . . . just don't do anything crazy."

The Hayate stood on the runway, washed in the clean sunlight. The propellers started turning, and a satisfying roar filled the air. At a hand signal from Ken, one of the ground staff pulled the chocks away. Ken nodded at Yamada, and taxied onto the runway. There were voices on his radio—loud, insistent voices. Headquarters was calling him. They were going to order him to stop.

Ken didn't want to argue. He switched the radio off and started down the runway on his own. At full throttle, he roared down the snow-dappled strip and lifted off. His guns were fully loaded and the plane was heavy, but his engine was running well.

He deliberately headed due north, away from all the hostile aircraft, then banked to the east and began a steep climb. Apparently the Grummans hadn't noticed him, for they all stayed in formation, heading east. Ken guessed the bombers were at 5,000 meters, their fighter escort another 500 higher. When he got up to 6,000 meters, he noticed three Japanese planes at 8,000. They looked like Shokis. Yes, three of them, heading straight down for the B-29s. Ken felt as if he were watching a huge movie screen. As the attacking planes closed in, the Grummans scattered like a school of startled fish, then swept back, several of them taking on each of the intruders. The first Shoki flared like a match and fell away. The second went into a steep dive and managed to escape. Making straight for the tail of one of the B-29s, the last of them was only seconds away from a collision when, like a moth flying into a light trap, it hit a curtain of bright tracer fire and dropped away, tumbling in a tailspin. The sight showed just how tight their defenses were.

Ken decided to go up to 7,000 meters. The sky was clear up here, his horizontal visibility excellent. 1,000 meters below him, though, was a thin layer of cloud that he could take advantage of for a sudden attack.

The air pressure dropped. Ken felt a stabbing pain in his ears. He blocked his nose and tried to swallow hard, but it didn't seem to help. The flu was doing this to him, just as Yamada had warned. He was about to switch on his thermal suit when he realized he wasn't wearing one. Still, the oxygen was flowing smoothly in his mask.

7,000 meters. He was right above Tokyo now. He watched as the B-29s started unloading their bombs on the city. Flowers of bright flame unfurled on the ground, one after another. Their aim was incredibly accurate: the bombs were dropping only on the districts that had survived the previous raids. There was scattered antiaircraft fire, but it had no effect at all. With the sun at his back, Ken stayed above them, waiting for his chance. Then, from somewhere out of the upper sky, he saw a single Hayate streak down toward the swarm of bombers. It was a Kamikaze, with a bright red rising sun on its fuselage. The pilot might have been one of the teenagers he'd taught to fly himself, a kid like PFC Honda. The pilot had obviously chosen a group of B-29s without a fighter escort, and he made straight for the lead plane. He took a hit on his right wing, and flames shot up. He flew on—on through a thicket of tracer—then crashed into its left wing where it joined the body. The huge frame of the bomber rocked, and burst into flames. Four, then six of its crew ejected. Their parachutes opened. The giant aircraft began to tumble, a trail of purple flames behind it, turning huge spirals in the sky. But what had happened to the Hayate? It must have burst apart on impact. But no, there was one of its wings, and a piece of its rudder, fluttering down. Apparently most of the fuselage was buried in the B-29.

After losing its leader, the rest of the formation was in disarray; the spacing between the planes was ragged, their payloads falling wide of the mark. Ken picked out the one at the rear. 1,000 meters above it, he pushed down hard on his control stick. *Mama, here I go!* Engine at full power, wind shrieking, speed 700 kph, no flutter. He knew every inch of his Hayate. The target plane pulled out of formation. *They see me coming. They're going to shoot.* Tracer bullets hurtled at him from every direction—like a bunch of bristling spines. *There it is.* The join on the main wing, only lightly covered by defensive fire: *that's what Haniyu must have aimed for.* 300 meters away now. He opens fire. The guns don't work. *What's wrong? Damn it, we're hit.* Puffs of white smoke from his fuselage and wing. He stabs at the firing button, but nothing happens. Either they've jammed or they've taken an enemy bullet. He's hit again, and again. Flames are now on either side of him. The fuel tank is on fire. *It's burning hot.* Another 100 meters. *My God, it's a huge plane.* The gunner on top swivels this way. *He's going to shoot. Crash before he hits me!* 50 meters . . . 20 . . . 5. A look of horror on the gunner's face. *I did it.* IMPACT!

A spray of yellowish powder bursts all around him. Powder? No, blood. *This burning smell, it's the smell of blood.* Down there the white city streets, Tokyo—no, rice fields out in the country, fields covered with old snow. *It's not hot any more.* The bomber is gone.

I'm swinging. Back in our house in Chicago—the swings on our bright green lawn. I'm swinging back and forth. I can see the leaves in the trees, now close, now far away. "Mama, push me harder." "Ken, be careful, you'll fall off." "Harder, Mama, push me harder!"

Someone's calling, "Lauren?" A man's voice. Not George, but Uncle Norman.

A nice voice says, "I'm over here, Daddy." And where am I? I'm swinging through the air. Ken Little, swinging on the bright green lawn, with Mama pushing me. Mama's white dress, her wedding dress, opens in the wind like a big white umbrella. Will Maggie wear a white wedding dress like that? I'm swinging, swinging. How do you say "I'm swinging" in Japanese? How do you say "I love you" in Japanese? I love you, Maggie!

It's not a white dress that opened up there, it's a parachute. My God, I've been thinking all this in English. I've been feeling this in English, dreaming this in English. What happened to my Japanese?

It's okay. Umi. The sea. I can remember "the sea" in Japanese. That blue expanse down there is water. A beach stretching below me like an undiscovered land, a soft white line of waves breaking at its edge. What country am I drifting to?

Wait, I know that beach. That's the Chiba coastline. Row after row of white waves ending on the shore. I'm swinging. The wind is warm, as if blowing from some southern land. The way it's carrying me, I'll probably make it to that field near the sea. I'm going to live. Maggie! I made it.

No movement in my right leg. It's completely numb. But now some-thing, some part of my body, is beginning to move. It feels like someone else's. I can move my right leg . . . and, God, there's a hell of a pain from my knee on up as soon as I start. But it doesn't matter, I can move. My arms . . . my left arm's limp. Why is it so wet? Blood. Drenched from my shoulder down, fresh blood. Dyeing my flying suit red, merging with the rising sun at my neck. My arm . . . feels like I'm dangling a hunk of red meat. I'm still bleeding, a spray of blood. Maybe I can untie my muffler with my right hand and press it against my shoulder. Strange that I don't feel any pain. Ah, now the muffler is all red.

A grove of pines by the shore, a breakwater. I want to make a good landing, but how can I on this useless leg? I know, I'll land with all my weight on my left leg. Like being tackled in rugby.

I'm down. I can see clear across the rice fields. It's warm here. Still winter, but the fields are covered with rape flowers. I'm home, back in my own country. Home from some strange, distant place.

People running through the rape flowers. Several men. Men in tat-tered clothes. They must be from the nearby village. "Hey, I'm over here!" I try to shout, but my voice is gone. Was I hit in the throat too? Anyway, I made it. I'm safe.

Ken raised himself with his right hand and nodded at his res-cuers—men with coarse, sunburned faces.

They didn't nod back.

"Amerika hei da!"

"Amerika hei da! Yatchimae!"

The men raised their bamboo spears. One of them thrust deep into Ken's chest. The sharp blade pierced his flesh, penetrated to the very core of his body. An older man thrust his spear into Ken's throat.

What's going on?

A third man aimed his spear.

"No!" Ken screamed in English. "No! I'm Japanese!"

But the sound just escaped through the hole in his throat like the whistle of a flute.

6

The snow had soaked Eri's white *tabi* socks. Her toes were numb, and she couldn't feel the thongs on her wooden clogs. The struts underneath were caked with mud and snow. Aware that she mustn't slip, she mustn't fall now, she walked carefully, a step at a time. It had never taken her more than a few minutes to walk the length of the road leading up to the gate of the primary school. But now as she marched at the head of her brother's funeral procession, the road seemed absurdly long.

"Eri, wait," her father called to her. He bent down and started scraping the mud and snow off her clogs with his hands.

The head of the Military Police stopped him. "I'm sorry, I should have noticed. Your Excellency, you mustn't get your hands dirty." So saying, he ordered an assistant to clean her clogs with a twig from one of the larches by the road.

Since Eri was carrying an urn containing the ashes of a Hero of the Japanese Empire, as soon as she stopped the entire procession behind her also stopped. Eri was followed by Anna carrying a photograph draped in black of Ken in uniform. Behind her came her father, and then a meandering line of dignitaries: the mayor, the station-master, the Chief of Police, the postmaster. The old soldiers of the Provincial Veterans' Association and the black kimonoed matrons of the Women's Patriotic League brought up the rear.

Eri began walking again, with her eyes on the ground. The people lining the road bowed deeply as the procession passed. One could tell at a glance which were the locals—in gray work clothes—and which the evacuees from Tokyo—wearing slightly better clothes. Several foreigners were among them, looking quite out of place as they stood there staring. The Military Police were out in full force, forming a solid wall of uniforms and sabers in front of the crowd.

When it had been announced that a municipal funeral would be held for the late Lieutenant Ken Kurushima, a dispute had immediately arisen between the military and civilian police forces over who would provide the official escort. The Military Police insisted it was only natural that they should do so, this being the funeral of an Army officer, while the regular police claimed it was their prerogative, because the late Lieutenant had been a resident of Karuizawa. A compromise was finally worked out, whereby the Military Police would escort the procession from the railroad station to the primary school where the ceremony was to be held, and the civilian police would line the road for the rest of the way, from the school to the Kurushimas' house. When Saburo heard about the dispute, he muttered that it sounded like a couple of gangs of small-time hoods quarreling over turf.

At first, Saburo had flatly refused when the mayor suggested a municipal funeral for his son. But the latter had begged him, saying the young airman's death at the hands of their American enemies had been reported in the newspapers, and the local government would lose face if it didn't do *something* to welcome the return of this Hero of the Empire to his hometown. To this, the Chief of Police added a patriotic appeal, saying a ceremony for the Lieutenant would help stoke the local people's resolve to fight on against the monsters responsible for his death. And finally the commander of the Military Police had put in a plea, mentioning that his superiors wanted the funeral to be in keeping with the dignity of the Army Air Corps.

Saburo gave in. Eri had been privy to all the political maneuverings at the police station, and now when she saw the extravagant escort of MPs they'd arranged, she had to bite down hard on her lip to keep from smiling. All that obsequious bowing and scraping by the commander—"Your Excellency, you mustn't get your hands dirty." Ha! Obviously the pompous old fool was worried that someone might take a picture of the Ambassador bending down to scrape the mud off her feet, and send it to the newspapers.

The procession wound its way to the front gate of the primary school. On entering, they all made the deepest of bows to the little building (there was one in every school in the Empire) in which the photographs of the Emperor and Empress were enshrined. Then they moved across the schoolyard, where the students were lined up in their black shorts. Eri felt sorry for the children, who had been standing there waiting for them, shivering in the cold.

After placing her brother's urn on the altar, Eri took a seat. Discreetly she slipped out of her clogs and rubbed her frozen feet together. But her middle toe and her little toe were swollen to twice their normal size with chilblains, and the rubbing only made them worse. She should have worn boots instead.

The Shinto priest glided solemnly up to the altar, and the ceremony began. Eri hardly listened to the speeches. All these long-winded eulogies by people who didn't even know Ken, who couldn't have cared less about him if they had known him—didn't any of them feel embarrassed by it all? She stared with hate in her eyes at the old men who got up, one after another, to drone on about the heroic young airman. Her gaze wandered over the crowd, seeing few faces she recognized. She looked at the shivering white knees of the schoolchildren. Then, with a start, she noticed the dazed look on her father's face.

Two days ago her father and Anna had suddenly returned from Tokyo, their faces streaked with soot and their clothes full of burn holes, and told them about a massive air raid, and how they had seen the whole city burning, and how they themselves had barely managed to escape the fire that had consumed their own house in Nagata-cho. As they talked, Eri noticed there was something wrong with her father. He would suddenly fall silent in the middle of a sentence. When she told him to go on—"Then what happened, Papa?"—he would start talking about something else entirely. To Eri's horror he began to remind her of poor mad Mrs. Hendersen. He would open his lips to say something, then stare emptily into the distance, his glasses resting on the tip of his nose. Yesterday and today he seemed to be gradually returning to normal, but now he had that dazed look again, his mouth open, gazing into the distance. It looked undignified. "Papa!" she whispered, nudging his arm with her shoulder. She was relieved when he answered sternly "What *is* it, Eri?"

Everyone stood up to sing "Should I set forth upon the sea," the hymn for the war dead.

> Should I set forth upon the sea,
> let my body sink into the waves.
> Should I set forth into the mountains,
> let my body turn to grass.
> I shall have no regrets
> should I die a soldier's death
> for My Lord the Emperor.

Ken had always joked that the hymn was all wrong. "With just the sea and the mountains, the Navy and the Army, it's behind the times," he said. "What about people like me—the fliers? When I go I want them to sing, 'Should I set forth into the sky, let my body glide through the air.'" If Ken only knew . . . She wished she had talked with him a while longer that day. "When will you be back?" she'd asked casually, and he had said, "With the war like this, who knows?" His smiling face was the last she had seen of him. She began to cry.

The official ceremony ended, they gathered up the urn and the photograph, and the procession formed up again. The sky had cleared. They passed through a phalanx of policemen, who lent an official, slightly sinister note to the proceedings. But the road was much more slippery than before, and Eri could hardly walk straight. As she led the marchers past the livery stable and onto the path that led to their villa, her muddy clogs slipped. It may have been because her tired legs faltered the moment she saw the roof of her house; anyway she slipped, and someone grabbed her around the waist, letting his hands linger there a few seconds longer than necessary. She immediately recognized the nicotine-stained fingers of the Chief of Police, and the stench of the cheap Asahi cigarettes he chain-smoked, as he said, "The urn must be heavy for a girl like you." *Heavy? You must be kidding. It's too light. It's obscene the way that Ken's become so light.*

Yoshiko came out of the house to meet them. Eri's father gave a brief speech thanking everyone, and then they all broke up, leaving the Kurushima family and a few close friends to go inside, shutting the sliding doors behind them.

Alice, Margaret, and Father Manabe, the new pastor, were waiting for them in the parlor. The pastor was there to perform the private ceremony.

"You must be freezing," said Alice. She was in black mourning clothes. "Come on in and warm yourselves by the fire."

Yoshiko put some more firewood in the stove, but the wood was damp and merely smoked. They looked around for some paper to burn, but they couldn't find any. Paper was scarce in the last winter of the war. Every sheet of newspaper was saved for toilet paper or for wrapping things in.

"Here, burn this." Saburo brought in a heavy bundle tied with string.

"Papa!" Anna grabbed him by the arm. "That's valuable, they're your diplomatic papers."

"Go ahead, use them. I don't need them any more."

"But, Papa." Anna untied the thick sheaf and laid the documents on the table. There were handwritten memos on Foreign Ministry stationery, typed documents in English and German, and notebooks in leather bindings. "We went all the way to Tokyo to save these. Didn't you say you needed them to write your memoirs?"

"Burn them," he said. "I don't need them any more."

Papa, are you in your right mind? Eri and her mother searched his face for a clue to his behavior.

Saburo looked at his wife and daughters. Stroking his white moustache, he told them, "I've left the Foreign Ministry for good. I sent in my resignation yesterday. My life as a diplomat has been an utter failure. I failed to stop the war. *I failed*, and the result is the death of my own son. Writing my memoirs would be an utterly pointless undertaking now. I want to burn it all. Burn that diplomatic life. If it can provide a little warmth for my son's funeral, that would be some consolation."

"Oh Papa, I understand." Anna started crying and pressed her face against his shoulder.

Saburo took a handful of documents and stuffed them into the stove. The papers smoldered for a few seconds, as if reluctant to burn, then burst into flames. The flames illuminated his haggard face.

"Let me do it," Anna said. Gently pulling the sheets out one by one, she fed them into the stove, then put firewood on top of them. The stove came to life and warmed the room with a pleasant crackling sound.

The pastor began the ceremony. They said a prayer for the dead, then sang a hymn. This, the last of Ken's many funerals, was his only Christian one.

Halfway through the ceremony, Margaret began to choke on her tears. Her choking turned into a loud cough. Eri rubbed her friend on the back as she clutched her stomach, doubled up with pain. Eri put her arm around her thin shoulders and led her out to the veranda.

"Thanks, Eri."

The two of them sat down in the wicker chairs. Margaret bent over and began to vomit. The painful retching continued for several minutes. Eri looked bewildered and afraid.

"Maggie, what's wrong?" She took out a handkerchief and wiped Margaret's forehead, pushing back the damp hair.

"It's okay, it's nothing." Margaret straightened up and gave her a cheerful smile, as if the whole thing had been a joke.

"Don't scare me like that." Eri was still feeling shocked, but was relieved by the bright expression on her friend's face. She smiled back at her.

Outside, the air was full of black butterflies, a swarm of them, fluttering over the snow-dappled garden. They rose so buoyantly, each in its own direction, that it took Eri and Margaret a few moments to realize that these weren't living things they were looking at but the ashes of Saburo's career rising from the chimney.

7

The radio in the Kurushima house was a German one bought years ago in Berlin, and when the Emperor spoke that August day in 1945 his voice came over loud and clear. It was the first time in history that an Emperor had deigned to address his subjects over the radio. But His Majesty's speech was full of difficult classical Chinese words—he might as well have been speaking in Latin—and although Alice could make out a phrase that sounded like "to bear the unbearable, to endure the unendurable," most of what the quick, high-pitched voice was saying was simply incomprehensible to her.

The Emperor's voice was quavery; he even stumbled on some of his lines. Alice was surprised how *undignified* he sounded. Could this really be the voice of His Imperial Majesty, the Son of Heaven, the Supreme Commander of the Armed Forces of Japan?

But Saburo recognized the voice right away and bowed his head from the very first word. "Yes, that's His Majesty," he said with a hint of nostalgia, and listened intently to the speech from beginning to end. When it was over his cheeks were streaked with tears. From the expression on his face Alice knew Japan had lost the war.

Saburo turned to his family. Eri was away at the police station working, but Anna and Yoshiko were there. "*Senso wa owatta,*" he said. "Japan has surrendered to the Allied powers." He started to repeat what he had said in English for Alice's sake, but she nodded and told him:

"*Wakarimashita.* I understood everything you just said in Japanese."

Since her son's death Alice had taken a sudden and enthusiastic interest in learning Japanese. With Saburo as her teacher over the last

517

few months, she had reached the point where she could get by in everyday conversation, and she was even able to write a few simple sentences in the complicated Japanese script. The notebook she always carried with her was now a vocabulary book, with page after page of Japanese words on one side and their English meanings on the other.

"What a stupid, worthless war," said Saburo, with a heave of his shoulders. "We've lost everything."

Alice gently tapped her husband on the arm and smiled. "Yes, but peace has come. Let's go tell Ken about it."

"Yes," he replied. "Let's do that."

Ken's grave lay among the trees in the larch wood behind the house. There was a little tombstone they had made by piling up pieces of lava from Mount Asama into a little pyramid. This simple grave bore no inscription, but the care the family took of it was obvious from the bouquets set round about it. The flowers were always kept fresh. Purple bellflowers and pink convolvulus, the wildflowers Alice had picked, swayed in the midday breeze. The cicadas cried loud and insistent, and the sky was filled with great banks of cloud. In Tokyo the heat must have been unbearable, but here in the highlands, deep inside the wood, the air was cool, and the moist surface of the moss growing on the grave looked almost refreshing.

Epilogue

Margaret Hendersen died of tuberculosis, not long after giving birth to a baby boy. "Our baby," as Alice called him, was fathered by Ken.

Ken Jr. was raised by Anna and Shigeo Yamada, who were married in 1946.

Eri married an officer in the U.S. Army of Occupation and moved to the United States.

Saburo Kurushima was cleared of all charges by the Chief Prosecutor in the international war crimes tribunal, without being brought to trial. This was partly on the strength of Congressional evidence given by Joseph Grew, former U.S. Ambassador to Japan, who thought it "exceedingly doubtful" that Saburo had known in advance of the Japanese attack on Pearl Harbor and described him as "decidedly pro-American in outlook and sentiments." Saburo died in April 1954, soon after hearing that Eri had given him a second grandchild. An obituary in an American newspaper called him "another victim of Pearl Harbor."

Alice lived on for another twenty years, sharing the small house that Anna and her husband built on the site of the old one in Nagata-cho which had burned down. At the age of eighty, she suffered a sudden heart attack. In the ambulance on the way to the hospital, knowing her death was imminent, she muttered, "*Watakushi wa Nihonjin desu*"—I am Japanese.

On a gravestone in Aoyama Cemetery, her name is to the right, with Saburo's on the left, and Ken's in the middle. Above the names are the words from Herodotus she chose as an epitaph for her husband:

IN PEACE, SONS·BURY THEIR FATHERS.
IN WAR, FATHERS BURY THEIR SONS.

The Author: Otohiko Kaga was born in Tokyo in 1929. As a teenager he became a cadet at the Junior Army Academy, and at the age of sixteen he saw his hometown go up in flames. After studying in postwar France, he became a professor of criminal psychology and counselor to prisoners on death row.

Turning to literature in his late thirties, he made his debut with "A Winter in Flanders," followed by "A Summer Never to Return," a novel based on his wartime experiences, which won the prestigious Tanizaki Prize in 1973. He achieved best-selling status in 1979 with "The Sentence," a massive novel about Japan's condemned prisoners, and then *Riding the East Wind* in 1982—works which established him as a master of the Western-style epic in a country where the short story and the novella had been the main vehicles of serious fiction. He has recently completed "The Eternal City," a trilogy about Tokyo in the 1930s and 1940s, crowning a career as an expert literary witness to the effects of war.

Riding the East Wind is his first novel to appear in English.

The Translator: Ian Hideo Levy was born in the United States in 1950 and educated in Taiwan, America, and Japan. He received the American Book Award for *The Ten Thousand Leaves*, a translation of the classic Japanese poetry anthology, the *Manyoshu*. With the publication of "The Room Where the Star-Spangled Banner Cannot Be Heard," which won the coveted Noma Prize for New Writers, he became the first Westerner ever to be recognized as a writer of original Japanese fiction.